# A Vineyard for Two

# Books by
# Laura Bradbury

**The Winemakers Trilogy**
*A Vineyard for Two:* http://bit.ly/AVineyardforTwo

**The Grape Series**
*My Grape Year:* http://bit.ly/2GNTSt9
*My Grape Paris:* http://bit.ly/2v2vjTP
*My Grape Wedding:* http://bit.ly/2v3gy2X
*My Grape Escape:* http://bit.ly/2v000sF
*My Grape Village:* http://bit.ly/2GRw1EC

**Other Writings:**
*Philosophy of Preschoolers:* http://bit.ly/2RKXaxJ

THE WINEMAKERS TRILOGY
BOOK 1

# A Vineyard for Two

## LAURA BRADBURY

Published by Grape Books

Paperback ISBN: 9780995917323
eBook ISBN: 9780995917330

Visit: www.laurabradbury.com

*To Franck, who teaches me about romantic love.*
*To Nyssa, who teaches me about selfless love.*
*To Thea, who suggested a Christmas novella that*
*somehow morphed into this (non-Christmas) novel.*

*C'est à partir de toi que j'ai dit oui au monde.*

—PAUL ÉLUARD

# chapter one

CERISE SWORE UNDER her breath.

"Why are you being so rough?" her youngest son demanded as she tried to do up the buttons on his dress shirt.

"Because you're squirming like a snake trying to shed its skin."

"I'm not!" Yves protested.

"Look, we're going to Maxime's funeral. I'm sad. We all are."

"Do you miss him?" Yves asked with the bluntness of an eight-year-old.

"*Bien sûr*," she said. "Of course." It had been so sudden. A massive heart attack had stolen Maxime from them five days before, just as he was crossing the courtyard to have their usual morning coffee together before Cerise went to work in the vineyards. Maxime had been the one who, in his retirement years, had devoted himself to teaching Cerise winemaking.

"I don't remember Daddy's funeral," said Yves, tilting his head in a way that squeezed Cerise's heart. His dead father used to tilt his head in the exact same way.

"Of course you don't." Cerise hugged her son's sturdy little body. "You were just a baby, *mon cheri*."

By teaching her winemaking, Maxime had also dragged Cerise back from the brink of depression after the accidental death of her husband.

She shook her head as if to clear it. If anyone knew how to weather grief, she did. Six years ago, in the space of a year, she lost both her parents and her husband, Antoine.

What made this time different was something she had to keep secret from her sons. She had to protect them from the dread that had lived within her in the week since Maxime's death.

The mere thought of the vineyards she'd toiled over for six years and saved from bankruptcy falling into the hands of Clovis, Maxime's grandson, had her unconsciously digging her nails into Yves's stomach.

He yelped.

"*Desolée*, Yves," Cerise said, blinking away tears of indignation. "I'm so sorry. My hand slipped."

Her older son, Marc—tall and slim with grave gray eyes that missed nothing—came into the living room, dressed neat as a pin. She worried for the umpteenth time that his father's death had robbed the eleven-year-old of a carefree childhood.

"Is Yves being difficult?" Marc shot his little brother a quelling look.

"Don't start, Marc," Cerise said. "He's almost ready."

"Stop wiggling!" Marc admonished Yves. "Can't you see you are going to make us late? That would show a lack of respect for Maxime."

"Marc, it is my job to order your brother around, not yours," Cerise reminded him. "Besides, you seem to have forgotten Maxime was always late—often hours late. He prided himself on it."

Marc clamped his lips together—a sign of disapproval she knew well.

She stood up and patted Yves on the head. "All done. We can go now." Yves had the same glossy brown hair and brown eyes as Antoine. The resemblance made her heart echo with loss.

# chapter two

MAXIME'S SERVICE WAS held at the Cathédrale Notre-Dame in Beaune. Cerise knew he'd always preferred the smaller, medieval church on the Faubourg Saint-Nicolas, but it was too small to house all the friends, family, and fellow winemakers who wanted to pay their respects.

Cerise walked hand in hand with her boys up the stone steps of the Cathédrale, her fingers numb with dread. Maybe there would be such a crowd she wouldn't even have to see Clovis, the man who could possibly inherit her vineyards. She'd exchanged a few polite words with him in the past, civil nothings at the winemaker gatherings that punctuated the calendar in Burgundy.

Even if she didn't have to talk to him today, however, she knew it would be only a reprieve. She'd have to deal with him eventually.

The crowd thickened as they approached the receiving line of Maxime's relatives.

"Why don't we just go inside?" Yves asked. He was about the height of everyone's waists. "What are we waiting for?"

"We have to give our condolences to Maxime's relatives, you little heathen," Marc said. Cerise raised an eyebrow at Marc—a warning.

"Why aren't we in the line?" Yves asked, unperturbed by his brother's insult. "Aren't we Maxime's family?"

"We were linked by friendship and the wine domaine," Cerise tried to explain. "But not by blood."

In his blithe way, Yves had pinpointed the crux of the problem. She'd rarely heard Maxime speak of Clovis. *How does someone who scarcely performed his role of grandson and heir possibly deserve my vineyards? He doesn't.*

They inched forward. High heels echoed on the smooth marble, and the hush of suppressed conversation filled the air. Cerise knew she didn't have to remind her boys what to do. Unfortunately, they knew how to behave at funerals. At Antoine's funeral six years earlier, she'd held a two-year-old Yves in her arms and grasped Marc's hand. He'd been unusually still and calm for a five-year-old. Cerise had wanted to believe at the time that Marc didn't really understand what was happening, or the permanence of his father's death, but as the years passed, her suspicion grew that he had understood everything.

Antoine's family had leased Maxime's family's vineyards in the Hautes-Côtes, a winemaking area above the prestigious wine-centered town of Beaune, for over two hundred years. The lease had passed to Cerise as Antoine's wife. It could be broken only by neglect, which was unthinkable, or Maxime's death.

Now Clovis was the logical heir to the vineyards Cerise had coaxed to life since her husband's death—the vineyards that had coaxed her back to life at the same time. She stiffened her spine, ready to face the enemy.

The greeting line was long and populated by Maxime's large and distant family—a scattering of aunts and uncles with some second cousins thrown in for good measure. Cerise let go of the boys' hands to greet them. Marc and Yves followed her example, far more solemn than little boys should be.

She didn't know any of Maxime's family nearly as well as

she'd known Maxime, but she'd crossed paths with them occasionally, like she had with Clovis. The wine world around Beaune was small, and her reputation as a winemaker had grown over the past six years.

Her shoulders dropped as she saw the end of the line. Clovis was nowhere to be seen. She wiped her hands on her tailored black skirt, offended on behalf of Maxime but relieved for herself.

She was just about to take the boys' hands again and make her way into the cathedral when she saw him—in the line but partially hidden behind one of the huge stone pillars that flanked the entrance.

Resentment rose up, seizing Cerise's throat. This flashy playboy who already owned and ran one of the wealthiest wine domaines in Burgundy wouldn't just be robbing her of her vineyards but also the food from her sons' plates, her passion, her pride—and her soul.

She lifted her chin and walked briskly to where he was receiving a suffocating hug from a middle-aged woman with a monstrous netted hat. *Serves him right.* When she had caught glimpses of him in the past, he was usually surrounded by such an impenetrable crowd of attractive women that she didn't even bother with a polite *bonjour*, but she knew today she had to at least try to be civil to Maxime's only grandson. Just for the funeral.

His eyes met hers, and his lips curved up. A dimple flashed high on his left cheekbone. Cerise managed to stop from rolling her eyes. Always trying to charm his way out of everything, this one. Her resentment grew into a multi-tentacled thing under her sternum.

He finally untangled from the woman, who had managed to kiss his face three times before barreling off to kiss someone else. Clovis wiped his face but didn't manage to rid himself of the hideous coral lipstick on his right cheek. Cerise pursed her lips. No. She wasn't going to tell him.

He put out his hand to Marc, who had no idea this man could be their ruin, so he shook it like the well-mannered boy he was. Next, he shook Yves's tiny hand. That dimple flashed again. Cerise forced a mental shake. As it always was at the wine events where their paths crossed, Clovis's appearance was a clear-cut provocation.

A well-tailored dark suit set off his wide shoulders and piercing blue eyes. Clovis had no right to look that good at his grandfather's funeral, never mind benefit from the genetic fluke that he was Maxime's only direct descendant.

He leaned forward and, placing his hands lightly on her shoulders, pulled Cerise in to give her *les bises*—light, customary kisses on each cheek. His touch was gentle, but she was furious at how it made her face flood with heat.

Cerise staggered back, blinking. Of all moments to get teary. *They must be tears of rage.* She wondered if Clovis knew how much she despised him. His effortless grace and easy life left her feeling cursed.

"This must be so difficult," Clovis said, still oblivious. "I've been thinking of you often in the past few days. Maxime always thought of you as the granddaughter he never had."

Cerise knew Maxime's greatest regret was that he'd fathered only one child—Clovis's father.

She remembered one winter evening over Maxime's kitchen table when they were drinking *Chartreuse* after she'd tucked the boys in for the night. How the monks managed to bottle the taste and smell of fresh mountain herbs was a mystery Maxime and Cerise had always tried, yet never succeeded, to unravel.

The conversation had somehow strayed to Maxime's son, a topic both of them usually avoided. Perhaps Maxime had drunk more than usual that night.

Maxime had dropped his head to his hands. "My son was a philanderer and a wastrel."

His grief had seemed to be focused on the person Clovis's father had been rather than the loss of him. Cerise often thought to herself that it was a good thing he'd died years before, wasting away in the hospital with advanced cirrhosis. It had saved Maxime additional heartache, in any case.

Clovis's mother had passed away of a sudden and swift-moving cancer when her only child was seven. Standing in front of him now, Cerise's heart squeezed, thinking how difficult it must have been for any seven-year-old, even Clovis. She hardened herself again. She could not afford to feel any sympathy for him.

"I adored your grandfather." Her voice cracked, and she regretted her words. She didn't owe him anything personal. She had reached the end of her civility. Cerise gave him a curt nod and turned to cross the threshold of the church with her boys.

"We have many things to talk about." Clovis's voice followed her.

She didn't even turn around. As much as the idea twisted her gut, he was right, but Maxime's funeral was neither the time nor the place for a brawl or negotiations. Besides, she needed to be feeling less emotional for that conversation to happen.

Cerise slid into one of the pews near the front, right at the edge so she could make a quick escape if Yves needed to use the bathroom or throw up—surprisingly frequent occurrences with him.

She sniffed the familiar odor of old stone and wood polish. If only she could shut off her senses like a light switch. This church brought back too many memories.

"That lady has whiskers." Yves pointed to the rotund Burgundian grandmother on the other side of Marc. Cerise narrowed her eyes at him, but when she snuck a glance at Marc's neighbor, she had to admit the lady's whiskers were indeed impressive.

Marc must have caught this because he said, "Don't worry, Maman, I'll make sure he behaves."

Nothing, of course, was better calculated to make Yves misbehave than the idea that his older brother was supervising him. Cerise gave Marc a firm shake of her head. He was only eleven. He would be more carefree if he still had a father.

The organ music became louder. Cerise had despised organ music since her parents had been killed in a car accident on the route de Pommard six months before Antoine's death. His funeral had clinched it: organ music was the soundtrack of incomprehensible tragedy.

Antoine had been her first love—they met in school when Cerise was only fourteen—and she knew he would be her last. She'd been young and happy with Antoine, but she'd become a different person since his death. Tragedy had a way of doing that.

When Maxime had finally persuaded Cerise to take over the vineyard lease under his guidance, she'd discovered herself in the scent of freshly turned soil in the morning, the acidic taste of a grape waiting to burst into maturity, the complex challenges of vinification, deciding just the perfect time to bottle her wine… Maxime had introduced Cerise to a new life, one she now needed like oxygen—oxygen that Clovis would likely rob from her.

Her ears pricked up as Clovis's voice came down the aisle.

She felt the weight of a hand on her shoulder. Cerise whipped around. Clovis stood above her in all his vexing perfection. She gave him the same deterring look she had given Yves just minutes before. He couldn't have it both ways: take away her vines and charm her while doing it.

"May I sit beside you?" he asked, an apologetic smile on his lips that would probably melt the defenses of most women.

Not Cerise. "Don't you have a designated seat with your family up front?"

He groaned. "I've hit my limit of smothering from great-aunts-once-removed."

Completely out of character, Marc burst out laughing. Cerise swiveled her head, and he clamped his lips together. She couldn't blame him. If he knew the context, Marc wouldn't find Clovis any more amusing than she did.

She gestured at Yves, Marc, and the whiskered lady. "There's no room."

Yves, who was fidgeting, piped up. "Yes, there is! Squeeze in!"

Cerise reluctantly slid over, and Clovis lowered himself down beside her. Having his large frame pressed against her side made her feel small. It dawned on her that was part of her problem with Clovis. The ease with which he seemed to move through winemaking and life only highlighted her struggles. He made her feel insignificant.

Someone like him could never comprehend those terrible months after Antoine was crushed under an overturned tractor while pruning the vineyards. He would never see Cerise's struggles—the grief and fear; learning to care for the vineyards under Maxime's tutelage; the backbreaking work; the years hail had swept in late in a black cloud, almost decimating twelve months' worth of labor when she had almost no wine reserves; trying to be both mother and father to her grieving sons—much less respect her for surviving them.

She scanned the crowd, wondering how she could escape with her boys, but the cathedral was packed.

Clovis leaned in toward her. "It's not only the great-aunts. This is a difficult day for both of us. I thought we could give each other moral support."

She stared straight ahead, indignation blocking all her

imagined retorts. Cerise had no intention of giving or receiving support from Clovis.

The organ player began pounding an alarming dirge..A hush fell over the church. *Merde.*

"I hate organ music," Clovis muttered, echoing her thoughts. She peaked an eyebrow in surprise. That was a coincidence—or, on second thought, maybe not. There was not much to love about organ music.

"Why aren't you a pallbearer?"

"Maxime specifically asked that the funeral people do it."

"Why?" Cerise demanded.

He shrugged. "No idea. It wouldn't be Maxime's funeral if there wasn't a bit of mystery."

That was true. Maxime was known for being enigmatic.

They all stood for the processional. As the priest walked among the pews in stately robes, a shudder ran through Cerise. For a thirty-two-year-old, she had attended too many funerals. Next came the sub-priests or whatever they were, just like at Antoine's and her parents' services. Then came the moment she had been dreading: Maxime's coffin being walked down the aisle by the sweating funeral home staff. An altar boy walked behind, dressed in a wide-sleeved white robe with a heavy wooden cross tied on a rope around his neck. He was swaying an ornate silver thurible full of smoking incense.

The cloying scent of the incense was even worse than the organ music and made her stomach revolt. She sensed a shudder run through Clovis, echoing her own.

"There goes the last member of my immediate family in France," Clovis murmured in the most desolate tone Cerise had ever heard. "I'm alone."

Cerise felt woozy from the familiar smells and sensations and couldn't process the sight of Maxime's coffin. She thought she had accepted his death, but she hadn't. Her vibrant, loyal friend was now lying in that box, lost to her forever. Her breath hitched on a sob. She could never thank him enough for what he had done for her, and now she'd lost the opportunity forever.

Clovis's hand moved closer to hers. It felt warm and solid. Cerise resisted the bizarre urge to clutch it like an anchor.

She saw Clovis was staring straight ahead at the coffin, his eyes shiny with tears. *I cannot feel sorry for him. I cannot have a chink in my armor.*

After a few moments of silence, the priest said a few words of welcome and invited them to join in a prayer. He asked the congregation to sit.

Cerise moved her hand away from Clovis's. For the ump-teenth time in her life, she cursed the sheer inconvenience of feeling everything so deeply. Emotions made it so much trickier to fight this man who possibly stood in the way of the life she had worked so hard for.

The reception was held at the medieval bastion on the private grounds of the Hospices de Beaune, the spiritual home of wine-making. The fact that the bastion had been offered for Maxime's reception was a singular honor. It was almost never open to the public and was used only to distinguish highly respected and connected members of Beaune's winemaking world. Maxime, of course, was both.

It was an imposing place, and Cerise wasn't surprised when her boys' mouths dropped open as she led them into the vast, echoing chamber. The vaulted stone walls were decorated with faded yet still exquisite Aubusson tapestries, which were set off by the red carpet on part of the floor. It took no effort to imagine this space when it was used as a medieval hall, complete with a jester performing on a lute and large jeweled goblets of mead and wine being passed around communal tables.

It was considered a privilege to be invited to an event at Le Bastion, but Cerise hadn't wanted to come here at all. She knew it would be considered odd, though, if she didn't make a brief appearance.

She didn't move in these exalted circles of Burgundy's most prestigious winemakers. For one, her vines were in the higher altitude Hautes-Côtes, so they carried less value than those on the lower slopes. Also, besides her vineyards and her boys, she was a practically a hermit. She had no time or energy left for socializing beyond her daily chats with Maxime. Her friends from her years with Antoine had slowly disappeared from her life, and she couldn't blame them.

Cerise saw many familiar faces in the crowd but no friendly ones. In her tailored black suit, and with her boys, she felt completely alone. *What I would give to be back in my vineyards.*

Clovis had left quickly after the service, whispering that he had to make sure his elderly relatives made it to the bastion. Cerise wondered why he'd bothered telling her, as if they were friends or something. Just because they both disliked organ music and felt alone today did not mean they had anything in common. Well, except those two things.

She took a kir from the table and stood awkwardly while Marc and Yves went off to explore the far reaches of the hall. She scanned the crowd for someone she could talk to until her aunt Geneviève, one of her only remaining relatives, swooped over. Hers was not one of the familiar faces Cerise had been hoping for.

She brought with her, as always, a cloud of Chanel N°5. Cerise coughed.

"Wasn't that a beautiful service?" Geneviève smoothed back

her lacquered, dyed blond hair. "All of Beaune was there, every-one who counts *de toute façon.*"

"Maxime would have laughed," Cerise said.

Geneviève clicked her tongue. "Always so disrespectful, but I'll forgive you. You did know Maxime better than I did. What I want to know is what's going to happen to your vineyards now? Who is going to inherit them? Logically it should be Clovis, but as he's already swimming in riches—"

"I'm aware of that." Cerise gritted her teeth. "I won't know anything until the reading of the will."

"You know, darling, if you ever are in a bind, you and the boys are welcome at our house." Geneviève patted her shoulder. "We would be delighted to have you."

Cerise was touched. She and her aunt didn't see eye to eye on most things, but despite it all, Geneviève had a good heart under all that makeup and hairspray, as well as an incredible amount of family loyalty. She gave her aunt a hug and for once didn't try to untangle herself right away.

"I wish—" Geneviève choked out.

"I know, I know," Cerise said, patting her back. She knew her aunt wished her sister—Cerise's mother—hadn't died. Cerise knew, too, that Geneviève wished she and her husband had been able to have children of their own. Her aunt and her uncle lived, just the two of them, in an immense house at the foot of the vineyards on La Montagne of Beaune. She also knew Geneviève wanted to have a closer relationship with Cerise, but not only was Geneviève an unrepentant snob, but also she compulsively tried to control the lives of everyone she loved.

Her aunt sniffed and rearranged her linen jacket. "Anyway, Cerise, what do you think of him? I was never friendly with either of his parents, you know, so I watched him grow up only from a distance. He always seemed like a pleasant boy, despite what must have been a wretched home life. I always felt sorry for him."

She followed her aunt's gaze to where Clovis stood in the middle of the room, surrounded by a trio of glittery women. They circled him like honeybees to a sunflower, surely eager to share their condolences and a lot more.

"You felt sorry for Clovis?" Cerise laughed.

"Of course! That dreadful father of his and his mother dying when he was only a boy—sometimes I worry your heart has hardened into a stone, Cerise. You were never like that before."

She knew "before" referred to her year of tragedy, but her aunt was wrong; that year hadn't turned her heart to stone. If anything, she felt things more acutely now, and she was far too emotional for her own comfort. She was just better at hiding it. "I don't think anyone needs to feel sorry for Clovis anymore."

"Well, he has turned out to be a wonderful winemaker. You have to admit that."

Cerise pursed her lips. "I think he was lucky enough to inherit incredible vineyards from his mother. I sincerely doubt he works much in the vines these days…if he ever did."

"I don't think you're right, but that hardly matters. Isn't he divine?" Geneviève sighed. "Those looks, that charm, those vine-yards, that fortune…it's too bad you don't throw your hat in that ring, *chérie*."

Cerise was surprised to observe that Clovis's eyes, far from looking gratified at his coterie of admirers, were darting around the room. "I'm not looking for another relationship, and even if I was, it would not be with a rich playboy," she said but kept watching Clovis. What was he looking for?

Geneviève blew out a puff of air. "What high horse are you on now? You would be lucky to find a new husband with such prestigious vines. You know that as well as I do."

How did her aunt always manage take her so quickly from affection to frustration? Geneviève had married well—to a man with holdings that included some of the most expensive appellations. Cerise couldn't see that Geneviève was any happier for it.

Her aunt dusted imaginary lint off Cerise's jacket. "You are a beautiful girl, but you need to care more about your clothes and your general appearance. You always look a bit wild, like you belong in the vineyards."

"That's because I do belong in the vineyards."

Geneviève ignored her. "You should strive to be more groomed, more *soigné*, like those ladies around Clovis."

Cerise shook her head in disbelief. "Grooming is for horses. Anyway, those ladies don't appear to be having much luck despite their blowouts and manicures." Indeed, Clovis didn't seem to be paying attention to them. His eyes still roved over the crowd.

That was, until they met hers.

His face transformed from annoyed to eager. If she didn't know better, she might have believed he'd been searching for her.

He began to move through the crowd in her direction.

"I must go, Tante." Cerise gave Geneviève a peck on each cheek. "I'll just find my boys."

With that, she sped off and located Yves hiding behind one of the priceless Aubusson tapestries, while Marc, furious, tried to impress the magnitude of this transgression on his brother.

Little boys were ticking time bombs. She wasn't leaving because of Clovis. Absolutely not.

# chapter three

*A* FEW DAYS AFTER the funeral, Cerise arrived early for the reading of Maxime's will at the notary's office in the nearby town of Nuits-Saint-Georges.

She had known Maître Gilbert since she was a child. Her parents had gone to him for all their legal work since well before she was born. Antoine's family had also been loyal to Maître Gilbert, as were most of the winemakers in the Hautes-Côtes.

The torn leather seats in the waiting room were sticky. It was one of those August days that already felt like an oven set on broil before nine o'clock in the morning. She berated herself for arriving early. She had never known Maître Gilbert to receive clients early—or even remotely on time for that matter.

She wondered when Clovis would arrive. As Maxime's principal heir, Cerise was certain he would be summoned to the reading. Vineyards were too valuable in Burgundy for no-shows, even for someone as wealthy as Clovis.

Her nostrils flared at the stale smell of tobacco and perspiration that permeated Maître Gilbert's waiting room. She'd barely slept again. She'd seen in the bathroom mirror that morning the dark half-moons under her eyes from this torturous uncertainty.

Earlier, she had gone out to work in the vineyards before it became too hot, feasting her eyes on row upon row of healthy green. As she'd de-leafed the vines under the rising orange sun, she found herself wondering if Maxime's will would allow her to keep the revenue from the wine she would soon harvest. Surely, Maxime would not have been so cruel as to cut her out entirely.

The problem was she had more riding on the upcoming harvest than she'd ever shared with Maxime. Her whole career. She should have told him when she'd had the chance.

Many times in the past few days she'd found herself at the cherry tree in the corner of her vineyards, which she believed lent her wine its unique flavor. She would lay both her palms against its gnarled trunk and pray.

She didn't pray to the Virgin Mary, like she had when she was a child—she hadn't done that since her husband and parents were taken from her. Instead she prayed to Saint Vincent, the patron saint of winemakers, that she would not lose her vineyards, Domaine du Cerisier. She had faith in him as much as anyone, which was to say not much.

She knew Maxime had considered her a de facto family member. Still, it was unheard of in Burgundy to divide up vineyards or give them away to anyone who wasn't related. The goal was always to keep everything intact and in the family line. Maxime had loved her, but he was a pragmatic Burgundian winemaker to his core. Yet…

Cerise realized she'd been chewing her lip, a habit she'd spent a lifetime trying to break. She picked up a *Paris Match* magazine from Maître Gilbert's waiting-room table and began reading about Princess Caroline's estrangement from Ernest of Hanover. Decades-old news.

"Brushing up on your history?" a man's deep voice asked from above.

Clovis looked annoyingly handsome, as expected. Wide shoulders, bright-blue eyes, chiseled cheekbones—but he didn't look as polished as at the funeral. He wore cotton shorts and a white T-shirt, and Cerise recognized the imprint of dirt and green stains from pruning on his clothes and hands. The same stains were on hers, even though she had stopped to change into clean clothes before coming to the notary. Cerise felt a spark of surprise. She must have caught him on one of the rare days he worked in his vineyards instead of just swanning around promoting them.

"I started leaf thinning late this morning, and I didn't have time to change." Clovis glanced at the shut door of Maître Gilbert's study. "Actually, I probably did. How could I forget Maître Gilbert is always late?"

Good lord. He was talking like someone who actually knew his way around a vineyard.

Clovis sat down beside her. "How are you fitting in your de-leafing in this heat? I can't remember the last time the leaves grew this much so late in the season."

"I got up early this morning and started," Cerise said, still confused "I'm used to doing most of it before the boys get up." She never thought she would be having such a conversation with Clovis. She remembered what was going to happen in Maître Gilbert's office in the next hour could leave her with no vines of her own to prune ever again.

Clovis smiled. "You must work fast."

"I'm a single mother. I have to be."

He held her eyes, and she couldn't help but blink. There was something unexpected reflected in his—if she didn't know better, she would say it was admiration. Her stomach did an odd flip.

"I've been marveling at you from afar, you know," Clovis said. "Maxime talked so highly of you—how you took a tragic situation and turned it around with grit and talent. I love your wines."

"You've tasted them?" She hated herself for not shutting him down, but she was just so shocked he'd tried them, and oh, how she missed talking wine and winemaking with Maxime.

"Of course. Your wines have an impressive following, but I'm sure you know that."

Cerise squirmed in her chair. The way he looked at her didn't just make her feel like the only person in the room but the only person in the world who mattered. Was he trying to charm her by pretending to be down-to-earth? She wondered if for nefarious reasons he was trying to lower himself to what he believed was her level. "Wild," as her aunt had decreed.

"I'm surprised to see you dressed like that." Cerise lifted her chin at him. "I didn't think you got out into the vineyards much."

He frowned. "What gave you that impression?"

"You're such a public person, always chairing wine festivals and snipping ribbons and being featured in magazines… How do you possibly have time?"

"It's not incompatible to be a serious winemaker and knowledgeable about marketing, you know," he said. "I did a marketing degree at school."

Now he was just pretending to be modest. She knew from Maxime that Clovis had graduated from the most prestigious business school in Paris. Still, in her experience being a serious winemaker left no time for anything else.

Clovis crossed his legs and leaned slightly toward her. She caught a whiff of the fresh earthiness of vineyards on him. It was mixed with something that made him smell even more pleasant. She wouldn't let it affect her, but it was a vast improvement on the tobacco and sweat of Maître Gilbert's waiting room that had invaded her airspace before his arrival.

Silence descended, and she noticed Clovis's eyes were, like her own, trained on Maître Gilbert's office door. Both were avoiding the question that was to be answered in that room and that felt like it was crushing her chest like an anvil. She couldn't stand a second more of not knowing. "Do you know how Maxime disposed of the lease for my domaine?"

Clovis turned to her, his blue eyes wide. "You get right to the point. *Your* domaine?"

A heartless answer from a heartless man. "Those vines are my livelihood. They are what puts food on my table." They were far more than that, but she wasn't about to share their emotional importance with him.

His eyebrows drew together. "You have no other income? Didn't your husband have life insurance?"

"Not everyone inherits a fortune like you," Cerise snapped. "Those vines were Antoine's life insurance. He didn't think he needed anything else."

He should have, of course, but she and Antoine were too busy being young and in love and having babies. The idea that one of them could cease to exist was unthinkable. Now, she often cursed their naiveté. Life insurance would have helped immensely.

"*Merde.* I didn't realize that," Clovis muttered. He sat back in his chair and eyed her with concern. "Did Maxime realize the vineyards are your only source of income?"

"Yes." Indeed, that was why she hung on to a sliver of hope that maybe he had found a way...

Cerise observed with a certain satisfaction that Clovis finally looked as troubled as she felt. "Do you know anything?" she pressed.

"No." Her instincts told her he was telling the truth. "Maxime never mentioned anything, and I haven't seen his will. You know he wasn't the sort of person who encouraged such questions."

"I guess not." Clovis was right. Until his collapse in the courtyard, Maxime had dwelled firmly in the land of the living. That was part of how he'd managed to drag Cerise back from the brink when she was so lost.

They lapsed into silence for a few minutes, but she couldn't seem to stop the skin prickling on her arm beside Clovis's, surely a physical manifestation of her resentment.

"Your sons are wonderful." He finally broke the tension.

She turned to him and again was surprised at what she saw in his eyes. Unless she was mistaken, that was wistfulness. Surely he wasn't the sort of man who longed for a child—unless to provide an heir for his fortune. Ah. That was it.

"Marc strikes me as an old soul," he said.

That was strangely perceptive. Marc *was* an old soul. She opened her mouth to warn him against making comments on her boys, but the door to Maître Gilbert's office opened, and the notary waddled toward them. He pumped Clovis's hand in a hearty handshake and gave Cerise two wet kisses.

The *maître*, rotund and smelling like the Waterman ink he always used to refill his fountain pen, rubbed his hands together. "Sad day. I think we all believed Maxime was immortal. Such a force of nature."

Cerise felt like yelling, *Tell me what the will says!* but managed to restrain herself.

Once they were settled in the office, Maître Gilbert took what felt like an eternity to make a few calls and locate some crucial papers on his massive oak desk. At last he buzzed his secretary to bring him the will. When she came in with a worn manila folder, she shot Clovis and Cerise a look of apology.

In his stately way, Maître Gilbert embarked on a pedantic reading of the pages and pages of legalese that introduced the will. She knew from experience that Maître Gilbert could never, under any circumstances, be rushed. This quirk of his had never felt as tortuous as it did today. Blood pounded in her ears. She began to tap her ballerina flat against the desk leg so as not to explode.

She heard a faint thumping sound and realized Clovis was tapping his foot on the other side of the *maître's* desk. Her eyes caught his. He shot her a rueful smile of understanding that she had to discipline herself not to reciprocate. Although his smile drew her in, this man was possibly minutes away from dispossessing her of Domaine du Cerisier.

Finally, Maître Gilbert got to the bequests and Maxime's many vineyard holdings. He listed many parcels that didn't concern Cerise and would be inherited by Clovis. So much wealth in those Côte de Beaune appellations, so much prestige, yet Clovis appeared impassive in the face of being pronounced a millionaire several times over. Of course he was blasé. He was already a millionaire thanks to his mother.

She began to feel more hopeful. Surely with all that Clovis was inheriting, Maxime must have realized he didn't need her vineyards, too.

"And as for Domaine du Cerisier," Maître Gilbert intoned, then proceeded to list all the parcels it comprised—parcels Cerise knew down to each individual vine. She couldn't breathe. Maître Gilbert read over the page silently. She leaned forward, unable to contain her impatience. The *maître* let out a long, slow whistle. "Well, now…that's an unusual arrangement. I wonder—"

"What is it, Maître?" Clovis said. "Cerise has been waiting long enough."

She felt a surge of appreciation, but it was quickly replaced by annoyance. "I can speak for myself, *merci*."

Clovis grimaced. "I was just trying to avoid calling the ambulance. You looked like you were seconds away from a stroke. Besides, I want to know, too."

"Why do you need to know?" she demanded, and in that moment, not for the first time since that horrible year of loss, the injustice of her life felt like too much to bear. She'd lost her husband and parents, and had fought so fiercely for everything she had, and now she might lose that, too. Compared to all that Clovis possessed and the life of ease he led, it crushed her. "Don't you have enough to satisfy you already?"

Clovis's mouth opened and then snapped shut. "I never said—"

"Figures," she muttered.

Maître Gilbert, who had been watching this exchange as if it were a riveting match at Roland-Garros, cleared his throat.

"Now, now," he reprimanded them like children. "This is not at all a good start."

"A good start to what?" she demanded.

The *maître* pursed his lips. "It is something I have never seen before in all my career."

"What. Is. It?" Clovis infused each word with impatience.

Maître Gilbert steepled his fingers and studied Clovis and Cerise. "Maxime has left Domaine du Cerisier to the two of you jointly."

"*Quoi?*" they demanded in stereo. Of all the things she had worried about, she had never even entertained this as a possibility.

"The lease is terminated with Maxime's demise, and Cerise is to cease rental payments. She is a fifty percent owner now." He arched a gray eyebrow at Clovis. "With you."

"A fifty-fifty split?" Cerise said, trying to wrap her head around whether this arrangement was better or worse than being completely dispossessed.

"*Oui.* It means you and Clovis are now equal partners."

*Worse.* "How could Maxime do this?" she burst out. "Why?"

"I don't know," Clovis said, but something strange was happening with his mouth.

"You're smiling!"

"Well...yes," he admitted. "I think we might work well together."

"I don't *want* to work with anyone, especially not you."

Again, *le maître*'s eyes ping-ponged back and forth between the new partners. "This should be interesting."

Cerise snorted.

"It could be worse." Clovis reached out and tried to touch her arm, but she snatched it away before he got the chance. *How dare he.* "This could work, Cerise. I'll do everything in my power to make it work."

"I don't want your promises or your partnership. I—"

"Another thing!" the *maître* interrupted with a sparkle in his eye. "Maxime left his house, adjacent to the vineyards—"

"We know where it is." She cracked her knuckles.

"Very well. It is now part of the same title as the vineyards and therefore is also co-owned by the two of you, as are all the outbuildings that make up the domaine."

Cerise hadn't considered that as a possibility, either. She and her boys lived in a small wine harvesters' house across the courtyard from Maxime's main dwelling. It was basic but big enough for her and her boys and, more importantly, right beside the vineyards.

Clovis owned half of everything. She pressed her fingers against her temples.

She had always loved Maxime's house, and it made sense to keep the entire domaine intact. The house was ancient and rambling and made of old stone. Maxime had painted the fading blue shutters himself years before. Plus, beneath it was a fifteenth-century cellar—one of the largest and most prized in the region. Her cellar. Surely—

"What about the cellar?" Cerise asked.

"I was just about to ask the same thing," Clovis said.

*Of course he was.*

The *maître* consulted the will again. "Co-owned, just like the rest of it."

Cerise swore under her breath. The cellar was also where at least half the art of winemaking occurred. She didn't think she could tolerate interruptions there any more than she could in the vineyards, or the vat room, or her house.

While the *maître* droned on with the rest of the will, she slumped in her chair, reeling.

After the reading, Cerise shook *le maître*'s hand mechanically, fixed a date to sign some apparently crucial conveyancing documents, and walked in silence out of the office. Clovis walked a few feet behind her.

"He enjoyed that, the old rascal," Clovis remarked once they were out in the parking lot that reeked of melting tar. If it was anybody but Clovis, and anything but her entire life, she would laugh.

"How much do you want for it?" She squinted up at him after failing to locate her sunglasses in her handbag. She cursed him for being so tall. "I can't promise to pay it off now, but if we agree on a price, my word is good."

Clovis tilted his head. "What are you talking about?"

"I'm going to buy you out."

"You are?"

"Of course."

"Don't I have a say in it?" he asked. His lips quivered, although he didn't smile.

"*Non*," Cerise answered. "Don't be ridiculous, and *don't* laugh at me." Buying him out was, of course, the only possibility. "Partners! Maxime must have been delirious."

"Why is that so terrible? You now own half of a domaine you only rented before. That's a win. Look, we need to discuss this partnership. I think we're both tired and overwhelmed with the new information. How about we go out for dinner next week and talk?"

"There's nothing to discuss," she said. "Except price and terms."

He lifted his hand, palm up. "I don't agree, but I must go home and change. I'm flying to London this afternoon, and I'm already running late."

Cerise made that throaty French sound of disgust. *Figures. He's probably going for some flashy wine event or his latest conquest.*

"I'm going to pretend that was directed at the caprice of Maxime, not at me."

"You can pretend whatever you want, as long as I can buy you out."

"You can't buy me out unless I agree to it, and I don't." He sighed. "I truly do need to leave, or I'll miss my flight."

One of his wine groupies would no doubt be waiting for him at Heathrow.

"On second thought, instead of dinner, come for a winetasting at my place when I get back," he said.

"Why would I do that?"

"What better way to get to know your new partner than tasting his wine?"

Cerise repressed a snort of contempt. As if he made his own wine, flitting off here and there all the time. Still, it would take tireless work to buy him out. She was sure his wine would fuel her motivation. He was all smoke and mirrors. Nobody could hide behind a winetasting, not even Clovis. It would prove he was no worthy partner, despite Maxime's caprice.

"Fine," Cerise said.

"And you could at least pretend like you don't hate me."

She rolled her eyes. He was probably right, though; being blunt and rude didn't seem to be getting her what she wanted. Still, she didn't have it in her today to be civil. "When should I come for the winetasting?"

"Any time after Wednesday. Just drop by when you have a chance."

It didn't sound like he even planned on being there. It would be one of his minions who would conduct it, no doubt. If she needed confirmation that Clovis considered her a nonentity, she had it. She nodded curtly.

Clovis reached out an arm as if to close the space between them, then apparently thought better of it and shoved his fist in his pocket.

*Wise choice.*

"Don't think of me as your enemy, Cerise. I had no clue what Maxime had up his sleeve, I swear."

She blinked in the bright sunlight. He seemed to need her to believe him. She couldn't imagine why.

"Whatever." She turned to leave before he tried to give her *les bises.*

She didn't look back, but she had a feeling he was still standing there, watching her cross the parking lot to her car.

# chapter four

CERISE HAD BEEN distracted all week. She itched to work in her vineyards, but she knew the season was drawing to a close and the vines needed to be left alone.

She paced up and down the rows with her unused secateurs in the pocket of her jean shorts and a wicker basket on her arm, picking off a grape here and there to press and test the maturity and aromas of the juice.

In her mind she organized what was left to do to prepare the cellar and her equipment for harvest. Marc and Yves were still on summer vacation and were more than happy to disappear in the hilltop forest behind the village with their friends, making forts and conducting wars with homemade slingshots made from hazel canes. They came home for lunch and dinner but otherwise enjoyed the glorious existence of feral children.

She found herself, as she often did, by the cherry tree in the upper corner of her parcel. She picked a grape from a promising-looking bunch and squeezed it between her thumb and forefinger.

The skin was robust and took some pressure to burst. The pulp inside was satisfyingly plentiful. Cerise popped it in her mouth and contemplated the tannins of the seeds and the strongly cherry-flavored pulp. Not quite enough sugar in the grape, but soon.

Wednesday had come and gone. Clovis had probably

returned from London, but Cerise was having second thoughts about going to his domaine for the promised winetasting. It felt like a waste of time playing polite when all she wanted to do was get down to negotiating the buyout.

She picked up the metal thermos of coffee she always left at the base of the cherry tree. The cherries were over, but many were still squashed on the ground, their rich, fragrant essence being soaked up by the soil. She never allowed anyone to pick or eat the cherries. They belonged to the vineyards, in the same way she did.

She settled on the ground, unscrewed the cap to her thermos, and poured the steaming hot coffee. She leaned against the tree trunk and took a sip. The bitterness grounded her in her body, as did the solid feel of the trunk against her back and the sharp scent of limestone-rich soil. All this felt real. The situation with Clovis and the partnership did not.

The worst part of the whole knot was the secret wine she had bottled last year. She called it Cerasus, after the Latin name for the cherry tree she sat against.

Domaine du Cerisier had always suffered financially. Its wines were the less valuable appellations, and three out of the six years Cerise has been winemaking had been blighted by catastrophic hailstorms that had decimated her crop yield. There was never enough wine to sell and barely any stocks left, so taking some of the previous year's grapes to concoct an experimental wine was madness. Still, if Cerasus was successful, it could save Domaine du Cerisier. But if Clovis discovered it and began to meddle, she would never get the chance to find out.

Again, she wished she'd shared her secret wine idea with Maxime when she'd had the chance. She was sure he wouldn't have foisted Clovis on her if he'd known what was at stake.

Sunlight filtered through the gently rustling branches above her, casting coins of sunlight that dotted her forearms and bent knees. She loved this tree. She couldn't stand the idea of it belonging to anyone else, any more than the vineyards. But now Clovis owned half the tree, and the vineyards, and Maxime's house, and her life. She hated it.

She closed her eyes and leaned her head back. The leaves rustled overhead. A tractor hummed in the distance. Even though vineyard tractors saved time and money, Cerise always insisted on doing everything by hand. People believed this quirk was because Antoine had been killed by a tractor, but that was ridiculous. It was a horrific accident, but it had been entirely Antoine's fault. He had been trying to drive it up a steep, muddy hill on a rainy day—something any wise person would know was dangerous. He had been impatient and slightly reckless like that.

Cerise eschewed the specialized tractors for pruning and harvesting because she was convinced that their use produced inferior wine. She used them only to transport her grapes during the harvest, and there was no way around that. Tractors were brute force, rather like Antoine had been. They ripped leaves and damaged grape bunches. They frequently harmed the precious roots beneath the ground. Cerise was firm in the belief that vines and grapes needed to be handled gently, lovingly, like a child... or a lover, although she hadn't had one of those since Antoine.

The scratchy bark felt pleasant against the back of her head. Her thoughts began to wander in that tangled, fractured way that presaged sleep. Clovis's face swam into her dreams, and then...a soft sound jerked her back to consciousness. Her eyes flew open.

There was Clovis, looking down at her with an intent expression.

"What are you doing here?" She squinted up at him. It bothered her that he hadn't invaded only her conscious thoughts but her unconscious dreams, too.

"I came at a bad time?" he said. "I know the sanctity of a coffee break."

He didn't mention the napping. Cerise scrambled to her feet, spilling coffee on herself in the process. "*Merde!*" She brushed the burning liquid off her bare leg as though she could also brush off his presence in her dream.

"Yes, coffee breaks are sacred." Her voice came out harsh. She had to remind herself that being rude hadn't advanced her cause at the notary's office.

"I wanted to let you know I'm back and available whenever you'd like to come for a tasting."

"Oh."

Their eyes caught, and she couldn't think of anything to say to this man. Dressed in beige cotton pants and a white linen shirt, he looked like someone who belonged in daydreams, not real life—certainly not as her new partner. It was all so ludicrous.

Clovis reached out again, as he had at Maître Gilbert's office. His hand didn't drop this time.

She remained suspended for several seconds as he moved his hand as if to cup her face, then she ducked out of his reach. *This is no dream.* She bent to pick up her thermos. When she stood again, his hands were in his pockets. She wondered if that surreal moment had happened. Better to pretend it hadn't.

"How was England?" she asked, attempting civility.

He didn't answer right away, but then he shook himself slightly. "It was fine, *merci*. Terrible coffee. Excellent crumpets. The queen still has her head. How were the past few days for you?"

"Aggravating," Cerise admitted. "It's driving me crazy that I can't ask Maxime why he left things the way he did."

Clovis nodded. "I've been preoccupied with the same question."

"Still have no idea?"

"No." He shrugged. "I know nothing for sure…"

Something in his tone made her narrow her eyes. "There's something you're not telling me."

He tilted his head to the side. "I have a hunch, that's all. Nothing more."

The sun slanted through his irises. She didn't think she'd ever seen eyes that shade of cobalt. "Come on."

He shook his head. "I could be wildly off. Besides, we'll never know for certain, will we?"

"Tell me anyway." Cerise crossed her arms. She needed to know what he suspected.

His blue eyes locked with her brown ones. "I'm almost certain my theory would offend you and make you hate me more than you already do."

"I don't hate you." Far in the back of her mind, she was vaguely aware that this situation was far more Maxime's fault than Clovis's. "Not exactly."

He arched an eyebrow.

"I resent you. It's not the same thing."

"It feels the same on the receiving end." That dimple flashed on his left cheek.

"How does it feel?" Clovis made her feel like an unimportant gnat, and she thought it improbable that her dislike of him had penetrated his defenses.

"Not good, Cerise. Not good."

"You look like you can handle it."

He crossed his arms in front of him and tilted his head. "Looks can be deceiving."

"Let's be honest here. I'm nothing to you, nor are these vineyards when it comes down to it. Look at all you've got."

His nostrils flared. "You don't know me. You have no clue what my priorities are."

That gave Cerise pause. Her resentment had transformed into a full-on attack. She blew out a breath. "I apologize. That was out of line."

"*Oui.* It was." They both crossed their arms and stared at each other for what felt like a long time.

"Do I really make you feel that way?" He finally broke the silence. "That horrifies me beyond belief. I don't know you well, but I would like to. You strike me as the most interesting person in any room. Besides, we're fifty-fifty partners now. I take that seriously."

"We're fifty-fifty partners for the *moment*," honesty compelled her to add. She took another deep breath. "All right. I think I've gotten out all my spite for the moment. Can you please tell me your theory about Maxime's intentions? I promise I won't get angry."

His eyes sparkled. The dimple made another appearance.

"When I make a promise," Cerise said, "I mean it."

It took a while, but Clovis finally nodded. "*D'accord.* Here's my theory, for what it's worth. I believe Maxime felt you and I would work well together and…well, be a good fit. I suspect he had been planning our fate for a while but was biding his time."

A shock of betrayal ran through her, followed by disbelief.

"A good fit? Like…romantically?" Surely Maxime would never manipulate her life in such a way—unless he thought it would make her happier. In that case he would have been capable of anything.

Clovis's eyes darted away from her for a few seconds. "Possibly. I think perhaps Maxime believed we would need each other once he was gone. I wouldn't be surprised if he felt we have both suffered enough in life. He knew I've always been lonely. He may have figured we'd be less lonely together."

*The meddling old—*

"What are you thinking?" he asked.

Cerise shook her head. "I'm furious at Maxime. I almost can't believe it, but—"

"But what?"

33

She didn't answer. "He must have thought I can't find a man on my own."

"I'm sure he didn't—"

"As if I need some sort of *matchmaker*."

"Well, do you?"

"No! Why, do you?"

"Well…" The dimple flashed like a flickering light.

"You're happy about this?" she cried.

Clovis took her two gesticulating hands in his large ones, stilling her immediately, perhaps from shock at a man's touch. It had been a long time.

"Maybe I should explain. I'd been asking Maxime to introduce us for some time, but he kept putting me off. I always believed it was because he didn't think I was good enough for you—a worry that, to be honest, I shared. Maxime throwing us together this way will at least give me the chance to get to know you better…if you'll let me."

"This is crazy. Until now you were barely aware of my existence."

He shook his head. "Wrong. Call it a gut feeling, but from what Maxime told me and from the little I've seen, and especially from tasting your wine, I began to think that perhaps we have a lot in common."

Cerise let out a puff of disbelief and broke her hands away. "Look at you. Look at me. We have nothing in common. You did this. Maxime acted on your suggestion."

"You knew my grandfather better than anyone. Do you honestly think I could compel that stubborn mule to do anything he didn't want to?"

Even through her anger, Cerise had to recognize he had a point. "No, but it's unnerving to think you've been…observing me. I'm neither a pawn nor a prize to be won. I am a winemaker with everything invested in these vineyards. This is my *life's work*, Clovis. How dare you or Maxime treat it like a game?"

He took a step back. "Trust me." He gestured wide with his arm, encompassing the vineyards, the domaine, and her. "None of this is a game."

"You don't even know me."

Clovis sighed heavily. "I realize how offensive this whole arrangement must seem. All I'm asking is that you come and taste wine at my domaine. I completely understand if you decide not to. It's up to you, I swear. I'm going to leave now. Please trust me when I say I would never dream of interfering with these glorious vineyards you have played like a Stradivarius. Never. I just want to know you better, and I would love the opportunity to spend more time with your sons."

"My sons? Why?"

He shrugged. "I guess I've never known what it is to be part of a family."

"Never?"

Clovis's shoulders dropped. "Never."

She felt that dangerous sympathy for him once again. She couldn't indulge it.

"I'm going now."

Cerise merely nodded, not trusting her voice.

He gave her a funny little wave and began to walk away. He paused after a few steps and sent a smile over his shoulder.

"What is that for?" Cerise asked.

"I'm just saving the image in my mind of Cerise under her cherry tree. It's quite a sight. I think my gut feeling was right."

"This tree is one hundred percent mine, by the way." She laid a hand possessively on its trunk. "It doesn't come with the vineyards!"

"How could that tree belong to anyone but you?" he said before striding away.

After she put the boys to bed that night, Cerise crept over the gravel courtyard that linked Maxime's house to the wine harvesters' lodgings she made her home. She hated looking across the courtyard to see Maxime's shutters all closed.

She could open them again. After all, she was half owner of the house, but somehow to do so seemed disrespectful. She hoped the house would come back to life at some point but not yet. She was so furious with Maxime, and he was dead, *damn him*. Her anger had nowhere to go.

She picked one of the long, intricate iron keys from the wad that dangled from her fingers and opened the lock to Maxime's front door. It was worn and smooth under her fingers.

Cerise had come here to try and find answers—different answers from what Clovis believed. She could not understand why Maxime had waited until his death to throw his grandson and Cerise together. He'd certainly made no effort to do so while he was alive.

She stood in the front hall on the cold marble flagstones, shot through with pink and ochre and mined from the local quarries. Her foot found that groove at the base of the curved oval staircase, worn away by hundreds of years of Maxime's ancestors. It spoke of continuity, safety, security...all the things the deaths of her husband and parents had robbed from her.

In the days after Maxime's sudden death, Cerise had ensured the house was thoroughly cleaned and the beds made up with fresh linens. Everything was perfect and ready to go, but she didn't know what it was ready for exactly. Things felt suspended

here. Even though that felt wretched and tragic, she was inti-
mately familiar with that state of being.

She made her way up the stairs, inhaling in the familiar
mustiness mixed with wood polish. It was good to check on the
place. Pipes could burst. Mice could burrow in. Her hand ran
over the banister, the wood slipping under her palm like silk. She
loved this house, and yet she didn't feel like she was the person to
fill it—not with the tragedies she brought with her.

She let herself into Maxime's room. The shutters were closed,
but she knew when they were flung open they looked out over
the domaine's glorious vineyards.

Even though they were higher-altitude vineyards, Maxime
had always said he found them more beautiful than his holdings
on the lower slopes, holdings that would now be absorbed into
Clovis's already prestigious domaine. How she longed to open
the shutters, but something stopped her. *Not yet.*

She perched on the end of the massive bed, facing the shutters. She kept circling around to the same question. Why, by
appointing Clovis her equal partner, had Maxime taken away her
freedom to choose?

The only answer was a creak of the ancient floorboards under
the bed.

She blinked away tears. She had rarely felt lonely before
Maxime's death. She was so busy with her boys and the vineyards, and Maxime was always there to talk to. Since Clovis's
brutal entry into her life, loneliness gnawed at her. She wondered
whether it was Maxime's death or Clovis's presence that was the
main culprit.

Maxime was beyond helping her find the answer. Like so
many things in life, she would have to figure it out herself.

# chapter five

CERISE WAITED THREE more days to go to Clovis's
domaine. She finally made the decision to go based on the
reality that Clovis was her legal business partner, whether
she liked it or not. Diplomacy was perhaps the only way to get
rid of him. Resentment and anger hadn't gotten her very far.

As she arrived in Morey-Saint-Denis in her clunky lilac
Citroen, she admired the charm of the little village. It wasn't
as outwardly glorious as its neighbors Gevrey-Chambertin and
Chambolle-Musigny perhaps, but it had a simpler feel that belied
the gorgeous wine it produced. Cerise liked that combination.

The village church was perfect, with a charming little
round window above the door. It was set in the middle of stone
houses with white shutters and window boxes overflowing with
red geraniums.

Winemakers like Clovis had it easier down here; the Grand
Cru appellations on their labels had so much prestige that
ensuring quality was not a necessity but rather a choice. Cerise
wondered which approach Clovis took. She would soon find out.
Nobody could hide behind a winetasting. The wine spoke for
itself, especially to finely tuned palates like hers.

She parked on the vineyard side of the road and entered the
domaine via a small door inset within the massive white metal

gates. The gates were closed, and a restrained gold plaque on one of the stone pillars announced she had arrived at her destination: Domaine de Valois—the winery Clovis had inherited from his mother. Geneviève had already explained that, adhering to the chauvinist Burgundy tradition, his father had taken over the domaine the day after the wedding because Clovis's mother had no siblings. After his death, it passed on to Clovis as their only offspring. Cerise suspected Clovis had been managing the domaine in all but name long before that.

In Burgundy, the least welcoming domaines were generally the wealthiest—those that didn't need or desire customers to wander in off the street.

Inside was a picture-perfect courtyard. A rambling two-story stone house stretched along one side, flanked by winery outbuildings for fermentation, vats, and barrels. The entire place was neat as a pin. There wasn't a single weed pushing between the pea gravel, and the shutters and doors were the same glossy white as the main gate. Masses of white hydrangeas lined the front of the house. Cerise wondered who had planted them. Surely not Clovis.

There was no reception she could see, so she walked toward the vinification area, which was surely being readied for the upcoming harvest. That's where the sound of a spraying hose and metal clanging was coming from, in any case.

She walked through the huge open doors and spotted a man who was definitely not Clovis high up on a ladder spraying out one of the large fermenting tanks lined up in a row. One of Clovis's many workers, to whom Cerise always referred in her head as his minions.

The man on the ladder must have possessed some preternatural sixth sense because he stopped spraying for a moment and peered down at Cerise.

"Pierre!" he yelled to some unseen person at the back of the vat room. "Turn off the hose!"

Pierre obviously heard because within seconds the hose only trickled water. The man began climbing down the ladder.

"*Bonjour*," he said as he reached the flagstone floor of the cavernous room. "My name is Jean. I'm the *régisseur* here." A régisseur managed the day-to-day operations of a wine domaine, and Cerise had heard through the grapevine that Jean was an extraordinary one. After wiping his hands on his cornflower-blue overalls, he held one out to Cerise.

"*Bonjour*." She couldn't help but smile at this man, with his bright-green eyes and flop of white hair over his forehead. "My name is Cerise Desloires."

He laughed. "I know who you are."

"But—"

"I should explain. I've been working in the wine world for a long time. I knew your husband. In fact, I was at your husband's funeral. What a loss—the whole wine community mourned along with you."

Cerise waved her hand. "I'm sorry, I don't—"

"Of course you don't remember me. I'd be surprised if you remembered any guests from that terrible day. I'm sorry for all the tragedy you've endured. It is more than anyone should have to bear."

Her throat closed off with emotion. There was a compassion in his eyes that had nothing to do with pity, and it brought tears to her own.

"Also," he continued, "you are one of the most talented winemakers of the Côte. I make it my business to know your wines."

"Really?" She was stunned at this piece of information. "*Merci*."

"You are a superlative winemaker, and I don't say that to many people."

"I'm flattered."

"It's the truth."

"I've heard of you, too," Cerise said. "The best *régisseur* in the Côte D'Or, perhaps in all of France."

Jean gave her a wink. "Something like that."

"I've also heard other winemakers are constantly trying to poach you from Clovis."

Jean flipped his hair out of his eyes and laughed. "Well…yes, but I don't like to bother poor Clovis with that."

*Poor Clovis?* Were they thinking of the same man? Speaking of him—

"I don't see Clovis here." She gestured around the vat room. "This is probably a bad time. I'll come back."

"Certainly not!" Jean grasped her arm. "I've received strict instructions from Clovis to keep you here and fetch him immediately. I hate to be ungallant, but he will never forgive me if I let you leave. You don't want to do that to an old man like me, do you?"

Cerise tilted her head. "I'll stay, but don't think I'm buying this 'old man' act for a second."

He grinned. "Ho! Pierre!" he called to the man fiddling with valves at the bottom of one of the tanks. "Clovis is in the plot of vines for Les Amoureuses. Go get him. *Allez!* Hurry up."

Pierre sped off.

"Impressive." Cerise was curious if Jean's natural authority extended to her business partner. "Does Clovis obey you like that?" She wanted behind-the-scenes information.

Jean chuckled and led her back out to the courtyard. "I was there the day he was born," Jean said as their shoes crunched over the gravel. "His father…well, I suppose I shouldn't speak ill of the dead, but I believe some people are never meant to be parents and inflict terrible damage when they are…but enough of that. I taught Clovis everything he knows about wine. It would be no surprise if he did defer to me, but that is not his character. He became his own man years ago. We are colleagues now; we listen to each other. I would never dream of ordering him around his domaine."

On the opposite side of the courtyard, Jean beckoned her down a steep set of massive stone steps that led to the cellars. At the bottom she inhaled that heady scent of wine cellars in Burgundy—a combination of humidity, limestone, and centuries of spilled wine.

Oak barrels were laid out side by side as far as the eye could see.

"These cellars are massive," she said. She had known Clovis's holdings were extensive, but to see this...

"Huge," Jean confirmed, leading the way to an adjacent room. "The few times we've tried to do anything with the floor in this cellar, we stumble onto Roman cellars a meter or so below. We've learned not to disturb things any more than strictly necessary."

They arrived in a room with bottles stacked in sections of stone shelves and bins lining the walls. The walls were black with mold, which meant this cellar enjoyed high humidity—every winemaker's dream. There had to be an underground spring or river close by.

In the middle of the room sat three barrels, turned on their ends, each with a few corked bottles on top that were labeled only with a scrawl of white grease pencil.

Jean went to an old sink built into the corner of the space and took clean glasses and a corkscrew from the rack above.

He brought them to the barrel closest to Cerise. "Clovis should be here soon."

He busied himself with tidying up the bottles, so she began to drift around the room, fascinated despite herself. She was drawn, of course, to the oldest-looking shelf with the moldiest bottles. The silence between her and Jean was a companionable one. Wine cellars were holy places. The world outside was silenced, time meant little, and pleasure and history were captured in the magic alchemy of wine.

"How far back do these go?" she asked. The tiny chalkboards in front of the individual stacks of bottles were so crumbled they were illegible.

"The ones after 1910 are marked. The ones before that…" He shrugged. "We just know they are from earlier than 1910, that's all. Clovis and I often play the game of trying to figure out the year of the unmarked bottles."

"How did so much wine survive the war?" Cerise referred the Second World War, when Nazis occupied Burgundy and drained local cellars of every bottle they could find.

Jean shrugged again. "We built fake walls, *bien sûr*, like most other winemakers. I was only a small child then, and my father was the *régisseur*, but I remember it was my job to capture as many spiders as I could and bring them to the newly built cellar walls so they would spin webs and make the walls look old enough to trick the Nazis."

Cerise laughed, charmed by this image of a tiny Jean, darting around the cellar with his spiders and his bright-green eyes. "I shouldn't laugh. I know that was a terrible time."

Jean nodded. "It was, so I feel ashamed that my memories are mostly good. The two Germans who lodged with us were kind, jolly men from Bavaria. They had no more desire to be here than we had to host them. They were blackmailed into fighting because otherwise their families would have been killed. They were kind and respectful—apologetic, actually. The local SS leader who came every once in a while to terrorize us was another matter, but the adults kept us children away from him. Our Bavarian guests also put themselves at risk to protect us."

Cerise was intrigued. "What were the other good memories, besides the spiders and the Bavarians?"

He sighed, leaning with one hand on the rim of the nearest upturned barrel. "I suppose the way we all helped each other. We knew without a doubt we were all connected. There were communal meals and late-night family gatherings and parties down in the cellars after curfew. It was such a time of solidarity. None of us were going to make it on our own. I miss that."

Cerise felt a surge of envy at Jean's experience. She'd never really had that feeling of teamwork with Antoine. Their roles had been so separate and distinct. Maxime had been her mentor, not her colleague. Her insularity since Antoine's death meant that all her old friends had drifted away. Cerise's life had become the antithesis of what Jean described. She felt an ache behind her breastbone she hadn't been conscious of before.

"You look somber," Jean observed.

"No, just thinking," she lied. "I suppose you heard of the way Maxime left things in his will?"

He rubbed his chin. "*Oui.* Odd, but then again, I would bet anything Maxime had his reasons. That man didn't do anything on a whim."

Cerise dug the toe of one work boot into the gravel of the cellar floor. Jean was right about Maxime. "The way he left things…it was a possibility that never even occurred to me."

"I don't think it occurred to Clovis, either, but somehow it makes sense. You couldn't find a better partner than Clovis, you know, or a more dedicated winemaker."

"Come on, Jean," she chided. "I know you must be loyal, but let's face it—you run things around here."

He shook his head, and his hair flipped to the other side of his forehead. "Outsiders might assume so, but trust me, Clovis is the boss. I assist him—that's why he can go away like he must. The fact of the matter is he has a talent I never possessed."

She narrowed her eyes. "Perhaps you're biased."

"You could say that," Jean said. "But you could also say nobody is better qualified to evaluate Clovis than me."

As she was pondering this, she heard a racket in the main cellar.

"Good God." Jean chuckled. "That must be Clovis. It sounds like he's sprinting."

Sure enough, Clovis came around the corner, flushed and breathing so hard Cerise wondered if he had run the whole way from his vineyards.

"You came!" he gasped, a hand to his heaving—and, Cerise had to admit—lovely and broad chest.

"A promise is a promise." Cerise acquiesced when Clovis leaned in to give her *les bises*. He smelled of the outdoors. Freshly crushed leaves, sunshine, and a slight tang of sweat. It was intoxicating in the same way as the wine cellar. "I told you my word was good."

He enveloped her in a warm smile she had to steel herself to resist. "Has Jean here been telling you all kinds of terrible stories of my misspent youth?"

"We hadn't gotten to that," Jean said. "So I suppose I'll save them for another time. I must check on Pierre. The elevator doesn't quite reach the top floor with that one." He tapped his temple to demonstrate, then turned to Cerise. "It was an absolute pleasure spending time with you. I hope to further our acquaintance."

"You're leaving?" Panic fluttered in her chest. Wine cellars were such intimate places, where regular rules felt suspended. It wasn't just Clovis she didn't trust, she realized with dismay. It was herself. She could still summon hate for him, but it was getting harder, and he was just so damn attractive.

"I'm leaving you in excellent hands." Jean withdrew with an inscrutable wink.

She was being ridiculous. Of course she could trust herself. She didn't even like Clovis. This winetasting was merely to socially lubricate the sale negotiations. Still, Cerise felt uneasy. Here in his wine cellar, reality and logic felt silenced in the same way as the noises from the courtyard above.

She was standing on the opposite side of the tasting barrel

from Clovis. The barrel between them was a good thing, she reasoned. It kept things safe and businesslike.

Clovis took a deep breath. "Thank you for coming."

She nodded, conscious of a trickle of sweat running down his throat. She was aware of an urge to reach across the barrel and wipe it away, but instead she followed it with her gaze until it disappeared beneath his blue cotton T-shirt. She cleared her throat. "So, what will we be tasting?"

"Would you like to start with a Bourgogne Blanc?"

"This is your cellar, not mine." She shrugged, feeling oddly hurt. Strange he would have her taste such a basic appellation. All he could offer her was plain white Burgundy? Even in the hallowed vineyards of the Côte D'Or, that was rather generic.

He went to the far shelves and plucked a bottle from the stack. In his slightly damp T-shirt and shorts from the vineyard, his muscles were on full display. Still, he moved with a lanky grace that was uniquely his. *Stop noticing*, she scolded herself.

He brought the bottle to the barrel and picked up the corkscrew made from a local grapevine.

Cerise couldn't seem to look directly at him, so she focused on his hands as he wound the corkscrew into the cork. They were shaking slightly, yet he must have done this a million times before. She wondered for the first time if maybe she wasn't the only one rattled about being alone together in the cellar.

Clovis poured the wine into glasses and passed one to Cerise.

Now, at least, she could concentrate on the wine, not its maker. She swirled it around, admiring its crystalline straw color. She buried her nose deep in the glass, sniffed, and was almost knocked off her feet by the citrus and hazelnut notes. "This is more than just a Bourgogne Blanc," she said, lifting her eyes so she could examine his face. "Where are the vines for this?"

"A little parcel a hectare or so above the Musigny plot."

"That's Grand Cru," Cerise said, wondering if he was trying

to trick her. "Why on earth would you be selling it as just a white Burgundy?"

He took a sip.

*God, he has a beautiful mouth, finely sculpted yet expressive.*

"I don't feel it has had the complexity and depth these past three vintages to warrant a Grand Cru label," he said, examining his wineglass instead of her. "When a truly worthy vintage comes along, the Grand Cru designation will come back. *Promis.*"

"Was this Jean's idea?" Cerise asked.

He laughed. "Jean tried to talk me out of it."

Maybe there had been truth in what Jean meant when he said Clovis was the boss. She had respect, despite herself, for that kind of rigor. *Merde.* It made him harder to dislike, and she was already struggling with that in this otherworldly place.

*Stop this. I don't want a partner. I am no longer the woman I was when I was married to Antoine—a woman who needed a man.*

She took a sip of wine and swished it around her mouth. Its satin texture introduced a gorgeous bouquet that included butterscotch among the notes she had smelled earlier. This wine… it might not be a Grand Cru, but it was *so* close. Whatever the appellation, it was playful, rich, and warm, and evoked a heady feeling of nostalgia. It was such a delicious wine that Cerise no longer felt like she knew up from down.

"What do you think?" Clovis asked, his expression so intent that his eyes appeared almost black in the dim light.

She thought she wanted to kiss him, his wine was that good. She shook her head to regain some rationality. "It's such a welcoming wine. It's got so much charm."

She swallowed another sip, and her eyes met Clovis's. It was an intimate thing, tasting someone's wine. It was like glimpsing into their very soul. Cerise believed it was the best way to discover hidden facets of any winemaker. If a winemaker didn't possess certain qualities, she found, they could never tease them out of their wine.

"It's lovely," she said, trying as she spoke to unravel the mysteries contained in her glass. "Truly, but there's something else…a longing, like for a different time—or maybe a different place." She shook her head again. "Sorry, I'm getting maudlin. That must sound like complete nonsense. Good wine makes me fanciful."

Instead of looking at her with ridicule or skepticism, his eyes were round in shock.

"What?" she asked, conscious of a desire to go around the barrel and wrap him in a hug.

"No one else has ever picked up on that. This is why I begged you here. I believe the best way to know a person is to taste their wines. I know it's an uncommon opinion, but—"

"I happen to share it." She tipped the glass and let the honey-toned liquid tantalize her palate and her mind all over again. Her joints felt looser, and she was aware of every particle of air between her and Clovis.

He moved across the room again, walking behind her. She couldn't seem to breathe as he passed close, then moved farther away. A clinking sound made her look up to see him choosing another bottle from the shelves.

With smooth, practiced movements this time—the nerves, if that's what they had been, had subsided—Clovis twisted the corkscrew into the new cork. She was hypnotized by the smooth play of muscles in his forearm, tensing and relaxing in sync.

He probably wasn't trying to seduce her, but his wines were accomplishing it anyway. She couldn't let that happen. She needed to keep things strictly business if she ever hoped to negotiate a buyout. She was far more vulnerable to his appeal down in his wine cellar than anywhere else, Cerise realized too late.

A buyout was the only way to achieve the independence she wanted more than life itself. She steeled herself against Clovis and tried to adopt a nonchalant tone. "What are you having me taste now?"

"Les Amoureuses." The name taunted her. *The Lovers.* She'd forgotten that his holdings included that Chambolle-Musigny appellation. It was one of his most famous wines.

He pulled out the cork. It slipped free from the neck of the bottle with a soft sigh. "I use a horse in these vineyards," Clovis said. "No tractors."

Cerise grasped this diversion from her unruly thoughts. "Why?"

"Because of the rocky topsoil. I think I may move entirely to horses, actually. I'm not a fan of machinery."

"I'm not, either," Cerise said when he handed her a glass and finally met her eyes. *If only his weren't so compelling.*

His opened wide. "*Eh merde.* That was an insensitive thing to say. Of course with Antoine's death, you would hate machines. My apologies."

She breathed a sigh of relief. The mention of Antoine would break the spell. It was the perfect reminder that she had already found and lost her soul mate. Romantic love was firmly a thing of her past. She waved her hand. "No need for apology. It was a tragic way for Antoine to die, but my dislike of machines has far more to do with how they damage the soil and roots. It's like allowing harm to a dear friend. Hmm, I'm sounding whimsical again."

"No," Clovis said. "You sound smart."

She smiled back at him, perhaps for the first time. He made a strange sound, as though swallowing a gasp.

"What vintage is this wine?"

"2005."

"You're having me taste the good stuff."

"Would I ever do otherwise?" His dimple flashed high up on his left cheek.

Cerise fought a magnetic pull toward this nemesis of hers. Antoine's ghostly presence was proving no deterrent for her desire to move closer to him, to run her fingers up the muscles of his forearms and feel the warmth of his skin.

Disconcerted, she stared into her glass and swirled the garnet wine around it. She buried her nose in the glass and inhaled deeply. Oh no. It was just as intoxicating as Clovis.

She cleared her throat. "There's a nice backdrop of *sous-bois* and mushroom. Red fruits above."

She was seduced by the notes of loganberry and red currant. This was a deep, complex wine. It was a fall-on-your-knees-in-love wine. Les Amoureuses. The spell tightened around her like a rope.

Her skin prickled with desire for Clovis, this man who held her fate. She was aware of only her glass and him. Her eyes flicked up and met his. The hands that crafted this… She wanted them caressing her. The mind that created this… She wanted it to want her.

She had to resist. She had to keep Domaine du Cerisier under her command, and the only way to do that was buy Clovis out. If she gave in to her lust, she would risk giving in to them working together, being partners together… She had to protect herself and her boys at any cost.

She tried to say something dampening, but no words came out. All she could hear was the thump of her heart and the shallow, ragged sounds of her breath. The ache to close the distance between her and man who made this wine pulsated to the ends of her fingers.

With intent expression in his eyes, Clovis placed his wine-glass down on the barrel and moved to her. His arms encircled her body.

Cerise froze. His touch made her feel warm and cherished. She wanted more. She couldn't let this continue. She tilted her face up to tell him.

"*Bonjour!*" A terrible French accent rang through the silence.

Clovis's arms dropped. "*Merde,*" he cursed under his breath.

She clutched the rim of the barrel, her knees watery. *What just happened?* "Who is that?"

"I have no idea." Clovis strode to the entrance. "But whoever it is, they must have let themselves in."

# chapter six

THE VOICE BELONGED to one of three young tourists, presumptuous enough to wander into Clovis's cellars. That was simply not done, but it wasn't the first time Cerise had heard of it happening.

Her mind raced with what might have happened if they hadn't been interrupted. They'd been close enough to kiss. Oh, how she'd wanted to, and oh, how she hated herself for it. She had been just on the verge of telling him nothing could happen between them…at least, she was almost sure she would have if they hadn't been interrupted. A niggle of doubt remained, reinforced by the frustrated longing that reverberated behind her breastbone. She should be relieved that nothing happened. She had to be.

"*Bonjour.*" Clovis turned to the tourists, a mask sliding over the raw emotion that had been on his face just a minute before. "And who are you? Please come in."

Seeing as they were here, Clovis had to invite them in. Cerise would have done the same—gritted her teeth and borne the intrusion. To be any less than hospitable was unthinkable for a Burgundian.

The leader of the pack was a tall, skinny boy of around twenty or so. He was dressed all in black with a porkpie hat perched on his unruly blond curls. The two girls with him wore an odd mishmash of prints and plaids that seemed too self-conscious to be unintentional.

"I'm Brent," the boy said, then waited expectantly, as if for a round of applause.

None came, and he continued in English. "I've heard this is one of the best wineries in the region, so of course I had to bring my friends to try it. Who are you?" He jerked his head at Clovis. The two girls gazed at Brent adoringly.

"I'm the winemaker here," Clovis answered. "My name is Clovis de Valois."

The boy laughed and rolled his eyes. "You don't seem to realize who I am. I'm an influencer. My assistant emailed ahead to book a winetasting, but nobody got back to her."

Cerise watched this unfold with amazement. Brent acted as though he was conferring a singular honor on Clovis.

"It's a busy time of year for us," Clovis said, his eyes flicking to Cerise and sparkling, inviting her to share his amusement at the sheer absurdity of Brent.

Well, there was no harm in that.

"We don't have much time for winetastings," he explained.

"But one post from me, and you could sell a huge number of bottles."

A snort escaped Cerise. Clovis's wine was purchased years in advance. Potential customers battled to even gain a spot on his waiting list. The idea that he needed social media celebrities for sales made her bite her lip to keep from laughing. Her eyes met Clovis's again, and although his mouth was schooled in a firm line, the dimple on his cheek kept flashing. She wasn't the only one having a hard time containing her mirth and welcomed the much-needed release after the intensity between them before.

Clovis just answered with a noncommittal "Is that so?"

"Yes." Brent nodded.

"Seeing as you're already here, what would you like to taste?"

The skinny boy mentioned the Bonnes Mares Grand Cru, which retailed at several hundred dollars per bottle.

Clovis's eyes widened. "I'm sorry, but all those bottles are sold. How about a Passetoutgrain?"

Cerise waited, wondering if the boy would realize a Passetoutgrain was the lowest-quality wine from Burgundy, even though Clovis's would probably still be excellent.

"Fine." The boy sniffed.

"Cerise, can you help me?" Clovis tilted his head to indicate she should follow him to the bottle bins.

The three intruders huddled together and occupied themselves by exclaiming over Clovis's ignorance, apparently believing that neither Clovis nor Cerise understood English.

She thought the spell had been broken with the intrusion, but standing close to Clovis in front of the bin, she craved the feel of his arms around her again. She knew she should be grateful for the tourists' intrusion, but her stubborn heart refused to feel thankful.

"There will always be a Bonne Mares for you to taste," Clovis whispered to her.

She looked forward to that, but...she shouldn't. Tasting his Bonne Mares would be far too risky. "Do you have any spoiled wine you could give him?" she asked to divert herself. "I'm curious if the famous Brent would notice a difference."

"Should I?" he mused. "I mean, ethically..."

"It's would be for research," she clarified.

The dimple flashed deep. "In that case, who am I to stand in the way of experimentation?"

"Exactly."

"Besides, that much pretension deserves a karmic correction."

"I couldn't agree more," she said, trying to remember the last time she had enjoyed herself this much. Despite her initial reticence, she was warming to idea of a friendship with this unnatural ally. Being sociable could only help the negotiations.

Clovis grabbed a bottle from the bin, then took another from an upturned barrel on their return. He eased the cork out of the one from the barrel, gave it a sniff, and shared a mischievous smile with Cerise over the bottleneck.

"Here we go." He poured it into three fresh glasses and passed one to each member of the trio.

Then he opened the other bottle, the one he'd taken from the bin, and poured a glass that he handed to Cerise. She tasted it, instantly recognizing his famed Bonnes Mares, with its rich flavors of Morello cherries and back notes of tobacco and truffles. This wine made her want to run her tongue down Clovis's bare chest, something she absolutely, definitively, could never do. He winked at her. *Mon Dieu.*

For several minutes she was absorbed in experiencing the wine, thinking of all the things she couldn't do to the gorgeous genius who'd made it. She looked up and saw a pained expression on Clovis's face.

Brent was rhapsodizing over the oxidized wine and giving his friends a winetasting lesson that showcased his ignorance.

She pointed to the wine in her glass and gave Clovis a thumbs-up, then looked meaningfully at Brent and rolled her eyes.

The boy must have caught it because he paused mid-exegesis and said to Cerise, "Who are you?" It was the first thing he had said to her since walking into the cellar. "Are you his assistant?"

"My name is Cerise," she said. "And I'm not Clovis's assistant." *Good God, that's what will happen if remain partners. People will assume I'm his assistant.* Her resolve reasserted itself.

"Cerise happens to be one of the finest winemakers in the region," Clovis said.

The boy's expression changed. "In that case we must come

and winetaste at your place. We could sell a lot of wine for you, you know."

Clovis mouthed, "Sorry."

The trouble was, unlike Clovis, she and her domaine could use the publicity. Her appellations were far less valuable than his and therefore more of a challenge to sell. She devoted all her limited time to making good wine and knew she had sadly neglected marketing.

Still, she had her pride. "I don't do winetastings," Cerise lied. "My domaine is too small."

"Are you on Instagram?"

"No," she said. "Neither are most of my clients."

The boy made a sound of disbelief. "Then how do you sell your wine?"

"Don't worry about Cerise." Clovis jumped to her defense in a way that made her wonder if he thought she couldn't fight her own battles. "Or me for that matter. Us Burgundian winemakers do just fine. We don't all live in your world, you know."

"Of course you don't," Brent snapped. "Otherwise you would have heard of me."

"I have no doubt," Cerise said placatingly, glad her life left her absolutely no time for social media.

"I'm sorry," Clovis said, casting a look of apology at Cerise. "I must get back to the vineyards."

"Can we come with you?" the boy asked. "For some photos?"

"I'll be doing dirty work today. It's not photogenic."

"Maybe you can just leave us down here in the cellars?" one of the girls suggested.

"No," he answered.

The boy clearly couldn't take a hint, as he didn't move, so Clovis had to lead them upstairs and out of the courtyard. Cerise brought up the rear to ensure no stragglers were left behind.

Between them they managed to herd Brent and his posse out of the small gate.

They started laughing as soon as Clovis shut the gate behind the "guests."

"I wouldn't have missed that for the world," she said finally.

Clovis wiped his eyes. "Part of me feels guilty about pulling such a trick."

"Don't."

He put a hand on his chest and sighed. "You're right. I haven't had that much fun in a long time."

That was true for Cerise, too, but there was that troubling moment before the intruders had interrupted. Her face burned with the memory.

The winetasting had not gone the way she'd intended. She had trusted the winetasting would reinforce her dislike of him, but instead it made him impossible to scorn. It complicated everything. As much as she was drawn to Clovis, she didn't want a partner. She needed to make her own mark on the winemaking world, and she couldn't do so with Clovis overshadowing her.

"I should go." She needed time alone to think. "The boys will be home soon."

"Wait." Clovis took a step toward her, and she wondered for a second if he wanted to pick up where they'd left off. She couldn't, not here in the lucid light of day, or anywhere else, she chastised herself. "Can you come for lunch on Sunday?"

"*Merci*, but I spend Sundays with the boys."

"The invitation includes them, of course," he said. "Like I said, I'd like to get to know them better, too."

She hesitated. There was no reason for him getting to know Marc and Yves better. She didn't plan on having Clovis in her life for long. Still, she remembered what Geneviève had said about his traumatic childhood and the longing in Clovis's eyes at Maître

Gilbert's office when the solicitor had mentioned her sons. There was a great sadness there that echoed with something in her.

Clovis angled her chin with his forefinger so she met his eyes. His touch was warm and electric. "Please?"

"Well, if you're going to resort to underhanded tricks like begging—"

"I am."

"What can I bring, then?" she said.

"Just you and your sons."

"That's not what I meant."

"I know, but I enjoy cooking. I'm thrilled to host the three of you. Besides, we have things to talk about."

She raised a skeptical brow.

"Work things," he clarified.

*"D'accord."* She opened the gate. "Until Sunday."

*"À Dimanche."* Clovis stayed inside the frame of the gate and waved until she drove off.

On the way home, Cerise remembered she needed a baguette for dinner, or maybe two as the boys' appetite has grown in direct proportion with the number of hours they spent building *cabanes* in the forest. It was easier to think of practical things like dinner than what had just transpired between her and Clovis.

She double-parked in front of her favorite boulangerie in Nuit-Saint-Georges. She had to get her head together before she saw the boys. She ran across the cobblestone street and opened the door of the shop, her arrival heralded by a little bell.

The place smelled of freshly baked bread and butter, and it was blessedly air-conditioned to preserve the beautiful pastry confections. She breathed in the cool air. This was good; she could gather her thoughts here. She took her place in line.

Maybe the pull she felt toward Clovis could be chalked up to the intoxicating effect of his cellars. He made wonderful wine. How vexing. It would be much harder to get rid of a partner she respected. She didn't feel ready to begin to sift through the complexities of his magnetic pull.

She caught a glimpse of familiar bottle-blonde, well-coiffed hair in the line ahead of her. She began to back out of the bakery. Not Geneviève. Not now.

Her *tante* Geneviève picked up her baguettes and turned to leave. Too late. She caught sight of Cerise right away.

"*Ma pétite* Cerise!" She embraced her warmly, enveloping her in a stifling cloud of Chanel N°5. Geneviève was dressed head to toe in elegant white linen, impeccable as always. "What a stroke of luck! How are you, *ma chérie?*"

"I'm fine, thank—"

"I've been in Dijon," her aunt breathlessly informed her. "The stores have started putting out their fall lines. The trunk of my Mercedes is packed with shopping bags. I'll have to get them in the house before your uncle sees them!" She tittered at her own joke. "Where have you been?"

"As a matter of fact, I've been to Clovis's for a winetasting." There was no point in lying. She knew it was likely the news would filter to her aunt sooner or later. "I'm on my way home."

Geneviève gave her a thorough once-over. Cérise had changed into a clean pair of shorts and a cotton T-shirt for the winetasting. She wasn't wearing a ball gown, but she wasn't wearing her dirty vineyard clothes, either, unlike Clovis.

Geneviève's mouth popped open in a round, perfectly lipsticked circle. "Is that so? Well, well, well…"

"It was just a winetasting." But even though Cerise hadn't yet figured out exactly what had happened, it was certainly much more than that. The memory of Clovis's strong arms behind her back, pressing her so close she could smell the crushed leaves on his skin, rocked her on her feet. No, it wasn't just a winetasting, but she could never trust her aunt with the truth. She could barely admit it to herself.

"Don't tell me you went dressed like that!"

"Of course I did. I just told you I'm on my way home."

"But you will never catch a man like Clovis dressed like a vineyard worker."

"I wish you would get rid of this stupid idea that I want to 'catch' Clovis. Besides, I do work in the vineyards," she protested. "Every day. I'm proud of that." Cerise couldn't count the number of times she and her aunt had argued this point.

"You must strive to be more elegant, my dear." Geneviève tsked. "I know you don't have your mother anymore to give you such advice, but I have told you before, it is not the same here on the low slopes as it is on your high slopes. The style is much more *soigné* down here. People will confuse you for a rustic!"

Cerise rolled her eyes. "Clovis came straight from working in the vineyards, without changing."

"But that's different."

"How?"

"He's the winemaker!"

"Tata, *I'm* a winemaker."

She sighed. "It's not the same, Cerise."

"I've told you before, I don't care what anyone thinks. If it turns off Clovis, wonderful." That didn't feel true, but logically it had to be.

"That is just silly," Geneviève said. "I don't say you will succeed, but now that you two are legal partners, think of your advantage—your access to him! He is a prize, my dear. You must at least *try*."

Cerise made a low, guttural sound of anger. "I'm not going to continue this conversation, Tata, because I'll say things I regret. How is my uncle doing?"

Geneviève rolled her eyes. "I see you're as willful as ever, but just know I always have your best interests at heart. Your uncle has a touch of the gout, but otherwise he's fine. He always asks about you. You must come over with the boys and visit more often."

Cerise smiled. "Give him my love."

Her aunt gave a shrug that indicated she was giving up, yet again, on bringing Cerise around to her way of thinking. "Think on what I said, *ma chérie*. I worry about you. You have been alone too long." With that, she floated out of the door, leaving Cerise to seethe in her perfumed wake.

# chapter seven

FOUR DAYS LATER Cerise was back at the gate to Clovis's property, this time flanked by her sons. It was open, so she ushered the boys into the courtyard. Marc and Yves stood still at the threshold, taking it in.

Yves glanced up at her. "Does a king live here?"

Marc snorted. "There are no more kings in France, Yves."

Yves pulled at Cerise's hand. "Is that true, Maman?" Cerise had picked him up a wooden shield and sword at the Beaune market, and since then he'd been enamored with kings and knights and dragons.

"It is. There haven't been any kings in France since the Revolution in 1789."

"Where did they go?"

She considered whitewashing the truth but then thought the better of it. "The Revolutionaries cut off their heads."

Yves brown eyes widened. "Awesome," he breathed.

"I knew you'd like that. I'll tell you more about it when we get home, *d'accord*? There might even be some books with pictures in them at Maxime's house."

Yves nodded vigorously. Cerise had a sinking feeling that guillotines were going to be the next thing that captured his lively imagination.

"Clovis lives here?" Marc asked, his voice incredulous. It was an awe-inspiring place.

"He does," she said. "Maxime once told me that Domaine de Valois—I guess it was called something else before Clovis's father took over—dates back to the fifteenth century."

That history emanated from the ivory stones around her, and Cerise sensed her boys felt it, too.

She wondered how badly Clovis's father had driven this domaine into the ground before he died and what it had taken Clovis to build it back up. The sheer weight of Clovis's inheritance started to reveal itself in all its complexity. If he had no children, Cerise had no idea who the domaine would pass to. She hoped it would be a good steward like Clovis because it hurt her heart to think of such a magnificent place that produced such magnificent wine falling into ruin.

She hadn't been proud of the fact that she'd devoted more thought than usual to what to wear to the Sunday lunch. She wondered if her aunt's advice at the bakery had insidiously burrowed into her mind. Regardless, Geneviève's insistence on "catching" Clovis had solidified her resolve to keep things strictly business. They had a buyout to negotiate. Cerise could not let their relationship be anything more than friendly, even though she couldn't bring herself to hate him anymore either. Today, she would allow nothing to ambiguous to occur.

Unlike her aunt, Cerise was neither a social climber nor a gold digger. She wanted her vineyards and her independence; that was all. Nothing irreparable had happened between them in the cellar. It was just a bizarre moment. They hadn't kissed. They could be friendly without any awkwardness.

It was one of those days where the temperature was pushing toward thirty-five degrees Celsius and the air felt like it blew straight off the Sahara. It was so hot that in the end Cerise had slipped on the coolest thing she owned—a simple white slip dress with a drawstring collar that tied at the nape of her neck, paired with hand-tooled leather sandals Maxime had brought her back from one of his many trips to Greece.

Cerise let Yves ring the bell, and Clovis opened the door almost immediately. She hung behind her sons, conscious of a sudden shyness. Orange roses framed the stone around the front door. She breathed in their delicate perfume and tried to steady herself.

"Welcome!" Clovis leaned down to the boys, then glanced over their heads at Cerise. He blinked. "Wow."

A shiver ran through her body. *Just business*, she reminded herself. Of course she was attracted to him. His currency was charm, after all. It didn't mean she needed to act on it. She nudged her boys to go in front of her.

Clovis turned his attention back to Marc and Yves. He shook their hands, one boy at a time, and chatted with them like fellow adults rather than children. "Welcome to *chez moi*."

From the smiles on the boys' faces, Cerise concluded they weren't immune to Clovis's appeal, either.

"Come in." He ushered them in the hall.

He wore blue shorts and a long-sleeved white cotton shirt rolled up to his elbows that outlined his muscular biceps in a way that made her yearn to run her fingers up and down them. She gave herself a shake. *Purely professional.*

Clovis was reputed to be so wealthy that Cerise half expected a servant to be lingering around, but he appeared to be alone.

The smooth flagstones at their feet echoed as they followed Clovis down the hall. The walls were lined with beautiful paint-ings—she spied a small landscape in the style of Renoir. He led them into a living room that boasted some beautiful antiques, but the couches looked deep and cozy.

A simple *apéritif* was set up on the coffee table—a bottle of cassis and a bottle of *crémant*, which were, of course, the ingredients to the local *apéritif* called kir. There was also some cubed *comté* cheese, rounds of *saucisson sec*, and a bowl of chips for the boys. Everyone sat down, and Clovis chatted with the boys about their school. He sympathized when they complained about a teacher who yelled a lot and punished the class by depriving them of gym.

Clovis groaned. "I hated when teachers did that. Do you play sports outside of school?"

"Rugby," Marc said proudly. He had followed in his father's footsteps and joined the Rugby Club of Beaune as soon as he'd turned ten.

"I like soccer," said Yves.

Marc made a sound of disgust. "A sport for drama queens."

Cerise rolled her eyes. Of course Yves chose a sport his brother disparaged. Logical.

"Which do you like best, soccer or rugby?" Marc asked Clovis, leaning forward with his elbows on his knees to wait for the answer.

She watched, interested to see how Clovis was going to extract himself from this diplomatic nightmare.

"Neither," he said. "I mean, I enjoy them both, but my sport was handball."

"Handball?" Marc and Yves echoed.

"Yes. I almost made it to the national team, but then...well, school, then the vineyards, came calling."

"Like they did for my *maman*!" Yves said, pleased. "She often says the vines need her to take care of them, just like we do."

"We have that in common." Clovis's smile moved to Cerise, like the warmth of the sun coming out from behind clouds. *Resist.* The way Clovis talked to Marc and Yves like small adults and the fact that he seemed genuinely interested in what they had to say blindsided her. She could never be with a man who didn't love her sons, but that didn't seem to be the case with Clovis.

*Wait.* She couldn't be with Clovis because she had to save her vineyard, her independence, her very sense of self... She could never let herself be subsumed by a man again.

"Yes." Yves squirmed on the couch. "But please don't bore us about the vines and stuff. That's all Maman and Maxime ever talked about."

"Yves!" Cerise sent him a look meant to nip such rudeness in the bud.

"It's boring!" Yves protested.

"What would you boys like to drink?" Clovis intervened. "I went out especially and bought Orangina."

Yves cheered.

"Orangina would be nice, thank you," Marc answered with his habitual decorum.

Clovis laughed—that inviting laugh that had taken her by surprise at the winetasting. "I'll go and grab them in the kitchen. I wanted to keep them cold on such a scorching day."

When he was gone, Yves hopped up from the couch, unable to sit still as usual.

"No touching," Cerise reminded him.

"Will you cut off my head if I do?" Yves's eyes sparkled.

"I wouldn't rule it out." Cerise grinned at him. "But I am serious about the not touching, you know."

He sighed. "I know." He roved around the room, his hands clutched tightly behind his back, inspecting every piece of furniture, the glossy books on photography and France and winemaking stacked artfully on the coffee table, and a cluster of photos on one of the shelves.

"Sit down," Marc said. "It's rude to snoop."

"He's right," Cerise admitted. "Although it's not your place to say, Marc."

"I'm not touching anything," Yves protested. "I'm just looking with my eyes, like Maman always tells me to."

Clovis returned with two opened Orangina bottles and a basket flowing with large *gougères* that filled the room with the delicious smell of melted Emmental and butter. He set the drinks down on the table. Fortunately, he didn't seem to mind Yves roving around the room.

"Who is this girl in your photos?" Yves pointed to one of the frames. "She's in one, two, three…four of them," he counted.

Cerise's heart squeezed oddly. She knew Clovis had girl-friends. That fact had no impact on her life; it shouldn't have an impact on her heart. Because she was sitting across the room, she couldn't see which photos Yves was pointing at.

"The little girl?" Clovis asked.

"*Oui,*" answered Yves.

"That's my daughter."

Cerise gasped before she could stop herself. "You have a daughter?"

He turned to her and smiled in a proud, shy way she hadn't seen before. "Yes. She's twelve and lives with her mother in London. That's why I'm in England so often."

"What's her name?" Marc asked while Cerise attempted to gather her scattered thoughts.

*Clovis, a father?* She'd never imagined that as even a remote possibility—not even for a second. She couldn't comprehend why she never heard about this from Maxime—or anyone else for that matter.

"My daughter's name is Emily."

"Emily." Yves considered this. "It's an okay name, for a girl."

"Cerise, you look thunderstruck," Clovis said.

"I guess I am. Why did I not know you have a daughter?"

"I don't keep it a secret." He shrugged. "But the situation is more complicated than I'd like." His powerful shoulders dropped, and he stared down at his hands.

"Complicated how?" she asked.

"I met Emily's mother when I was a student, studying for my marketing degree in Paris. I did three months of work experience in London, and...well, Emily was the happy result of that. Her mother and I didn't stay together. It wasn't"—he glanced at the boys and then back to Cerise—"that sort of relationship."

*But it was enough of "that sort of a relationship" to produce a child.*

Yves brought over one of the framed photos and passed it to Cerise. She should reprimand him for breaking her no-touching edict, but she was burning with curiosity. Emily was adorable. If Clovis's daughter was now twelve, this must have been taken three or four years previously. She looked every bit the British schoolgirl, even though her proper English school uniform was a bit rumpled. She was missing both front teeth. She had her father's startling blue eyes, and her blonde hair was pulled back in two skinny braids under a royal-blue bowler hat.

Cerise couldn't get enough air into her lungs. *What a thing it would be, to make a child with Clovis.* She shook that thought out of her head. That had to be Geneviève speaking, not her. "Does she come here to Burgundy to visit?"

"There is nothing I would love better." His voice broke, and he paused to clear it. "But her mother is an anxious person and doesn't let Emily out of her sight."

"Even with her own father?"

His blue eyes darkened several shades. "When Emily's mother, Patricia, began taking medication to treat her anxiety, I had high hopes that maybe..." He'd been clasping his hands together, and now he let them fall to his knees. "*C'est comme ça.* I would never want to do anything to upset Emily or her mother, so I go over there at least twice a month." He glanced up at Cerise. "You still look stunned."

"I guess I never pictured you being a fellow parent."

He had begun to pour two glasses of kir, but he paused for a moment and studied her. "Why?"

"You seem too..."

"Too what?"

"I don't know. Serene, I guess? Like you haven't been humbled by life." Cerise regretted the words as soon as they came out.

A muscle twitched near Clovis's mouth, and his eyes hardened, but instead of responding he turned his attention to Marc and Yves. They had already guzzled their Oranginas and were peering out the window to the large garden at the back of the house, which boasted a swing set.

"You can go outside if you'd like," Clovis told them. "I installed that for Emily when I thought she might be able to visit me a few years ago. I'd be delighted to see it being used."

Cerise braced herself. Clovis had every right to be angry with her.

They hurried out of the room, Yves making his departure on the heels of a loud Orangina burp. Clovis passed her a kir and held out the basket of *gougères*.

Hesitant, she took one but didn't eat it right away.

"I know you have suffered far more than most." There was steel in Clovis's voice. "But do you think you're the only one to have struggled?"

"No," she tried to explain. "I just didn't imagine you had." She cursed her lack of filter.

"Do you know how much I grieve over the fact that Emily has never been able to travel to France with me, to discover where half of her comes from?" He held his body stiffly. "Do you know what it is to be separated from your own child?"

"No," she admitted. "I don't. I can't imagine."

"How about watching my mother die of a horrific cancer when I was only seven?" His finely sculpted nostrils flared. "Do you think I didn't suffer from that?"

Cerise realized what a grave mistake she'd made. She flushed with shame. Her own experiences weren't supposed to harden her toward others, but that was how she was acting. "No…I'm sorry. That must have been terrible. What I said was unfair. I apologize. It's just that you exude this…I don't know, this aura of ease. It's galling."

Clovis had been sitting in an armchair, but now he moved to the couch beside her. The couch was soft, so it gave way under his weight, pushing them closer to each other. Every cell in her body was aware of his proximity. "Did you ever stop to consider that air of ease might be armor?"

She hadn't, and that delicious smell of fresh leaves and oak and his own scent muddled her thoughts even further. She wanted him, but she could never have him. She needed to shut herself off to him, but in doing that she'd been heartless.

"What I want to know is why you have so many prejudices about me," he said, his voice low and earnest. "I wish you didn't. Whether you like it or not, we're partners now. We're going to have to work together."

She couldn't seem to look up. She was rigid with mortification at being in the wrong and confused that what she wanted to do in that instant was sink into Clovis's arms.

Instead, she leaned away from him and stared at the floor. "Part of it might be that you're so ludicrously handsome," she muttered. It was true. She couldn't be near him, especially so near that she could feel the heat from his skin, and remain unaffected.

"What?" He laughed. In a second the tone of the room changed again. "That's not what I thought you were going to say."

She sent him a tentative smile. "You look a bit stunned."

"Touché."

She leaned back in the couch and studied his striking features. "Come on, you must know it's true."

He twisted so he also leaned against the couch cushions,

and he studied Cerise with his cheek resting against his fist. That liquid heat she'd felt at the winetasting rushed through her again. "What about you?" he said. "Should I make all kinds of assumptions about you simply because you're one of the most beautiful woman I've ever seen?"

She searched his eyes, which had shifted again and were now focused on her with laserlike intensity. "You're serious," she concluded with wonder.

The way he was looking at her right now, with such hunger... it had the magic of making her feel beautiful. She needed to stop this. *My vineyards, my independence...*

Clovis tentatively stroked her straight dark hair. "You must know it's true."

His touch felt protective and tender. His hand moved leisurely to the back of her neck, and with deft fingers he twisted up her hair, which she had foolishly worn loose on such a hot day. She opened her mouth to say something but couldn't find any words. She had to move, but her limbs were frozen with the need to see what Clovis was going to do next.

He leaned forward and gently planted a kiss at the nape of her neck.

"Oh." The lone, soft word popped out of her mouth like the cork being released from a wine bottle. She had to stop this, but it felt too good.

"I have been wanting to do that," Clovis murmured between applying more kisses to that sensitive spot. "You have the most provocative neck I've ever seen."

"Oh my God." Cerise sighed before reason could assert itself. *Purely professional.* The words now felt so weak she barely recognized them. She didn't want a partner, or a man, but she did want to be touched the way he was touching her—more than anything.

His face swam in front of her field of vision. She ran a finger up the sharp line of his right cheekbone. *Cerise, stop this before it's too late.* His eyes drifted closed. He exhaled, as though relieved of a great burden.

They leaned into each other. All the while her mind muttered in the background about her vineyards, her career, her boys…but somehow the kiss felt unavoidable. More than anything, she had to know what it felt like to kiss him.

It was so much softer than Cerise had expected. Gentle lips among the bristles of his stubble. He tasted of blackcurrant and butter and deliciousness that made her hunger for more. She knew this was a terrible mistake, but at the same time a rush of joy made her angle her head to deepen their connection.

Kissing Clovis was even more delectable than tasting his wines.

His hand stroked her back, tracing the bumps of her spine. In one fluid movement, his arms wrapped around her and drew her closer so she was almost sitting on his lap. She was being reckless, but it felt as though she had been asleep for years and he was gently teasing her awake. She slipped her arms around his warm torso.

She didn't ever want to sleep again. Their kiss became hungrier.

*More* was her only remaining thought. *More, more, more.*

Somebody groaned, and Cerise suspected it was her.

A clatter sounded in the hallway, and they both sprang apart, just in time.

Yves burst into the room. "I'm hungry." He narrowed his eyes. "Why are you sitting so close?"

She dared not look at Clovis. She was having a difficult enough time catching her breath as it was.

Yves turned his attention to his mother. "Why are your cheeks red, Maman? Are you angry?"

She leaped up off the couch. Clovis moved to do the same, then quickly sat back down and pulled a red throw cushion over his lap. He cast her a rueful glance.

Her entire body vibrated like the village church bell ringing

Angelus, but luckily there was not as much outward evidence of it for her. She felt completely bewildered but couldn't resist meeting Clovis's gaze. She bit back laughter.

Better offense than defense. "That's a rude question," she said airily. "Where's Marc?"

"In the bathroom."

"How was the swing set?"

"It was great! I came in only because of Marc, who kept nagging that I was going too high and I was going to break the swing set—or my neck."

Marc came into the room just then. "And you would have!"

Cerise needed time and solitude to process what had happened with Clovis, but that would have to come later. Right now she needed to be a mother.

"Marc." She summoned a warning look in her eyes.

"Did he come in and declare he was hungry?" Marc ignored it. "Of all the little ruffians…"

"Do you think Clovis appreciates this kind of behavior?" she asked in her parenting voice, a voice she was reluctant to use in front of Clovis, but she knew her boys were heading for a fight.

She sensed, rather than saw, Clovis stand behind her. "I think lunch should be ready now." He brushed his hand on Cerise's lower back in a gesture the boys couldn't see. She should step out of his reach, but his touch was feather-light, and their connection rushed through every cell in her body.

# chapter eight

CLOVIS GUIDED HER out of the room, his fingers still grazing her spine in a way that shook her to her core.

She would have to stop this. She knew she'd been weak and made a terrible mistake. She needed to clarify things, but there was a delicious scent guiding them to the kitchen. As they walked down the hall, the fragrance of meat braised in onions and reduced wine reinforced the sensation of being entranced.

In the kitchen, Clovis, or a servant—though there still appeared to be none of those around—had set a rectangular pine table for four. There had to be a formal dining room in a house such as this, but she was charmed that he had eschewed formality for warmth. She was beginning to understand this was a side to him she'd never anticipated.

"Please, have a seat." He left her side but not before tracing a slow, promising circle on her low back. He went to the pale-blue Lacanche range in the corner of the kitchen.

"I love this table," Cerise said as she made sure the boys sat down properly. She settled in her chair and admired the table-top's honeyed patina and plentiful gouges.

"I do, too." He ladled something from a yellow stone-ware Dutch oven into a casserole dish. "It was originally my great-grandmother's. It's been in this kitchen for as long as I remember. It was probably handed down from her great-grandmother."

Cerise's mind and body were still in such a tangle that she was grateful for an innocuous topic. "And so on, and so on, back to the dinosaurs…"

"Exactly."

"Did you make some of these grooves?" she asked, inspecting them.

"Many. There were lots before me, though. Pine is such a soft wood. Is there a child alive who can resist digging in a thumbnail and leaving their mark?"

Yves, who had been doing just this, yanked his hand away and hid the offending appendage on his lap.

"I know about your parents, of course, but are any of your grandparents still alive?" Clovis asked.

"I have my father's mother, who moved down to Uzès a few decades ago," she said. "She's in a retirement home now. The rest…no. I was close to my maternal grandmother, but she passed away just before my parents' accident. I'm grateful she was spared that, at least."

"Yes," he agreed, still busy at the stove. "Although it did leave you even more alone."

"Once Antoine died, yes. I have my boys, though," she said, conscious of their presence. Marc was watching her, as usual. She blew him a kiss, and his serious expression melted into a smile that was all too rare.

"Do you enjoy cooking?" Clovis asked he took something that smelled like garlic and onions out of the oven. He shook off his oven mitts.

Watching him cook was unbelievably intriguing. She stared, remembering the feel of those clever hands tracing the curves of her face, lifting the hair off her neck… Wait. He'd just asked her something. "Excuse me. What was your question?"

"Do you enjoy cooking?"

Cooking was a nice, neutral topic, except that her answer was complicated. She used to enjoy cooking, when she and Antoine could sit at the table together with the boys, but when he died, that enjoyment evaporated. She was still a good cook, but it had become a utilitarian thing—one more chore after a long day of winemaking. Ideally, she would like to cook not just *for* someone but with someone.

She imagined what it would be like to cook with Clovis. There would be coordinated movements in a fragrant kitchen, brushing past each other like dancers, tasting each other's creations… It would be the most extraordinary foreplay. She quivered. This was a complication she hadn't anticipated. Clovis had a gift for reawakening all the pleasure censors in her brain.

She admonished herself again. *The kiss happened, but I need to stop things now.* Despite idle daydreams, there could be no concocting delicious things with Clovis in the kitchen…or anywhere else for that matter.

"Cerise?" Clovis prompted. She still hadn't answered.

"Maman?" Marc said. The troubled crease had reappeared between his brows.

She shook her head. "I guess I don't have an easy answer. I used to enjoy cooking but not so much now."

"I hope you enjoy eating." Clovis looked over his shoulder and smiled. Absorbing his warmth felt so easy, so natural. It went with the fragrance of the food, and the worn pine table, and the feel of his hand on her back.

"No worries there," Yves answered for her.

"Do you enjoy *boeuf bourgignon?*"

"We love it," she said. The boys nodded. "It was my maternal grandmother's specialty." It was the epitome of French simplicity, but if well executed, it was truly sublime. "Besides, what self-respecting Burgundian would admit to not liking *boeuf bourgignon?*"

"Not one." Clovis laughed. "But if it was your grandmother's specialty, maybe it wasn't such a wise choice after all."

It was her turn to laugh. "You don't strike me as easily intimidated."

"About most things, no, but when it comes to grandmothers' specialties, all bets are off." He brought a small dish of escargots from the stove and placed it in front of her.

Even though her stomach growled in anticipation, she looked up to see Yves's and Marc's eyes fixed on her plate. "Go ahead and give it to one of the boys," she said to Clovis. "I swear, no matter how much food they inhale, they always adopt an expression of starving orphans."

Clovis shook his head. "I can't do that. Ladies first. I am sure your boys, as gallant Frenchmen, wouldn't have it any other way."

Yves and Marc exchanged a questioning glance, then nodded fervently, gazing up at Clovis.

The boys were duly awarded when he brought them each a dozen piping hot escargots. "*Voilà!*"

"*Merci!*" both said, watching Clovis with a certain reverence.

When she was young, Cerise's grandfather had cooked dozens upon dozens of escargots on Christmas Eve. He would forage for the snails, then purge and clean them. Nobody did that anymore. Escargot was one of her favorite dishes. Even though it was hot outside, it was lovely and cool in the stone kitchen. Clovis could not have chosen better.

"*Miam!* Escargots!" Yves popped one in his mouth.

Clovis joined them, then picked up the bottle of red Hautes-Côtes de Beaune Cerise had brought and poured some for the adults.

With the help of the thin little escargot fork and clamps, Cerise dug in. Her mouth reveled in the perfect combination of parsley, garlic, and butter. Clovis could cook. She took a slice of fresh baguette from the full basket in the middle of the table.

"Delicious," she declared after she had eased at least half of them out of their shells and into her mouth. "Do you make your own escargot butter?"

"Of course," Clovis answered. "My grandmother—my mother's mother—would disinherit me from the grave if I didn't. She taught me how to cook."

"She taught you well."

Her boys, who couldn't talk because their mouths were full, nodded vigorously in agreement.

She sipped her wine. It boasted notes of spice, with a rich cherry to follow. It made her proud, just like Marc and Yves, who were doing honor to Clovis's snails.

Clovis took a thoughtful sip, then gave her a long look with his blue eyes.

"What?" she asked.

"I constantly marvel at the wine you create. In Burgundy so many winemakers are handed Stradivariuses with their prestigious vineyards but never learn how to make music with them. You don't have a Stradivarius to play, but you create wines that taste like you do."

For a few moments, she couldn't find any words. "That's a lovely compliment. *Merci*." She could defend herself easily if Clovis was rude, but she felt unarmed against his kindness.

Their eyes stayed locked until Yves asked for more escargots. Luckily Clovis had anticipated the appetites of ravenous boys and made extra.

She was surprised that, despite having next to nothing in common with Clovis, the conversation flowed without effort. Yves's presence generally made this easy, and Marc as well to a lesser extent, but even without their contributions Cerise and Clovis found an endless supply of things to talk about.

They swapped tales of the winemakers they knew in common and all the latest vineyard gossip: who had inherited which vines, who had been irrigating at night on the sly—a crime that in Burgundy warranted stripping of a winemaker's appellation status—and their guesses as to what day the wine authority would *lever le ban* and allow the harvest to begin.

Luckily, Clovis's lunch was so good that Yves was too busy eating to complain about the shop talk. Marc had always been interested in winemaking, and Cerise sensed that he could have a future as a fine winemaker ahead of him. If she could buy out Clovis and save Domaine du Cerisier with her secret new wine, that was.

The *boeuf bourgignon* that followed was served with potatoes sliced paper-thin and soaked in an unctuous *gratin dauphinois* that Cerise decided would have won praise even from her grandmother. The two dishes together were rich, succulent, and tender.

She was surprised to find Clovis was as knowledgeable and nuanced in his views as his wine. It became clear that, as Jean had told her, he had his own opinions.

She felt a stab of guilt that she'd held so many prejudices against him. They couldn't possibly proceed as partners in her vineyards, but the other... No, she couldn't entertain that until things were settled with their shared inheritance. That moment in the living room had been yet another moment of weakness. It couldn't happen again.

She scraped a gooey slice of perfectly ripe Époisses cheese on a piece of baguette and washed it down with a Bonnes-Mares that Clovis had brought up from his cellar that morning. This entire meal, she realized, was every bit as seductive as the wine-tasting had been.

His charm hadn't been oversold. She had to steel herself against his effect on her. She straightened her spine. She must be stronger. She would be in no position to negotiate a buyout if they became physically involved—or bottle her secret wine. Her whole world was at stake.

Just as Clovis was pulling ramekins of chilled chocolate mousse from the fridge, the doorbell rang.

She shot a questioning look at Clovis.

He shrugged. "I have no idea."

He left the room, and shortly afterward a babble of voices could be heard in the hallway.

Clovis reappeared in the kitchen with three people at his heels. They all looked vaguely familiar—she suspected they were fellow winemakers and she had seen them at the Copavit or one of the wine events around Beaune.

"Cerise," he said, taking her hand as she stood up from her chair. Her fingers curled reflexively around his. She commanded herself to straighten them. "I'd like you to meet my friends Luc, Gaspard, and Amandine. The first thing you should know about them is they have an uncanny knack of arriving just as dessert is served."

All three came forward and gave Cerise *les bises*. She introduced her sons, who returned their *bises* just as she had taught them.

Clovis, in the meantime, slid three extra chairs around the table.

His friends settled in. It was obvious from the way Amandine reached across the table and turned the wine bottle around to examine it, then poured some for herself and her friends in the extra glasses that had magically appeared, that they stood on the most casual terms with Clovis.

"Sublime!" Luc sighed after taking a sip. "Round in the mouth…such finesse. I would hate you if I didn't love you, Clovis."

She missed Clovis's response because Amandine turned her clear green eyes on her. "I feel like I need to tell you something."

Her heart began to beat faster. So many of her friends had dropped away, or maybe she'd been too preoccupied for them.

She couldn't remember how to act around people her own age and wondered if she was about to be ambushed.

"I'm a massive fan of your work," Amandine said, blushing under her blonde bob. "I'm aware of the challenge you faced, and ever since I tasted your first vintage I've been keeping tabs on what you've been doing."

"Really?" Cerise was flattered, as she didn't think any friend of Clovis's could be a slouch where wine was concerned.

"*Oui.* I love it when woman winemakers succeed. A rising tide lifts all boats, *n'est-ce pas*? I've been hoping for a chance to meet you."

Cerise laughed, touched by Amandine's honest and sincere praise. Maybe this whole friend thing was easier than she remembered. "That's lovely to hear. To be honest, I don't get beyond my vineyards very often."

"Like all good winemakers." Amandine nodded. "I figured as much."

"Maman," Yves said plaintively and tugged her arm. "I'm bored."

"Do you like comic books?" Clovis must have heard him. "I kept all my old ones. Do you want me to show you were they are? You can take your chocolate mousse with you."

Both boys nodded enthusiastically, and Clovis led them out of the room. Cerise gave him a grateful smile and turned back to Amandine. "In any case, thank you."

"Amandine here is not the only one. I'm also a huge admirer of your wine," said Luc, who must have been listening. He was fair and blue-eyed, extremely handsome but with a boyish energy that made him seem younger than Clovis, even though they were probably around the same age.

"You have finesse," said Gaspard, who had a wiry build, a prominent nose, and shaggy dark hair. "You coax something out of your wines that is truly unique."

She was not used to such flattery. "*Merci*," she said again, then tried to shift the conversation from herself. "Tell me where you all work. I'll have an easier time placing you if you tell me what is written on your wine labels."

They laughed.

"I run the family vineyards in Savigny-les-Beaune," Luc said. "Domaine Ocquidant."

"Ah!" Cerise said. "I love your Serpentières."

"Excellent taste." Luc nodded. "That's my favorite, too."

"I run my family domaine with my brother in Aloxe-Corton," said Gaspard. "Domaine Chapuis. Corton-Charlemagne and all that."

"Nice." She nodded. All winemakers, like she'd suspected. "How about you, Amandine?"

A shadow crossed Amandine's brow. "My younger brother runs our family vineyards in Pernand-Vergelesses."

"We're practically neighbors then," Cerise said. She lived only two villages away from there. "I love Pernand wines."

"Not her brother's!" Gaspard banged the table with his fist. "Amandine is a brilliant winemaker. She graduated at the top of our class at the wine school in Beaune. She was one of the most promising students they'd ever seen. Her younger brother has no idea how to make wine and doesn't care."

There was a fervor in Gaspard's eyes as he spoke that led Cerise to question if Gaspard and Amandine were indeed just friends, but the exasperated way Amandine looked back at him made her think not.

"If he's a bad winemaker, why is he in charge?" Cerise asked.

"Did everyone just expect that you would take over the vineyards when your husband died?" Amandine demanded. There wasn't a winemaker in the region who hadn't heard Cerise's story.

"No...even I didn't," Cerise admitted. "It was Maxime who convinced me, then helped me fight for them."

"Exactly." Amandine crossed her arms. "You and I don't have penises, as if *that* has anything to do with being a good winemaker. Honestly..." She scowled. "It's a nightmare. I do all the work, but he takes all the credit, and even then he manages to screw things up."

Gaspard made an odd hissing noise. "Amandine! Listen to me. You have to go out on your own." It was clear from Gaspard's exasperated expression that this was not the first time they'd had this exchange.

Clovis came back into the room and sat down beside Cerise. He rolled his eyes at the argument, which he'd probably heard before.

Amandine sighed. "With what money? You know the price of vines around here. You're a dreamer."

"I know you could raise some," he insisted.

"Anyone around here would be glad to help you," Clovis said. "I've already told you I'd invest."

Amandine let out her breath in a burst. "I won't do business with a friend." She fixed Clovis with a hard green stare. "I've already told you that. Besides, it would be a bad investment. Nobody knows who I am or what I can do because they have no idea I'm the one making the wines—or trying to, anyway."

Clovis shrugged and got up from his chair. "It doesn't change the fact that I am always here to help if you change your mind."

Cerise felt the truth of Amandine's words course through her. It was a bad idea to do business with friends, yet she couldn't avoid doing business with Clovis. It would be so much simpler if he was easy to hate or not her business partner.

Gaspard opened his mouth again, and Clovis, who was puttering around with the coffeemaker, joined them at the table and clicked his tongue. "Gaspard and Amandine, can we argue about this later? I am delighted you all feel so comfortable around my table, but this is Cerise's first visit, and I was *hoping* to make a good impression." He sat down again.

The three of them muttered apologies, then everyone dug into the *mousse au chocolate*. How had Clovis known to make extra? The mousse was a distilled, decadent indulgence. Cerise knew it wasn't good she was aroused by the fact he'd made this. She couldn't allow him to cook for her again—her restraint was already sorely tested.

"How's the love life, Luc?" Clovis asked after a moment of contented silence. "Are you still seeing that woman from Chagny?"

Luc looked up, his blond hair messy. "God no."

"Does it *ever* last long with you?" Amandine rolled her eyes.

"None of us can throw that accusation around," Gaspard pointed out. "Remember? We're all hopeless at relationships."

"Valid point," agreed Luc. "Besides, never mind about the woman from Chagny—guess who is coming to stay for three weeks over Christmas?"

"Who?" Clovis asked.

Luc's expression was that of an eager puppy. "Stella and Sadie from New York."

"Who are Stella and Sadie?" asked Cerise. It may have been an inappropriate question in any other circumstances, but Clovis's friends had treated her with such a complete lack of ceremony that nothing seemed inappropriate.

"They lived here in Beaune for three years when they were in elementary school," Clovis explained, his eyes connecting in that electric way with hers. "Their parents became great friends with Luc's. Luc has been in love with Stella since grade one."

"This is it." Luc took a deep breath. "This time I'm finally going to tell her how I feel."

"You say that every time they visit." Gaspard groaned.

"This time I mean it."

"So your plan is to forsake all women while you wait for Stella?" Clovis asked.

Luc blushed. "Well…it wouldn't do for me to get out of practice."

Clovis chuckled. "I didn't think so."

Amandine snorted and shook her head. "Men." She rolled her eyes at Cerise.

Luc steepled his fingers on the tabletop. "I know it sounds crazy." He looked at his friends, his good-natured face open and suddenly serious. "But Stella is the one. If I can have her, I won't need all the other women."

"*All* the other women?" Cerise raised a questioning brow at Amandine.

Amandine just shook her head, clearly exasperated.

"I don't think it sounds crazy." Clovis reached over and patted Luc's shoulder. His blue eyes flicked to Cerise's for a split-second. "It doesn't sound crazy at all."

They downed strong espresso to finish the meal, which, Cerise had to admit, was perfection. She would have thought Clovis would serve flashy, experimental things in something avant-garde, like test tubes. Instead, his cooking was generous and simple.

After the coffee, Yves returned to the kitchen. "Marc says I'm cheating."

"Cheating at reading comic books?" Cerise asked.

"Clovis also lent us his pack of Tarot cards," Yves explained.

"Well, are you cheating?" Luc asked.

"Maybe a bit," he said. "But it's only fair. I'm younger."

She knew Marc and Yves had arranged to meet their friends in the early evening in the forest to continue building their fort.

It was time to leave, and not only because she needed to escape Clovis's ambit to regain some self-control.

"I should get the boys home." She called Marc into the kitchen.

"I wish you could stay longer," Clovis said, a wistful smile on his lips. "But I understand."

She wondered how much he truly understood—if he knew how strongly she was attracted to him but how she could never let it go further than it already had.

Despite Cerise's protests that they could see themselves out, everyone got up from the table and walked them to the door. Clovis walked beside her. "We didn't end up discussing business." His lips quirked. "I became rather, er…distracted."

She searched his eyes. She didn't know what that kiss in the living room meant. She wondered what it meant to him, if anything.

"Me too," she admitted. "It was…"

"Astonishing," Clovis said. She had been about to say "crazy" but swallowed it. She would set the record straight with him later, but in front of his friends and her sons was neither the time nor the place.

"*Merci* for the lovely afternoon," she said instead. "It was… unexpected."

The dimple on his cheek appeared. "I'm going to find out what you mean by that. I must return to London tomorrow. Emily is in a school play. Can I come to your place when I get back so we can, well—"

"Discuss the inheritance?" Cerise said. *Just business from now on.*

"That's what I was going to say." His eyes sparkled with their shared…Cerise didn't even know what to call it. She knew she should act aloof, but the mischievous invitation in his eyes was impossible to resist. It had been a long time since she had felt such complicity with someone. *How inconvenient.*

They reached the entryway, and Luc was the first of Clovis's friends to give her *les bises* and say goodbye. He embraced her warmly. "We were all so thrilled when Clovis told us how Maxime had left things," Luc said. "And that he's going to be working with you. You will see how talented he is."

Cerise stiffened, shocked that Clovis had already discussed the inheritance with his friends—before anything was even decided.

"We haven't decided how we'll arrange things at Domaine du Cerisier," she said stiffly.

"But he has so many ideas for your vineyards!" Luc said, not picking up on her lack of enthusiasm. "Just think of the possibilities."

Her blood turned cold. Clovis had no intention of listening to her plan to buy him out. How dare he have ideas about her vineyards. She had made it so easy for him.

That was what this lunch had been about—seducing her into forgetting she needed to be independent. The kiss, too, she realized with mortifying clarity. It had all been to manipulate her into compliance. He wasn't attracted to her. He had never been attracted to her.

"*Au revoir,*" she said. *I have to get out of here, or I might scream.* She gave Clovis, Amandine, and Gaspard a curt nod instead of the polite *bises* and dragged her boys out the door, ignoring their protests.

Her face burned as she stalked across the courtyard to the gate, and it had nothing to do with the orange afternoon sun. She was so naive. When she thought of how Clovis had made her feel and how quickly she had succumbed to his charm, her skin prickled with annoyance.

She could hear Clovis's raised voice directed at Luc, asking him what idiocy had just escaped his mouth. Of course Clovis would be upset his duplicity had been exposed by his feckless friend. Excellent. Thank God Luc was feckless. It was the last time Clovis would make a fool of her.

She had risked her work, her future, and her sons' future—for lust. How base.

If she wanted to take a lover—and given how fast she had caved with Clovis, perhaps she needed to—she would pick some-one who wouldn't be involved in any aspect of her life outside the bedroom. There was too much to lose and nothing to gain.

# chapter nine

ONCE SHE GOT the boys off to play with their friends the next day, Cerise went into her *cuverie* and attacked the pre-harvest preparation with unusual violence.

She had woken up that morning still in a state of incandescent rage that Clovis had so easily made a fool of her. She was furious with him, but she was even more livid with herself.

He'd never had any intention of listening to her proposal. He hadn't taken her seriously from the start. She turned on the hose full blast and climbed down a ladder into one of the huge maceration vats to spray it out.

Thank God he had left for London. It would give her a bit of time to strategize before the inevitable confrontation. Then, the harvest would be upon her. Maxime's timing had been atrocious, foisting this predicament on her just before the most critical time in the winemaking year. The entire winemaking calendar hinged on the harvest. The grapes had to be brought in carefully and at just the right moment; otherwise the entire vintage could be ruined.

Of course, there was the matter of her secret wine—Cerasus. If she couldn't get rid of Clovis, he would eventually notice the discrepancy in the previous year's yield as well as that from the imminent harvest. She planned to hive off a quarter of her grapes to create a second batch. She knew it was a massive risk. If the first vintage failed, she would have reduced the domaine's revenue by a quarter for nothing. Now that Clovis was her legal partner, he could even accuse her of theft.

After the lunch at his house, she had no idea who he really was or what he was capable of. What she had seen of him so far was all smoke and mirrors.

Maybe she shouldn't risk Cerasus this year. Yet she wholeheartedly believed it could be the making of her reputation as a winemaker and the one thing that could ensure the future of Domaine du Cerisier. If the previous year's batch was a success, she would need a second vintage to sell. The time to make that second vintage was this harvest. There were no second chances in winemaking. Before Maxime died, she had made the decision to bet on herself. She couldn't let Clovis stop her now.

She had no idea how she was going to keep all this from Clovis when he came back from England. What a mess.

She lost track of time in the vat. When she finally shut off the hose, she heard her name being called. She seriously entertained the idea of pretending she wasn't there, but it hadn't been Clovis's voice—she was starting to recognize his.

She climbed out, soaked to the skin and dripping water all over the concrete floor.

Luc was standing at the bottom of the ladder. "It's me, Luc," he announced unnecessarily.

Cerise sighed and dropped the hose to the ground with a hollow clatter. "Yes, I see."

She felt a stab of anger, then tried to reason with herself. She owed Luc a thank-you. If he hadn't blurted out the truth, Clovis could have strung her along for who knew how long.

She gave him the *bises* but arched her body back so she didn't get him soaked, too. There was no point in showing how upset she was. She had her pride. Too much of it, Maxime had always chided.

"*Bonjour*, Luc. *Ça va?*" She kept her voice steady.

He shrugged. "I'm on my way to my vineyards, but I'm not well. I'm not well at all."

"Why?"

"Clovis is extremely upset with me."

"That's unfair. You were just telling the truth. Now I know his true intentions. I'm grateful to you."

Luc's shoulders sagged. "That's not what I meant yesterday. Clovis never said as much. I just assumed… I mean, I never imagined you wouldn't want to work with him or that you could afford to buy him out."

One look from Cerise cut him off. He was right, of course. Vineyards in this prized area of Burgundy were ridiculously expensive, even in the more modest appellations like hers. It would take decades for her to pay off Clovis's half. Even if she could buy him out, he would still be in her life, not as her partner but as her lender. Still, it was better than being forced to work with someone who had already concocted "plans" for the vineyards without even considering her wishes.

Luc waved his hand in apology. "Of course, that's none of my business."

"*Non*," she agreed.

"What I don't understand is why you hate the idea of the partnership. Clovis is a brilliant winemaker. You couldn't find a better partner."

She couldn't find the words to begin to explain to Luc the years of struggling to change from Antoine's wife to a confident winemaker in her own right.

"Clovis is used to owning and ruling things," she said instead.

Luc seemed to consider this. "Well…yes, he is extremely competent, but I don't believe he always needs to be in charge."

"Men in Burgundy generally do. Look at his life, Luc. What *isn't* he in charge of?"

"His childhood certainly wasn't in his control. Now, his daughter," Luc answered. "If Clovis was hiding a tyrannical disposition, don't you think he would have gone to the courts to insist Emily come over to France by now, or dragged her back from London himself?"

He had a point. If what he said was true, Clovis was being remarkably understanding about Emily. Still, personal life and business were two different things.

"You couldn't find a more loyal friend," Luc continued. "Just think of the things you could—"

"I don't want a partner," Cerise said. "Any partner."

He studied her with a thoughtful expression. "I see," he said finally.

"Good."

He turned to leave, then turned back to face her again. "Please don't blame Clovis for my words yesterday. He was thrilled for an opportunity to get to know you better and learn more about how you coax such extraordinary wine from your vines. To be honest, I think he's…I think he's been lonely for quite some time. He needs good people around him."

Cerise snorted.

"You don't believe me?"

"He's got all three of you, and Jean, and Emily over in London. Besides, is he ever photographed without scads of women clinging off his arms? Don't tell me he's lonely. I don't buy it."

"A person can be in a room of people and still feel lonely."

She knew that truth too well. Still… "Forgive me if I'm skeptical about that applying to Clovis."

Luc shrugged. "All I hope is that you get to know him better before deciding anything. I don't know what I would do without such a friend in my life."

This gave her pause, but she couldn't afford doubts.

She nodded, then walked him to his car. On the way they passed the cherry tree.

"I've always been intrigued by this tree." Luc touched its gnarled trunk as they passed. "Not to mention how you manage to make that one tree give all your wines a cherry flavor. We all wonder over it. Clovis always says you have a gift."

She smiled. It was difficult to stay annoyed at Luc, with his quick eyes and open face. There was something solid about him. She had the same instinct about him as all of Clovis's friends she'd met the other day—they were people worth knowing.

"You're not angry with me?" Luc asked as he got in his car.

"No," she said. "Just out of curiosity, does anyone stay angry with you for long?"

He grinned. "Nope."

After Luc left, Cerise slid into the cool of Maxime's shuttered house instead of heading back to work in the vat room.

She told herself it was because she would need to move herself and her boys into the big house in a matter of days to make room for the harvesters who would be sleeping where they normally made their home.

The truth was she was still searching for an answer from Maxime. He had only ever talked perfunctorily about his grandson, Clovis. Now she wondered how close the two of them were and why Maxime was so convinced the partnership was such a good idea that he'd written it into his will.

She went to the den, which was walled with Maxime's books. She began plucking his favorite volumes from the bookshelves and flipping through them. She inhaled the scent of old leather and yellowing pages. She felt for a moment that if she turned quickly enough, she would catch Maxime ensconced in his favorite leather armchair, watching her. He had always tracked down early editions if he could find them. Perhaps he'd left a note for her. If he had, perhaps it would be in one of his favorite books.

There was nothing in Victor Hugo's collection of love poems or Jean D'Ormesson's *Le Vent du Soir*. Nothing in Sartre's *Le Sursis*. Just book pages…

Cerise's thoughts meandered back to her conversation with Clovis. The talk they'd had before the kiss. His blue eyes had gone dark when he mentioned his mother's death. She wondered if there was a similar pain in her eyes when she talked about Antoine.

Cerise doubted it. The uncomfortable fact was even though she and Antoine had been in love, she was a different person now from the young woman who'd married her high-school sweetheart. She missed his ready laugh and sparkling brown eyes, but even though their marriage had worked for her then, it wouldn't now. More troubling still was she preferred who she was now.

She and Antoine had been so young and quickly swept up with the births of Marc and Yves. Before his death, Cerise had no notion of her talents or abilities, and no opportunities in which to discover and test them. She was aware only of a vague frustration, of wondering late at night: *Is this it?*

It was understood between them that Antoine oversaw the vineyards, the harvest, and the vinification. Cerise helped a bit as she could but never considered herself qualified to do more. The few times she made suggestions, Antoine had laughed at her affectionately. Now, she marveled at the fact that her husband's patronizing attitude hadn't made her furious. She had fallen into the traditional role of wife and mother because she hadn't known any different—neither of them had.

After he died—after that terrible black hole of grief swallowed her for months—Maxime threw her a rope in the form of a challenge. He asked her to at least try to work the vineyards with his guidance. He lured her by framing the winemaking as self-sacrifice. She would be doing this for her boys, he convinced her, and for Antoine's memory.

But as the months and then the years rolled by, marked by the rhythm of the vines, Cerise had blossomed. She had unarguably become a far better winemaker than Antoine ever was. It began to dawn on her that Maxime's challenge was far less about her sons and far more about giving her the gift of self-discovery.

Maxime had been eccentric but wise, at least when it came to her. Surely he'd left an explanation. She pulled Dino Buzzati's collection of short stories, *Le K,* off the shelves. It had always been a favorite, yet...nothing.

Now, Cerise knew what she could do, who she was, and where she wanted to take her winemaking. No one would stand in her way. It hadn't been an issue with Maxime. He was so much older—past the age of needing to prove anything to himself or others. When she came to him for advice, he gave it, but he took an entirely hands-off approach, letting her make her own mistakes so she could learn from them.

No man near her age, especially not a man like Clovis, would be contented working under her direction or as her equal, especially if they were romantically involved. She never again wanted to be patted on the head and laughed at affectionately. She never wanted another partner.

# chapter ten

A FEW DAYS LATER, Cerise still had no answers, although she had gone into Maxime's house several times when she thought of a new spot where he may have hidden a letter or clue. He had always liked a game, damn him.

Now, though, she was preoccupied with her grapes. They were nearing maturity, and she went out into the vineyards and tasted them every day, bringing a few back to juice and test, evaluating when she should start the harvest. The wine authority had given the region the green light the day before, but she always liked to wait a few days after that—her grapes grew at a higher altitude, and she strove for peak maturity.

She had exhausted herself cleaning every inch of the *cuverie* and her wicker harvesting baskets.

She used a tractor only once a year, and that was during the harvest to haul grapes. There was no other way, really. She had changed the oil in it and made sure it was working smoothly. She set about moving her family into the big house.

The sun beat down on her as she moved the last mattress from the attic of the harvesters' house to the main sleeping room. Her boys had helped her for several hours that morning, but she had finally released them to play with their friends in the cool shade of the forest.

The heat made the intense physical labor even more exhausting, but she was glad for it. It made it easier for her mind not to wander to Clovis or her conversation with Luc. Clovis would probably getting back from London soon, so she knew her reprieve was about to end.

By noon she had to retreat inside Maxime's house for a cold shower to wash off the sweat and dust from the attic. She made a quick lunch of a *salade composé* with *frisée* lettuce, some *lardons*, and hard-boiled eggs cut into slices. She added some halved walnuts, then took her plate outside to the wooden table and benches she had installed under the twisted wisteria. She poured a glass of chilled white from her small Aligoté parcel and sat back with a sigh of pleasure.

Waiting longer to harvest always came with the risk of a freak hail storm or other disaster, but those extra hours in the sun and a higher sugar content in the grapes could also make the difference between a good wine and a sublime one. This was especially the case with Cerasus, which would be unfiltered and unsulfured like the year before. There was nothing to hide behind—every nuance would show up in Cerasus. That was both its strength and its downfall. This also meant, of course, that if she waited too long—even a day—she could be faced with rot, and her secret batch would be ruined.

Her calculations were interrupted by the sight of Clovis approaching across the courtyard. Her reprieve had ended.

He waved at her—the nerve!—but at the sight of him drawing near, tall and broad, memories of their time together rushed back. *It was all an act on his part. Resist.*

He held up a hand. "I'm so sorry to interrupt your lunch. I'm sure you've been working hard all morning in this heat. I was doing the same. I returned from London yesterday, and I just felt I needed to clarify things after Luc's enthusiasm got the better of him at our lunch."

This was the last thing she felt like doing, especially now her heart had jumped at the sight of him. Even in his work shorts and T-shirt, he looked handsome. She remembered the gentle brush of his mouth against her neck and shivered despite the heat.

"No need," Cerise said, proud of her neutral tone of voice.

"I won't take more than a minute or two of your time," he said, polite but implacable.

She knew she would have to deal with him eventually, so she gestured for him to take the chair opposite her. He nodded his thanks and sat down. This was the perfect opportunity to set a new precedent for their dealings.

His face was tight. The thought that he was nervous entered her mind, only to be banished. She was the one whose body and mind were running amok. Clovis wasn't the type to get nervous. But then she remembered his trembling hand pouring the first bottle at the winetasting, when they were finally alone in the cellar.

"Please, eat." He gestured to her plate.

"I've lost my appetite," she said. It was the truth, but after it came out, she realized it sounded more surly than disinterested. He didn't disgust her—he should, but unfortunately he didn't. When he was near her, she didn't seem to have room in her mind for anything but his presence.

His mouth dropped open. "Wow…really? Am I that bad? I think you got the wrong impression from what Luc said."

"Luc came to explain." When she thought back to that conversation, she realized she'd been just as troubled before Luc's visit as after. Luc's belief in Clovis's good intentions had muddied waters that were better clear.

"He did?" Clovis's brows drew together, his eyes translucent in the bright light. "My friends deserve gold medals in meddling, especially Luc. I told him emphatically not to bother you with explanations. He never listens."

"Neither do you," Cerise said.

"What do you mean?"

"From what Luc said, I inferred that you were never prepared to seriously consider my offer to buy you out."

"That is partially true." Clovis searched her eyes. "I'm not ready to consider it *yet*."

"What are you waiting for?"

"I just... I was thinking..." He paused. "I'm going to be completely honest."

"Please," she said, exasperation seeping into her voice.

His eyes met hers. "I was looking forward to learning from you and getting to know you. It seemed as if that was Maxime's intention."

Cerise couldn't break away from his azure gaze. "Do you know that for sure?"

"Not exactly, but us being partners was his dying wish. I believe we need to at least try to honor it."

She opted not to tell him about her unfruitful search for clues. "Neither of us can know what he intended." Maxime was gone. She knew what death meant better than most.

"To be honest, that has been driving me crazy." Clovis ran a hand through his already messy hair. "It is so like Maxime to leave us like this, without any explanation."

"We agree on that, at least." She smiled at him for the first time since he'd arrived. "He always loved a riddle."

Clovis's dimple flashed, and his appeal increased again, if that was possible. *Mon Dieu.* She had to handle him like live dynamite. If she let herself, she would be prepared to do any number of things to make that dimple appear again.

He let his hands fall open on the table. "I truly respect you and your winemaking. I would never step on your toes or tell you what to do. How could I, after all, when we are equal partners?"

"This is Burgundy," Cerise said. "When a woman and a man winemaker work together, who do you think gets the credit?"

"I think you underestimate the reputation you've already made for yourself."

"Why do you want to get to know me better?" She narrowed her eyes at him, assailed by an unwelcome thought. She had come across people who were vampires of tragedy and drawn to her suffering, like those bystanders who craned their necks at bad traffic accidents. Cerise could never understand what kind of twisted satisfaction they got from secondhand grief, but they did. She had developed an instinct about people like that. She hadn't thought Clovis could be one. "Is it pity? The tragic widow thing?"

His breath came out in a puff of disbelief. "*Purée,* Cerise! Look at yourself. How could you ever be an object of pity?"

Her instincts had been right. That wasn't it.

"It's definitely *not* pity," he continued. "I came across that kind of person after my mother died, the morbidly curious. I would never—"

"Sorry." She knew she owed him an apology. "Of course you wouldn't. Why do you want to work with me, though? You have everything you could ever need down at your domaine."

He leaned back in his chair and tilted his chin. "You really think so?"

"Of course."

Clovis shook his head, exasperated. "You're wrong."

"Then why?"

He blew out a breath. "I want to work with you because you fascinate me." He began to tap his fingers on the tabletop. "I suppose it's no secret that I'm attracted to you."

Heat rushed from the tips of her fingers to the ends of her toes.

"I have no desire to usurp your vines, it's just…you carry an electrical field around you that makes me feel more alive when you're near."

Her face burned—and other parts of her as well. He made her feel alive, too, but she had to forgo that.

"I've been wanting to know you for a long time," he said.

She blinked. "You didn't even know I existed before Maxime died…or barely, anyway."

"I knew."

He watched her with an intensity that made all the words Cerise wanted to say clog in her throat, blocked by a wave of lust so powerful it was all she could do to keep from lunging across the table for him. She couldn't. Maybe he didn't want her vines—she still wasn't sure about that—but he definitely wanted *something* from her.

"I have a proposition," he said.

"What?" Her voice sounded gravelly, like it had come from far away.

"Let me help you with your harvest."

"I don't need help." Her brain was telling her to stay stubborn, even though her longing was louder than her reason. Anyway, it was a lie. This was the first year she was heading into harvest without Maxime. She had her amazing harvest captain, Jorgé, but he was only one person, and she had no clue how they were going to handle all the harvesters and the sorting table without Maxime's calm assistance. But if Clovis was around, he would find out about Cerasus, and then she had no idea what would happen. It was too risky.

"I want us to see for ourselves before we decide on anything like a buyout."

"See what for ourselves?"

"If Maxime's final wish of us as partners has any validity."

His argument made sense. Maxime had often been inscrutable, but Cerise had never known him to do anything without a reason.

"You couldn't possibly leave your domaine during harvest," she reasoned. "No winemaker can, unless they're the kind who doesn't actually do any winemaking, which I don't believe you are, not anymore."

"Anymore?"

Cerise nodded.

"That's progress, I suppose." He chuckled softly. "We're starting the harvest tomorrow afternoon. Jean and I always have it planned out well in advance. Besides, our starts will surely be staggered by a few days because you're at the higher altitude. Do you have an idea when you're starting?"

"Two or three days from now. I'm still debating it."

He nodded. "You'll decide what's best."

She bristled. "I know I will."

He frowned at her. "That's what I just said."

She bit her lip.

He gave her a long look. "Can we just give it a try, for Maxime? I won't meddle. I promise."

If he could stick to that promise, she could use the help. She had a feeling that if she didn't acquiesce, it would be harder to get rid of him. If he stayed true to his word and didn't meddle, he never needed to know about Cerasus. It was tempting.

"I don't know," Cerise said, gnawing on her lower lip.

"Please, could we try working like partners, just until *la paulée?*" *La paulée* was the huge celebration held at each domaine on the last night of harvest.

"That was underhanded, using Maxime."

He shrugged. "Maybe, but I think he would approve. He never hesitated to use emotional blackmail to reach his nefarious ends."

She smiled as she remembered how Maxime had used her boys to blackmail her into taking over the vineyards. "True."

"After *la paulée*—"

"What happens after *la paulée?* This arrangement needs an end date."

"You make your decision as to whether you want me as your partner."

"You'll respect my decision?" She was skeptical.

"Absolutely."

Cerise considered his promise. Agreeing to a trial period might pave the way for the buyout. Even though Clovis wasn't holding it over her head...yet, half of Domaine du Cerisier was his by law. Maybe she owed him a trial. Her moral compass, damn that thing, told her she did.

"All right," she finally agreed. "But I need to be clear-headed for this to work."

His eyebrows drew together. "What do you mean by that exactly?"

"Just that... This may sound presumptuous, but can we agree to be only winemaking partners during the harvest?" The idea of having him so close and never touching him made her physically ache, but it was for the best.

"Why?" he asked, not defensively but rather sounding honestly curious.

Cerise cleared her throat. "Well...it's just I think if we get involved physically, a clear-headed decision would be impossible for me."

Clovis cocked his right brow. "I would certainly hope so."

She laughed despite herself. "You think highly of your skills."

"Yes."

"So you *are* the playboy I thought you were."

"Correction. I *was* that playboy. No longer. Besides, the reason I think neither of us would be left clear-headed is because I've experienced the chemistry between us."

She did her best to look unimpressed even though she pulsed with the urge to find out if his confidence was justified. She remembered the warmth of his breath on her exposed skin, then the gentle touch of his lips. "Yes...well, we're not going down that road."

"Never?"

"Certainly not before the partnership issue is decided." She tried to look far more resolute than she felt.

He nodded, disappointment but not reproach in his eyes. "If my willpower is to last, I should leave and let you eat."

Cerise stood and moved around the table to walk him to his car.

He gestured for her to sit down again. "I can see myself out. Eat."

She didn't sit down. He was so close now she could smell his fresh, masculine scent. Her fingers itched to reach out and touch him.

Instead of walking away, he took a step toward her, which had them standing mere inches apart. All her instincts wanted to close that gap. She needed to feel that jolt of pleasure again.

"I have one last question," he said in a voice so low it was almost a whisper.

"What?" She met his eyes, and a flash of connection ran through Cerise like an electric shock. *I know you.* A field falcon flew overhead, the whoosh of its wings echoing the whoosh of her heart.

They had just started to get to know each other. How could she feel that Clovis had somehow been part of her life forever?

It must be her imagination. She needed to resist him, even if felt impossible.

"I won't come any closer if you say no," he said. "But could we seal our agreement with a kiss instead of a handshake?"

The sunlight filtered through the wisteria, rippling over them like a river of gold. At this precise moment, she was not at all convinced she was going to succeed.

"A kiss?" Her voice came from far away.

"Just one."

"Why?" But she needed it, too, to tide her over the coming

weeks. Otherwise she would be mooning around, unable to do the Herculean work the harvest required.

"Like a squirrel storing up nuts for winter," Clovis said.

She laughed at this perfect image. A vision popped into her mind of her and Clovis lying in bed after making love, chuckling about something silly. One kiss couldn't cause too much harm if it stopped there, and she would make sure it did. Just one kiss…

"One kiss." She tried to school her features to appear forbidding but knew she was failing. She took a small step closer. The crickets in the nearby grasses began to chirp, and the delicate perfume of late summer roses wafted on a light breeze.

Clovis took one more step, then Cerise did, until they were touching.

She closed her eyes to savor the thrill of his body against hers. She felt his heat through his worn T-shirt and could feel his ragged breaths on the crown of her head. It was as if there were charged atoms pulling them together, fusing them. He had been right about their chemistry.

She lifted her hands and placed them on his biceps just where the sleeves of his T-shirt ended and the smooth, warm curves of his biceps began.

He exhaled. "How do you do it?"

"What?"

"Make me feel so much."

She made a small shrug. She understood exactly what he meant, and there were no words, really, to explain it. She couldn't let herself experience it beyond one kiss, but goddamn she was going to grasp every second of bliss from that. She would store it up to relive when she had to be strong.

What came next was unexpected. He took her hands gently in his, unbent her fingers, and raised one hand to his lips. He placed a reverent kiss in the middle of her palm. It was softest of contacts, but it vibrated through every cell in her body. He did the same with the other hand, and she wondered if she would shatter into a million pieces.

"Those two don't count," he murmured.

"Okay."

He returned her hands to where they were. His fingertips moved around to her back and traced the grooves of her spine through her shirt. Her eyelids floated closed. It had been so long since someone had touched her in a way that was meant solely to give her pleasure. She was slammed with the magnitude of what she'd been missing these past years.

Their lips touched, and their bodies melded like quicksilver.

The kiss began as tentative but became hungry. Clovis's soft, clever lips set every nerve in her body alive and filled her with a yearning ache, shattering every vestige of her self-control. The ache grew into desperation as she felt his long stiffness against her hip.

"Cerise," Clovis moaned against her mouth.

This close to him, she was intoxicated with his taste of salt, limestone, and vineyard. She slipped her hands under his shirt and raked his back with her nails. He freed a primal part of her that had been buried since Antoine's death.

"*Mon amour*," he murmured between kisses. It took her a few seconds to register. *My love.*

She sprang back, breathless. "What did you just call me?"

"I'm sorry," he gasped. He leaned down and put his hands on his knees, as though catching his breath after a long race. "I just…I didn't mean to frighten you."

"Well, you did." She didn't know what this wild magnetism was between them, but it wasn't love. She had had a husband, and she didn't want another. They barely knew each other, even though that was not how they were acting. "How can you love someone you hardly know?"

He stood up again, hands out in apology. He watched her

intently for a moment, then gave a funny little nod, as if to him-self. "You feel like home."

"What does that mean?"

He shook his head. "Never mind. I get carried away when it comes to you."

"Me too," she admitted. It was a relief to share her con-fusion, even with Clovis. "It's not love, for God's sake, but we're dangerous."

He held up a palm. "Believe me, I know."

Cerise pointed to him and then back at herself. "This is exactly why the strictly business part of this partnership trial is so important." It physically hurt to say that and forgo the sensa-tions that left her limbs feeling heavy, but she had to think of her vineyards, her boys, Cerasus—everything she had momentarily forgotten in those minutes of unmitigated bliss.

"I promise I will remain completely in control from this moment on. I won't let my true feelings get in the way during the harvest."

"Your true feelings? You mean lust, right?"

Clovis watched her for a few seconds, then took a deep breath. "Whatever you want to call it, Cerise."

She nodded. "We can't do this again." She was reminding herself as much as him.

"Ever?"

Cerise hesitated. She didn't want to draw a line across him forever. Just the knowledge that he was a possibility made her feel more alive than she had in years. She wasn't prepared to give that up. "Under the right circumstances." She shrugged. "You never know, but we're a long way from that. We have a harvest to get through."

His eyes shined. "A handshake to seal the deal?" He put out his hand—a part of him she knew could make her lose all sense of propriety and logic.

She stared down at it. "No way."

His dimple flashed. "I respect that."

"*Au revoir*, Clovis." She waved him away. She tried to get back to her salad when she heard him pull out of the courtyard, but her appetite didn't return. She seemed sustained by his presence alone.

# chapter eleven

~

THREE DAYS LATER, she went out to the vineyards before her sons woke up to go to school. They had started two days earlier. Summer was over, although the weather hadn't received the message.

The crickets chirped as Cerise picked a grape off a lovely cluster. She burst the sturdy Pinot Noir skin between her fingers, then took a tiny bite with her front teeth, measuring its sweetness, firmness, and acidity. She popped the entire grape in her mouth and tried to detect every nuance of flavor.

Everything was ready for her to pull the trigger. Her harvesting team was in place and had been informed that this year things might look a little different with Clovis's involvement. Many other winemakers had started already. Clovis had begun his harvest, and she hadn't seen him since their kiss. Their *second* kiss, although she still marveled over exactly how she'd let that happen.

She was never in a rush for the harvest to begin. It was wonderful in many ways—the security of finally getting the precious grapes safely juiced, seeing her harvesters again, and the huge release of *la paulée*—the traditional meal and all-night party on the final night.

However, the harvest was also a massive undertaking.

Managing so many employees was her least favorite part. Every year a few loose cannons and the odd romance-turned-sour slipped into the mix, and a handful of harvesters ended up more interested in crying and complaining than harvesting grapes.

This year she wanted to be certain that her choice to begin the harvest was not influenced by any desire to see Clovis again. She missed feeling the way she did when he was near, and as much as that knowledge scared her, it enticed her as well. She swallowed the grape in her mouth. Her grapes were perfect. Clovis had nothing to do with it.

She smiled privately to herself. "Tomorrow." She touched the closest grape cluster. "Tomorrow is the day."

She pulled out her cell phone and made the necessary calls as she weaved between her rows of vines. Her last call was to Clovis. She wondered if he would still be so keen on helping her, seeing as she had put an end to any possibility of further…um, physical entanglements, not to mention the fact that he was in the thick of his own harvest by now.

"*Allô?*" he answered.

"*Salut.* It's me, Cerise."

"I've missed you."

She opened her mouth to say she'd missed him, too, then closed it again. *Strictly business.* "How's your harvest going?"

"Nice yield so far and excellent quality. A poor harvester stepped in a wasps' nest and had to be taken to the hospital, but he's recovering."

"Oh, thank God. I hate it when harvesters get injured. I always feel so guilty. Anyway, I've just made the call. I'm going to start tomorrow."

"What time?" he asked.

"I'm aiming for right after lunch if I can swing it."

"I'll see you tomorrow morning then," he said. "I imagine it'll be a zoo with all the harvesters arriving."

"Oh...okay." He clearly wasn't wavering from his plan.

"A deal's a deal." He chuckled. "I'm looking forward to it."

"Me too." Cerise was shocked to realize it was the absolute truth.

The next morning her harvesters began to arrive, and she was up to her ears in completing their temporary employment paperwork and directing them to their designated beds in the harvesters' house.

By nine in the morning the sun was beating down on Cerise's dark hair. It was going to be scorching. She could tell by the particular smell of the pea gravel releasing every drop of moisture and the sweat beading at her hairline.

Surely Clovis wouldn't arrive so early. He would have things to do at his domaine first. She tried to discipline herself not to watch for him among the groups of harvesters.

At nine fifteen, though, she spotted him walking toward her, chatting idly with a lanky German harvester who came every year. Her heart missed a beat. He was dressed for a day of hard work and smiling at Cerise in a way that kindled something in her chest even hotter than the sun.

"You came," she said, shading her eyes with her hand as he approached. She felt rattled by his nearness, as if he alone caused a disturbance in the air around them, or maybe it was the combination of them together.

He sent her a quizzical smile. "*Bien sûr* I did. How can I help?"

She had just finished checking in a freckled Irish girl named Fiona. Fiona was on her way up to the harvesters' quarters to drop off her things, but she had stopped to introduce herself to some fellow workers on the way.

Cerise nodded toward the girl. "How long do you think she's going to last?" she asked Clovis in a low voice.

He squinted at Fiona. "Her skin is so fair—almost translucent. I would say only a few hours, if that. If she were my harvester, I'd be tempted to advise for her not to go out in the vineyards at all in today's heat. She'll wilt within minutes."

"My thoughts exactly." Cerise tapped her pen against her clipboard. "But I'm not sure what to do with her...or how to replace her."

He reached out and touched her arm, probably to get her attention as she was deep in thought, but the contact felt like the time she had accidentally put her hand on a neighbor's electric fence.

"I have somebody working at my sorting table who wants to harvest," he said. "We could swap them. Fiona can come with me, and I'll send you my person."

She hesitated. There was a possibility that he just trying to offload his deadwood, but she had to *try* to trust him. He was right. A deal was a deal.

"I don't hire or keep on slackers," he assured her.

How inconvenient that he seemed to have a knack for reading her thoughts. Since their last kiss she'd had many, *many* thoughts about Clovis she'd rather keep secret.

"The grapes look good?" he asked.

It took a moment for her to return to the present. "Perfection. I don't want my grapes to wait a minute longer," she said, realizing only after the words were out that in fact they were no longer *hers* and arguably had never been. "I mean...*our* grapes. For the time being, anyway."

He clicked his tongue. "You promised to wait until the end

of harvest to make your decision. I won't expect one before then. If fact, I'm quite sure I don't want it before then."

She nodded. "Wise."

He rubbed his hands together. "So, I'll talk to Fiona about the swap. Otherwise, what else?"

"Even low-level things?" Cerise asked, not to test him but because that was where she really needed help.

"Of course," he said. "If I recall, my promise was I would help you with anything you need."

She ignored the glint in his eye when he said this and turned her attention to a new group of harvesters making their way up the drive.

She waved at the harvesters' house behind them. "Can you make sure everyone has a bed and settles in quickly? I'm going to check in these new arrivals, then double check the tractor again, and then make a beeline to the kitchen to make sure the cooks have lunch ready on time. I'd like to start harvesting by two o'clock if we can."

Clovis glanced at his watch. "I'll make it happen."

"Could you also get everyone to the table by noon sharp? I always find that tricky—like herding cats."

His mouth twitched. "Anarchist cats, more like."

"Aren't all cats anarchist?"

He titled his head. "That's true, actually. In any case, everyone will be there at noon. *Promis.*"

Cerise liked the definitive tone of his answers. Employees who peppered her with questions were all too common. He seemed like one of those rare people who figured things out on his own and found solutions instead of problems.

She turned to leave, then remembered. "I guess you should know I moved into Maxime's house with the boys like I do every year." Her voice came out defiant.

He shrugged. "Of course. You didn't need to tell me. Anyway, I don't think of it as Maxime's anymore."

"You don't?"

"No."

"What do you think of it as?" Cerise said.

"I think of it as our house. Yours and mine."

She was stunned by the image that flashed in her head. Living there with Clovis and her boys and— She gave her head a firm shake, then raced off toward a cook who was leaning from one of the outbuildings, calling her. She tried to push aside the daydream—at least until she could savor it later, when the day was done and she was alone in bed.

Cerise reassured the cooks that yes, they would indeed have enough food. She went through this every year. The older Burgundian women never felt they had ample food for the harvesters unless there was enough to feed an infantry battalion. There were always far too many leftovers for Cerise's fridge and freezer to hold, and she and the boys ate for months on the frozen surplus. She tried to give food away, but every winemaker she knew was likewise drowning in leftover *boeuf bourgignons*, *coq au vins*, and *blanquettes de veau*.

Cerise stacked empty baskets on the cart eight high and strapped them in.

When Antoine had been the winemaker, he had opted for newer (and easier) plastic tubs for harvesting, but Cerise had gotten rid of them before her second harvest.

She liked to minimize the contact her grapes had with plastic as much as possible. She believed—whether it was superstitious or not—that the traditional wicker Burgundian harvesting baskets gave something extra to the flavor of her wine. She wondered idly whether Clovis was of the same mind.

She saw him again after the lunch bell—a large repurposed cowbell Maxime had picked up near Gstaad in Switzerland—clanged out over the courtyard. He was seating harvesters around the two large wooden tables that lived in the barn for most of the year and were dragged into the stone outbuilding that doubled as the dining hall during the harvest.

"How did it go?" she asked him.

"Fine. Everyone has a bed. You set it up perfectly in there."

She knew from experience that it surely hadn't been as simple as that. Harvesters often came as groups of friends, and the bed swapping as they got settled was a logistical nightmare.

"That's the result of hard-earned experience," Cerise said, remembering her mistakes of the early years, when she had tried to make everyone happy, and Maxime had merely looked on with amusement at the resulting chaos.

Clovis smiled knowingly. "I'm sure we could regale each other with grape harvester stories until the wee hours."

She was struck by a sudden vision of doing exactly that, but in her mind she and Clovis were not seated at a dinner table or side by side on a couch but lying intertwined in bed on a hot night, with the window cracked open to let in cool night air. They were sated and naked, laughing softly in the dark. Her head was on his chest, and he was stroking her hair.

Clovis interrupted her daydream. "By the way, I found a harvester from Bavaria—from what I could understand, anyway—already drunk and half-passed out behind a barrel in the courtyard. I put him to bed. Don't be surprised if you don't see him until tomorrow."

"What if he—?"

"I made sure to turn him on his side and leave a bucket beside him."

Cerise was impressed despite herself. "Wow. You handled that like an expert."

His eyes fled hers. "Yes, well," he muttered. "I had a lot of experience with my father."

A wave of remorse rocked her on her feet. She'd inadvertently poked at what she was starting to see was a painful bruise. "I'm so sorry. I never—"

"I know," he said and waved her concern away. It didn't go, though. Her childhood had been loving and stable. It wasn't until she was an adult that her life blew apart. To have that happen as a child…she couldn't even imagine what Clovis had endured. She wanted to wrap her arms around that rock-hard torso and hug him tight.

"I talked to Fiona," he said, changing the subject.

"Fiona?"

"The Irish girl."

She tried to get a grip on herself. "What did she say?"

He sighed. "I failed. She didn't understand your concerns. She swore to be immune to the effects of the sun and heat. I tried everything I could think of to persuade her."

She arched an eyebrow. "Do you believe her?"

"Of course not. She may be used to the sun in Ireland, which is to say—"

"Not much sun at all," Cerise completed for him.

"Precisely. Almost every single harvester I've had with that complexion has dropped like a fly in the vineyards."

She gnawed her lip.

Watching her, his eyes sharpened with intent.

"I was sure I could convince her, but she has a stubborn streak that I would respect if it didn't mean you're going to end up with a heatstroke patient," he said finally. "I want to be able to solve this problem for you. I'm frankly embarrassed that a young Irish lass has defeated me."

"We tried," she reasoned. "We'll take every possible precaution with her, but I guess she'll have to find out the hard way, like so many of them. Did you look at the weather forecast?" It was slightly cooler where they stood in the stone outbuilding, but because the huge doors were open for the harvesters, not by much. Sweat pooled between her breasts and behind her knees. It was going to be brutal in the full sun of the vineyards.

The delicious scents of fresh parsley and savory puff pastries wafted from the direction of the kitchen, but Cerise felt almost too hot to eat.

"It's supposed to get up to thirty-eight this afternoon," he said. "It's going to be blazing out there."

He looked at her in a way that made her heart do an odd thump.

The cooks began to parade out of the kitchen with huge platters of *pâté en croute*, little rounds of *saucisson sec, jambon perseillé,* and *gougères*.

"Do you have a seat?" she asked.

He pointed down the table at one of the only remaining spots. "Right there."

"Sit down then. I have to do my spiel. Um…do you want to say anything?" The idea that he would, and that as a partner it would be justified, made her doubly determined not to cede to her self-indulgent fantasies.

Clovis shook his head. "You would hate me if I did that. I'm no masochist, Cerise. Anyway, you're the winemaker here, not me."

That was a relief, but it still didn't erase the fact that she'd felt beholden to ask in the first place.

Cerise waited until everyone was seated. She clapped her hands and gave a short speech of welcome, talking about this year's grapes and her plans for the harvesting order. She also joked about a few of the regular harvesters, who took it with a sparkle in their eyes, and underlined the care that was required when handling the precious grapes.

As she reached the end, she lifted up her right hand and gave a sign to the kitchen staff to bring in the kir.

At the sight of the garnet mix of white Aligoté wine and blackcurrant liqueur, everybody erupted in an impromptu *ban bourgignon*, the traditional Burgundian drinking song that mainly consisted of clapping and singing la la laaaaaas.

Cerise could feel her face infuse with pleasure and pride. Morale was excellent. There were no delays. Better yet, Clovis was here to witness her achievement. He could see for himself that although his help was appreciated, she would be just fine on her own.

She realized her legs ached. She'd been on her feet all morning. The only remaining spot required squeezing in tight beside Clovis. She hesitated. The physical closeness might be…unwise. Still, she needed to eat. She slid in between him and another harvester she had met only briefly at check-in.

The side of his body was rock hard pressed against hers. She wanted to explore his torso with her fingertips, discover the grooves and valleys. *Stop that.*

Clovis had already began to taste the first course of *jambon perseillé*, which Cerise always sourced from Charcutier Raillard in Beaune, along with tiny, vinegar-infused cornichon pickles.

"Delicious," he said, moving over to give her room. "Raillard?"

"Where else?" She started eating hers. Eating during harvest was a matter of fuel as well as pleasure. The first taste of the traditional jellied ham with vinegary pickles and a fresh kick of parsley made her close her eyes in pleasure. Without meaning to, she let out a funny little noise.

She opened them again to see Clovis with his fork hanging midair a few inches from his mouth, watching her.

Her whole body vibrated under his gaze. Neither the food, nor the heat, nor the other harvesters were enough a distraction. *Damn.*

Luckily, Jorgé burst into the barn where they were eating. She knew he was driving up from Portugal, where he had been visiting his grandparents, but she hadn't expected him until the next day.

"Jorgé!" she cried. She quickly realized she was too tightly jammed in to get up, but she waved him over.

"Cerise!" He gave her hearty kisses on the cheeks and hugged her for good measure. "I drove all day and night. I couldn't miss the first day of your harvest!"

"I am so, so happy you're here," she said, grinning up at him. Jorgé was still young, just barely twenty years old, but he had been helping her with harvests since he was fifteen and had decided the French baccalaureate wasn't for him. His parents were vineyard workers, so he knew what he was doing. He had a warmth and solidity about him that made him seem older than his years, and he had proved time and again to be a huge asset during harvest. He had become more a friend and colleague than an employee.

"I'm starving," he said.

"Here." She gestured to her seat and finally managed to unwedge herself, purposely avoiding Clovis's reaction. "You eat. Once the cooks catch sight of you, they'll make sure you're well fed. I'll finish eating in the kitchen, and then I should do some last-minute prep."

"Can I help you?" Clovis said.

She waved away his suggestion. Time alone with Clovis was exactly what she was trying to avoid. "No, no. You should get to know Jorgé here. Clovis, this is Jorgé, a key member of the harvesting team. He sets a flaming pace in the vineyards—you'll see. Jorgé, this is Clovis. My new…partner. For the time being."

"Oh!" Jorgé said, then turned to look at Clovis. "Oh," he said in a different voice. "You're the—"

"Yes," Cerise cut him off. She had poured out her distress about Maxime's will on the phone with Jorgé when he was in Portugal. "Clovis."

Jorgé, being a well-brought-up boy, stuck out his hand. "Nice to meet you."

Clovis gave him a long look, then shook it. "I don't believe you really think that," he said. "But I will change your mind."

Cerise looked from her friend to Clovis, then left in a hurry. Distraction. Distraction was the name of the game.

# chapter twelve

THE SECOND DAY of the harvest dawned—the first full day. The afternoon before, Cerise had managed to keep herself so busy with her harvesters and the cooks, as well as the first batch of sorting and pressing, that she had managed to avoid Clovis almost entirely.

Soon after breakfast the harvesters began work in the lowest section for Les Hautes-Côtes de Beaune and, despite the lead blanket of heat, were snipping off bundles of grapes at a steady pace. At the end of the afternoon, she left the vat room for enough time to survey the scene with satisfaction.

The rhythm of the harvesters snipping grape stems, calling over to the porters to take full baskets to stack on the tractor, their laughter, and the unlabeled bottles of wine being passed along the rows of vines for constant refreshment was like an orchestra playing the most enchanting symphony. There were few things more gratifying than a harvest running smoothly.

Jorgé ran up and down the rows, working faster than anyone else. He helped novice harvesters hone their snipping technique and gave them tips to preserve their knees and backs.

Clovis was ensuring the wine baskets were properly stacked on the flatbed tractor attachment and firmly secured. That was a crucial job, and from the looks of it, he was ensuring that the grapes were protected as if they were his own. Which, Cerise reminded herself with a stab of consternation, they were.

She approached him from behind. Before she said a word, he spun around as though sensing her presence. "Shouldn't you check in at your domaine soon?" she asked. "I can take over here. Everything seems to be humming along nicely."

She knew from experience—she supposed they both did— that things could, and did, go wrong on a regular basis. He should really grasp this window of smooth sailing to check on things at Domaine de Valois.

"I probably should," he admitted. "Although Jean has phoned me several times. It sounds as if he has everything under control." He glanced over to Jorgé, moving nimbly between the crouched harvesters. "You were right about Jorgé. He has the makings of a fantastic *régisseur*."

She shaded her eyes from the sun's glare. "The thought has crossed my mind, too, but I've been waiting for him to express interest."

"That's wise," Clovis agreed. "Who knows? He might want to be a fighter pilot or undersea diver. I wanted to be both those things when I was younger."

"You didn't want to be a winemaker?" She was so close to him she could smell that unique interplay of dirt and vines, combined with the tang of salt from his skin and then another heady scent that was distinctly his. It was fast becoming her kryptonite.

He shook his head, and Cerise found herself fixated on the subtle play of his throat muscles above the stretched collar of his T-shirt. "Winemaking was the last thing that interested in me. Unfortunately, I was plagued with ear infections when I was little, so my damaged eardrums eliminated my dream careers."

"Were you sad?"

"Inconsolable for about a year or so. Still, I am one of those lucky people who went into their profession out of obligation but ended up falling in love with it."

She blinked. "Me too." She was unnerved by such a powerful tug of attraction and searched wildly for another topic. "Do you think Fiona is holding up?"

He followed her gaze to the row where Fiona was harvesting. On Jorgé's advice she had tied a white T-shirt around her head, and Cerise noticed Jorgé giving her a steady supply of water and preventing the wine bottles from being passed to her. Jorgé seemed to have designated himself Fiona's guardian angel.

"Looks like Jorgé is taking excellent care of her," Clovis observed.

She nodded. "One of the things I love most about Jorgé is his kindness."

"Some people are keepers, plain and simple." Clovis cast her a long, azure look.

She didn't break the connection between them, even though she knew she should, until Jorgé brought another basket of grapes for Clovis to secure on the tractor.

"Go back to your domaine for a while," Cerise said, reason reasserting itself. "Jorgé said you were here all yesterday afternoon. I need to get back to the vat room to check the *pressoir*."

"I'll just whip down and put out any fires, then I'll be back. Is there anything I can do for you when I'm there?"

"Actually..." Cerise hesitated. This was a lot to ask someone, especially a man she barely knew. Still, Maxime had done this every year for her, and otherwise she didn't know how she would manage.

"What is it?" He tilted his head.

"It's an unusual request. I don't even know if they'll let you do it."

He chuckled. "Now I'm curious. You have to tell me."

"On your way back, could you pick up Marc and Yves from

school in Beaune? They just started on Monday. It's Saturday, so they're finished at noon. I know it's out of your way."

His eyes widened, but he didn't look angry, or shocked, or... Then a smile lit his face.

What a glorious thing it would be to be on the receiving end of that smile every day. "It's difficult to manage the harvest and the first week of school at the same time—"

He placed a hand on her arm, and she stopped midsentence, stunned again by that electric shock.

"It would love to."

A good chunk of the stress she hadn't realized was weighing down her shoulders lifted.

"What school do they go to?"

"Saint-Coeur. You know where that is, just on *le boulevard*?" It wasn't as if there were many schools in Beaune.

He lips twitched, and he looked suddenly mischievous. "Saint-Coeur...I remember it well, though perhaps not as well as they remember me."

Cerise found her lips curving in amusement. She sensed a story behind his words. "What did you do?"

"I went to Saint-Coeur up until grade ten, but then...well..."

"Well what?"

"I was expelled."

Cerise choked back laughter. "Really?" If either of her boys *dared*— She was going to expire of curiosity. "What did you do?"

He shook his head. "I don't think I come off well in this story. I'm trying to make a good impression on you, remember?"

"Now I really have to know." Why did she want so badly to hear about Clovis as a young truant? There was something about that playful, slightly naughty glint in his eyes that drew her in, even though she knew she shouldn't care.

"I'll tell you when I come back with the boys, but *not* in front of them."

Exercising considerable willpower, she resisted the desire to pester him further. "Their teachers might give you a hard time about picking them up. I just met them myself two days ago, briefly, but—"

"Don't worry." He waved a hand dismissively. "I was always good at charming teachers."

"Not enough to keep yourself from getting expelled."

"That was a *male* teacher."

She chuckled. "I should have known."

He checked over the baskets as Cerise asked Jorgé to take over the loading. There was nobody else besides Clovis she trusted enough to ensure the grapes' well-being. She wondered why she already trusted him so implicitly with them. She had to be more cautious. If she trusted him with too much, he was bound to find out about the grapes she was secretly diverting for Cerasus. She had a special vat for those, and she took care of that when nobody was paying attention. The workers in her vat room were used to the "don't ask" policy.

Clovis turned to leave, then paused. "Will the boys be frightened when I show up? I don't want to put them in a difficult position. I know Emily's mother gives her strict instructions not to leave school with anyone but her."

She shook her head. "You'll find I'm a laxer mother—or maybe just tired. They know who you are, and for some reason they seem to like you." It surprised her that he was so thoughtful of their well-being, but then again he, too, was a parent.

"For *some* reason?"

"I mean, they took to you quickly. You have a way with children."

"I think I might," he said. "Sadly, with Emily, I haven't had much opportunity to find out."

She quickly sped over to the *cuverie* after he left so she could oversee the sorting, destemming, and pressing. She also secretly removed the baskets of grapes she'd earmarked as Cerasus and made sure they were destemmed and placed in a smaller, separate vat at the very back of the room.

She had an excuse ready—that she was doing something slightly different with the vinification in the small vat. A half-truth was the best kind of lie. Antoine had been a specialist at those. He'd say he'd be home in time for dinner. Perhaps he intended to be, but he rarely was. He'd say he would come to her twelve-week ultrasound appointment. Same. That he wouldn't use his tractor in the vineyards when they were muddy and dangerous. Maybe he underestimated the danger, but he did it time and again—until he became the victim of his own recklessness.

If the workers, and especially Clovis, discovered her "vinification experiment" went so far as removing her wine from appellation status altogether, they would be horrified. The appellation—or the accreditation from the wine authority which guaranteed potential buyers that wines had both quality and regional authenticity—was what sold Burgundian wines in France and around the world. The risks Cerise was taking with the creation of Cerasus meant it would never qualify for that seal of approval the words "appellation contrôlée" on the label would give. Without the appellation, initially at least, she couldn't charge much for each bottle but...if it became a celebrated wine, the price would continue to rise with demand. It alone could be capable of ensuring the future of Domaine du Cerisier.

The risky techniques Cerise used to create Cerasus and attain the purity she dreamed of meant it would never qualify as an appellation wine. It would need to be very special indeed to sell. If it was, it could sell a lot. A big gamble but potentially a big payoff, not just financial but artistic, too. Winemaking was an art, and Cerise finally felt confident enough to stretch her wings and innovate.

If only Clovis hadn't been added to the equation at the worst possible moment for Cerasus…

He might even have a legal case against her for fraud if he found out. Then she really would be at his mercy. She would accept his help during the harvest, but that was all, she reminded herself again.

Her boys had always loved the festive atmosphere of the harvest: the delicious, communal meals; helping in the vineyards on the weekends; and the joyous bustle that took over the courtyard. There was always someone to kick around a soccer ball or talk about dinosaurs

They had been passed around from cook to harvester to harvester since they were babies, but now that they were older, it dawned on them that Cerise didn't have much time during the harvest. They didn't like that part. Maxime had filled in beautifully for her when he was alive. Now, without realizing it, she was asking Clovis to do the same by picking them up from school.

For the last few years, the scorching summers meant the harvest coincided with the shaky start of the new school year when Marc and Yves were coping with so many new things—new class formations, new teachers, and for Marc this year his move from elementary to middle school.

If it wasn't for the harvest, she would be making an extra effort to be present for them. As it was, she was almost completely absent. It was the week of the year when she felt her single-parent status the most acutely.

The syrupy smell of crushed grapes in the *cuverie* was almost overwhelming. The extreme heat probably meant the grapes were going to start fermenting much sooner than usual.

Once she felt confident the sorters were doing their job meticulously, and she had finished diverting her Cerasus grapes—for the time being, anyway—she headed back to check on the harvesting in the vineyards. More specifically, she needed to check on Fiona. That girl worried her.

Earlier, she had asked Fiona if she wanted to come inside and help in the *cuverie* or, better yet, refresh herself with a little nap in the harvesters' house.

It had backfired. The Irish girl, instead of slowing down, sped up as result of her concern. Cerise felt a mixture of annoyance and grudging respect. Grit showed up in the most incongruous people. Oh well, she had tried. At least the work day would be over soon.

As she approached the lower vines, the dust rose up from the dry limestone soil as Clovis's blue Mercedes—she shouldn't trust anyone who drove such a flashy car—appeared in the distance.

She heard Jorgé shout over Clovis's engine.

"She fainted!" he yelled. His head popped up between the rows, and he frantically waved Cerise over.

She broke into a run. Jorgé was squatting in the dirt, holding Fiona's strawberry-blonde head on his knees. A wet white T-shirt had slipped off her head.

"She's still breathing, I checked." Jorgé's liquid-brown eyes met Cerise's.

"Pulse?"

"Steady. I've been soaking the T-shirt every fifteen minutes or so for the past hour and begging her to go in or at least rest in the shade."

"This isn't your fault, Jorgé," Cerise tried to reassure him. "But we have to carry her out of the sun now."

"Yes," he agreed. "But where?"

They looked around them. The nearest tree provided only a smidgen of shade. "I think we need to get her to Maxime's house," she said.

"In the tractor?"

Cerise glanced up. The tractor was almost fully loaded with baskets. They'd have to drive it at a snail's pace, or their precious cargo could be splattered all over the gravel roads.

"Clovis's car," she answered.

Clovis joined them just then, not even out of breath from running. She was happier to see him than she could have imagined a month ago at Maxime's funeral. The boys followed in his wake but hung back when they saw Fiona unconscious.

"We'll have to use your car," she said to Clovis, never tearing her eyes away from Fiona's flushed face.

"Of course," he said. "When I saw, I drove in as close as I could."

"Is she dead?" Yves's voice came out small and scared.

"No, no," Clovis reassured him. "Just heat exhaustion. She's fainted, that's all. Don't worry."

He picked up Fiona and carried her gently but rapidly to his gleaming car. Jorgé and Cerise ran after his long, powerful strides. Was it wrong that she wondered what it would feel like to trade places with poor Fiona? Yes, it was wrong, not to mention wildly inappropriate. She opened the car door. Before she hopped in, her brain finally caught up with her actions.

"I need you to stay here and oversee things, Jorgé," she said. "Downplay it, okay? Everything will grind to a halt if you leave."

"But—"

"We'll take good care of her. I promise. I need you here."

He gave her a reluctant nod.

"Can you make sure the boys are kept busy? It will be easier at the house without them."

Jorgé nodded. "Of course, but—"

"It's just heat exhaustion," she said as Clovis settled Fiona, still unconscious, into the luxurious leather back seat. "She's sweating, so it's not heatstroke. Clovis and I know what to do."

The cool air from the car's powerful air-conditioning enveloped her like a cold shower. This was perfect for Fiona, but they had to leave right away, or the car would begin to heat up.

"Tell her…" It was the first time Cerise had ever seen Jorgé at a loss for words.

She reached out and patted his shoulder. "I will," she said simply. This was more than just protectiveness. Jorgé clearly had feelings for Fiona. That was incredibly quick. Interesting.

"If anything happens to Fiona, I'll never forgive myself," he said.

"Neither will I," she said. "But I promise you, it won't."

She slammed the car door, and pebbles spurted under Clovis's tires. They were off.

She stayed in the back seat with Fiona while Clovis drove with single-minded focus toward Maxime's house. It was the ideal place to take her. The several-feet-thick stone walls made it cool, even on the hottest days.

She reached for Fiona's hand. It was hot and dry in hers.

"Go faster!" Cerise urged Clovis.

"I'm going as fast as I can without hurting either one of you," he said, glancing at them in the rearview mirror.

"You don't want to damage your shiny car," she muttered.

"Don't be ridiculous."

The worst of it was that Cerise knew she was being ridiculous. Adrenaline did that to her.

Fiona's eyelids flickered, and she murmured something Cerise didn't understand.

"Fiona?" she said. "It's Cerise. You passed out."

This time the girl's eyes snapped wide open, revealing pale-green irises. "Feck." She even moaned in an Irish brogue.

"I didn't understand what she just said," Cerise said to Clovis as Fiona's eyes fluttered shut again.

"I'm not completely clear either," he said, spinning into the courtyard and parking right by Maxime's front door. "I speak fluent English, but Irish always sounds to me like an entirely different language."

"You get her out. I'll open up." She extracted a big lump of old metal keys from underneath a fossilized nautilus Maxime had found in one of the vineyards. She used the largest iron key to unlock the door, then stepped into hall, relieved to feel its coolness.

"Let's put her on the living room couch," she said, calling out to Clovis, who was extracting Fiona from the car.

Fiona must have come to again because she pushed away Clovis's offer of assistance. "I can walk on my own!"

Clovis looked over to Cerise. "Sure she's not related to you?"

"Shut up." Cerise wasn't sure whether to laugh or act dignified. "It's completely different."

"Is it?"

Fiona tried to shake off Clovis's support again.

"Will you at least let me hold your arm?" he asked in what sounded like an extremely good British accent. "I'm French. You must indulge my gallantry."

"Oh, all right," Fiona said and took his arm. "But I'm a feminist, you know."

"I happen to adore feminists."

Fiona smiled up at him. Cerise was reminded it was dangerous to be attracted to a man who could charm women so easily.

They took a few steps, and Cerise, watching Fiona closely, saw when she staggered again. Fiona tried to cover it up, but she would have fallen if Clovis hadn't been holding her so securely.

Cerise took her free arm once they'd crossed the threshold.

"Are you dizzy?" she asked, steering her to the massive over-stuffed couch Maxime had bought only two years before.

"A wee bit," Fiona admitted as they settled her on the cool fabric. They made her lie back, and Clovis propped up her head with a cushion.

"Are you feeling any better?" Cerise asked in stilted English, a far cry from Clovis's plummy accent.

Fiona closed her eyes. "Yes, it's lovely and cool in here. I'm just so embarrassed. I cannot fecking believe I passed out. You warned me."

Cerise decided this was not the moment for I-told-you-so. "That's nothing to be ashamed of," she said and looked up to see Clovis watching her, not Fiona. "I admire your...how do you say in English? Grit." She took Fiona's small-boned hand in hers. "Don't blame yourself. We need to cool you off so this doesn't turn into anything more serious."

"Then I can go out in the vineyards again?" Stubbornness blazed in her pale eyes.

Cerise exchanged a look of disbelief with Clovis.

"We'll just take it one step at a time, *d'accord?*" she said, her eyes warning Clovis from saying anything further. He gave her an infinitesimal nod. Good. He understood that to ban Fiona from anything would be the surefire way of ensuring she would find a way to do it.

"I'm much cooler already," Fiona said. "Go back to the vine-yards. I'm fine."

"First, would you like some tea?" Cerise asked. "I'm also going to get you a liter of water. I want you to drink it over the next while."

She nodded. "Rehydration. I understand. Tea would be grand."

Cerise went to the kitchen, and Clovis followed her. She was unsure of what to do. She couldn't stay here and nurse Fiona and be in the vineyards and the *cuverie* at the same time. She knew more grapes earmarked for Cerasus would be arriving any time.

As she reached for the kettle, Clovis made her pause by putting his hand on hers. She looked up and almost got lost in his thoughtful expression. She was glad he was here with her and that she was not dealing with Fiona alone, but she could not let herself... She would lose herself if she followed her instincts rather than her reason. She wiggled her hand free.

"I'll take care of the tea, the water, and Fiona," he said, seeming unperturbed. "You need to get back to the *cuverie*."

She squeezed her hands to her sides to keep from touching him. She was surprised he instantly knew what she needed to do and where she needed to be and didn't question it. She wondered how he would react if he knew exactly why she so urgently needed to go back to the vat room—to use their grapes for an experiment that risked the financial well-being of the entire domaine. He would not take it well. Cerise was certain of that.

She nodded. "I can't leave things there for too long. You know how to—?"

"Treat heat exhaustion? Yes."

"I think with Fiona, you'll need to—"

"Make sure she doesn't escape?"

She laughed. "You understand our patient, I see."

"Perfectly." He dug in his shorts pocket, then handed Cerise his car keys. "Take my *shiny* car, and send someone to relieve me later on?"

"Of course and...sorry about that."

"You were stressed," he said. "Don't worry about it. Fiona and I will be just fine."

"*Merci.*"

He shook his head and gave her a little push on the small of her back. "There's no need for sorrys or thank-yous between partners."

# chapter thirteen

CERISE FLOORED IT to the vineyards. Clovis's car purred, but her mind clunked around in circles.

The ease with which he had designated himself caretaker of Fiona, instead of assuming that Cerise, as a woman, would automatically take that role, startled her. When Antoine was alive and someone got sick, it was Cerise's responsibility, even if she was sick herself. Worse, it had never crossed her mind when Antoine was alive that things should be any different. Being with a man now would revert her to the person she had been then, and she never wanted to go back.

As soon as she arrived in the vines, Jorgé ran to her.

"How is she?" he asked, his eyes wild.

"She had already regained consciousness by the time we got to Maxime's." She put an arm around his shoulders. "Clovis is staying with her, but I'm positive it was just a bout of heat exhaustion. Nothing serious."

Jorgé put a hand over his heart. "Thank God." He sent up a little Ava Maria and then crossed himself.

"It wasn't your fault." She squeezed his shoulder. "You know that, don't you?"

He stared at her, his brown eyes wide. "I just… Fiona is special."

"Oh?" Cerise said, trying to leave it open-ended. "You mean you have feelings for her?"

"Yes." He didn't hesitate.

He had only just met Fiona the night before. Cerise marveled at his audacity in declaring himself so definitively.

She wondered if Clovis was already discussing with Fiona the original plan of having her work at a sorting table at Domaine de Valois. Now that she knew Jorgé's heart, moving Fiona would be far more complicated. Cerise would never do anything to hurt him.

She went to check the loaded tractor. Jorgé had done a superb job, but without him in the vineyards, the harvesters had slowed down a little.

"How were the boys?" she asked.

Jorgé laughed. "They didn't need much help from me. I gave them each a pair of secateurs and a bucket, and then Marc took things in charge. He knows his way around a grapevine, that one."

Indeed, she found Marc a few rows over, bent over a grapevine, explaining the fine art of grape cluster triage to Yves, who, for once, seemed to be listening.

She listened to Marc for a few minutes and then gave him a hug from behind. "You're sounding like an expert, Marc, and your cutting technique is flawless."

He turned slightly and smiled up at her. "I like it in the vineyards. It just feels like I belong here."

She kissed the top of his head. His dark hair smelled of the vanilla shampoo she strong-armed them into using once every three days, mixed with the scent of vineyard dirt. "That's because you do."

"And me?" Yves piped up.

"Marc is teaching you well." Cerise smiled again at her sons. She had to keep these vineyards healthy and in her possession so she could pass on Domaine du Cerisier to them. They had lost their father. Life owed them something good, but Cerise no longer trusted life, so she would provide it herself.

The basket set between them was already three-quarters full. They were getting older, her babies. Maybe they really could start to help—Marc, definitely.

"This tractor is ready to go to the *cuverie*," Jorgé called over to her.

"Do you boys want to go for a tractor ride?" Cerise asked them.

They shook their heads. "No, we want to stay here in the vineyards," Yves said.

"We still have work to do," added Marc.

Children of her own heart.

Jorgé stopped with the boys on his way back from the vineyards, but Cerise was nowhere near finished her work in the vat room, especially with Cerasus. When the dinner bell rang, she told them to go on without her.

She was only vaguely conscious of the harvesters making their way to dinner and then straggling back out a couple of hours later. Marc came to check on her after they ate, but she asked him to put Yves to bed and then go to bed himself.

She ensured the crushed grapes were settling in the vat reserved for Cerasus, then became conscious of a loud rumble from her stomach.

She was starving. She had no idea what time it was; she hadn't even gone to the house to check on Fiona, Clovis, and the boys. There would be plenty of food in the makeshift dining area in the barn. She'd sneak in there. She checked her watch. Ten o'clock. Her body was adamant; she had to eat.

She made her way stealthily across the courtyard, cursing the light crunch of pebbles under her boots. If she bumped into anyone, they would want to chat, and she might die on the spot fantasizing about leftover couscous or *pâté en croute*.

The inside of the barn was dark, but she crept in and felt her way to the kitchen door. Before she could open it, she noticed a sliver of light underneath. *Merde*. She didn't want to talk. She just wanted food.

She turned the handle and pushed, only to see Clovis installed on a stool at the counter that served as a prep area, with an assortment of *terrines, pâté*, and cheeses scattered in front of him. He'd scrounged a baguette somewhere and poured himself a glass of wine from one of the bottles she always left for the cooks.

His eyes met hers. "I'm not stealing your harvest food," he said. "I was hungry."

Was she that territorial? She held up her hand. "Not mad. Starving."

She went over and tore off a piece of baguette, picked up his knife, cut a slice from the huge terrine, and put it on the bread. She took a huge bite and chewed, her eyes almost rolling back in her head with pleasure at the meaty taste of terrine atop the pillowy baguette.

When she looked at Clovis again, he was holding out a little cornichon pickle for her. She added it to her feast and took another bite. Terrine was always better with a cornichon; the vinegar kick was a perfect foil to its earthiness.

Clovis thrust out another stool from under the counter. She sat down beside him, and they silently demolished five slices of *pâté en croute*, half a round of Époisses, several large wedges of Citeaux cheese made by the monks up the road, a hunk of *saucisson sec*, and a silky-smooth *pâté de foie*.

Finally, Cerise dropped her knife and picked up her wine-glass. "*Dis-donc*, that's better."

He let out a deep sigh and let his knife drop, too. "Perfect."

"You missed dinner?" It was then she remembered she'd promised to send someone to the house to relieve him earlier. She clapped a hand over her mouth. "*Merde.* I got so busy in the *cuverie* I completely forgot to send in a reinforcement."

Clovis picked up his wineglass with one hand and waved away her concern with the other. "Jorgé came right after he finished in the vineyards, and by then Jean had called. With this hot weather, he wanted me to make a decision about the maceration temperature, so as soon as Jorgé arrived, I took off down there."

Cerise nodded, but that couldn't be the whole story. "Why are you back here?"

"I left my cell phone, and also I wanted one last look at Fiona. Once I did that my stomach was turning inside out, and I snuck in here. I grew up raiding harvest kitchens."

Cerise could picture him as a bright-eyed, dark-haired little imp, escaping his unhappy home life in the warm embrace of the harvest kitchen and its cooks. She was certain they must have cosseted and spoiled him, knowing the family he had to return to after the harvest. She hoped they gave him lots of hugs.

"How's Fiona?"

"She'd doing fine now."

"I thought she would. She revived quickly."

This was so comfortable. Eating. Chatting. At times like this, she felt as if she'd known Clovis forever. She remembered what he had said after their final kiss in the courtyard, about how she felt like home to him. At the time it had sounded ridiculous, but maybe she was beginning to understand.

He nodded, busy unwrapping the skin from a slice of *saucisson sec*. "Of course she wants to be back in the vineyards tomorrow. I didn't suggest the option of coming down to work at the sorting table at Domaine de Valois again because I didn't think Jorgé would thank me for that."

Cerise snorted. "Yeah. He thinks he's in love with her."

"You don't believe him?" Clovis watched her over the rim of his wineglass.

She rolled her eyes. "I don't think you can fall in love that fast. Lust, maybe. Not love. Do you believe him?"

He broke her gaze and began wrapping up the remains of their meal to put in the fridge.

"Well?" Cerise prompted.

"I think I do believe in a sudden lightning bolt of love," he said, his back turned to her as he opened the fridge door. "I didn't used to, but life has a way of surprising us."

Could he be talking about her? She quashed down an irrational spark of hope that flashed through her heart. She shook her head. She no longer believed fairy tales existed. Jorgé and Fiona were as touching as they were absurd. Before her marriage to Antoine and her year of losses, Cerise probably had believed in love at first sight, too. Part of her wanted to return to the innocence and idealism of Jorgé and Fiona, but that was impossible. She was no longer that person, and it served her well in so many ways.

"Was it love at first sight with Emily's mother?" Cerise asked, then regretted the question as soon as it was out of her mouth. She shouldn't have asked something so personal, but for some mysterious reason she wanted to know.

He shut the fridge door and turned around again. "No. It wasn't like that. I was so young then and very…um, restless."

She became aware that she and Clovis were alone again. They'd been chatting in such a friendly way, but suddenly it no longer felt comfortable. Now, that magnetic charge between them made her squirm.

She searched for a way to neutralize the atmosphere. "What did you do in the house while you watched over Fiona?"

He smiled. "I read a bunch of Maxime's old hunting periodicals."

"Planning on shooting a wild boar?"

"*Sûrement pas.*" He shook his head. "I never understood what Maxime liked about hunting. Honestly, all those wine-soaked men stalking the forest, armed to their teeth... I'm far more scared of them than any wild boar." He leaned his chin on his hand in a way that made her think of Rodin's famous sculpture. She couldn't seem to tear her eyes away.

"I guess the periodicals made me feel closer to him somehow," he mused. "It was strange being in his house. He rarely invited me up here, and after you arrived he actively discouraged it. I could never figure out why."

Guilt settled over Cerise. "It must have felt unfair that your grandfather devoted so much time to me and not to you. It *was* unfair."

Clovis shook his head. "No. We were close. It's just that we always saw each other on my turf, not his. It was like he avoided throwing you and me together."

Clovis hadn't exactly been on her radar, but she had known he was Maxime's grandson. It struck her how strange it was that she'd seen so little of him when Maxime was alive. She'd always assumed they didn't get along, but that didn't appear to be the case. She bit her lip, mulling it over.

"Please stop that."

Cerise looked up. His hands were balled into fists on the counter, his voice strangled.

"What?" Even before she asked the question, she became aware of every charged particle of air around them. She pulsed with the knowledge that if she just reached out, she could touch him. She had to stay in control. She reminded herself of her boys in the vineyards that afternoon, working so hard and loving it. Domaine du Cerisier was not only her future; it was their future, too.

"I know I made a promise not to touch you, and I'll honor that even if it kills me, but—"

"But what?" The idea that he could be suffering with as much lust as she was thrilled her to the core, even though she knew how wrong it was.

"If you keep biting your lip like that, you *will* kill me."

Cerise couldn't think of anything to say, so she just watched him and waited...

He pushed himself away from the fridge and took a few steps closer. With his right index finger, he touched her lip just below where her teeth had it in their grip. The heat of his finger singed like a brand. If only he wasn't Clovis and hadn't inherited half of Domaine du Cerisier with her. If only he was a handsome stranger she wouldn't have to deal with tomorrow. She could slip her hands under his shirt and do all the things she fantasized about.

"You make it difficult not to kiss you when do that." His voice was rough, and his face was tight with restrained lust.

She could not take one more second of the desire in his eyes without giving in to hers and ducked her head. "I do that when I'm thinking or trying not to laugh," she mumbled.

"I know. It comes with a little pucker between your brows." She could hear him shift his body, restless. "I want to kiss that away, too. Desperately."

"I—I didn't know."

"I believe it. It does something to me. I can't explain it. I'm overtaken with a blinding desire to pleasure the thoughts right out of you."

"Oh." Every inch of Cerise's skin yearned for him to do exactly that.

"I'm keeping my promise, but it's taking every ounce of self-control I possess."

If only they could just have one night, with no strings

attached. But there was no changing the fact that she couldn't negotiate after that. Hell, she probably wouldn't be able to think straight for days, maybe months. She stared at the grooves in the worn countertop. *If only there was a way to have him—and not the consequences.*

She took a deep breath and looked up. "I'm struggling, too. I'd love to have meaningless sex with you, but you're not a stranger anymore. That makes it impossible."

Clovis jerked back as though she'd slapped him. "Meaningless sex?"

She regretted her words as soon as they flew out of her mouth. She didn't want a relationship or, God forbid, a second husband, but she hadn't meant for it to come out so crudely.

His eyes moved over her face, then he gathered up the final things on the counter and put them away. "You're right," he said without meeting her eyes. "It's a terrible idea. *Bonne nuit,* Cerise. Sleep well." He turned on his heel and walked out.

She was left alone in the empty kitchen, repenting her misstep. Still, the truth remained that she couldn't allow herself to have anything besides meaningless sex with Clovis or anyone else. She might start to care, and that would make her far too vulnerable as well as erode her hard-won independence.

She thought back to their impromptu dinner. There was something about his presence... She wasn't just attracted to Clovis; she actually liked him. In that case, it was probably for the best that she had made him angry. It slashed the chances of them indulging in their attraction. It didn't feel like it was for the best, though. Not one bit. With a heavy heart, she finally flicked out the light and headed to the big house.

# chapter fourteen

THE NEXT MORNING when the alarm rang at five o'clock, Cerise noted the absolute stillness of the gauze curtains in Maxime's bedroom and the chorus of crickets playing outside the window. It was going to be even hotter than the day before.

She had thrown off the white sheet and duvet that covered the large bed during the night and slept completely naked.

She'd barely slept, bothered by how Clovis had left the night before and how she had obviously hurt him.

Her shorts and T-shirt lay in a pile where she had discarded them on the wood floor. She showered and headed downstairs to make the boys' breakfast but stopped short at the sight of Clovis fiddling with the coffeemaker on the kitchen counter.

"*Bonjour?*" The word came out as a question.

He spun around, the hurt of the night before apparently forgotten. "Ah! *Bonjour!* I thought I'd bring fresh baguettes. Did you sleep well?"

"Not really. About last night—"

"Don't even think about it," he said and leaned over to give her the *bises*. She kept it brief, resisting the urge to linger. The problem was she *was* thinking about it and regretting the way it ended. He seemed emotionally lighter than the night before, perhaps because she had eradicated all of his desire for her with that one impulsive sentence. Logically, that was a positive development if it was true, but it felt wretched. She could hear Yves and Marc stirring. She couldn't talk of it now, even though she longed to. Her boys would be arriving in the kitchen at any moment.

She eyed the four baguettes at the center of the table. "It was thoughtful of you, but we don't usually eat a baguette each, you know."

"You don't?" He was measuring the coffee grounds. "I did when I was a boy. I just wanted to be sure we had enough."

Cerise busied herself getting the milk, jam, and butter out of the fridge while she madly searched for a neutral topic of conversation. "Hey, before the boys appear, you never told me why you were expelled from of Saint-Coeur."

"I'd rather not—"

"You promised."

He flicked the switch on the coffeemaker and leaned against the counter, looking so tall and lean and sexy Cerise began to overheat. "I really don't want to tell you."

"Why?"

"I was young, stupid, and hormonal."

"Sounds like a great story."

"I'm not proud of it. I came here this morning determined to be helpful and a good friend to you." He winced as he said that last word. That irrational flash of hope returned. Maybe his desire hadn't completely vanished. "I feel like maybe…just maybe, I can rebuild my reputation with you, and this story could undo all that."

She gasped. "Is it that bad? Excellent. I can't wait any longer."

He nodded, his eyes cast down to his feet.

"I won't judge you. I promise."

He fixed her with those blue eyes and studied hers in such a way that she felt he was penetrating her soul. "All right," he said at last. "But keep in mind the boy I was at fifteen was a far cry from the man I am now."

"Keeping that in mind." She nodded.

"I was caught with another student doing something not very Catholic under the altar of the school church."

Cerise let out a burst of laughter. "Who was she?"

"She was two grades above me, but we were just over a year apart in age, and I was…uh…advanced in that department. She was deep into philosophy."

"Let me guess? She was a nihilist."

He raised his brows, impressed. "Correct. She wore a pair of heavy black glasses I just wanted to whip off her, as well as other things."

She had to grab on to the back of the nearest kitchen chair she was laughing so hard. "How old were you?" she finally gasped.

Clovis blushed, a fascinating sight she wanted to reproduce again and again. "Fifteen."

"But wait…you said you were thrown out of school. Just for that?"

"Well, that and the fact that I took the blame while my par-amour escaped. They never found her, and I would not tell them who she was. They held the threat of expulsion over my head to try to scare me into giving up her identity, but it didn't work, so they had no choice but to follow through."

"During World War Two you would have been useful in the French Resistance."

"It's funny you mention that. When they were threatening me, I rather imagined myself as a young Resistance fighter being interrogated by the Nazis."

She could just picture it and burst into laughter again.

A few moments later, she clutched her stomach, trying to catch her breath. "Thank you. I can't remember the last time I laughed so hard. *Mon Dieu*, my stomach hurts."

Clovis eyed her narrowly, but his dimple flashed. "So gratified to have provided you with such entertainment."

"You did." God, she did really like him. Meaningless sex was definitely off the table. She had no idea what that left.

"You're not mad I let myself in?" he asked, clearly seeking to change the subject.

A while ago she might have been, but not now. She shook her head. "Did you use your key?"

He found four glass breakfast bowls for their coffee and hot chocolate in the cupboard and set them on the table. "I didn't have to. You left the door unlocked."

Cerise tried to remember, but she'd been so unsettled when she got home, she couldn't. "That's entirely possible."

"Sleeping with an unlocked door—"

"I don't need you to look after me, Clovis," she reminded him.

"I know, but I can't help thinking it would be nice if we could look after each other. That's what friends do, isn't it?"

Marc and Yves came in then, delighted to see Clovis. That was good, because looking after each other sounded so wonderful that Cerise was at a loss for words.

Clovis was a big help at breakfast, spreading butter and jam on Yves's numerous slabs of baguette. Her youngest son did, in fact, eat one full baguette—and half another one. Clovis accompanied the boys to help in the vineyards while Cerise could leave directly for the *cuverie* to get Fiona settled at the sorting table. With Jorgé now infatuated with her, there was no way she could suggest moving her down to Domaine de Valois.

Time flew by. Things were so hectic in the *cuverie* that she didn't make it out to the vineyards until it was time for the *goûter*—the snack of coffee, wine, and baguettes with *pâté* and *saucisson* that was doled out of the domaine's ancient Citroen *camionette* at about ten thirty every morning.

Jorgé passed her a glass of white wine as soon as she reached the *camionette*. The harvesters were sitting around in the dirt, trying to manufacture some shade out of their kerchiefs and hats. Even the short five-minute walk from the domaine to this section of the vineyards left sweat beading on her brow. Her breakfast with Clovis had left her feeling she had lost track of her bearings but also oddly contented in a way she was not accustomed to. Maybe they could be friends.

"How is Fiona doing at the sorting table?" Jorgé asked her.

"Off to a good start." Cerise smiled. "The other sorters are determined to make her fluent in French. They're starting with the swearwords."

Jorgé's deep-brown eyes shone. "Good. Those are the most important ones in a foreign language."

"How are the boys?" she asked, scanning the vines with a hand shading her eyes. "I don't see them."

"' I sent them down to the kitchens with the task of checking on whether lunch would be on time."

"Lunch is always on time."

"I know," Jorgé grinned, clearly pleased with himself. "Really, it was just to get them out of the sun for a bit. They won't stop working, those two. I figured the cooks would tempt them with treats to stay for a while in the shade of the kitchen."

"Brilliant, my friend." She glanced up the dusty vineyard road at the sound of an engine. When she saw who was bearing down at her, she used one of those rude words herself.

"What?" said Clovis, who was within earshot as he fiddled with the tractor that would shortly be hauling the next load of grapes to the *cuverie*. "Who's that?"

"Ah! I know who it is." Jorgé chuckled. "But I didn't think she would come for a visit during the mess of the harvest."

"I wish," muttered Cerise. "It's my aunt Geneviève." She squinted at Clovis. "Remember the one who was at the *apèrtif* after Maxime's funeral?"

He nodded. "I know her husband quite well. She's the one who glides around in a cloud of Chanel, *nest-ce pas?*"

"That one." She groaned. "She'll find a way to humiliate me in front of my harvesters. Guaranteed."

Neither Jorgé nor Clovis argued otherwise.

Her aunt's convertible hummed to a stop, and she emerged a minute later in impeccable white linen. She was like Teflon. Her clothes repelled the dirt that stuck to everyone else.

Geneviève threw her arms up in the air. "Cerise! I've come to see how our lady winemaker manages the harvest."

Cerise leaned forward to reluctantly give her *les bises* but kept her arms crossed. "Pretty much the same as any male winemaker." She coughed at her aunt's overpowering perfume.

But Geneviève was no longer listening. Instead, she fluttered up at Clovis. "*Bonjour*, Clovis. How do you manage to look so handsome with all this dust and muss? It was so kind of you to help Cerise at such a critical time. My husband and I have been sick with worry about how she will manage with Maxime gone. Thank goodness she has you."

Cerise felt the rage she always felt sooner or later in interactions with her aunt begin to roil in her chest, but before she could respond, Clovis did. "Cerise is more than capable of managing the harvest herself. Far more capable that most of us male winemakers, as a matter of fact."

Geneviève tittered and placed one of her manicured hands on his exposed bicep. "*Bien sûr* you would say that. You're so gallant."

Cerise could see surprise in his face—he had underestimated

who he was up against. "As a matter of fact," he persisted, "she let me come here as a favor. She was not initially supportive of my interference at Domaine du Cerisier."

"Interference!" Geneviève exclaimed. "Maxime left you equal partners. She has no right to make you feel unwelcome." Geneviève turned her wide blue eyes at Cerise. "I thought your mother brought you up better than that, Cerise, but ever since Antoine died, well...you haven't been the same girl you were before."

Before Cerise could open her mouth to speak, Clovis stepped back from Geneviève's touch and said in a stiff voice, "Thank God she discovered that core of steel inside her. She would have been decimated by tragedy otherwise. Her strength is perhaps the thing I admire most about her."

*Stop, Clovis. Just shut up.* If this was him looking after her, she neither wanted nor needed it in her life. His overbearing defense didn't leave her a chance to speak for herself, and it was making her harvesters look between her and Clovis wonderingly.

Geneviève gasped. Her hands flew to her cheeks.

Cerise took her aunt by the crook of her arm and tried to drag her away from the crowd of harvesters munching baguettes with *pâté*, reveling in this prime entertainment. Clovis might think he had deterred Geneviève, but Cerise knew better.

Geneviève, amazingly strong when she was meddling, stood her ground. "You admire our Cerise?" She pressed a palm against her heart. "You must be halfway in love with her. Oh! This is even better than I'd hoped."

"*Arrêt,* Tata," Cerise snapped but to no effect. Clovis didn't deny her aunt's conclusion, which created a knot of confusion and anger in Cerise.

"*Mon cher* Clovis! It is what her uncle and I were hoping, *bien sûr,* but with the disheveled way she dresses, we didn't believe it was a possibility. Cerise would be a most...stimulating wife, I promise you! She has so many qualities, you know, but they are sometimes hard to see through that tough exterior."

He was opening his mouth to respond, but Cerise hissed at him, "Don't say a word more. You have said too much already. If you think I'm so capable, why can't you just let me handle this?"

She managed to drag her aunt away and asked her to leave in no uncertain terms. As usual, Geneviève acted like she was at a loss as to why Cerise found anything she said the slightest bit offensive. And maybe, Cerise thought as she stormed to the *cuverie,* Geneviève didn't realize what she'd done wrong. Clovis, on the other hand, should have known better.

Cerise managed to avoid Clovis until breakfast the next day, the fourth day of the harvest and the third full day. Well, not avoid, precisely, but she kept busy, came to meals a few minutes late, and made sure she was seated on a different side of the long table. A few times she furtively observed he was trying to catch her eye, but she was having none of it.

She had gone to bed before the end of dessert the night before, yet sleep had eluded her, and she'd spent hours staring up at the long crack that looked like a crescent moon on Maxime's bedroom ceiling. Damn Clovis for being like all men and not letting her fight her own battles. It wasn't like she hadn't proved herself time and again. He had made it clear that his version of "taking care of each other" really meant him taking care of her.

As she showered and dressed, she fumed that men always treated women with such a patronizing attitude. Antoine had been the same. He hadn't done it in a cruel way; it just never crossed his mind to treat her like an equal. For a while she was beginning to hope maybe Clovis was different, and she was incredibly disappointed to discover she had been wrong.

She arrived in the kitchen just as Yves did. She bent down, gave him the *bises*, and took him in her arms for a long hug.

"Where's Clovis?" he demanded when he pulled himself free. "Didn't he come with fresh baguettes?"

She hated to admit it, but even though she was still furious with him, the kitchen seemed emptier than it had yesterday. That was ridiculous, but then found she had grown used to her heart and mind disagreeing since Maxime had thrust Clovis into her life.

"Just because he came once doesn't mean he's coming every morning," she explained. "He came yesterday only because we had some vineyard stuff to discuss."

"He told me it was because he liked have breakfast with us," Yves grumbled as he sat down.

"Never mind. It's nice to have breakfast just the three of us, isn't it?"

Yves shook his shiny dark hair. "It's not as fun as when Clovis is here."

A familiar guilt sat heavy on her shoulders. She couldn't take away the fact that Yves and Marc didn't have a father. She tried to be the best mother she could, but moments like this were a sinking reminder she would always fall short. She could never be two people. She could be only herself, and that would never be enough.

Marc came into the kitchen.

"Clovis isn't here today. He's not going to come every day," Yves informed him as Marc sat down. Cerise poured hot chocolate.

"That's too bad," Marc said. "I like him."

She turned from the boys to slice the leftover baguette and hide her confusion. She wouldn't have thought Marc would welcome anyone new in their life, especially not a man. He was as suspicious and protective as they came. She wondered how Clovis had conquered her intractable son so handily.

Someone rapped on the front door.

"It's Clovis!" yelped Yves and leaped up.

Her heart missed a beat. "It's probably not," she called out to Yves, but he had already gone to open the door. Surely it couldn't be Clovis, not after how she had told him off in the vineyards. Maybe he'd humiliated her by coming to her defense with Geneviève, but she'd scolded him in front of the harvesters. That was hardly better, and the truth of that sat heavy with her.

Yves was right. Shortly after she heard the large front door creak open, she heard Clovis's warm, deep voice responding to Yves's high-pitched one. He had come. Despite everything, he had come, but was it for her or for her sons?

*"Bonjour!"* he exclaimed, arriving in the kitchen with fresh baguettes under his arm. His eyes moved fast over Cerise and focused on Marc and Yves, who were bouncing around in front of him.

Maybe she deserved that.

"You're just in time!" Marc exclaimed, shaking Clovis's hand in greeting. "Maman was about to toast yesterday's baguette. Blech. Fresh *tartines* are so much better."

Clovis set the bread down on the table and took a deep breath. *"Bonjour,* Cerise." He stepped over and gave her quick *bises* on each cheek. No lingering.

"It was nice of you to come," she said, too disconcerted to meet his eyes.

"Was it?" he asked pleasantly enough, but there was a chilliness in his eyes as she passed him a bowl of coffee. He watched her over the glass rim as he took a sip, still standing up. "I'd like to talk about yesterday, if you can spare a moment. You were extremely preoccupied yesterday afternoon and evening."

"It's fine." She waved her hand. "It's in the past."

"I'd still like to talk about it," he said, implacable.

"All right. Maybe later this afternoon?"

He nodded. "Yes."

This formality between them made it feel like ice instead of blood was running through her veins. It was a far cry from the night of their kitchen raid.

Yves jumped up, dragged Clovis to his seat, and began to pepper him with questions about the fine art of constructing forest forts. Clovis, as it turned out, had much advice to give on the subject.

Clovis was meticulously polite to Cerise. She drank her coffee and munched her *tartine*, but her favorite breakfast tasted like dust in her mouth. His well-bred manners stung like lashes of a whip. She couldn't bear a minute more of this torture.

She got up from the table. "I need to get to the *cuverie*. Marc, are you all right to get you and Yves down to the bus stop in time, or would you like me to drive you?"

Marc looked up at her. "You don't need to drive us," he said. "We'll be fine, Maman."

"Maybe Clovis can take us to the bus!" Yves suggested, excitement in his eyes.

Cerise and Marc opened their mouths to protest, but before they could, Clovis patted Yves's small hand. "It would be my pleasure, Yves, as long as it isn't a problem with your mother and brother."

"It isn't," Yves answered, sure of himself.

"There is no need—"

"It is not a question of need." Clovis glanced up at her, his eyes translucent. "I would like to."

She didn't know what else to say, but now she had another worry to add to her long list: how her boys would cope with Clovis leaving their lives as suddenly as he'd come into it.

"Thank you for the baguettes," she said robotically, then escaped.

She burst out into the courtyard and took a huge gulp of morning air. Damn Maxime for pitching her into such an unwinnable predicament.

In the middle of that afternoon, Cerise was in the *cuverie*, overseeing the pressing of the latest Pinot grapes from the midlevel vineyards. She had already filled two massive vats with grape juice, and the heady odor of fermentation began to sneak into every corner of the room. Her worries had been justified. The hot weather was causing fermentation to happen much faster than usual.

She had given everyone who worked in the vat room a thorough lecture on safety and avoiding the risk of carbon monoxide intoxication. The toxic fumes were rising fast from the vats due to the heat. Luckily, besides Fiona, she didn't have workers in the *cuverie* unless they were experienced.

When she had just seen a batch of grapes through the *pressoir*, she went to the sorting table, where Fiona was doing precise, speedy work with the grapes as well as making rapid progress on her mastery of French expletives.

"You're doing an excellent job," Cerise said in English. "I just wanted to check you understood what I said about the carbon monoxide. You're at less of risk because the sorting table is farther away from the vats, but if you start feeling light-headed, tell someone and go outside."

"Right." Fiona nodded. "But no need to worry. I feel grand.

I admit I'm glad to be in the shade. You were right; I would have fainted again. Us bloody Irish, eh?"

"Luckily the Irish have many other qualities." Cerise patted her back. "Keep up the good work."

"With the swearing or the grape sorting?"

"Both."

As she headed back to the pressing machine and vats, Clovis arrived outside with another load of grape baskets, full to the brim. A bolt of joy lit her up—it should have been from the beautiful grapes ready to be transformed into wine, but it was in fact due to the sight of Clovis disheveled from working and glowing with sweat. She could almost catch his scent over the heady fermentation.

Her heart sank as fast as it had soared. She had managed to alienate him. She should be relieved. She was not. She felt like a magician when she made wine; too bad she couldn't transfer some of that power to her personal life.

She knew he was waiting for her to initiate their talk. So far she'd put it off, but she hated this feeling of distance between them. She wondered why it felt so unnatural.

She went out to meet him at the tractor, determined to be fair and hopefully show she was not a complete shrew.

"These look incredible," she said, running her hand over round, dark purple bunches in the closest basket. Under Clovis's oversight, the baskets were efficiently and securely piled while ensuring the delicate grapes assumed no damage. "What a satisfying sight."

He nodded. "Your harvesters are a wonderful team."

"I think you and Jorgé lead by example."

His left eyebrow quirked. "Was that a compliment?"

"Yes."

"Feeling a tad guilty perhaps?"

She sighed. "I have a temper, as you saw yesterday, but I give credit where credit is due."

He clicked his tongue. "It just so happens I have a temper, too. Your aunt made me—"

"Protective? Overbearing? All those things I made it clear I didn't want you to be?"

He bit back a grin. Cerise felt a ripple of relief that his lips were no longer pressed in that firm line. He shrugged. "Maybe."

Her shoulders dropped in relief. "I honestly don't know how my uncle puts up with her. She would provoke the Pope."

"I really think she would." He chuckled.

"I'm sorry for going ballistic on you, but I've told you before that I can defend myself."

"I know." He loosened a strap on the grape baskets, looking so chastised she had to resist the urge to kiss his frown away. "Rest assured, it's not just you. Ask my friends. It's my nature to defend anyone I care about. It's annoying, I know. I try to control the impulse, but I don't always succeed, as you saw yesterday."

*He cares about me?* Cerise rolled that piece of information around her mind like a loose pebble. "You were so cold this morning at breakfast."

His dimple flashed. "I was polite."

"Yes. Meticulously polite. It was a living nightmare."

He laughed. "You avoided me all day yesterday and a good chunk of today."

She tilted her head. "Fair point." She sighed. "I guess we're both appalling."

Clovis enveloped her in a grin, one that had so much warmth that all the ice between them melted. "We can be appalling together. That sounds like fun, actually."

A panicked voice shouting in the *cuverie* snapped them both to attention, and they ran inside. There was an urgency to the sound that couldn't be dismissed.

Clement, one of her oldest *cuverie* workers, was the source.

He was perched at the top of a ladder attached to one of the full vats. He was half bent over the rim, shouting, "Yannis! Yannis!"

Yannis was another worker in the vat room, a middle-aged man who had been working at the domaine during the harvest for years.

"What happened?" Cerise demanded at the foot of the ladder.

"Yannis! Last I saw him he was up here on the ladder taking a sample of the juice, and then…he just disappeared."

# chapter fifteen

"GONE?" CERISE DEMANDED.

"I think I saw his hand," Clement said, his voice choked.

"Clement, get down," she said. "Now." She ran to the wall to retrieve a long metal pole with a curved end she had mounted there a few years previously when she had almost been overcome by carbon monoxide vapors while evaluating the contents of a vat.

Clement stumbled down the ladder, and Clovis lifted him off the last few rungs. Her heart pounding, Cerise climbed up the ladder at light speed and began plunging the hook into the vat. *Please, God, no.* She had to get Yannis out.

Within seconds Clovis was on the other edge of the vat. He must have grabbed the spare ladder. She felt an overwhelming wave of relief. She didn't have to save Yannis on her own.

"Anything?" he called to her.

"No, *merde*…wait! I just hit something hard, but it's near the bottom." Her heart lurched. "*Non!*"

She thrust the pole to Clovis and heaved herself over the rim. As she splashed into the macerating grapes, her head began to spin. This was reckless, but she didn't know what else do to. Fermentation and its killer carbon monoxide were deadly. *Don't pass out. Just don't.* She had to get to Yannis. She dived down, blind, kicking her feet wildly until her fingertips hit the bottom of the tank. Leftover stems scratched her skin, and the crushed grapes were viscous and thick as she splayed her hands to reach out farther. She felt a solid appendage and grabbed it, not taking the time to figure out what it was. She pulled it up behind her, kicking frantically, sure her lungs were going to explode. Her head popped out, and she gulped at the air—a bad idea. She had gulped mainly carbon monoxide. Her consciousness began to gutter like a dying candle.

"Here!" she shouted up to where she thought Clovis was, although she couldn't see anything. She felt the hard hook beside her and guided it to what she guessed was approximately the middle of Yannis. *Please let Yannis live.*

"I've got him!" Clovis shouted, and her vision cleared enough that she could see him leaning down into the vat and pulling Yannis's inert form out of the grape soup. She would never be able to deadlift an unconscious person the way Clovis was doing. *Oh, please, let Yannis merely be unconscious.*

Clovis seemed to pass Yannis to somebody behind him. "We've formed a chain," he called down to her. "I'm going to get you out."

She surveyed the rim. It was too far away to climb out on her own. Her consciousness went black for a time. "Please," she called when she found her voice again. A few more seconds, and she was going under.

He lowered the hook to her. Her movements felt clumsy, thanks to the carbon monoxide. She grasped the hook, and using it like a lever, Clovis maneuvered her out of the crimson mash.

He was so strong, she thought vaguely. She felt as though she were looking at herself through a blurry window, and her thoughts were as clumsy as her movements. She gripped on to consciousness and clung tightly to the pole.

Quickly, Clovis's strong arms were under her armpits, lifting her out of the vat. Her muscles screamed, and her head swam. She wanted to cling to him, but she needed to get to Yannis.

"Yannis!" she cried as her feet found the ladder. Her eyes began to focus as she looked down. Yannis lay on the cement floor in a puddle of juice and grape skins, completely still. Several workers were performing CPR on him. She made a move to scramble down the ladder, but luckily Clovis's arm held her in an iron grip.

"You'll fall if you try to get down on your own. I can't believe you're still conscious."

She nodded, cognizant enough to realize that if he let go, she would end up sprawled on the concrete beside Yannis, probably with her head cracked.

The sound of her heart pounding in her ears was almost deafening. Yannis had to live. He had to…but Antoine hadn't. She marshaled her emotions. She would be no use if she indulged in old trauma.

She felt Clovis's solid body behind her, holding her securely as they climbed down. He didn't release his grip until her feet touched the solidity of concrete floor.

She staggered to Yannis's side and kneeled by his head. "Any response?"

Clement was giving him vigorous chest compressions, while another worker gave mouth-to-mouth at regular intervals. A third, Philippe, held his fingers at Yannis's inner wrist to feel a pulse.

They shook their heads, grim.

"You called for an ambulance?"

"Of course," Clement gasped and wiped a trickle of sweat out of his eyes.

"I can relieve you." Clovis crouched beside Clement after a few more compressions.

Clement leaned back on his heels and knuckled his eyes. "It happened so fast."

Nobody answered. The truth was that accidents always did

happen in a split second. That's what Docteur Beaumont had told Cerise about Antoine's death: *it was instant.* One moment everything was fine; the next everything changed. Docteur Beaumont meant it to be consoling, but instead it had made Cerise ever-conscious that tragedy could befall at any moment. It was terrifying every second of every day to care for and love others.

Clovis began compressions with more energy than Clement, whose strength must have been flagging.

She remembered what Docteur Beaumont had taught her about CPR: if it wasn't absolutely exhausting, you weren't doing it right. Cerise shuffled on her knees to Clovis's side, ready to take his place when he needed a break.

She looked at Phillippe with a question in her eyes. His mouth was a thin, straight line, and he shook his head. "Nothing."

Cerise remembered another thing Docteur Beaumont had said—about how when CPR didn't seem to be working, a last resort was pounding the chest with the fist, like in a fight to the death. It had sounded barbaric at the time, but now…there was nothing to lose.

"Pause for a second," she told Clovis.

"We can't give up!" Clement cried.

"Nobody's giving up," she snapped, and before any of them could protest, she brought her fist down on Yannis's chest as powerfully as she could. The tiny bones in her fingers screamed with pain. *Bordel de merde,* that hurt.

Clovis merely nodded in approval as she did it a second time, then he seamlessly resumed his compressions.

On his third compression after her punches, a guttural moan emerged from Yannis's throat, and he began to cough. Clovis flipped him on his side.

"We've got a pulse!" Phillippe cried as Yannis regurgitated what he had swallowed from the vat. A siren sounded in the distance.

Cerise sat back on her heels. "I was so scared," she murmured to no one in particular.

Yannis's eyelids flickered, and he was trying to talk. The paramedics swarmed around and took over.

Clovis told them the whole tale succinctly, and in under five minutes the paramedics had stabilized a now-conscious Yannis and left, sirens blaring, to whisk him down the hill to the hospital in Beaune.

Cerise stood up, trying to hide her unsteadiness, and thanked everyone who helped bring Yannis back. Clement and Phillippe agreed to follow the ambulance to Beaune and promised to phone her with any news. The paramedics had spared a moment before they left, however, to reassure everyone that Yannis seemed as though he would recover.

"Drive safely," she called to Phillippe and Clement as they drove away. It was only at that moment she realized they had an audience. The other workers in the vat room were huddled over to the side, their eyes wide, pale with shock.

She began to shake. She had to escape their gaze. She couldn't let her workers—or Clovis for that matter—see her weak.

She headed outside, but Clovis followed her and took her arm. "Let's sit on the bench." He pointed to the bench beside the huge barn doors to the vat room, under the wisteria.

She shook her head. "I need to—"

"Just five minutes." He sat down and patted the bench beside him. "You're shaking," he observed.

"No—"

"So am I. It's the adrenaline leaving your body. That's how humans are wired. It'll pass. We just have to shake our way through it. We might as well do it together."

*Just like being appalling together.*

A wave of emotion welled up in Cerise and threatened to escape in a sob. She tried to remain rational. This was probably the aftermath of the adrenaline rush, too. Her teeth began to chatter. She sat beside him.

"Thank you for what you did in there." She wrapped her arms tightly around her torso. She hadn't known what to expect from Clovis, but he'd kept a cool head, and if he hadn't been there, she doubted anyone would have had the strength to pull her and Yannis out of the vat. They had worked together as a team—a real team—and in doing so, they'd probably saved Yannis's life.

She leaned forward, wondering how she could have prevented the accident from happening in the first place. It shouldn't have happened at all. She racked her brain to figure out what she had neglected to do or say.

"It wasn't your fault," Clovis said after a few minutes of silence, punctuated only by the sound of her teeth clacking together and the cooing of the pigeons that nested in the eaves.

She dropped her head in her hands. "I must have missed something."

He took her hand in his. She remembered vividly how at Maxime's funeral she had fought the fleeting urge to grasp on to his hand like an anchor. This time she didn't resist and squeezed back. "No. Your safety protocols are top notch, and you've done a superb job of training your workers in first aid. This was a freak accident. Nobody can prevent those."

She wasn't sure. She had to figure out a way of preventing them in the future. She leaned back again but held fast to the mooring of his hand. The shakes were becoming less violent.

"Bit better?" Clovis asked.

She nodded. "I probably won't be great until I hear from the hospital, though. You?"

He crackled the knuckle of his right index finger with his thumb. "Same."

Their eyes caught under the dappled shade of the wisteria, and gratitude for Clovis rushed through her. She couldn't have saved Yannis without him. He didn't try to talk her out of her shakes or her delayed fear. He just ensured that whatever she needed to go through, she wasn't doing it alone.

"Your muscles must be screaming from swimming in that grape muck." He beckoned with a finger. "Come here."

Before she could question what she was doing, he gathered her in his warm arms. The sound of his steady heartbeat made her entire being exhale. The shakes stopped completely. He made no move to kiss her. He just held her against his heart and ran his hands up and down her back and arms, lightly massaging away the pain and fear. For once, she accepted the deliciousness of being cared for.

Cerise had no idea how much time passed. She had no thoughts of moving until she heard one of the cooks calling her from across the courtyard. Slowly, regretfully, she disentangled from the man she could no longer think of as her nemesis. In the space of an hour he had proved himself to be a true partner. It was, she reflected, the most powerful aphrodisiac that existed for her.

"Do you want me to see the cook while you take a quick shower?" he asked, keeping his hand on her shoulder, his touch maintaining a link between them.

"Why? Oh...I must be stained with grape juice, aren't I?" She smiled to think of the sight she must present. Wouldn't it be perfect if Geneviève could and see her now.

He nodded, a smile in his blue eyes. "You're crimson."

She held out her hands and inspected them. They were a deep, unmistakable magenta. "Oh my God. I didn't even stop to think—"

"It's very fetching."

"Is my face like that, too?" she asked.

He nodded, and that divot in his cheek reappeared. She fought the urge to kiss him in that precise spot.

He started laughing, and Cerise joined in. It was a welcome release after the stress of the past hour. Finally, she put her hands on her knees and took a bracing breath. "Okay. I need to go. I'll shower first because I don't want to frighten anyone, although I'm not sure how much of this I'm going to be able to get off. Um…Clovis?"

"Yes."

"I couldn't have saved Yannis without you. *Merci.*"

He tucked a loose strand of juice-soaked hair behind her ear. "My pleasure."

"I'm so glad the boys are at school. I wouldn't have wanted them to see that."

"No." His face tightened. "There are things children shouldn't see."

"Thank God you insisted on this trial period," Cerise said in a quieter voice. "I believe it saved Yannis's life."

He shrugged. "You're the one who thought of hitting his chest. It might have gone another way if we weren't both there."

She wanted to say something about the fact they made good partners but didn't know how to put all these emotions that were whipping up inside her into words. "*Merci,*" she said instead.

"*De rien,*" he answered. *It was nothing.*

But it wasn't nothing, she thought as she hurried to Maxime's house, her heart in a whirl. It was something. Something decisive.

## chapter sixteen

JUST AS SHE finished her shower, Cerise's phone rang with the welcome news that Yannis was out of danger, and according to the paramedics, her punches may well have saved his life. She knew the truth, though. If it wasn't for Clovis, Yannis wouldn't have gotten out of the vat in the first place. Before she hung up, she asked Clement to phone Clovis right away.

She inspected herself in the bathroom mirror. She had managed to scrub off the worst of the purple stain on her skin, but parts of her retained a vaguely lavender hue. She shrugged. She didn't have the time or inclination to worry about that. She had to get back to the *cuverie* and ensure things were returning to normal. It wouldn't do for her grapes to be languishing in baskets outside the vat room.

She was so occupied setting things back to rights in the *cuverie* that she didn't see Clovis again until dinner. She arrived late, and Jorgé and Fiona beckoned her to sit with them and tell the tale of the near-drowning. Her boys had walked straight to the vineyards from the school bus and were now being spoiled by the cooks and had been invited to eat in the kitchen. She caught Clovis's eye at the opposite end of the table and lifted her hand in a wave. He smiled and winked back. An invisible tether of kinship joined them.

Over an enormous couscous packed with lamb, vegetables, and chickpeas and the briny fragrance of pickled lemons and *ras-el-hanout* spice, Jorgé marveled over Yannis's accident.

"I've heard of it happening," he said between bites. "I mean, we all have, but I just never thought it could happen here."

"Me neither," Cerise said, grim. "I've already laid down a new rule. Everyone who climbs up the ladder to the vat *must* be spotted by someone on an adjacent ladder."

"Smart," he said. "No other domaines are taking safety that far, you know. It means you'll need more manpower."

She shrugged. "If I have to be the one to set the new safety standard, so be it."

"Still, it would not be the worst way to go for a winemaker, drowning in fermenting grape juice... It has a certain poetry to it."

"Don't be ridiculous," said Fiona in French. "I'm sure Yannis did not look poetic, near dead on the vat-room floor."

"I can confirm he did not." Cerise appreciated the astringent quality of Fiona's pragmatism.

After cheese, exquisite apple tarts, and espresso, she thought it would be prudent to turn in for the night. It was already getting close to eleven o'clock, and her desire to gravitate to Clovis's side was becoming overpowering. The boys had headed for the big house after dessert, and Yves would be waiting for her to kiss them good-night.

She didn't feel sleepy, but bed would be the wise place to be after such an eventful day. She waved *bonne nuit* to the table and walked through the courtyard to the sounds of crickets and gravel crunching beneath her feet.

Once she had tucked in the boys, she went to Maxime's bedroom window and gazed down into the courtyard. There was no sign of Clovis's Mercedes. He must have left for the night. She missed him, she realized with dismay.

Nothing could happen between them until the harvest and the buyout were complete, of course, but if it ever did, it would have to be because she initiated it. Clovis was proving to be a man of his word, which was both reassuring and vexing. In the dark of Maxime's bedroom, she finally admitted to herself that she wanted Clovis in every possible way, more than anything.

It was another sultry night, and even with the shutters and windows wide open, not so much as a wisp of breeze dispersed the heavy warmth. She tossed and turned. Despite Clovis's lovely massage on the bench, her muscles ached from the adrenaline and effort.

She longed for his touch. Thank goodness he was back home at Domaine de Valois. Finally giving up on sleep, she threw on shorts and a tank top and crept downstairs. Marc and Yves would be fine—they almost never woke during the night. Besides, it wasn't like she was going off the property.

Once past the front door, she saw lights on in the harvesters' house and heard the faint hum of festivity echoing through the night air. She could never figure out how they could carouse so late into the night, then get up early to work in the vineyards.

A full moon lit up the sky. Her head spun with the unfamiliar notion that the world was full of possibilities. Around the side of the house, she used a huge iron key to unlock the small wooden door that led to the cellar.

She slinked down the stairs and flicked on the dim lights at the front of the cellar. The comforting dankness belowground welcomed her like an embrace. She exhaled.

This was the only place she seemed to be able to think clearly. It was her refuge, her laboratory, and her church.

She went to the barrels she always visited first—in the farthest, darkest corner of the massive cellar. More by touch than by sight, she found the box of matches and iron *rat de cave* candlestick made from a forged iron coil she kept on an overturned barrel.

The spark flamed. She breathed in the sulfur from the freshly struck match. Once she lit the candle, a soft yellow glow poured over the back corner like honey.

She reached for the long glass tasting pipe that hung on the wall and a clean wineglass she stored in a secret compartment on the overturned barrel.

Cerasus. Her secret. Clovis had helped her save Yannis today without hesitation. Suddenly, it felt wrong not to tell him about her project. He was operating on good faith; she was the one being duplicitous. That truth settled like a lead weight in her stomach.

She uncorked the barrel, drew out a little of its contents with the pipette, and lifted her thumb to release the wine into her glass. She swirled the liquid and inhaled deeply. It was close to being ready, although it would be difficult to decide when to finally bottle it. Like so many things in winemaking, and in life, she would just have to trust her instinct would take the lead.

She imagined how people would react when she pulled Cerasus out of the appellation system. Shocked? Surely. Disparaging at first? Definitely. Intrigued? Without a doubt. It simply wasn't done in Burgundy.

She took a sip. She had gone so far in her search for purity; she worried perhaps she'd gone too far. She wondered if the wine would stand up to bottling and potentially travel without sulfites, without filtering… Yet when it came to ensuring the future of Domaine du Cerisier for her sons, half measures just wouldn't be enough.

She swished the wine around her mouth, trying to discern every nuance in its bouquet. She let it sit on her tongue. It tasted so… Excitement mounted despite her natural restraint. She tried to gain an even deeper understanding of the flavor profile.

"Cerise?"

She almost dropped the pipette. That was Clovis's voice. His feet crunched on the gravel as he made his way toward her. Her heart skipped a beat. *Merde*. He knew nothing about this wine. She knew she had to tell him but wasn't sure how or when. She was sure he was going to be angry, or worse, hurt and betrayed—done with her for good. She'd be if the tables were turned.

"I thought you went home a long time ago," she said. Every cell in her body yearned with the need for him to touch her again. Somewhere deep in her heart, her instincts had accepted him completely, yet all the practical barriers of their business partnership remained. She took a step back, trying to barricade herself against his effect on her.

He shook his head. "I spent a long time at the dinner table and then…I don't know. I didn't feel like going back to my house. I still feel unsettled."

"I didn't see your car." *Merde*. Now he'd know she'd looked for it.

"I parked it on the road outside the gates."

She nodded. So he knew. It felt for the first time like revealing her true self to him didn't really matter after what they'd just been through together. "I fell into bed exhausted, but… Do you think it's the adrenaline?"

"Probably." He leaned against one of the barrels that contained her precious experiment. "That and the full moon."

She needed to tell him about Cerasus but had no idea how. "Of course. That always make me restless. It is so beautiful."

"It is." Clovis was looking steadily at her. "It would have been a shame to sleep through that."

"Yes." Her voice sounded strangled.

"What are you tasting?"

She studied him in the flickering candlelight. Now was the time, but fear tightened her throat. For one, there was the question of his reaction. Second, winetasting with him would be intimate, like it had been at Domaine de Valois, especially with this wine. It was risky, but then she remembered sitting on the bench with him while she shook and…not having to be alone for once. The part of her that used to love rock climbing and roller coasters and loving without fear woke up after years of being asleep.

"I'm going to let you taste this because I believe you can keep a secret." The words felt rash but right.

"Do you really?" His eyes flashed with something that looked like relief. "What changed?"

She shrugged "This afternoon."

"Finally." His voice was low. "I thought I'd never gain your trust."

"No," she said. "Here." Before she could reconsider, Cerise slid the pipette into the barrel and filled it with her secret wine, then let it drain into a glass she plucked from nearby. She passed it to him. *Will he understand?*

He met her eyes and took a sip. She stared at his lips—those perfectly sculpted yet generous lips that had created such sensations on her neck…and the rest of her. She wondered what his lips would feel like on her collarbone, or behind her knee, or between her breasts. She shivered, and it had nothing to do with the cellar's dampness.

Clovis moved the wine around in his mouth thoughtfully, then suddenly frowned and held his glass in front of the candle flame. Backlit by candlelight, her wine looked like some sort of magical elixir. He stared at it. "What is this?" She couldn't read his voice.

"Do you like it?" She heard a small noise at the other end of the cellar but couldn't tear her gaze from Clovis as she awaited his opinion. The fact that they had acted as true equals—a team—that afternoon operated on her like the most powerful aphrodisiac.

"Like it? This is…like no other wine I have ever tasted, Cerise. It's extraordinary. It has a purity, strength, *delicatesse*…"

"It's a secret. I should have told you when we learned about how Maxime had left things. My own little experiment."

He nodded slowly. "I know this sounds ridiculous, but this wine is *you*."

She blushed. She should have guessed he would uncover the most important secret about Cerasus so quickly. How had he known? She had realized the same thing over the past several months. "I used the grapes grown closest to the cherry tree. Are you angry?"

His eyes widened. "You're telling me now, aren't you?"

She gestured at the glass in his hand. "Obviously."

"Then I'm not angry." He took another sip. "You've devised a different winemaking process, haven't you?" he asked, taking another sip.

"Yes." She heard that noise again but reasoned it must just be one of the village cats that occasionally slipped in and out of the cellar. "No sulfites, extended maceration, no filtering, eighty percent new barrels… Right now I'm trying to decide how long the barrel aging should be. What do you think? I'm making it up as I go with this one."

"I think you don't need my input. I wouldn't dream of interfering in your brilliance. What do you call it?"

"Cerasus. I won't be asking for appellation status."

"Latin for *cherry*," Clovis mused. "Perfect." His gaze lifted from the wine to her. "It's sublime." There was something in his eyes that convinced Cerise he was talking as much about her as the wine. "How did you keep this a secret?"

She squirmed under his gaze. "I kept you mainly in the

vineyards, and none of my *cuverie* workers talk. I needed you most in the vineyards, though. That, at least, is true."

She fought the urge to close the distance between them. She wanted to lean into his chest, hold him in her arms and sink into him, body and soul. It took every ounce of her self-discipline to resist.

She knew Clovis wouldn't make the first move. He would keep his word, especially after the scene in the vineyards with Geneviève. If anything were to happen, she would have to be the seducer.

The entire day still felt so surreal, and she felt so…incomplete. She wondered how, just hypothetically, she could break his willpower. Her ideas made her skin grow hot.

A heavy silence settled between them. Clovis emptied his glass.

"Do you want to taste more?" she asked.

His throat muscles convulsed as he swallowed. Was he suffering as much as she was? "Yes, please."

Instead of picking up her pipette, Cerise dipped her index finger into her wineglass, then dabbed a bit of wine on her clavicle. *My God, I am going mad*, she thought, but her self-control shredded into useless tatters. "Maybe you can help me." She met his smoldering gaze. "I've been wondering what it tastes like here, but I can't do that on my own. Can you—?"

For an unbearable moment he just stared at her, his blue eyes dark, saying nothing. Then, finally, "Are you asking—?"

"Please." Any remaining logic was consumed by the conflagration ripping through her body. She popped the cork back in the wine barrel and waited.

He moved toward her, and the air felt heavier. Oh God, this near, he was redolent of lemon and salt and wine. He dipped his head down, and his tongue darted out and gently licked the wine. Cerise trembled, the need to get closer to Clovis hijacking her sanity. His lips pressed against her overheated skin. His mouth felt glorious, absolutely perfect. It didn't linger on her nearly long enough.

"And here..." She dabbed another drop under her jawbone. Clovis took his time. He was *so good* at taking his time.

"I can't believe I'm reminding you," he said as she dipped her finger in her glass a third time, "but...our agreement? I promised myself I'd be gentleman, but my self-restraint has limits." That dimple appeared. "You're leading me over the edge—you know that, don't you?"

"*Oui.*" She was too drunk with need to begin to explain how their saving Yannis had clinched it. It sounded bizarre, and she didn't understand it herself. "You promised you'd help me with my winemaking," she reminded him instead.

"I did." They were standing so close his breath was warm against her face. "Oh, and how I meant it."

She dipped her wine-soaked finger between the curves of her breasts. His tongue swooped down. She felt herself softening... melting like candlewax exposed to an open flame.

"This is in the way," she mumbled and pulled her tank top over her head. He paused for a moment as he undid her bra with a deft flick of his fingers. *He is good at that, too.* He began kissing her everywhere. *Oui.* There, *there.* She grabbed on to the rim of the barrel behind her for support. Cerise noted with a certain smugness that they were both shaking again.

"Who was I kidding?" Clovis murmured between kisses, each more delectable than the last. "I was never much of a gentleman anyways."

"Thank God for that," she gasped and threw her head back.

He chuckled and wedged her between his tall, muscular body and the barrel of wine.

His hands slid from her hair down to her waist and encircled it, and his thumbs brushed the soft skin of her lower back. She felt desperate to feel more of his bare skin against hers. Her shorts dropped to the ground, and fumbling, she managed to free his as well.

His length pressed firmly against her bare thigh. Hunger for him exploded like sparks behind her eyelids.

"Rules are going to be broken," Clovis warned.

"Then let's break them together."

She felt even more heat and a twitch against her leg in response.

Cerise trembled. It had been a long time for her—there had been no one since Antoine—but this pleasure… It ached like exquisite pain.

She tugged off his T-shirt and explored his powerful back muscles with her fingertips. She moved her hands up to the biceps that had helped her save Yannis. He wasn't just beautifully made; he used his strength for good.

He groaned and lifted her hair to kiss her neck. Her focus narrowed to his touch and the candlelight flickering over their almost-naked bodies.

"Cerise," he sighed, his hands in her hair and his lips against her ear. "I don't want this to stop."

She kicked off her lacy underwear. "Me neither." She slipped his underwear down, and he sprang free, thoroughly ready.

He lifted her in his arms so her legs straddled him. He held her there, against the barrel, effortlessly, like she was as light as a butterfly.

"*Oui*," she whispered. "Yes." They were going to plunge together.

He entered her slowly. Her gaze moved up to his eyes. His reflected how she felt—full of wonder. She dropped her head and kissed that magical spot on his left cheek where that elusive dimple hid.

"*Oui,*" she gasped again, reveling in a sense of completeness that stunned her. Her imagination had been working overtime, but this was far beyond anything she had conjured there.

As he began to move inside her, she clung to him, reveling in the sensation of their joining.

"I have been wanting this for so long." He brushed the damp hair from her forehead so he could kiss her deeply. "Wanting you…"

"This feels—" was all Cerise could gasp a while later as he filled her to his hilt. Even though there were no words for what she was feeling, she murmured all sorts of things she would never dare say—until he made her cry out his name.

A few moments later, he cried out hers.

# chapter seventeen

THEY STAYED JOINED until their breathing slowed and Clovis's heartbeat once again became as steady and reassuring as a metronome under Cerise's ear.

She reeled from the revelation that he knew exactly how to unlock her. It felt disloyal to think it, but Antoine had never truly figured that out. She closed her eyes to banish Antoine from her mind. That was a different life, with a different Cerise.

"I certainly wasn't expecting this when I came down here," Clovis said. She felt the brush of his fingers as he smoothed them over her bottom. She knew from his voice that he was smiling, even though her eyes were still shut. "Forever dreaming about, *bien sûr*, but not expecting."

She laughed softly against his chest. Her feet felt the ground again as he lowered her down the length of his body, handling her as gently now as a fine Limoges tea cup.

"And you such a gentleman," she said in mock reproach.

He bent to the ground, picked up her underwear and bra, and passed them to her with a rueful smile. "Not so much, as it turns out."

"Thank God for that."

He chuckled and slipped on his black boxer briefs. The sight of how snugly they hugged his thighs and everything else left her feeling like she was going to combust again.

"You didn't let me fall when I was against the barrel," she pointed out. "That was gentlemanly."

He kissed the tender spot under her earlobe. "Never."

She found herself smiling. She had expected to regret giving in like she had, but she just felt...happy. She didn't know how long the afterglow was going to last; she might as well enjoy it.

He gently helped her dress. She was clumsier than usual from the intensity of it all.

"It goes strongly against the grain with me to put clothes *on* you," Clovis said. "But I imagine it must be close to one o'clock; we have an early morning tomorrow. You must be tired. Or, rather, *we* must be tired," he corrected himself.

"Are you?" she said, struggling to do up her bra. Wordlessly, he turned her around and did it for her, dropping a gentle kiss on the tip of one shoulder blade, then the other, and finally on the nape of her neck. She shivered and was shocked to feel her desire multiply exponentially so soon.

He took a moment to consider. "Oddly, no."

"Me neither." In fact, she felt stronger, braver, more energetic than she could remember. They finished dressing. "The thing is, I was tired—exhausted actually—but now...I feel I could complete the entire harvest on my own in the next few hours."

His dimple appeared. "Well, perhaps you can take on the world now, but you might not be feeling that at five tomorrow morning unless you manage at least a few hours of shuteye. I'll go home so you can sleep in peace."

"Deciding what's best for me again?" she chided him but with a chuckle.

He lifted his palms. "Guilty."

She studied him in the candlelight. His eyes glowed, and she had never seen his features so relaxed. She didn't want him to leave. "What if you… What if you don't go home tonight?" she blurted out, shocked when the words escaped her mouth.

He arched a quizzical eyebrow. "You mean, sleep here?"

"Yes."

"In the cellar?"

"No," She tried to keep a straight face.

"With the harvesters?"

"No." She rolled her eyes. "You'll be swinging by here first thing in the morning anyway, right? What about making it easier and spending the night in the big bed…with me?" She shrugged, struck by shyness. "It's only practical."

"Let me get this straight. You're inviting me to spend the night in your bed because it's practical?"

She felt her face burn. "There might be…other reasons."

"I was just teasing you." He leaned forward and dropped a tantalizing kiss on her lips. "I'm thrilled to accept your invitation, not to mention surprised."

"Have I been that standoffish?"

"Yes." He pulled her away from the barrel and into his arms. "But I suppose you had reasons for your wariness." He held her like that for some time, then finally pressed his lips to the crown of her head before pulling back a bit. "Aren't you concerned about the boys seeing me in the morning?"

It was kind of him to think of that. "We'll be up well before they are."

Clovis nodded and reached for her hand. "In that case, *mon trésor*, can I escort you to bed?"

"Yes, please."

He swooped her into his arms and carried her up the steep stone steps. There was nobody to be seen now in the courtyard. It was just them and the full moon.

In Maxime's bedroom, they took time undressing each other a second time. They made love again, slower, then again. They shared unspoken secrets in the twisted white sheets while silver light bathed them through the open shutters. He called her *mon trésor* too many times to count. *My treasure.* That was exactly how he made her feel. She kept waiting for the regret to strike, but it had apparently fled along with her caution.

Cerise was woken up by a broad hand stroking her forehead and gentle kisses on her shoulder. Pigeons cooed outside the window.

Clovis's lips were close to her ear. "I hate to tell you this when you're sleeping so soundly, especially as I could watch you forever, but it's five o'clock. What time do the boys get up for school?"

She opened her eyes and drank in the glorious sight of Clovis's cerulean gaze and bare torso. "*Bonjour toi.*" She rolled toward him and buried her head in his chest. The light dusting of hair tickled her nose, and his skin was warm and firm. Everything about him was just right—like a perfectly balanced wine, precisely calibrated for her palate. She wanted to stay in bed with him all day. She searched for misgivings but found none. Clovis and her together just felt right. She wondered if it could last… she couldn't know that, or how Clovis felt, but at least she could enjoy it while he was here.

He kissed her temple. "You're not the only one who wants to stay in this bed." He gathered her in his arms. Need pulsed deep within her. This didn't feel like it was going to be just a one-night stand. A harvest affair was neither unusual nor very different, but his gentle kisses combined with the way his hands claimed her unequivocally did not signal that Clovis had any regrets.

"We can be quick," he whispered, urgency and humor mingled in his husky morning voice.

She chuckled. "I don't need convincing."

He entered her quickly, taking her breath away while her readiness stole his. She gave free reign to her desire, not even attempting to pull back at any point. Clovis's hunger matched her own, then egged her on until they completed together in an explosion of suppressed cries and whispered wonder.

After, Cerise lay half on top of him, trying to catch her breath. The scent of crushed grapes from yesterday's harvest wafted up from the courtyard below. The crickets sang even more joyfully, it seemed.

*It wasn't like this with Antoine…* Cerise shut down that thought right away and eased out of bed to ensure it stayed banished. The two men weren't comparable. Cerise and Antoine had been each other's first. They were so young, and they didn't know anything but each other. There was something to be said for experience, she mused as she pulled fresh clothes from the antique wooden dresser. Experience, plus that connection between her and Clovis that she still didn't understand.

*Stop it, Cerise. The physical connection is one thing, but I mustn't confuse it with everything else.* Yes, she liked Clovis, and yes, sex with him was far more powerful than she ever could have imagined, but her reasons for wanting her independence, in both Domaine du Cerisier and life with her sons, remained unchanged. Could she have Clovis in her life and the independence she craved? *You are getting ahead of yourself.* Clovis hadn't even revealed his sentiments.

"I'm going to hop in the shower." She pointed at the bathroom.

He blew her a kiss, got out of bed, and began to gather his clothes. She longed to know what was going on in his head.

Cerise allowed herself one last, lingering look at his splendid physique. It didn't just *look* beautiful; the way he wielded his strength with such gentleness, the way he moved and touched and kissed and held her was also beautiful. She left the bedroom humming "L'Encre de Tes Yeux," an unabashedly romantic ballad she had thought she didn't like anymore.

He was gone when she returned to the bedroom. She reasoned he must have headed down to start breakfast. She needed to decide what to say to her sons. She may have no choice but to admit Clovis had spent the night, but she didn't want to...not yet anyway.

Their affair could end up being short-lived, even though that idea made her heart squeeze, so there was no reason to upset the boys over something so fleeting. She took a few deep breaths to steady herself as she combed her air with her fingers and twisted it into a fat knot on the top of her head.

There was no sign of him downstairs. She had a flash of doubt about confiding the secret of Cerasus in him last night, but...no. He had given her no reason to distrust him—on the contrary.

The boys would be emerging any minute, so she busied herself measuring the coffee and heating milk in a dented metal casserole dish that probably dated from the second World War.

With Clovis gone, it would have been easy to start wondering if she had made a massive error in sleeping with him, yet her body did not agree. It still hummed with pleasure. *No, I wouldn't have missed that for all the world.* Still, she had to remain cautious. He had to be made to realize that getting closer to her did not equate with moving toward partnership in Domaine du Cerisier.

Yves came bounding downstairs and, after giving her wet kisses to say *bonjour*, sat down and groused about the fact he had to go to school when he'd rather be harvesting.

"It will be the *paulée* in a few nights," Cerise said. "Besides, on Wednesday you can help all afternoon."

"Promise?" Yves pleaded with brown eyes that were identical to Antoine's. They made her promise herself that no matter how many days things lasted with Clovis, she knew she could never accept a dynamic with him that fell into traditional roles like it had with Antoine.

"Promise."

"Pinky swear." Yves held up a crooked finger, and she knew what to do. She crooked her own around it, and they shook. She poured warm milk over hot chocolate powder in his bowl.

"Where is the bread?" Yves asked. "Is Clovis bringing it?"

*Merde.* She'd completely forgotten to go to the boulangerie for baguettes—again. Yves was not the only one who wanted to know Clovis's whereabouts.

There was a knock at the front door. Her breath caught.

"That must be him!" Yves hopped off his chair.

"I don't think—" she began, but Yves had already run into the front hall, paying her no attention.

Within seconds, he led in Clovis, looking handsome and disheveled—she felt a thrill that she had done that to him—and carrying three baguettes under his arm.

"I thought I'd bring the baguettes again today," he said, scanning the table and counters. "Ah! Good. You haven't gone out to get any." He sent her a smile that was somehow as intimate as their escapades of the night, topped off with a wink.

Cerise just stood there, her heart exploding with delight. She tucked the memory of her happiness away, in case things went sideways.

Yves sat down again, beaming up at him. "See, I told you it was Clovis," he said, reproach in his voice. Marc came in, and Clovis had to stop and shake his hand in a manly *bonjour*.

"I thought I'd beg for a fresh coffee before starting the day," he told Marc.

"We're always glad to have you," Marc said, favoring Clovis with one of his rare smiles. "Is Maman working you too hard? I've heard some people say she's a harsh taskmaster during harvest."

Clovis sighed, his eyes meeting Cerise's for a mischievous

second. "She is a taskmaster," he admitted, his dimple appearing briefly, although he managed not to smile. "But I don't mind."

She bit her lip as the combination of intense lust and trying not to laugh bubbled up inside her.

"Would you like a *café au lait?*" she asked with forced formality.

"You know he has it black, Maman," Marc reminded her. "Just like you."

"Right," she said and turned to pick up the coffeepot with one hand and two glass coffee bowls with the other.

"How rude of me!" Clovis said. "I have neglected to say *bonjour* to you, Cerise." He moved around the table.

*Right!* They weren't supposed to have seen each other yet, according to the boys, let alone spent the night intertwined in the big white bed upstairs.

He stood in front of her, blocking her view of her sons. Her skin tingled with anticipation having him so close, but because both her hands were full, she couldn't give him the covert touch she longed to.

His blue eyes sparkled as they held hers. She marveled at how he was able to invite her to enjoy their shared secret without saying a word. A steady pulse of need thrummed in her veins.

"*Bonjour,*" he said in a formal tone belied by a devilish smile. "How did you sleep?"

"Not very well." She shook her head in mock regret. "I was very preoccupied."

"I'm sorry to hear that."

She bit her lip. "Oh, don't be. Thank you for bringing baguettes. So thoughtful. I'm sorry to hear you feel I work you too hard."

He gently kissed one of her cheeks, the soft feel of his lips both a memory and a promise. "I'm not complaining. I'm also not responsible for what I do to you tonight if you bite your lip again." It was the quietest of whispers in her ear. Cerise felt like she was dissolving right there, against the counter.

"What are you whispering about?" Yves demanded. "It's rude to have secrets. You always say so, Maman."

Clovis moved away quickly and sat between Yves and Marc. "Just harvesting matters."

Marc, in the meantime, was subjecting Clovis to a thorough inspection. "Why are you wearing the same clothes as last night?"

Cerise bit back a smile at Clovis's confounded expression. He clearly hadn't factored in Marc's attention to detail.

He sent her a desperate look, but she just served his coffee and schooled her features to remain neutral. She sat down in the empty chair. "Yes, why *is* that, Clovis?"

"There's no point in changing often during the harvest," he finally said. "Harvest clothes are pretty much good only for the garbage afterward."

"Maman changes every day," Yves pointed out.

"So I see," he said, nodding.

"And you have changed every day so far," Marc continued his investigation.

She had to bite her lip again.

"Yes, well, not *every* day. Today proves that, right?" he said.

"Hmm." Marc remained noncommittal.

With that, they sipped their coffees and hot chocolates and ate copious amounts of fresh baguette slathered with unsalted butter and homemade apricot jam. Apparently, lovemaking with Clovis made her ravenous.

From his narrowed eyes, it was clear that Marc had them under heavy surveillance, but she tried to act as though she didn't notice. Finally, she checked her watch and stood up. "You're going to miss the bus, you two. Come on." Now that they had adjusted to the routine of the new school year, she felt confident they could take the bus by themselves.

She beckoned them into the front hall, where they picked up their *cartables* for school and put on their shoes. She bid them each goodbye with a kiss.

Yves peered up at her as he clung to her neck for a few seconds after the kiss, as he always did. "You look different," he said at last.

"Do I?" she said, unable to keep the surprise out of her voice. "How?"

"Brighter," he said and, with a last peck on her cheek, skipped out the door to catch up to his brother.

She returned to the kitchen, still dazed.

"What?" Clovis paused in clearing the table.

She shook her head. There was no point in mentioning it to Clovis. He could get the wrong idea. "Nothing." Instead, she went to him and took his face in her hands. He was so gorgeous she almost couldn't bear it. They sank into a long, breathless kiss that left them both wanting more.

"Do you think we could…?" Cerise felt his readiness. She couldn't be close to him without feeling empty, needing.

Clovis groaned. "You already know my answer. You do crazy things to me."

She reached down to undo his shorts, but then she heard a knock on the door and then, "*Allô?*"

"Who—?" she blurted out.

"*Dieu*, not now," Clovis growled. He sat down in a hurry on the closest kitchen chair and pulled it near to the table to hide his impressive erection.

Luc appeared in the kitchen.

"What are you doing here?" Clovis demanded. "Why aren't you at your own domaine?"

Luc rolled his eyes. "Good morning to you, too."

Cerise gave him *les bises*. "We just finished breakfast, but do you want some coffee? I was going to serve us another one before getting to the *cuverie*."

Luc took the seat beside Clovis. "That would be perfect. Doesn't sound like any of the harvesters are awake yet. Quiet in the courtyard." He looked at his friend. "I hope some of Cerise's good manners will rub off on you, my boorish friend."

"Why *are* you here?" Clovis narrowed his eyes at Luc.

"I heard about the incident with Yannis yesterday. As you can imagine, the news is traveling fast through the winemakers on the *côte*."

Cerise dropped her head into her hands. "Crap." She'd been so consumed with Clovis that she'd forgotten about the ripples Yannis's accident would make. She wanted Domaine du Cerisier to be known for its incredible wine, not its history of accidents.

"No one thinks it's your fault, Cerise." Luc patted her hand. "It could happen to any of us. The main thing people are talking about is how you two saved his life. I wanted to come and check on you. I'm sure it was quite traumatic. You've both experienced enough of that in your lives."

She smiled at him. Luc had an inherent kindness that was rare and precious, but it also came with a certain naiveté. "Life doesn't seem to work that way," she said. "Unfortunately, there isn't a quota on hardship." Clovis could have grown hardened and cruel with the childhood everyone said he'd had, but instead he'd become gentle and loving. It was a miracle, really, and he deserved all the credit. "Clement called from the hospital yesterday. Yannis is doing extremely well," she continued. "That makes the whole thing easier to handle."

"Cerise was brilliant. She dove into the vat to get him."

Luc nodded, bathing her in his warm smile. "I heard."

"Thank you for coming to check on us," Clovis said. "You're a good friend, better than I deserve."

Luc shook his blond head. "Don't be ridiculous. You're family."

Cerise had forgotten how nice it was to have friends who dropped by, checked on one another, shared a coffee or glass of wine and a chat. She's had that before Antoine died; maybe she'd been wrong to let her old friendships slip away.

"Any further news from Sadie and Stella?" Cerise asked.

"Yes!" Luc said, eagerness making his eyes seem even bluer.

"Really, Luc? Stella?" Clovis groaned.

Luc turned to his friend. "Look who's talking. We don't choose who we fall in love with; fate chooses for us." His eyes shifted to Cerise for an instant before returning to Clovis. "I love her. Stella is the only woman for me. You of all people should understand."

Even though he had glanced at her, Cerise couldn't be sure if Luc meant some other woman or her. Both possibilities filled her heart with turmoil. She couldn't stand the idea of him with any other woman, yet she didn't know if he could love her and give her the autonomy she needed.

Clovis nodded, oddly engrossed in a spoon he'd been fiddling with. "Any further communication from her?"

"A few messages with some photos. *Amazing* photos. She's stunning. She wrote that she can't wait to come to France and see me."

"Just—" Clovis interrupted.

"Just what?" Luc said.

"Just be careful there. Is Sadie is coming, too? Will she be doing any field work while she's here?"

Luc rolled his eyes. "Not as far as I know. She said something about needing to get away from work for a while. She's an anthropologist specializing in the Gallo-Roman period," he explained to Cerise.

"Really?" she said. "That's fascinating."

Luc nodded. "Sadie's brilliant. She always felt like one of my sisters. I adore her, just in a different way from how I feel about Stella, but she's one of my favorite people."

Cerise smiled, but behind the smile she was shocked to realize Clovis was now one of her favorite people. The thought of losing their physical connection was devastating, but losing him as a friend…that would be even worse.

"I should get outside and start the day," she said. Clovis and Luc made a move to get up, too, but she waved them down. "You two catch up. No rush." She bid the men goodbye and crossed the courtyard to the *cuverie*, her thoughts more on Clovis than her grapes.

# chapter eighteen

CERISE SPENT THE next several hours absorbed in outlining the new safety protocols for the *cuverie* and overseeing the sorting, pressing, and destemming. She also reassured everyone about Yannis, who was up and alert and enjoying a nice *café au lait* with a *pain au chocolate*, according to the nurse she had spoken to earlier that morning. She'd also said Yannis was an incorrigible flirt, which pointed to a full and speedy recovery.

Clovis briefly stopped by the vat room to tell her he was going to his domaine for a quick check before lunch. She wanted to give him a kiss, but instead they shared a smile that was perhaps even more intimate.

About a half an hour before the lunch bell, it dawned on her that despite almost a complete absence of sleep the night before, she was working with a novel and seemingly unbounding energy. She had always found joy in her work, but it seemed to multiply tenfold when she had Clovis to share it with.

Maybe Maxime had not been so misguided after all, at least about them being personally compatible.

She was coming down a ladder after spotting Clement at the rim of a vat when she was intercepted by a tall, skinny man holding a camera.

"Can I help you?" she asked. Most tourists knew better that

to stumble in off the street during harvest. The real winemakers were all too busy to give tastings.

"I'm here from *Vino Veritas* magazine. I'd like to do a story on you and this domaine."

"Surely you don't mean now?" It was unimaginable that a wine journalist of all people would think of asking at this time of year.

"Yes."

She waved her hand to show all the activity around him, in case he hadn't noticed. "I'm in the middle of my harvest."

"We wanted to do a big online feature to appear in two or three days. We have a massive audience." She knew he wasn't lying about the audience. Everyone in the industry clamored after exposure in *Vino Veritas*.

"Can't it wait until after I get my grapes in?"

"I realize how inconvenient this is, and I apologize, but it can't wait. It's our editor's orders. If you can't, we'll have to go to our number two choice."

Cerise fought against her initial instinct to give him the boot, and not politely either, but with Cerasus coming out, and Yannis's accident, the attention might put the focus back on her wine, where it needed to be. She wouldn't dream of mentioning anything about Cerasus yet, of course. She still needed to get the wine bottled and ensure it was good. It was a secret shared only with Clovis for now.

Marketing was the part of her job she both hated and neglected, but she always felt guilty that she was doing her domaine a disservice by being so reclusive.

As she was deciding how to answer the journalist, Clovis walked in. His eyes scanned the *cuverie*, lighting up when they connected with hers. His hair was damp from a shower, she imagined, and he wore fresh clothes. She wanted to do only one thing at that moment, and it wasn't give an interview. It had to do with Clovis and a large bed with crisp white sheets. She couldn't believe she still wanted him with such urgency considering the number of times they'd been together in the past twelve hours. Where was it going to stop?

The journalist brought her back to reality by sticking out his hand to Clovis. "Monsieur de Valois! I know you by reputation, *bien sûr*. I'm from *Vino Veritas*. We want to do a feature on this vineyard," he explained, although Cerise didn't see why he had started to address Clovis instead of her. "It can't wait until after the harvest. My editor is insisting it run in the next couple of days, especially now since the accident."

Clovis's eyes shifted from Cerise to the journalist. "What did Madame Desloires tell you?" She was shocked to hear him use her full married name, then remembered the journalist had called Clovis by his full name. He was demanding the journalist treat her with the same respect.

"She hasn't yet."

"Give me a moment." She gave the journalist her best replica of a gracious smile, then gestured to Clovis to draw away to consult in private.

The journalist frowned and pulled a package of Gitanes from his back pocket. "I'll be outside." He stalked off.

She pulled Clovis to the other side of a large stainless-steel vat, still in view of the workers. She tugged on her messy bun. "Of all the times to ask a winemaker for an interview! Any wine journalist should know better."

He nodded and reached his thumb to touch her bottom lip, which she realized belatedly she was gripping with her front teeth.

His touch rampaged through her body. "But I realize it would be great publicity." She had to try hard to remember the journalist was waiting outside.

He nodded. "I hate to say it, but it's true. I don't agree with everything they print, but the publication has countless readers. Everyone in the industry reads it."

She raked a hand through her hair and found a tiny green grape leaf, which she plucked out and, in an unthinking gesture, passed to Clovis. He tucked it in his pocket. "I know. But I'm terrible at giving interviews. Journalists always want to take the tragic-widow angle instead of asking about my wine, and now with Yannis's accident, it would be their perfect segue into those questions. I get defensive."

"No!" he said with mock shock.

"It's true." She half smiled, half grimaced. "Plus, I need to stay in the *cuverie* after yesterday to ensure nobody gets lazy about the new protocols. Honestly, this 'journalist'—"

"I happen to be excellent at publicity," he said. "Do you want me to take the journalist around and give him enough information so it promotes the domaine? I don't know everything—far from it, but I think I know enough for an article."

"Not a word about Cerasus," she reminded him.

Clovis shook his head. "Of course not. I would never break your trust."

She sighed a breath of relief combined with thwarted lust. "I know you wouldn't. That would be fantastic, actually."

"It could leave you to concentrate on your workers and your vinification."

"Yes," she said. "I'll have to make it up to you." She brushed the front of his shorts with her hand, as if by accident.

His gaze flew to hers. "How does anybody work feeling like this? I just want to—"

"I know," she said in an equally low voice. "This is why we made the 'nothing physical' pact, I guess."

"We were so wise back then," he mused.

"Yes." Cerise sighed, running her eyes longingly up the curved muscles of his arms that had held her last night.

"But not having nearly as much fun."

"To be honest, I think wise us were a bit boring." She found herself smiling like a lovesick teenager, which was exactly how she felt. How was she ever going to negotiate a buyout in this state of mind?

"Tonight." His eyes bored deep into hers. "I'll make it up to you."

"God, yes."

"That reminds me of something you cried out last night."

"Hmmm...I don't remember," she lied.

"Don't worry. I'll remind you when we are back in bed."

"I'm counting on it." His crooked smile broke the last veneer of her reserve. She took a furtive look over her shoulder and, seeing everyone was preoccupied or far away, leaned in to kiss him. He pulled her closer, and their bodies melded together. Her stomach lurched with the wondrous sensation of falling, knowing he would be there to catch her.

Somebody cleared their throat from the other side of the vat.

"*Merde,*" Clovis mouthed against her ear, making her shiver.

She couldn't repress a chuckle. "Duty calls."

They reluctantly pulled apart. They strolled from behind the vat and ushered the journalist outside again, explaining their plan.

Despite her apprehensions, the journalist was enthusiastic about Clovis filling in for her. That was a bit odd, seeing as he'd said he wanted to interview Cerise specifically. Then again, she'd always found wine journalists a strange breed.

Clovis was absent at lunch. Cerise knew he was probably still with the journalist, but she missed him anyway. She ate quickly and went back to the *cuverie*. As she was busy solving a draining issue with the sorting table, Amandine wandered in.

"*Bonjour!*" Cerise said, giving Clovis's friend warm *bises*. She had no idea why Amandine would visit during harvest, but the way Clovis's friends randomly appeared was endearing. Those were the kind of friendships she wanted in her life again, she realized.

"You look...different." Amandine's brown eyes squinted at her.

Cerise felt a flutter of panic and wondered if Clovis had branded her body somewhere visible; it certainly felt as though he had. But, no, that was impossible. "Louis, take it slower," she instructed one of the sorters as she tried to school her face into an expression of nonchalance.

"How are your grapes?" Amandine asked.

Thank God she had let it drop.

"Lovely juice. Excellent color." Cerise beckoned her away from the table. "Want to taste?" She opened the spigot on one of the vats and poured Amandine a glass of largely unfermented juice, known locally as *verjus*, or "green juice." It was bitter, and too much would hurt even an iron stomach, but to an experienced winemaker, *verjus* gave a glimpse into what the wine could eventually become.

Even though Amandine was officially second in command at her family domaine, after her brother, or perhaps even third in command if her father was involved, from what Clovis and his friends said, she was an excellent winemaker.

Amandine swashed the *verjus* around in her mouth and smacked it between her lips to taste properly. "That's a fine start." She gave Cerise a nod. "I can tell you subscribe to the same philosophy as me—wine is made three hundred and sixty-five days of the year, not just during the harvest and vinification."

Cerise nodded. "Exactly. How's your harvest going? I'm surprised to see you here, to be honest. I know how hard it is to get away."

She stared down into the juice. "Normally I wouldn't leave at all during the harvest. We don't have a large domaine like Clovis's that requires an experienced *régisseur*. He's hit gold with Jean, you know."

"*Oui.* Jean is a treasure." Cerise blushed at the mention of Clovis's name, not to mention the incendiary things he had done to her the night before.

Amandine's eyes went round under her blonde bangs. "That's what's different about you! You slept with him!"

*Merde.* Cerise opened her mouth to deny it but then realized the futility. She seemed physically incapable of not smiling. "Yes."

Amandine whistled, slow and low. "That was a terrible idea."

She bristled. Sure, Amandine was Clovis's friend, but Cerise barely knew her.

"Do you want to know why I left my domaine in the middle of the harvest?" Amandine asked.

"What does that have to do with Clovis and me?"

"Everything."

She crossed her arms but didn't say anything.

"My brother," Amandine steamrolled on. "He's making all the wrong decisions, trying to cut corners at the sorting table, doing sloppy work. How can I make good wine out of sloppy work?"

Cerise just looked at her.

"Impossible! Precisely," Amandine continued as though she had answered. "I complained to my father, and he brushed me off, told me my brother, as the only son, is the indisputable head."

"That's garbage," Cerise gasped, appalled for Amandine despite herself.

"I know. That's why I have to warn you. As wonderful as Clovis is, he's still a man. Don't go into a partnership with *any* man. You have your independence now, and that's a gift. You have to fight to keep it."

Clovis couldn't be compared to Amandine's cretin of a brother. "But—"

"*Non!*" Amandine shook her head. "Even though Clovis is my friend, as one female winemaker to another, I beg you—please don't give up control of your vineyards to him."

"I have no intention of doing that. Anyway, he *owns* half of them," she pointed out the obvious. "Maxime took care of that. Did you forget I've already lost my independence?"

"I forgot." Amandine grimaced.

"But I'm still following through with my plan to buy him out."

"That makes it even worse that you slept with him."

"Why?" she demanded, even though she had been of the same mind a mere twenty-four hours earlier.

"Because sooner or later, you are going to have to fight him for control and ownership. It's going to be a hundred times more complicated now you have slept together."

"Clovis isn't like that," she began. "Besides, this is probably just a short-term thing between us. It's just…" She shrugged. "Harvest insanity."

"Are you sure he knows that?"

Cerise froze. She had made her feelings about a longer-term partnership quite clear, but—

"Look," Amandine said. "I've known him for a long time, and when I see him with you…it's different. I wouldn't be so sure he wants just a fling."

She wasn't sure if she wanted just a fling either, but she couldn't see how it could possibly work out longer-term. "He's had so many women—"

"Yes, but do you know what he wants deep down, more than anything?"

"What?"

"A family. A family like he never had. I have this feeling

maybe he thinks you are the key to that, Cerise. Tread carefully. He's not nearly as bulletproof as he seems on the surface."

Maybe it was just the carbon monoxide rising from the vats, but Cerise's head started to spin. "Let's get some air," she said and hurried out into the sunshine.

The heat meant there was no respite from feeling she was being slowly suffocated.

Amandine squinted at her. "Even if you changed your mind about buying him out, and he proves to be the perfect partner, who do you think the wine world will defer to? It won't be you."

She thought of the journalist's enthusiasm when he learned he was being toured around by Clovis instead of her. As much as she wanted to, she couldn't completely dismiss the truth in what Amandine said. The winemaking world in Burgundy was dominated by men. She was one of the exceptions.

"Remember," Amandine continued, "this is coming from someone who loves Clovis like a brother." A bitter sound escaped her mouth. "He is far more of a brother to me than my own has ever been. But as wonderful as he is, it would still irk me to work under him. Can you see that? I want to be known for *my* work. I don't want anyone else taking the credit for my wine. Of course not an incompetent like my brother, but not even a dear friend and talented winemaker like Clovis."

Cerise backed up and sat on the rickety wood-and-iron bench. She dropped her head into her hands. It was still spinning. "Do you really think he believes I've changed my mind about the business partnership just because we've slept together? What a mess."

Amandine sat down beside her and patted her back. "If it was just one night, maybe you can still undo it."

"But, Amandine." She lifted her face to this unlikely confidant. "I don't want to undo it. I mean, I know I'll probably have to eventually, but not yet."

The combative look on Amandine's pixie face shifted to wistfulness. "I wish I felt that for somebody."

"You never have?"

She shook her head. "I've felt that way about winemaking. Always. But never about a man... Well, maybe except..."

Cerise waited for her to finish, but she didn't.

They both squinted into the sun for a while, each lost in thought, until Amandine cleared her throat.

Cerise sighed. "I didn't realize how much I needed this thing with Clovis until it happened last night," she admitted. "But now...he's hard to willingly give up so soon. It feels impossible."

"I always believed that vines, no matter what it says on the legal papers, belong to the people who love them most," Amandine said.

"I don't think that's a popular opinion in Burgundy."

"Maybe not, but do you believe it?" Amandine waited.

That was just not the way things worked. Still...she thought of her loving tours through the vineyards, talking to her vines. No matter what Maxime's will said, or what was happening between her and Clovis, in her heart Domaine du Cerisier was still hers, not Clovis's. "I do."

# chapter nineteen

*C* LOVIS SENT WORD through Jorgé that he needed to go to his own domaine to help Jean resolve a pressing crisis and a crucial valve on one of the vats. He missed dinner, which left Cerise alone to weigh with the truths in Amandine's warning against her need to be with him.

She stripped off her clothes and collapsed on the bed without even closing the shutters against the setting sun. She pulled the thin sheet over her shoulders and breathed in the smell of Clovis from the night before. Feeling conflicted yet comforted, she tumbled down a black well of sleep.

Sometime later—she had no idea how long, but the sun had set and the crickets' song thrummed outside—she woke. The creak of the bedroom door had interrupted her sleep. The light of an almost full moon shone through the open windows, making the bed glow white with its light. Clovis's face was visible in the crack of light from the hallway. His head was tilted.

"*Salut toi*," she murmured. "You came back up?" Acting on pure instinct, she reached out to him.

He came into the room and perched on the edge of the mattress, taking obvious care not to disturb her. "I missed you too much." He caressed the tender skin on her forearm with his thumb. The reverberations of pleasure convinced her she should just turn off her mind and all her futile reasoning and store up every second of this while it lasted.

"What time is it?"

"About one in the morning," he said. She wrapped both arms around his waist in time to pull him down. It was perhaps misguided and mistaken of her, but somehow in the moonlight it made sense.

"What is this?" He raised his left eyebrow.

"Stay."

He looked at her, wonder writ across his features in the silver light. "The thought of coming back to you was the only thing that got me through crawling around in grape juice under my vat for hours, I swear." He leaned in, and they explored the endlessly fascinating terrain of each other's mouths. At moments like this, autonomy didn't feel as important as being loved by him.

She ran a fingernail down his thigh. He trembled under her touch.

Clovis laughed softly. "You make it impossible for me to go slow. I have my standards, you know."

Cerise pulled him down beside her. "Standards are overrated. At least the kind that keep you from this bed."

"Anything that keeps me from you is overrated," he murmured in her hair. He took off his clothes in record time and slid between the sheets. Quickly, his hands were skimming her naked curves.

"I need you," he said as he eased into her.

"Me too," she answered with a gasp.

"I need you so much it terrifies me." His whisper was almost inaudible.

"Me too."

Cerise could feel he was holding his desire on a tight leash, and that fueled her own unrelenting hunger for him. He moved slowly and deliberately inside her. She was again stunned at the alchemy of their connection. In his arms she felt cherished. She felt whole. She felt vibrantly alive.

With a sinuous movement of her hips, she spurred him on. He paused for a moment to fill his lungs with air, then quickened and deepened his pace to match hers. They abandoned any last shreds of restraint.

Their eyes locked as they reached the peak. Cerise saw the wonder in her heart reflected in his eyes.

Afterward she lay with her head nestled in between his neck and shoulder. He ran his index finger up and down the curve of her hip and waist.

"Amandine came to visit today," she said. She didn't feel ready to tell him about their confusing conversation, but she felt a compulsion to share the fact of her visit nonetheless.

"Did she?" Clovis sounded a bit surprised but not enough to interfere with his caresses. "Has she murdered that useless brother of hers yet?"

Cerise chuckled. "No, but I think it's just a matter of time."

He sighed. "She was brought up to be the traditional daughter, to be married off to a rich winemaker who would bring more vineyards into the family. That would never work, of course. Amandine has always had more winemaking talent in her pinky than anyone else in her family. If she was the traditional wine-making wife she was brought up to be, she wouldn't be nearly as interesting."

Cerise rolled half on top of his solid chest and raised her head so she could see his eyes. "I was a traditional winemaker's wife. Unlike Amandine, I guess I didn't know any better."

He watched her. "But you loved Antoine, *nest-ce pas*? Love makes it different. Also, you were young."

She shrugged. "Of course I loved Antoine, but—"

He squeezed her thigh. "You can tell me anything. I'm hard to shock."

It took a few moments to find the words. "We were head over heels in love, but like you said, we were so young." She took a deep breath, and the next words came out in a rush. "I never want to go back to who I was before Antoine died. When we were married, I was so unsure of myself. I think it was only when I discovered winemaking that I discovered who I truly am."

He shook his head slightly. "I would never want you to go back, Cerise. I want the woman here in bed with me, with all her scars and strength and talent and grit."

She pressed her face against his chest, enjoying the tickle of his chest hairs.

"Who would ever want you to go back to being a traditional wife?" Clovis stroked her hair.

She chuckled. "Besides Geneviève?"

"I'm not so sure. She loves to harass you—that's obvious— but I think she's also a little in awe and probably, deep down, extremely proud of you."

"Interesting theory, but I'm skeptical."

"Don't forget, I'm a father, and I believe Geneviève considers you her de facto daughter. The things I love about Emily are the unconventional things."

"Like what?"

"The fact that she is obsessed with space—her room is full of books about black holes and exploding stars."

Cerise rested her chin on his chest, and he ran began tracing the contours of each vertebra down her back. Bliss. Her eyes drifted closed. "What else?"

She could feel a soft laugh reverberate deep inside him. "She can't sing in tune but dreams of being a pop star and belts out off-key songs all the time, even at school. She insisted on learning the banjo and takes lessons twice a week, much to her mother's horror. She doesn't suffer fools, whether it be a teacher or a fellow classmate. She'll let them know exactly what she thinks."

Cerise warmed at the obvious love he had for the quirks of his daughter. "It must be so hard living far from her. If it was my boys... Well, I can't imagine."

Clovis's chest stilled, and she almost sensed a black hole of grief opening inside. "It's terrible." His voice was quiet. "I hate it. I want to be part of her life every day, but her mother doesn't want me in that role. I've dreamed my whole life of a family of my own. When I was growing up, I had friends whose houses were full of laughter and good cooking and affection. There was yelling sometimes, too, of course, but I always knew there was love behind it."

Amandine had been right about his desire for a family, Cerise realized with a sinking in her gut. "Your house was never like that," she guessed.

"No. My house was empty and sad and bitter. I swore when I was old enough, I would create a loving family. So far I've failed."

She nodded against his chest. Her case was different. Until Maxime died, she'd felt her life was complete. She had her vines and her sons, and she had a friend in Maxime. She never questioned that maybe it wasn't enough. Then Clovis was made her partner, and...she realized how much she'd been missing.

But from what it sounded, Clovis wanted everything. She couldn't give him that. Despite his assurances that nobody wanted her to revert to the role of a wife, Amandine was right. That was just the way the tide ran in Burgundy. If she had him as a husband or a winemaking partner, let alone both, she would never again get credit for her wines.

"I'm so sorry," Cerise said because it was true and also she didn't know what else to say. She dropped a kiss on his shoulder.

He lifted his head slightly and kissed her temple. "Sleep?" he suggested with a quirk of his mouth. "Don't forget it's my *paulée* tomorrow night."

She'd forgotten. The harvest finished tomorrow at Domaine de Valois. In the evening Clovis was throwing the huge party to celebrate its success. Cerise wanted to stop time; their idyll would all be over so soon.

"Sleep," she said and let herself be drawn back into him as he curled his large body around her smaller one. In his arms she felt protected from reality, from her own thoughts, from the future… *He feels like home*, she thought just before falling asleep.

The morning was full of good news. Jorgé and Clovis kept coming back to the *cuverie*, where Cerise was working with full loads of beautiful grapes, with reports that the harvesters were working like a well-oiled machine.

Fiona had made the surprising leap from a mere beginner to one of the leaders of the sorting table. To make the day even better, Yannis made his grand entrance in the *cuverie* just as Clovis had stolen a kiss from Cerise behind a vat and was heading to the kitchens to make sure the cooks were ready for lunch.

Everyone stopped what they were doing and broke into a spontaneous *ban bourgignon*. Yannis smiled sheepishly and, without saying a word, walked to Cerise and enveloped her in a long, heartfelt hug.

"*Merci*," he whispered in her ear. "*Merci, merci, merci.*"

"It was my pleasure," she murmured back, her heart filled with relief. "I cannot tell you how happy it makes me to see you walk in here."

He held her at arm's length. "You saved my life, Cerise."

"Not just me," she said, pointing at where Clovis was standing off to the side.

Yannis went to Clovis and took him in the same bear hug. Clovis hugged him just as tightly. Yannis finally stepped back and beamed at them.

"How are you feeling?" Clovis asked.

"Reborn," Yannis said. "It's amazing the high one can get from almost dying."

Oddly, Cerise felt like she was experiencing something similar. With Clovis, her eyes were opened to a new sort of existence.

"How are your ribs?" she asked. She remembered how hard her fist had come down on them and had a vague recollection of hearing a sickening crunch in the panic of those moments.

Yannis hooted with laughter but then grabbed his side and winced. "That's what hurts the most! You broke two."

Clovis crossed his arms and raised an eyebrow at her, clearly impressed.

"Remind me never to get in a fistfight with you." Yannis laughed.

"Me too," Clovis said.

"Those punches of yours saved my life." Yannis rubbed his side. "That's what the paramedics told me and the dozen or so doctors I saw. Thank God you punch like a man."

"Wrong. I punch like a woman. You just underestimate my gender."

Yannis shook his head. "Trust me, I won't anymore."

"You'll be happy to know I've named a new *cuverie* rule in your honor. 'Yannis's law' decrees that anyone who climbs a ladder to the top of a vat has to have a spotter."

"That's a bit embarrassing, but…it's a good idea. I don't remember anything, but I must have passed out up there and fallen in."

"I'm glad you're here to help me make sure it's enforced," Cerise said, then clapped her hands. "Time to get lunch, everyone, where we can toast Yannis's resurrection. Besides, you all know how the cooks hate it when we're late."

A round of cheers rose and then another *ban bourgignon*. Yannis was hoisted up on the shoulders of Clement and a few other *cuverie* workers. Cerise, Clovis, and the rest of the crew paraded to the lunch barn, where a succulent *boeuf bourgignon* was waiting for them to celebrate their friend's triumphant return.

# chapter twenty

THAT EVENING, CERISE made her way to Maxime's house earlier than usual to shower and get ready for Clovis's *paulée*. He'd left for Domaine de Valois after lunch to make sure everything was well in hand.

As for Cerise, her afternoon had been just as satisfying as the morning, and she was trying to look forward to an evening of celebrations at Domaine de Valois without worrying about the end of her own harvest, which was drawing near. What would mean for her and Clovis?

Clovis had made a point at breakfast of inviting her boys personally, and they were bursting with excitement about the evening in front of them.

*La paulée* was not only a celebration for adults; it wouldn't be a Burgundian *paulée* without children underfoot. Marc and Yves knew they would be spoiled by the harvesters and cooks. They had run straight to Maxime's house from the school bus to get ready.

She found the boys dressed and playing a spirited match of Tarot in the living room.

"Who's winning?" she asked when she peeked around the corner.

"Yves," Marc said. "But I'm letting him win."

"No, you're not!" Yves's mouth dropped open with indignation.

"You're both looking handsome." She went over and kissed the tops of their heads. She sniffed. "And even more miraculous, you're clean!"

"We wanted to make a good impression at Domaine de Valois," Marc said, looking back at his cards.

"Yes," Yves chimed in. "Geneviève told us how everyone on the lower coast is rich, so we didn't want to look like tramps."

Cerise smiled. "Don't believe everything Geneviève tells you, but if it convinced you to shower and wash your hair, I'm grateful. I'm going upstairs now to get ready, *d'accord?*"

They both nodded, rapidly turning their attention back to the game of Tarot.

When she toweled herself off, she chose a lilac sundress she'd bought on a whim at the summer sales in Dijon a few years earlier but had never worn—there had never been the occasion. She didn't have many nights left with Clovis. That reality made her want to howl in frustration.

She had always loved the sundress. It had a tight embroidered bodice, spaghetti straps, and a full skirt that stopped above the knees. That wasn't why she chose it, though. She picked it because it had a long row of tiny little buttons going down the back, and she wanted Clovis to undo them slowly—one by one.

She planned to store every second of that process in her memory for the day they would have to face the fact that perhaps they wouldn't be able to make their envisaged futures align.

She reached around her back to do up the buttons but managed only the bottom few, and those with considerable difficulty. She hadn't thought this through. Maybe Marc wouldn't mind helping her.

There was a knock on the bedroom door.

"Come in," she said, figuring it would be one or both of her boys.

Clovis opened the door. He paused on the threshold for a charged moment, then closed it quietly behind him. An intent expression sharpened his features that sent a surge of heat from Cerise's toes to the top of her head.

"You have a habit of showing up where you're not expected," Cerise said. "I thought we were meeting you directly at Domaine de Valois."

"I missed you." He moved slowly toward her. "I figured maybe I could give you and the boys a drive down. Given how you look in that dress, I think this might be the best idea I've ever had."

Her heart skipped a beat as she surveyed how his linen shirt the color of wine and khaki shorts highlighted his glorious body and tanned skin. "You came at the perfect time. I was just wondering how I was going to get these buttons done up."

He came and stood behind her so they were both reflected in the massive gilded mirror. His hands settled on her shoulders as if they belonged there. He was so much taller than her, yet being with him somehow highlighted her different, contained strength. Being with Clovis made her see herself differently—as an explosive force in a small package, like fireworks.

He looked down at the buttons. "Are you certain you want me to button these up? As I've said before, dressing you feels counterintuitive."

"You're buttoning them up so you can *unbutton* them later," Cerise clarified.

"Ah. In that case…"

With his tongue caught between his teeth in concentration, he began working where she had left off. He dropped a kiss on her spine before he set to work on the next one. *Every moment. I need to remember every moment of this.* She shivered.

"My hands feel too big." He completed the second button. "These are fairy buttons."

"You're doing fine," she said, barely able to stand the pleasure of his fingers dancing against her skin. "But if it's too difficult, I could ask one of the harvesters…"

He placed another kiss on her next vertebrae—a kiss that lit up every cell in her body. "Absolutely not. This is my job from now on."

"Really?" she asked.

"For as long as you want me."

*Even if I still want you buy you out?* But then Clovis kissed her back again, disintegrating all thought.

When he was done, his mouth moved to the sensitive nape of her neck. He anchored her with firm hands on her hips. She slid around to face him. In one fluid movement, he lifted her onto the antique dresser. He pushed up the skirt of her dress carefully. She noticed his hands shook slightly as they moved under the lilac fabric.

"Are you nervous?" she whispered, a smile in her voice.

"A bit," he whispered back. "Mostly, I'm overwhelmed by you in this dress."

With measured, deliberate gestures, he raised her slightly and slipped off her wisp of underwear. Her entered her with exquisite slowness, holding her hips steady.

A sob rose in her chest. She wanted to weep with relief at being connected with him again—and weep that this magical harvest was ending. Time felt suspended, and they were both quiet so as not to be heard by the boys.

Only the creaking dresser, moving like a metronome, marked their joining. Their breathing became deeper and more ragged. She wondered how this could possibly feel so *right*.

"I want this to last forever," she sighed on the tail of a gasp.

He stopped and pulled back his head just enough so he could meet her eyes. He kissed her hard then, with a new note of possession that broke Cerise's last layer of resistance. Their eyes met in silent recognition as they broke apart together.

"Clovis," she whispered a few minutes later. His arms were still around her, and her head was against his chest, listening to the reassuring beating of his heart.

He pressed a kiss under her jaw. "*Ma Cerise,*" he murmured.

*My Cerise.* It was a common enough expression of affection in France, used in anything from friendship to children to passion, but it brought back her unease. He'd never used it before. If he started to feel possessive about her outside the bedroom, it would be a problem. She had made the decision long ago that she would never again belong to anyone but herself. She nestled her head on the curve of his shoulder, her mind churning.

After a few minutes, Clovis helped her down and tried unsuccessfully to comb her now-tangled hair with his fingers. She found the attempt—and the feel of his hands, still slightly clumsy from the aftermath of their joining—endearing.

He drew her close again and rested his chin on the top of her head. Finally, he took a step back so he could gaze down sheepishly at her. "I know I've delayed us getting to my *paulée,*" he said. "But I wouldn't have missed that for anything in the world."

"Me neither," she murmured.

He took a step back and clasped her hands in his, his eyes glowing. "I want this to last forever. We can build a life together, a real family. A true partnership. It's everything, Cerise. *You* are everything."

She drew back. "Wait."

"What?" His eyes were round.

The time had come to set things straight between them. It was only now she realized she had waited far too long. "I love being with you. I can't even begin to tell what this has meant…us together. It's just…I'm not sure we have the same definition of a true partnership."

Clovis stumbled back until his legs hit the edge of the bed. He sat down and rubbed his knuckles over his thighs. "Did I misunderstand this week?"

"It has been… It's been everything, Clovis," she said, desperate not to hurt him. "But I've explained before that I'm not looking to be anyone's wife."

He looked up. "And I told you I'm not like Antoine was. Besides, we don't have to rush into marriage."

"It's nothing to do with how I feel for you." She sat down beside him on the bed, wanting more than anything to put her arms around him, but he sat rigid. "I'm just not ready to throw everything in with one person like I did with Antoine—children, love, work—"

"What do you mean?"

"It means—it means I still want to buy you out."

He stood up and began to stalk back and forth in front of the dresser. "But didn't I prove to you this week that we could get more done together than separately?"

Cerise didn't know how to answer. He was right; they could accomplish far more together, but that didn't change her need to accomplish it on her own.

"Do you not enjoy working together?"

She watched him, feeling she was tearing both of them up with each word. "I do."

He gripped the edge of the dresser, facing her. He took a deep breath, as if trying to collect himself. "Explain what you need," he said finally. "I think I'm seeing only part of the picture."

She sighed. "For starters, I'm a woman in the wine industry.

You're a man. If we publicly become partners, you will get all the credit, particularly with Cerasus on the horizon."

He considered this. "But I would never *take* the credit." Clovis shook his head, clearly frustrated. "You must know that. Besides, you've already established yourself. I just want to help you, support you, so you can devote your time to exercising your talent as a winemaker. I just want to love you, Cerise."

The emotion in his face made her want to abandon all her principles about autonomy and throw herself in his arms.

Instead, she asked a question. "In your mind, why does partnering in the vineyards equate to love?" She thought she knew, but she wanted to hear the explanation from Clovis himself. She needed to understand.

He rubbed his forehead. "You know my history…my family."
She nodded.

"When my mother was alive, she and my father always lived separate lives. I don't want to be one of those couples—or families—who never see each other." He dropped his hands between his legs. He looked up again, his eyes pleading. "Surely you must know—work life and family life for winemakers are one and the same. I want a real family, a real partnership with you."

Cerise knew he was speaking the truth. Winemaking was nothing if not all-encompassing. It was the exact opposite of an office job with regular hours that didn't need to be considered outside the workplace.

"I've always longed for a family," he continued. "I cannot remember a time when I haven't dreamed of a life that was everything that my parents' was not."

"Okay," Cerise murmured, but he barely paid attention. Her heart sank. She was not the person to give Clovis what he wanted, and it pierced like the sharpest blade.

"When I found out about Emily, I proposed to her mother,

even though I was young then and still sowing my wild oats, and Emily's conception was just a one-night stand."

Cerise didn't know he had proposed. The idea sat like a lead ball in her stomach. "What happened?"

"She said no, obviously. She initially didn't want me to be part of Emily's life at all, but I refused. I couldn't have a child growing up thinking her father didn't love her. That was unthinkable."

She was blindsided by the thought of how wonderful it would be to have a child with Clovis. Antoine had been a good father, but she had a feeling Clovis would appreciate the miracle of children and parenthood in a way Antoine couldn't have when he was in his early twenties and trying to create a reputation.

"I made sure I was there for the birth," he continued. "From the day Emily was born, my heart was split. Half of it remains in England with her. It tortures me that I can't see her more often or be part of her daily life."

She tried to imagine how it would feel to be separated from her boys. The mere thought made her chest ache.

"The last thing I want is to cause my daughter stress or pain." His shoulders slumped, a defeated posture that seemed so unusual on him. "I take what I can get and try to give her no reason to doubt my love for her."

Cerise sensed there was something else. "But?"

"But to have a such fractured relationship because of geography and her mother's anxieties…" Clovis wore a wretched expression that tore at her heart. "Cerise, it's killing me."

It took a few minutes to untangle her thoughts. His torment was so sincere, and yet… "Being partners with me in the vineyards can't fix that."

"No," he admitted. "I wouldn't expect it to, although I admit to daydreaming about having Emily here and introducing her to you and the boys. What I'm trying to explain is that my childhood and the situation with Emily have taught me with absolute certainty what kind of relationship I want. I want a family. I need someone who is all in."

"Can I be all in if we don't partner in Domaine du Cerisier?" She tried to swallow the lump in her throat.

He shook his head. "I don't think so."

"Then I don't think I can give you what you need." Her voice came out low, full of regret. "I need to be independent in this domaine for my sons' future because I am a female winemaker in a macho industry, so I don't feel frustrated, so I don't end up resenting you—"

"I think you're scared."

"Why would I be scared?"

"Because of what happened to Antoine and everything you had to cope with afterward."

Anger sparked behind her breastbone. "How is wanting my independence being scared?"

"What I meant is that you're too scared to see that with the right person, you can have both love and independence."

Indignation and anguish warred inside her. "How about this? You are too scared to admit that a healthy relationship does not require us to be partners in everything."

His eyes blazed, and she was sure that hers blazed back. *Impasse.*

"Do you still want me to come with you to the *paulée*?" she demanded, having a hard time understanding how they had moved so quickly from that moment of transcendence on the dresser to this.

He checked his watch. "*Merde.* We're so late already."

"Do you?"

His eyes rose to hers again. He raked his hand through his hair. "Of course I do. *On y va.*"

# chapter twenty-one

LA PAULÉE WAS always a festive event, with many speeches, toasts, and songs. The celebration at Domaine de Valois would surely be no different, even though Cerise felt too frustrated and somber to be able to take it in.

The drive down to Domaine de Valois was awkward, but fortunately Marc and Yves spent the journey peppering Clovis with all sorts of questions.

As soon as they arrived in the courtyard of Domaine de Valois, the harvesters, who had been imbibing in all the wonderful free wine, seized the four of them. They festooned them with bracelets and necklaces of intertwined grape leaves.

On Clovis they perched an artfully woven crown of grapevines. Cerise soon hardly had time to think, let alone keep track of Clovis and her boys. The harvesters grasped her arms and immersed her into their chorus of traditional wine songs all Burgundians knew by heart.

Clovis laughingly joined some of the harvesters in an impromptu jig, but Cerise saw his smile was forced and never reached his eyes. She was swung into dancing by a small bald man with merry brown eyes. She caught a glimpse of Yves cheering on someone's shoulders and Marc doubled over with laughter about something.

When she finally escaped to stand behind one of the barrels stood on end in the courtyard to serve as makeshift *apéritif* tables, she saw Jean approach. She almost didn't recognize him at first out of his *bleus de travail* and wearing a nice pair of pants and an ironed plaid shirt. It was those kind, sparkling eyes that gave him away in the end.

She had no idea why, but her eyes welled up with tears. She tried to blink them away. Jean had known Clovis forever; maybe he could explain why Clovis was so stuck on this partnership.

"Cerise." He grasped her shoulders and gave her a sound kiss on each cheek, then gave her a narrow look. "What happened?"

"How did you know?" she asked, astounded. "Did he say something?" She looked over to see Clovis still being whirled around by his harvesters.

"No. I can just see it in your eyes, and Clovis's."

Jean would see right through any denial. "We got in a big fight before we came here. Things…well, things have been…so good, but then we started talking about Domaine du Cerisier—"

"The partnership?"

She met Jean's eyes. "Yes."

"Let me guess. He wants it, and you don't?" Jean's eyes were full of understanding, not censure.

"Yes." She bit her lip. "He just doesn't understand my need for independence, and frankly, I don't understand him. He wants all or nothing. I can't give him all, so I guess—"

"You just need more time to find some middle ground," Jean said. "Both of you."

She shook her head. "I don't know, Jean. He was so angry, and so was I."

He reached out for her, took her in his arms, and patted her back. She didn't realize how much she had been missing her father until this moment. Tears began to collect in her eyes again. "I see the difference in Clovis," he said, his voice low just for her. "And

I see you when you look at him. You two just need time. Can you promise me to give it that?"

"Well—"

"I'll extract the same promise from Clovis, never fear."

"I'll try," she said, not wanting to promise something she couldn't be sure to deliver.

"That's good enough for me." Leaving her with a final kiss on the cheek, Jean went off to talk to Clovis.

Cerise was left standing there, wondering if there was any middle ground between what Clovis needed and what she needed. If there was, she couldn't see it.

Clovis spent much of the meal going back and forth to the kitchens to help ensure the cooks and kitchen staff also enjoyed the celebratory night instead of working the whole time. Her heart ached when she looked at him.

It was clear by the way the harvesters patted him on the back and the older women bestowed him with juicy kisses that he was loved. That was no surprise to Cerise. Now she just had to figure out how exactly to try moving forward with him. She had so much thinking to do.

During one of the rare times he was able to sit for a moment beside her, just as a parade of fruit tarts began to flow from the kitchen, she said, "You should be proud of yourself. This is the *paulée* of a happy harvest." Jean would be proud. She was trying.

The corners of his mouth twitched up in something that wasn't exactly a smile. "Yet I was barely here. I'm not sure what to think about that."

"Maybe it means we could run two separate, independent domaines."

He searched her eyes. "So that's really what you want?"

"Yes." Trying did not mean lying to him. The hurt in his eyes was immediate. He said nothing but simply nodded.

This wasn't going well.

One of the cooks came up behind Clovis and grabbed his arm to coax him to dance with her. He was gone again. Guilt and anger created an unpleasant mix in Cerise's chest.

Quite some time later, as she finished pushing pear-and-ginger tart around her plate, the harvesters positioned Clovis at the head of the table and began chanting "*Choisi, choisi, choisi!*" Choose! Choose! Choose!

"What's that all about?" Cerise asked her neighbor, a taciturn and extremely rotund harvester who hailed from Alsace and who was getting quietly and steadily inebriated.

He hiccupped before answering her, bathing her in aromas of Clovis's fine wine. "Tradition at this domaine. The owner must take his crown of grape leaves and use it to crown his 'queen' of the evening. He has to choose one of the ladies." He took another slug of wine and shrugged. "Or a man I suppose. Each to their own, I say."

Cerise felt a sliver of doubt slide down her backbone. "Who does he normally choose?"

"One of the cooks."

"Ah." She wasn't sure whether to feel relieved or disappointed. It wasn't the kind of thing where he would choose her, then. That was good, because the day before she would have been convinced he would choose her. After the hurt in his face she'd just seen, she was no longer certain of anything.

The chant got louder and louder until Clovis raised his hand. Quiet rapidly descended on the table. "*J'ai choisi!*" he announced. He had chosen.

Surely it wouldn't be her. The cooks here were superb. They deserved it far more than she did. She had just rejected him as a business partner. Still, she found herself holding her breath.

"Cerise" His voice rang out. All faces turned to her. She could feel her cheeks flame red with adrenaline and, yes, a shock of pleasure. Maybe Jean was right. Maybe all wasn't lost.

The drunken Alsatian elbowed her. "That's you, isn't it? Get up there."

On her way to the head of the table, the crowd broke out in loud and sometimes slightly slurred renditions of *le ban bourgignon*.

Clovis smiled as she approached, but there was a hesitation in his eyes that hadn't been there before.

He laid the crown on her head, but his dimple didn't flash.

"Kiss, kiss, kiss!" the table chanted.

Clovis leaned over and gave her a brief kiss on the mouth. One that seemed so distracted that she shivered.

But the table broke out into cheers and more *ban bourgignons*. They at least were content.

At a tug on her sundress, she looked down to see Marc dragging a green-faced Yves behind him. The smell of vomit wafted off her younger son.

"He was determined to eat one slice of every single tart," Marc said, doing a poor job of hiding his disapproval. "I warned him not to, but as usual he didn't listen to me. He threw up on himself."

Cerise bent down and scrutinized Yves. "You're going to throw up again, aren't you?"

Yves nodded, then gagged.

Marc hustled him outside, and Cerise turned to Clovis, who had clearly picked up on what was going on.

"I'll drive you home right away," he said.

One of the cooks, a young woman she had chatted with earlier named Lynette, was standing near them.

"You can't go!" Lynette said to Clovis. "You have to be here to uncork the Balthazar!" A Balthazar was a massive wine bottle containing the equivalent of sixteen regular bottles of wine, and the uncorking of a Balthazar was an occasion of much pomp and ceremony. Lynette was right; Clovis had to stay.

"But I have to take them home," he insisted.

"I'll take them," Lynette said. "You know the harvesters would never understand if you weren't here."

"But—" Clovis said.

Cerise held up her hand. "She's right. Thank you, Lynette. This is so kind of you. I can't guarantee you're not going to have your car vomited in."

Lynette shrugged. "It's a crappy old Renault. Smells a bit like vomit anyway."

"In that case…" She shot Clovis a rueful look and hurried out after Lynette. There was still so much to say, but as any mother knows, a vomiting child takes precedence over everything.

She found Marc in the courtyard, holding Yves around the shoulders while he threw up behind a barrel that had been set on end for the *apértif*.

She took over Marc's position and soothed Yves as best she could. "My stomach hurts," he wailed.

"That's what you get for being a glutton," Marc said.

This made Yves cry harder.

Cerise gave Marc a quelling look, comforted Yves as best she could, and asked Lynette, "Where's your car?"

"Just outside the courtyard." She began to lead the way. "We kitchen staff have to get here early, which means we get the best parking."

As she half walked, half carried Yves to Lynette's car, she thought back to what her son had left in the courtyard.

"That vomit behind the barrel is going to smell," she said as she wedged Yves in the back seat and cranked open the window.

"I'll make sure somebody cleans it up," Lynette said as she revved up the motor.

"You're an angel," Cerise said and meant it.

Climbing into the Hautes-Côtes was slow because any time Lynette accelerated over twenty kilometers an hour, Yves would start crying that they were going too fast and he was going to throw up again. After what felt like an interminable trip, they arrived at Domaine du Cerisier.

She thanked Lynette profusely and hustled the boys into Maxime's house. Even though she was exhausted, she dealt with Yves's dirty clothes and upset stomach and finally managed to get both boys to bed.

She had to get Marc to undo all the top buttons of her dress until he got to the ones she could reach. The entire evening was a disaster.

When he was done, she gave him a kiss. "Thank you, *cheri*. I don't know what I would have done with Yves without your help."

He shrugged. "Did you and Clovis have a fight?"

She thought she'd hid it so well. "Yes, but it's nothing you need to worry about." She squeezed his shoulder.

"I like him, Maman," Marc said, looking up at her face, his gray eyes serious. "I like him very much. So does Yves."

Where was this coming from? "Why are you telling me this?"

"I just think you should know."

She couldn't give Marc any sort of guarantees about what the future held for Clovis's presence in her life, but she now knew that anything she did affected her boys as well as her. She was almost knocked off her feet with a wave of confusion and fatigue. "Thank you for telling me."

When she began to take her dress off, something slid off her head. Through all that, she'd still been wearing the grapevine crown Clovis had set there. She picked it up off the tile floor and placed it carefully on the bathroom counter. It felt silly, but she didn't want it damaged.

She stood in the shower for a long time, her thoughts wandering as beads of cool water ran in rivulets between her breasts and down her spine. *What I would give at this moment to have Clovis with me.* But no, she was used to dealing with everything on her own. It felt dangerous to suddenly need someone so badly. If she got used to him in all aspects of her life, like he wanted, and it didn't work out—she'd learned the hard way that people disappeared—she would be so much weaker than before.

And yet she longed for him as she crawled between the sheets. He had looked so hurt when she initially explained she didn't want anything long-term. His pain had made her heart ache. That made her as uneasy as the heavy, humid air outside that felt like the harbinger of a thunderstorm and echoed Cerise's own heart—charged with conflicting energies.

She tossed and turned before at last falling into a fitful sleep, with dreams of love and loss. She was woken up at some point by her own whimpering. She sat up. *What is that noise?* It sounded like the tap in the bathroom. She threw on a robe. Her mind spun. Maybe she had left it on, or God forbid, maybe Yves was sick again. She rushed into the bathroom and was dumbfounded to see Clovis standing in front of the sink, drying his hands on a towel.

"Yves?" The question died on her lips. She didn't know exactly why Clovis had come, but neither, at this point, did she care. Relief rushed through her limbs. *He's here, just like on the bench after we saved Yannis.*

"Damn," said Clovis. "I was hoping not to wake you. He's all right. I came here because…well, I wanted to check on all of you. I felt terrible letting you leave like that with no one here to help you."

"I've dealt with worse on my own," she said, leaning against the doorframe, thinking about that winter two years before when she and both boys had come down with a terrible flu.

"I know you have." He set the hand towel on the counter and turned to her. "But the simple matter is that I don't want you to have to anymore." He leaned against the counter and crossed his arms. "Does that make you angry?"

She shook her head. "No. I thought you were the one who would be angry after our conversation before *la paulée*."

He merely shook his head. "I was, but then I talked to Jean. Anyway, I checked on Yves first. I came in here to wash my hands."

Cerise braced on the counter herself, bewildered by this abrupt change in subject. "And?"

"He must have thrown up again in his sleep because he was covered with it. Same with his sheets."

"Oh no!" She yelped and made a move to rush to Yves's room. Clovis held her back with a light touch to her arm. "Was it like he was in the middle of a barf sandwich?" She clapped her hand to her mouth. "He's done that a few times before."

There it was—the dimple. Seeing it, her lungs felt like they could expand for the first time since their earlier conversation. "That's exactly the state he was in. Perfect description. It's fine. I wiped him off and found him a fresh pair of pajamas. While he was changing, I stripped the bed and put on a fresh pair of sheets—I knew where Maxime kept them."

"But the—"

"I scraped off the worst and threw the dirty sheets and pajamas in the washing machine. They'll be clean by tomorrow morning. Yves seems fine now. When I left him, he was sleeping soundly, and his skin tone looks much better. I think that was the last hurrah."

Cerise stayed against the doorway, at a loss for words.

"What are you thinking?" he asked, eyeing her narrowly. "Did I overstep?"

"You did all this while I was sleeping?"

"Yes."

At that moment she realized with absolute clarity just how much she loved Clovis. She would try. She would do everything in her power to find a workable middle ground, as Jean had made her promise. She couldn't choose to be alone, not when she could have this man by her side. That would be insanity. She had to have faith in him and in herself. It felt like jumping off a cliff, but they could do this, and she knew, looking at him now, it would be worth it.

She wrapped her arms as tightly as she could around his torso and gave him the mightiest hug she could. The linen of his shirt was soft against her cheek. She looked up at his face. "This is the most romantic thing anyone has ever done for me."

He slipped his arms around her, and his mouth quirked to one side. "Really? I just figured if I dealt with it, you wouldn't have to."

"Exactly," she said. "You know what?"

"What?"

"I think I love you, Clovis."

He laughed then, his eyes bright with wonder. "If I'd known it would only take cleaning up Yves's vomit to make you say that, I would have overfed him days ago."

"You should have."

He ran his hand through her hair. "And you, Cerise… I think I've loved you forever."

Pure joy made her lips curve. "Can we go to bed now that's clear?"

He blinked. "What? I figured after our argument I'd be going back to Domaine de Valois to sleep."

She ran her hands up the flat planes of his back, her heart pounding like it might explode. "No. Not tonight. Maybe not for a long time. Did Jean bring up the concept of 'middle ground' to you at *la paulée*?"

"He may have mentioned something about that foreign concept." He squeezed his arms around her to emphasize he meant it as a joke.

"Well, maybe we can explore that."

"Tonight?"

She chuckled. "No, not tonight."

"Thank goodness for small mercies." He reached behind her, plucked her grapevine crown off the counter, and settled it back on her head. He dipped down and met her lips in a long, slow kiss that promised many more. "Let's go to bed, my harvest queen."

She led him by the hand and gently pulled off his shorts, linen top, and black boxer briefs. Thunder sounded in the distance.

He growled softly at her as he picked her up and tossed her on the bed. "Tonight, I'm going to guarantee you don't change your mind about loving me."

She fanned her fingers out across the exquisite pattern of his chest muscles. "How, exactly?"

He crawled on the bed to join her. "You'll find out."

"Hmm." She dropped her robe and stepped forward to press her body, naked except for her crown, against his.

"I do have one question," she murmured as she lured him under the sheets.

He cupped her bottom with his large hands and moved her on top of him so they were face to face. He stroked the curve of her waist. "What's that, *mon amour*?"

"When you put the crown on my head at *la paulée*, why didn't you kiss me...you know...like you just did?"

He continued to caress her back and thighs. She straddled him and moved her hips so he slid inside her. She exhaled at the feel of him.

"I remembered Geneviève—and our talk before *la paulée*." His voice came as more of a gasp. He moved slightly inside her, and she groaned—a conversation within a conversation. "I wasn't sure...oh my God, you're killing me...where we stood and how you would like me broadcasting our relationship...in front of my team of harvesters."

"I wouldn't have minded," she said, moving slowly but implacably, enjoying every second of his torment at her restraint.

"Can I make up for it now?" Clovis convulsed under her.

"Let me think," answered Cerise, still torturing him with tiny, teasing movements.

"Please?"

"*D'accord*. If you insist."

He flipped her onto her back and loomed over her. She grabbed the back of his neck to draw him down for a kiss. "Storm's coming," she murmured against his lips.

They had fallen asleep tangled in each other's limbs, but a crack of lightning that lit up the bedroom made her jump awake. She looked immediately to Clovis, whose eyes were wide, too.

"That was clo—" he began, but before he could finish, a boom of thunder shook not only the window panes but also their bed.

They both leaped up at the same time. "I'll check on the boys," she said.

"I'll go through the house to unplug everything and make sure the windows are closed." He pulled on his boxer shorts.

Five minutes later they reconvened in the bedroom, the house and the boys amazingly still asleep and secure, and fell back into bed.

Clovis pulled her against him and curled his large body around her. His hand ran down the side of her rib cage and over her shoulder, making her shiver with pleasure. She was crazy to have thought she could ever give him up. She didn't know exactly how it had happened, but she needed him like she needed wine-making, oxygen, and strong coffee first thing in the morning. More, even.

"I always loved thunderstorms," she said. "Until I became a winemaker and realized they usually bring hail."

"I don't think this one is supposed to. I think we're safe. Anyway, almost all your grapes are in, aren't they?"

She snuggled against his chest.

Just then another lightning strike hit with a boom that shook the entire house.

Cerise whistled. "That was right on top of us."

"You know what I've always wanted to do?"

"What?"

"Make love during a thunderstorm."

Cerise could tell he was waiting for her response. "Interesting..." She tapped her fingertips on his forearm wrapped around her torso.

"How interesting?" His finger drew a circle around one of her breasts.

She reached down between them. "Let's just say you have my attention."

Their joining was as violent as the storm outside. The cacophony of the wind and thunder gave them permission to be noisy. Neither asked to take what they needed. It felt to Cerise like the lighting and thunder inhabited their bodies until the final, definitive explosion.

"I love you," she murmured to him again at the end, just as lightning lit up the bedroom like the swooping strobe of a lighthouse. Now the words were out, she couldn't see an end to them.

# chapter twenty-two

THE FINAL TWO days of Cerise's harvest went like a dream, mainly because she found herself so madly in love with her partner that the pigeons seemed to coo harmoniously, the *verjus* had never tasted so delicious, and the future had never felt so full of joy.

They'd agreed to finish up her harvest and then work on finding their middle ground after the *paulée* at Domaine du Cerisier.

After Antoine and her parents died, she could never have imagined she would feel this way, but it was as if by accepting Clovis into her heart, she also, after so long, said yes to life. She still felt hollow terror in her gut from time to time that losing him would break her, but fear was largely overshadowed by happiness.

The last vine was harvested midafternoon. Cerise was promptly festooned in vines and lifted on top of the tractor carrying the last load to the *cuverie*. It was driven by Clovis, who must have brought the crown from his *paulée* she'd left in the bathroom at Maxime's and perched it on her head, calling her queen of the harvest again, his new nickname for her. She laughed, but she believed the crown belonged there.

The harvesters barely let her leave to shower and change for the *paulée*. Clovis had to go down to Domaine de Valois to check on the beginning of his vinification.

She dressed in a pale-yellow sundress and made sure the boys were wearing clean shorts and T-shirts with their leather sandals. She warned Yves not to indulge his gluttonous eating habits again. The boys appeared to love having Clovis around, and they both struck her as more contented than she had ever seen them.

The courtyard was packed with raucous harvesters draped in grapevines and passing unlabeled wine bottles around. She was always generous with wine during the harvest but especially at the *paulée*.

Cerise and her boys' arrival was greeted with a loud cheer and a round of *le ban bourgignon*. Yves was plucked up and put on Jorgé's shoulders. He shrieked with laughter.

She scanned the courtyard for Clovis, but he was nowhere to be seen yet.

Finally, the old cowbell rang, calling them to the table. Another loud cheer rose, and everybody stampeded inside, including her sons. Cerise stayed in the dusty gravel courtyard, waiting for her love.

She was rewarded with the sight of Clovis waving at her from the far corner of the courtyard. He stole her breath but in the best possible way. He was wearing a white button-down shirt, open at the neck, and a pair of twill shorts. His face broke into a smile. He was here. All felt right with the world.

He walked toward her, hands outstretched. "You look like a dream," he said after kissing her soundly. "Now I'm going to be distracted through the entire meal, fantasizing taking that dress off you."

The buttery smell of freshly baked *gougères* floated out to the courtyard.

She just stood there, smiling at him. "I've missed you."

He kissed her again and laughed. "I left only three hours ago."

"Still."

"I've missed you, too." He drew her into his arms again. "I am so in love with you."

"Same," she said, enjoying his familiar scent and the feel of his arms around her—and that flame that always sparked between them. Home.

"You know we still have to figure out this vineyard thing," she reminded him, not for the first time. It was the only possible pitfall that remained.

"Shh," he murmured in her ear, his warm breath making her shiver. "I have complete faith that we will, but we agreed we'll do it after the harvest, *n'est-ce pas*? You deserve to celebrate tonight. You've earned it."

She nodded against him.

"What's this thing poking me?" he joked after a few moments of enjoying holding each other. "You wore my crown."

"I did," she said. "It's getting a bit dry, but—" She shrugged. "It's sentimental."

People started to call Cerise's name from inside the barn.

"I'd like to be alone with you somewhere," he sighed. "But I think you're needed."

The shouts got louder.

"Duty calls," he chuckled, turned her, and pushed her gently into the stone building.

The waning sun made the inside of the barn dark, blinding her momentarily. Clovis's hand was on the small of her back, guiding her. An anchor.

When the harvesters spotted her, they broke out into *le ban bourgigon*. There were many shout-outs to *l'amour* that made her blush, but she couldn't deny that love, even if it complicated things, should be celebrated. She was going to have to give Maxime credit after all, heavy-handed matchmaker that he was.

Just as she stood at her spot at the head of the table and gestured for everyone to sit down, Amandine burst into the barn. She clutched a bunch of papers in her hand. Her normally pale skin was flushed red. She was shaking.

"*Mon Dieu.* What has her brother done now?" said Clovis, standing at Cerise's side.

"She looks so upset," Cerise said in a low whisper. "Let's get her outside. I doubt she wants to melt down in front of all these people, and it looks as though she's not far from that."

He nodded. "I'll let the cooks know to start the service, and then I'll be right out."

She went over and took Amandine's shaking hand in hers.

"Let's step out for a moment," she said calmly and began to lead Amandine outside.

"No!" Amandine said. "Everyone needs to hear this! I will not demean myself by protecting him."

Cerise was now certain that Amandine was put in this state by her contemptible brother.

"Come," Cerise urged and guided Amandine, whose back felt rigid with fury, out to the courtyard. It took considerable force.

Clovis joined them almost immediately. He gave Cerise a small nod to let her know that the cooks understood.

Amandine glared at him. "You!" she shouted at him, her voice dripping with loathing.

*Clovis?* Amandine was making no sense, but then again she didn't seem like she was in her right mind.

He held out his hands, palms up. "I'm just here to be your friend."

"Friend?" She spat on the ground. "Never."

Cerise stared down at the spittle. She had no idea why Amandine could be angry with Clovis, but her skin prickled with foreboding. Things had been too good.

"What's happened, Amandine?" Clovis asked, his voice steady.

Amandine opened and shut her mouth a few times, then shook the papers in her hand. "This! This is what happened!"

He took them from her, but before he could even cast his

eyes down, Amandine raged, "Did you think she wouldn't see this? How *dare* you!"

He stared at her, his brows furrowed, as if desperately trying to comprehend. "I am so confused right now. Please tell me how I can help."

"You? Help?" Amandine put her hands on her hips and snorted. "And to think I thought of you as my friend!" She pointed to Cerise. "You did this to Cerise, but trust me, as a fellow female winemaker I will side with her against you."

"Against Clovis?" Cerise touched her chest, where it felt like a block of ice had formed. "Explain yourself, Amandine."

Amandine's round eyes turned on her. "You haven't seen it yet? No, of course you haven't; otherwise he wouldn't be here." She pointed at Clovis, whose tanned skin had drained of color.

"Seen what?" He stared at his friend. "This?" He waved the papers. "What is this? It just looks like a website printed out."

Amandine shook her head with patent disgust. "This," she said, speaking slowly and clearly, to brook no argument, "is the article in *Vino Veritas* by the journalist who interviewed you the other day."

"It's out already?" Cerise said. "I completely forgot about it."

"So did I," Clovis said.

"You won't forget it after you read it, Cerise." Amandine stepped over and squeezed her shoulder. "I'm sorry. Cerise should be reading it first." Amandine ripped the papers out of his hand and thrust them at her.

With encroaching dread, she took the bundle. She had no idea what she was going to discover, but given Amandine's reaction, she couldn't delude herself that it would be nothing. She stared at the printed pages and could feel the weight of Clovis's hand resting on her back as he read over her shoulder.

The title was a shock unto itself. "Clovis de Valois reasserts his rights over Domaine du Cerisier."

"What the hell?" Clovis muttered.

She scanned the article.

"'We all must acknowledge Cerise has done a brave job under difficult circumstances,' says Monsieur de Valois as he picks a stray grape off the vineyards that wine lovers will rejoice to hear will soon be under his brilliant guidance."

Now the ice filled her veins.

"'Family lines count for a lot in Burgundy,' says de Valois, 'but so does talent.' Indeed, de Valois need not be modest about his winemaking genius. This is displayed in every bottle that comes out of his Domaine de Valois. Wine lovers from around the world are united in their anticipation to see that same genius emerge from Domaine du Cerisier in the years to come."

*Clovis couldn't have...surely...*

"Although it seems incredible to many that Clovis de Valois would interest himself in lesser appellations such as the Hautes-Côtes, he explains, 'Burgundy is all about the producers. You can own a lesser vineyard, yet play it like a Stradivarius, whereas you can also own a Stradivarius and play it like a ukulele. I will play this vineyard like a Stradivarius, and I will relish the challenge.'"

He had told her she played her vines like a Stradivarius. It was his expression.

"Cerise." Clovis's voice behind her was strangled. "You have to believe me. None of this came from me. That journalist twisted everything. I said *you* were the one who played this vineyard like a Stradivarius, not me."

She felt like she was being shredded by her doubts. She hadn't had a good impression of that journalist, but this was so...awful. She kept reading, searching for proof that Clovis didn't do this.

"'We have one new exciting wine coming out of our domaine. We have called it Cerasus. It is a wine I have created in such an original manner that I've removed it from the appellation system completely to be able to produce unfiltered, pure—'"

Her hands drained of their strength, and the pages floated down to the gravel at their feet. Nobody knew of Cerasus besides her and Clovis. That one detail…it made it all real.

"Cerise," he burst out. "You can't possibly believe I said that."

She had to admire his talent. He'd made her truly believe he loved her for more than just her vineyards. All he had ever wanted was control. He'd just reached and taken credit for Cerasus. He'd never wanted her. The knowledge she'd been such easy prey elicited a powerful wave of nausea.

He appeared in front of her and grasped her hands. "I swear I have no idea where he got that from. I gave all the credit to you. I said I was going to be taking a step back. If you love me, you *have* to trust me—"

"Amandine," she said without looking at him.

Amandine was immediately at her side. "Yes."

"Can you please escort Clovis off the property?" Shock made her voice scratchy.

"Right away," Amandine said, and she tried to tug Clovis toward his car.

"I'm not going anywhere!" He stood his ground. "Hear me out. I didn't do this. I would *never* do this."

She felt frozen. All of her. Her heart, her skin, her mind. "How did the journalist know about Cerasus?" she shouted. "You're the only person I've ever shared that with. The only one."

"I know how this looks, but you know me, Cerise—" Out of the corner of her eye, she saw his hand reaching for her.

She snapped, "Don't you dare touch me."

He jerked his arm away and stepped back as if she had physically struck him. She wanted to.

"I don't know how this happened," he said, his hands out in front of him. "But I will find the answer. I love you. Can't you trust me?"

"No." She shook her head. "I did, briefly, but I'll never make that mistake again."

Amandine pulled on his arm harder. "Come on, Clovis. Haven't you hurt her enough for one night?"

"Amandine, I would never do this. You know me."

"I thought I did," she said and pulled on him again. "Come on. I'm going to follow your car home so you don't come back."

Cerise silently took the grapevine crown off her head and thrust it at Clovis. The fairy tale was over.

"I can't believe you assume I did this," he burst out in parting as he finally let Amandine lead him away. "After everything that has happened between us…"

Her last sight was of his blue eyes against a white face as he shook his head at her.

One of the cooks peeked out of the barn, and Cerise beckoned her over. "Can you tell everyone I'm ill, and let Marc and Yves know I have gone to Maxime's to lie down? They can come home and put themselves to bed when *la paulée* is finished."

The cook nodded, her eyes round. She must have seen the whole thing, or most of it anyway. The harvesters would get a story closer to the truth than any Cerise could make up. She no longer cared about anything except getting to her room before the ice that now encased her heart began to melt.

# chapter twenty-three

CERISE CLOSED THE heavy wooden door to Maxime's bedroom behind her. She opened one of the drawers in the commode and took out her laptop, which had sat unused for the entire duration of the harvest. She sat down on the bed and flipped it open.

She found the online article quickly. She read it over again, and then again and again and again. She wasn't quite sure what she was searching for. Perhaps a glimmer of hope that maybe Clovis couldn't have done this. Each read splintered her heart a bit more. It was there in bold black type. He had mentioned Cerasus to that journalist. There was no room for doubt.

Had her fear at committing to him been instinct warning her? She should never have let down her guard—not for a second. Life should have taught her that by now.

She put the laptop away and found herself at the window, hypnotized by the white linen curtains moving gently in the breeze. She attempted to reconcile the man she had shared those miraculous hours of pleasure and self-discovery with and the man who could be capable of such betrayal.

She hadn't seen even a glimmer of the pretentious, preening winemaker portrayed by the article when they were together. It's who she thought he was before she got to know him. Who was the real Clovis?

Memories began to roll through her mind, reframed in light of the article.

He had probably strayed into the cellar that night she first seduced him to spy on her work or gloat over his future holdings. Then, of course, he had been so resistant to the idea of a buyout. He always pushed that conversation off to a later date, surely hoping to have such sway of her by the time the question presented itself that she would change her mind. She knew from Maxime that Clovis hadn't lied about his wretched childhood, but now she realized what a perfect weapon it had been to use against her.

Maxime couldn't have known the truth of Clovis's duplicitous nature, or he never would have left them partners. She was sure of that. Clovis had tricked the ultimate trickster. She was out of her league.

The more her thoughts circled, the more Clovis lumping the vineyard partnership with their relationship became hideously logical. What didn't make sense was how he had made her feel and what she was supposed to do with her love for him.

A wave of nausea swept over her, and she ran to the bathroom just in time. It was as if her body was trying to rid itself of Clovis's treachery.

When she finally staggered to her bed, she curled into a ball, not bothering to get between the covers. She should be incandescent with anger. She should feel grateful she had found out before it was too late.

Instead she wept. Her happiness had been whole and shining only a few hours before. Now, once again, it was shearing off into a million pieces.

She was awoken by a loud knock on the front door.

She went to open it and saw immediately that Clovis carried a key in his hand—surely his key to Maxime's house.

Under the hall light his face was still ashen, and his eyes were such a deep indigo they were almost black. There were dark half-moons under them.

"Cerise." He grabbed her hand. "You have to listen to me. I can't—" His voice cracked. "This is a horrible error."

*More lies.* She twisted her hand out of his. "Is that the key to this house?" she demanded, struggling to keep her voice steady. "Were you going to let yourself in if I didn't answer?"

He looked at the key, as though astonished to see it in his hand. "No, I—"

"Get out."

"I won't. This is as much my house as yours. You owe me the benefit of the doubt. I won't move until you listen."

"I owe you nothing! You tried to trick me, and you got caught," she said, glaring into his beautiful, terrible face. "Now you can't accept it."

He crossed his arms in front of his chest. "You are talking like a crazy person, Cerise."

"I will never let you make a fool of me again." She pointed to the courtyard entrance opposite the front door. "If you ever felt anything for me, get out."

She could hear him swallow. "If you think so little of me that you believe that *merde* the journalist wrote, maybe you are not the person I thought you were."

"Leave. Now." Her voice came out as a fierce growl. Part of

her wanted to beg him to prove the journalist had made it up, to take her in his arms and show her how much he loved her, but that was only weakness.

He silently turned and walked back where he came from. She was not going to watch him leave. Her heart aching, she slammed the door. She slid down against it until she was crouched on the cool flagstone floor in the front hall. She held her knees.

Amandine was right. Sleeping with Clovis had been a disastrous idea.

When she heard her boys stirring, she managed to shake her head and command her legs to move. Just like after her parents and Antoine died, she would be strong for them, even before she could be strong for herself.

She willed them not to ask her any questions about the previous night. She wasn't sure she could answer without falling apart. Marc and Yves were subdued at breakfast, and because it was the weekend, Marc concocted a plan to take Yves to the woods behind the vineyards and build a fort.

As he finished his *tartine* of baguette, Yves asked, "Where's Clovis, Maman?"

Cerise saw Marc give Yves a swift kick under the table but pretended not to notice. "We won't be seeing him as much now the harvest is over," she said in a brisk voice. "He'll be busy catching up at his own domaine."

"Will you miss him?" Yves asked, even though his question earned him another kick.

"Of course not," she lied and gave each of the boys a kiss goodbye.

When the door closed behind them, however, she sagged down onto the nearest kitchen chair.

Without Clovis, everything hurt. Making the coffee. Trying to drink it. Buttering the boys' *tartines*. She missed him—or at least the man she had thought he was—with every cell of her body. Her skin yearned for his touch; her eyes yearned to see his smile; her heart needed his love…

Missing him made her furious with herself because she was grieving someone who had never existed. The article was concrete proof of that. She may have been able to hear him out if it wasn't for the mention of Cerasus.

She dug a deep gouge into the soft wood tabletop. The man she had fallen in love with was a figment of her imagination. The quicker she could accept that, the better. The Clovis she fell in love with was gone, just as surely as Antoine.

So she would grieve him, just like she had done with Antoine and her parents. At least grieving was something she knew how to do.

She went out to the courtyard to bid goodbye to her harvesters and send them off with their paychecks and bottles of wine. She pretended like nothing had happened the night before except a brief moment of illness at dinner. She was aware from people's sorrowful expressions and the somber feel of what was usually a joyous moment that everyone knew. Still, Clovis could try to take everything away from her, but he would not have her pride.

After lunch, Marc and Yves went back to their forest fort, so Cerise began to return their belongings to the harvesters' house.

During the harvest she had begun to contemplate staying in

Maxime's house. It was bigger, more comfortable, and she had loved being there with Clovis. She secretly entertained the idea that she and Clovis could live at Maxime's, together with the boys. She'd been such a fool.

The sight of the key in his hand, plus the uncomfortable knowledge that he owned half of it, had decided her in an instant. She was moving back to the harvesters' house now that it was empty again.

Legally he probably owned half of that as well, but it didn't feel that way. She had never slept with him there. She'd lived there alone with the boys before he became part of her life. She had grieved Antoine and her parents and Maxime there. Besides, as far as she knew, she possessed the only key.

She took over the last load and was locking Maxime's now-empty house when Amandine came across the courtyard.

Amandine gave her a hesitant wave as she drew closer. "I came to see how you are doing, like I promised." She looked around the property and up at the big house, where Cerise had drawn the shutters closed once again. "It's so quiet here now."

Cerise nodded. "The last harvester left before noon."

Amandine narrowed her eyes. "You look terrible."

She shrugged, overcome by exhaustion now that the indignation and panic to move had burnt themselves out. "He came by this morning."

Amandine's green eyes went wide. "Clovis?"

She gestured Amandine to a simple bench made from three massive slabs of local stone to the left of the front door. Amandine sat down.

"*Oui*." Cerise stretched out her legs in front of her to soak up the September sun. Maybe it would help the aching in every muscle and every bone. "He woke me up by pounding on the front door. He had his key out to use if I didn't answer."

Amandine sucked in her breath. "The nerve."

Cerise nodded. If there was one thing Clovis possessed, it was nerve. She thought back to how he'd said she needed to hear him out because she *owed* him. Nerve was something he had in abundance.

"What did you do?" Amandine called her back to the present.

"I told him to leave and never come back."

"Did you listen to him at all?"

Cerise was confused by the question. "No. Why would I?"

Amandine shook her head. "Of course you wouldn't. Last night he appeared at my house and swore again that he had boasted of *your* successes during the whole interview. He promised me he changed the topic to you every time the journalist wanted to talk about him."

Cerise couldn't keep her heart from squeezing with hope that this whole thing was a mix-up, but no...there was Cerasus. There was no way the journalist could have known about it unless Clovis let it slip. He had betrayed her secret. Wanting things to be different was denial.

"You listened to his lies?" Cerise demanded.

"Of course not." Amandine waved that idea away. "It's just that...I've never known him to lie to one of his friends. Ever. It's just strange, you know, when I consider it with a cooler head."

"Maybe he saves his lies for when he needs them to be believed."

Amandine cracked the knuckle of her index finger. "I've always thought, until last night, that he was incapable of dishonesty."

"You certainly expressed no doubts last night."

"No." She grimaced. "I have a terrible temper. My brother drove me to the brink yet again yesterday. I see red and then...well..."

She turned and examined Amandine's face, which was pinched into an odd expression. Was Amandine having doubts about her accusations? "I know he's lying," Cerise said, her voice hard.

"How can you be sure?"

"I had a secret wine project nobody else knew about. I told that secret to one person in the world—Clovis."

"Not even Maxime?"

"No. He wouldn't have approved, so I never asked permission. That wine was mentioned in the article."

"Oh!" Amandine snapped her fingers. "The unfiltered wine? What is it called?"

"Cerasus," she grunted.

Amandine whistled low and long. "Are you sure nobody else knew? Not even your cellar workers?"

"Nobody. I made sure of it."

She sighed. "I guess the evidence is clear then. What troubles me is that it just doesn't reconcile with the Clovis I know. I was enraged by my brother last night, and then I stumbled on that article, and—"

"Have you considered that maybe you didn't know Clovis at all? Maybe none of us did."

She didn't answer right away. "I guess that's possible."

"I can't think of any other explanation, Amandine. Believe me, I've been trying."

Amandine sighed. "You're right, of course. I should get back before my brother completely ruins our vintage." She stood up and kissed Cerise *au-revoir*, but there was doubt in her eyes her words couldn't dissemble.

When Amandine left, Cerise sat down again. She lost track of time on the bench until the boys' voices came ringing over the hill. She stood up and plastered a smile on her face to welcome them.

They were chattering of their adventures and a wild boar they were convinced they had heard grunting. Marc kept glancing at her, trying to be covert but failing. He was worried about her, she knew. She took their hands and led them into the harvesters' house. The pea gravel crunched under their feet, a melancholy sound today.

Yves glanced around the domaine, suddenly subdued. "It feels lonely here now."

"It always feels like that when the harvest is over," she answered with false cheer.

"It's not that." Yves shook his head. "It's because Clovis isn't here."

"Don't be silly," she said, her voice sharper than she intended. "How could the three of us possibly feel alone when we have each other?"

"I feel what I feel," Yves said, ignoring the dark looks coming from Marc.

Cerise gritted her teeth and glanced over her shoulder to Maxime's house. The closed shutters reminded her of the closed eyelids of a dead person. Whatever she and Clovis had, it was gone.

She felt what she felt, too, even though it would be so much easier if she didn't.

# chapter twenty-four

DAYS TRUDGED BY, each as gray and shapeless as the one before, even though the sun continued to blaze and the vinification was progressing as planned.

Cerise reasoned if she just kept putting one foot in front of the other, she would eventually be able to shake her shroud of grief. The evenings were the hardest. She would exhaust herself during the day in the vat room, breaking the caps on the pits and skins with a large pole and mixing in the juice to add color and tannins to the wine. She worked at a manic pace to quiet the lurching in her mind. In the evening, though, after she had helped the boys with their homework and tucked them into bed, she crawled into the single bed she'd bought after Antoine died and closed her eyes, only to find sleep had abandoned her yet again.

Clovis had made no further attempt to contact with her, and nighttime was when her barriers were weakest and doubts took root.

No matter how hard she tried, she couldn't reconcile the Clovis she had known in Maxime's huge bed with the man who had betrayed her. She remembered how his pupils dilated with pleasure when he was inside her, how they had whole conversations with their eyes…

Perhaps that was ruthless triumph she'd seen, not a shared sense of wonder. It was bewildering to be so mistaken in someone.

During those lonely hours she indulged in rare moments of self-pity. First her parents, then Antoine, then Maxime, and now Clovis... Of course Clovis was still alive, but his loss was somehow felt as keenly as the others. In a way, she admitted to herself, it was harder with him because he still walked the earth. If she'd only listened to her instinct—been more guarded.

About two weeks after the harvest, Luc appeared in the *cuverie* while she was busy organizing the wine being transferred from the vats to the barrels. The heady presence of carbon monoxide in the air made Cerise feel ill more than ever before–surely because it reminded her of when she and Clovis had saved Yannis and then made love in the cellar that evening. She had to take frequent trips outside to clear her lungs and head.

She was deep in thought—not about the logistics of the transfer, as she should have been, but wondering what had been Clovis's motivation when he'd helped her save Yannis. It had to be part of his larger scheme, but she couldn't figure out where it fit.

Luc's cough jerked her to the present. She whirled around, heart pounding. Some untamed part of her thought—hoped—it was Clovis. When she saw it was Luc, her body flooded with a ludicrous disappointment that enraged her.

Cerise leaned over and gave him *les bises*, not because she was feeling particularly warm toward Clovis's friend but because being rude would prove she was angry instead of indifferent.

"*Je te paie le café?*" she asked, inviting him in for coffee as an impervious person would do.

"Yes." Luc's blue eyes widened in surprise at her reception. "That would be nice."

She made him an espresso from the machine in the vat room, then made herself one. They chatted of their vinification and traded a bit of gossip about the winemaker in Gevrey who had been stripped of his appellation status and the barrel maker in Chaux who had been hauled off to rehab in Dijon.

Once they both had their espressos, she asked, "Did Clovis send you?"

Luc grimaced. "*Oui*...and no. He made me swear I wouldn't come up here and talk to you."

Cerise's heart leaped, but she pushed hope back down. "Then why are you here?"

"Clovis didn't do it. He didn't tell the journalist any of that rubbish."

"I don't want to argue this." She stiffened.

"He doesn't know how or why the journalist made that up. He's become obsessed with trying to track him down. I pity the journalist when Clovis finds him. I've never seen him this furious."

As much as she yearned to believe Luc, Cerise knew beyond a doubt that Clovis had betrayed her secret of Cerasus. That certainty was brutal, but it was also safe—a place she could retreat to in moments of grief or doubt. "There's no point, Luc. I was an idiot to be taken in, but I will not be fooled by Clovis twice. I have proof he did it. *C'*ést tout."

Luc leaned against the stone wall, staring intently at his beat-up sneakers for a while. "I haven't experienced what you and Clovis seemed to have during the harvest," he said at last. "But when I saw you together...well, it gave me hope I could find that for myself in the future."

"With Stella?"

He looked up. "You remembered?"

"It seems to be my curse to remember everything." She grimaced. Indeed, she remembered the feel of Clovis's lips making a slow path down her spine, the light pressure of his fingertips against her scalp, lifting her hair, the unbearable want just before he entered her...

She shook herself. It *was* a curse.

"Yes." He nodded. "With Stella."

"What's she like?" Cerise seized the opportunity to divert Luc. Talking about Clovis was like pressing on a bruise.

Luc smiled in a way that lit up his entire face. "She's the most beautiful woman I've ever encountered. I've been in love with her since I met her when I was seven years old. She's like…I don't know…she's blinding like the sun. Do you want to see a picture?"

"Of course." She indulged him even though she was overcome with bitterness to think of others experiencing love when it was denied to her.

He pulled his phone out of his back pocket and tapped it a few times, and then, still staring at his screen, a goofy look spread over his face. He passed the phone to her.

She took it, fully expecting to be bowled over by Luc's soul mate. She wasn't.

The Instagram feed was filled with professional-looking photos of a tall blonde girl with bright-blue eyes. In each photo—and she was front and center in every single one, which indicated to Cerise that her main interest was herself—she was posed in a way that perfectly set off a variety of outfits.

"So?" Luc prompted.

She didn't know what to say. This Stella looked to her like a cipher with no discernable personality. Each post was bogged down by a sort of conformity, an opaqueness that hid any actual character. Or maybe there was simply no personality to hide, Cerise considered.

It was odd; Luc was such a warm person. She wouldn't have pegged him as the type of man who fell for physical beauty alone. On the other hand, she was suffering right now precisely because she couldn't judge people's true character, so…

"She's very attractive," she said. Something prevented her from using *beautiful*. Maxime had always said for a person to be beautiful, man or woman, there had to be a spark of something they had endured, something they had transcended. Stella didn't have that.

"She's stunning," Luc agreed. "I'm embarrassed to admit it, but her Instagram feed is the first thing I check every morning."

"She must spend a lot of time on it," she observed, wondering if he would pick up on the reserve in her voice.

"I don't think so," he said. At that moment, she realized just how naive he was. "Stella's so naturally gorgeous, I think she could snap a photo of herself getting out of bed, and she would look incredible. Look! She did!"

He passed the phone back to Cerise. He had enlarged a close-up of Stella smiling in bed with a cappuccino. She wore skillfully applied "natural"-looking makeup, and her hair was far too perfectly messy to be natural. Also, there was no way on earth she could have snapped the photo, which was taken straight on at a distance, of herself. It was incredible that Luc had never asked himself who was in the bedroom taking shots of her.

"Who was that red-haired woman in one or two of the photos?" Cerise asked. "She didn't look thrilled to be in front of the camera." She could relate to that reserve.

Luc smiled warmly, quite different from his smile when he spoke of Stella. "Oh, that's Sadie. She's Stella's younger sister. Remember I told you about her? The anthropologist."

Cerise nodded. "I respect her scorn for social media. She's got incredible hair and intelligent eyes."

His smile got wider. "You're right about her being smart. Her specialty is Gallo-Roman ruins, so she often does a bit of research while she's here. She'll be coming with Stella." He sighed. "Poor Sadie. It can't be easy being Stella's sister."

"I don't know." She pursed her lips. "There's something about her. She looks interesting."

He nodded. "She's also the funniest person I've ever met.

Nobody can make me laugh like her. It's just when Stella is in the same room, it blinds you to anybody else. Like I said during the harvest, Sadie and I are old friends. She's the best."

"Old friends are a good thing to hold on to." Cerise set down her empty espresso cup. "I didn't, and I regret it now. By the way, I won't hold it against you that you are siding with Clovis."

Luc set his cup down, too. "Even though he's enraged, he wouldn't want anyone to take sides. Why don't you have any old friends?"

She shook her head. "I did when Antoine was alive—our school friends, mainly. They drifted away after his death. Sometimes I wonder if they thought tragedy was contagious and I was infected. To be fair, I had so much to do between the vineyards, our boys, and my grief, I guess I wasn't very social either."

"That's sad."

She merely shrugged.

"I hope you consider me a friend, even if I'm a new one," he said.

She began to walk him back outside. "That is kind of you, Luc." Even though he was naive and seemed to live in a world of fairy tales, his intentions seemed pure. But she was a realist—there was no way he could remain friends with Clovis and with her.

"I have to leave you here, I'm afraid. I must get to back to working on that transfer."

He nodded, a thatch of blond hair falling over his left eye. "I know this probably won't make a difference, but I've never seen Clovis in such a state as he is right now."

She made a noncommittal sound. "That's a shame, but he'll get over it." She was sure there were replacements for her already lining up.

Luc grimaced. "I'm not so sure."

Cerise decided she'd had enough moping around at her domaine. She was determined to get back to her weekly trips to the Saturday morning market in Beaune.

The boys always loved the outing because Yves knew she would pay for a few rides on the carousel on the Place Carnot. Marc had declared six months before that he was too young for such childish antics. The boys would meet up with many of their friends from school in Beaune and play happily on the *place* while Cerise chose her provisions in peace.

She dreaded the possibility of bumping into Clovis, and she couldn't shake the feeling of exhaustion and illness from her body, but she refused to avoid going into Beaune any longer. Her defiance unfortunately didn't eliminate the worries that circled her mind. Would he see her but ignore her? Even though she didn't want to talk to him, she thought her heart might shatter.

She missed him beyond anything she had thought possible. How blissful it would be to sink into his embrace and forget about the article…except she couldn't forget his betrayal. The idea that she might see him with another woman made the nausea she'd been struggling with rise in her throat.

Still, she had to go. It was a beautiful fall day, and it was part of her routine with the boys. Keeping things on an even keel for them overruled everything else. Besides, they had to eat, and the market was hands-down Cerise's best source of local, seasonal food. Even if she'd completely lost her appetite, her boys certainly hadn't.

She parked her Citroen like she always did in the parking lot at the boys' school, skirted the Porte Saint Nicolas—the little mini Arche de Triomphe—and led the boys down the rue de Lorraine with a market basket on her arm.

Before they arrived at the Place de la Halle, Cerise could smell the scent of farm bread and smelly cheese mixed with the syrupy overlay of squashed plums and figs. Usually it made her stomach rumble, but today it just made it lurch.

She gave Yves four green plastic merry-go-round tickets from her bag, and the boys dashed off to do their socializing in the Place Carnot. She scanned the crowd and sighed—in relief or consternation, she wasn't entirely sure. No Clovis.

She began her typical tour at Yann's for organic vegetables, then went into the market hall for cheese and a *poulet de* Bresse.

She was waiting in line for spit-roasted chicken from Rotisserie 21, relieved to be almost finished. For once, she didn't want to linger at the market; she wanted to just collect Marc and Yves and get home.

It was always busy at the rotisserie because it sold the best roasted chickens and the vendor always threw in extra roasted potatoes. For her boys, extra potatoes would be a sign that life had returned to normal, and they didn't need to worry about her. There were ten people or so ahead of her, and of course, because this was the Saturday market and the vendor liked nothing better than to chat with his regulars, the buzz of chatter filled the air. Nobody was rushed—nobody except Cerise.

She was chewing on her lower lip when she caught sight of the back of Clovis's head in line in front of her. She picked up her basket, which she had set on the ground beside her caddy, but he turned, and their eyes met. His eyes filled with a flash of joy, then widened with something else entirely. She couldn't escape now—that would make her look ridiculous as well as scared of a confrontation. She was a lot of things, but she was not the one at fault.

He left his place in line and came over to her. "Cerise? I can't believe this."

Dammit. As tall and broad and blue-eyed as ever. Luc hadn't been wrong—Clovis's cheekbones jutted out from his face, and there were dark circles under his eyes. Still, she wanted to sink into his familiar scent of grapes and crushed leaves. He smelled like *hers*…except he wasn't…not anymore. In a way, he never had been.

"Clovis" was all she seemed able to say.

"I've been searching high and low for that journalist." His words came out with a suppressed enmity that she had never heard from him before. "I finally found out he either quit or was fired from the wine magazine—there are conflicting stories—and he has been sent by *France Info* to the Middle East. He is the only one who can prove I haven't been lying to you. I will find him, but in the meantime, I can't believe you are willing to just throw away—"

A perfumed wall of indignation inserted herself between Cerise and Clovis. Geneviève. Of course.

Cerise braced herself for her aunt's criticisms that she hadn't locked in Clovis when she'd had the chance. But Geneviève's first words were, shockingly, not for Cerise.

"How dare you!" Geneviève raged at Clovis. "How dare you betray my niece in such a heartless manner! Don't think I didn't read that article. Everyone has, and I cannot explain to you the depth of your wickedness for discrediting all Cerise's hard work and talent."

"*Tante*," Cerise tried to interrupt weakly. She didn't like her aunt fighting her battles any more than she enjoyed Clovis doing it.

Clovis just stood there, horror in his eyes. "But—" he began.

"You're a horrible man, and my niece should not have to spend one more second in your vile company." The lacquered blonde hurricane didn't let him finish. Geneviève put her arm protectively around Cerise's shoulders and turned her away. "Come, *ma chérie*. Let's have a glass of something with sustenance."

She steered Cerise away from the rotisserie lineup. Cerise had never realized that her perfectly groomed aunt possessed such physical strength. Genieviève's cloud of Chanel N°5 blessedly replaced the haunting familiarity of Clovis's nearness. She tutted at Cerise. "You poor thing, just trying to do your *marché* and to be confronted with *him*. In public, no less. How dare he!"

Before she knew what had happened, Geneviève had settled her in a leather booth in the Brasserie La Concorde on the Place Carnot. Geneviève was greeted by a wave from a man behind the bar. She was a regular here.

They had checked on the boys on their way through La Place Carnot, who were more than happy to stay on the place, kicking a ball around with their school friends.

"What will you drink?" Genèvieve asked her. "Never mind. I'll order for both of us." Even though most people were still enjoying espressos at this time in the morning, she beckoned the garçon with a lifted finger and ordered two large glasses of Gevrey-Chambertin. "Nothing like Gevrey for heartache." Geneviève patted her hand once the garçon left. "It's a wine that settles the soul."

She was still reeling that her aunt had defended her and not Clovis. She couldn't make sense of it.

"You do not look at all well." Genèvieve surveyed her critically. "Much too thin and pale. Clovis did, too, come to think of it, but I feel no sympathy for him. Have you been eating?"

She shrugged. "I haven't had much of an appetite."

"Even so, you must eat, Cerise. I would have come up to see you earlier, but your uncle whisked me off right after the harvest to a ghastly wine expo in Bordeaux. It also took a few days for the news to filter to me."

"Well…*merci* for standing up for me back there."

"How could you think I would do anything different? I consider you like my own daughter, and I am a lioness—a lioness, I tell you!—about the people I care about. I thought maybe Clovis was the answer to what was missing in your life, but I was mistaken. I always admit my mistakes, *ma chérie*."

"So, you read the article?" They both nodded thanks to the waiter who brought them glasses of wine and a small plate of cubed *comté* cheese.

"Yes. When your uncle showed it to me, I was paralyzed on the spot. Paralyzed—I'm not exaggerating! Clovis tricked us all. I simply could not believe he downplayed all your success and had the gall to declare he was taking back the property. You are fifty-fifty partners, after all."

Cerise hadn't forgotten that fact. She couldn't get Clovis completely out of her life because they would have to settle the partnership one way or another. Amandine's warnings of the danger of mixing love and business had been uncannily astute.

"You didn't give him control, did you?" Geneviève asked.

"Of course not. He managed to deceive me, but I gave up nothing." Except her heart.

Geneviève sighed in relief and sat heavily back in her booth. "Thank God for that. But…what are you going to do? How are you going to get rid of him once and for all?"

Cerise shook her head. She had no idea. Sometimes she wondered if she hadn't found a solution yet because there was a part of her that still, even after everything he'd done, wanted him back. He was so angry and frustrated; was that the reaction of a guilty man? But such reasoning was foolish. She couldn't indulge it, even after seeing the haunted look in his eyes. She reminded herself of Cerasus. She couldn't afford to be naive, not ever again.

She sipped on the wine. Its depth, blackcurrant notes, and strong structure did rub down some of the sharp edges of her anguish. "It's a question of two things. First, I need to find the money to buy him out, and second—and perhaps a much more difficult problem—he has to let me do it."

Geneviève waved her hand. "Don't worry about the money. Your uncle and I want to help with that. We've already discussed it, as a matter of fact."

Cerise choked on her wine. "What?" she spluttered.

"Yes. You are our only heir, you know. Who else are we going to leave everything to? Whether we pass some of it on to you before or after we are dead in the form of an early inheritance... does it really matter?"

"But no! You can't do that. I had no idea."

"Of course you didn't. We couldn't let you know before you had the opportunity to prove yourself, which you have done beautifully, my dear."

"But I can't accept!" Cerise said. "I haven't been much of a niece for you. Not the kind of niece you probably wanted, in any case. Surely—"

Geneviève placed her hand over Cerise's. "My dear. We understood. You had more than enough on your plate. Besides, I know it's partially my fault that we...well, we don't always see eye to eye on things. We both have strong personalities. That's a family trait."

She felt a warmth grow in her chest and spread down her arms. Family. How she had missed it. She wasn't at all keen on taking Geneviève's money—depending on anybody was never a good thing—but maybe Geneviève's presence in her life could make her feel less alone. Her heart ached a bit less. She didn't know if it was the wine or her aunt's loyalty.

# chapter twenty-five

**B**Y THE MIDDLE of October when the vineyard leaves burst into crimson, yellow, and orange, Cerise was convinced her heartbreak was killing her, despite momentarily perking up every time she talked to Geneviève, which was quite often these days. Time wasn't healing, as it had done with Antoine and her parents. With each day that passed she felt worse.

She'd been beyond tired ever since the night of her *paulée*. Heartbreak could explain that, of course, but she was baffled by her constant nausea. Maybe she had caught a virus she just couldn't shake, or maybe she was truly ill. The idea of pregnancy had flitted across her mind but she had never felt sick with her boys, not even for a second.

She tried to put on a cheerful face for Marc and Yves, but that act was the most tiring thing of all. Clovis's betrayal had not only blasted her heart and soul but also shattered her body. Worse, she had no idea how to put herself back together again. She was starting to fear that perhaps it wasn't possible.

She couldn't let anything happen to herself. Her boys needed their mother. It was because of Marc and Yves that she finally dragged herself to the family doctor. He would either tell her she was dying or could help her. Both seemed preferable to her current state of wretchedness.

Docteur Beaumont welcomed her with a warm handshake and the dignified, formal kindness that had put her at ease since she was a child. She lowered herself in the leather chair across from his desk and tried to explain how she'd been feeling, her stomach turning at the whiff of cigars that always lingered in Docteur Beaumont's office. He was of the "do as I say, not as I do" school of medical thought.

He straightened his tie. He wore a suit to the office every day, even though he ran what would definitely be called a country practice. As far as Cerise could tell it looked like the same suit he had been wearing since she was a little girl. There was something reassuring in that—a reminder of a time when she didn't have to look after everything herself, when there were people who looked after her, and not because they were trying to steal her vineyards.

Docteur Beaumont steepled his fingers on his desk. "Emotionally, how have you been feeling? Has there been any crisis I should be aware of?"

She hung her head and muttered about an affair gone wrong.

"I might have heard something about that. When exactly did this happen, this affair?"

"During the harvest."

"Is there a possibility you might be pregnant?"

"*Non.* I never felt sick with the boys, remember?"

He nodded. "Oh yes, that's right. Still, every pregnancy is different, and if it was a girl that could also explain the nausea." His gentle eyes searched hers. "Maybe we should have you do the quick test, just to be sure."

Wait…had she had her period since the harvest? She honestly couldn't remember. She barely kept track of it at the most uneventful times.

"I suppose it could be the slimmest of slim possibilities." Her voice emerged quieter than a whisper.

Docteur Beaumont wordlessly passed her a urine stick and nodded toward the bathroom door.

A few minutes later she returned it to the doctor without looking at it. She knew from the boys that stick tests required waiting for a few minutes to get a reliable answer. Her nerves simply couldn't take it. The seconds ticked by, tortuous.

She couldn't be pregnant. Fate couldn't be *that* determined to complicate her life so completely. But then…her hand stole across her flat abdomen. No baby could ever destroy her life.

Docteur Beaumont finally flipped the stick over and raised his eyes to meet hers. "*Félicitations?*" Congratulations? The word was a question.

"I'm pregnant?" Cerise demanded, her hand pressing protectively over her belly button. She marveled how she had never entertained that possibility for more than a few seconds.

"Yes." Docteur Beaumont's eyes searched hers. "We'll do a blood test too of course but these sticks are reliable. Am I correct in thinking this is not entirely welcome? If that is the case, we can discuss—"

"*Non!*" The word exploded out of her mouth. It came from some visceral depths within her that she hadn't been conscious of until that second. "There is no need to discuss 'options.'"

A minute or two of silence passed between them.

"I know this is an impossible question," Docteur Beaumont said at last. "But how are you feeling? Emotionally, I mean."

"Confused…but I'll figure it out." She rubbed her stomach. "We'll figure it out."

He nodded briskly. "All right then, my dear. In that case, I'll be here to support you every step of the way."

"*Merci.*" She sat, trying to digest this new reality, as he wrote out requisitions for bloodwork and an ultrasound and a referral to a new obstetrician, seeing as her old one had retired, as well as a recommendation for prenatal vitamins.

After passing her the wad of paperwork, he reached across the expanse of his desk and grasped her hands. He squeezed them, a gesture so paternal and absent from Cerise's life now Maxime was gone that she felt the sting of tears in her eyes. "It's important you rest, Cerise, particularly after the emotional turmoil of the past months."

"How much do you know about that?" She felt the warmth of a blush stealing up her throat.

"*Ah, ma petite* Cerise," he sighed. "This is a small community, and I have known you forever. I know the broad outlines of what happened. I know you're no longer with the father of your baby. Clovis de Valois is indeed the father?"

"Yes."

"Will you tell him?"

She hadn't considered this. What a disaster. They co-owned vineyards and a house, and now they were going to be parents. And she had thought it was going to be difficult to excise him from her heart and life when only vineyards were involved...

Their disastrous situation just became impossible. She needed to figure out a plan to protect herself and her baby before telling him anything. "Not right away."

She saw hesitation in the doctor's eyes.

"I will tell him," she said. "I just need to figure some things out first."

He nodded and let go of her hands. "I'm estimating you're about six weeks along. Does that sound right?"

She nodded slowly.

The exhilaration and completeness of her and Clovis during the harvest rushed back. Somehow, it made complete sense that they had made a baby.

Again, there was no understanding how the man who had

gazed at her with such a glow in his eyes and moved his hands over her body with such infallible instinct could be the same man who had betrayed her so utterly. Even after weeks of pummeling her brain, it was like a complex algebraic equation she couldn't solve. Each time she tried, her heart throbbed with pain and confusion.

Maybe what Luc and Amandine had told her about Clovis not betraying her to the journalist was right. Maybe the journalist had fabricated the entire thing. But…it always came back to Cerasus. The mention of Cerasus was Clovis's indictment. She would be an idiot to trust him and his protests of innocence. Even though it was torture, it was far safer to be a realist.

Cerise held the secret of her pregnancy close in the days that followed. Only she knew, besides of course Docteur Beaumont and her new obstetrician in Beaune.

The vines blazed vivid orange, red, and yellow—a last blast of glory before another year of hibernation. The nausea continued, but she felt revived to know its cause was a new life growing inside her. She had no idea how she was going to cope with a newborn and the vineyards, let alone vineyards she co-owned with the baby's estranged father, but somehow all of those problems took a back seat to the fact of the baby.

In a twisted piece of mental gymnastics, her brain settled that she was having a baby with the person she had believed Clovis to be at the moment of conception. Her love. The man who had brought her back to life. That man had vanished just as surely as if he had died, and the person who looked like him was someone else entirely. Logically, it made no sense. That didn't matter. In her heart it did.

As it had with her boys, her love for her baby grew every day. This time around, so did her fatigue, whereas in her previous pregnancies she'd been bursting with superhuman energy.

Now that Cerise had transferred her wine to barrels, which were now aging in the cellar, she indulged in cat naps after her post-lunch coffee at the base of the cherry tree. She felt like she could never get enough sleep.

She fretted over how she was going to do all the work on her own, tired as she was, but the October sun warming her face soothed those worries for the moment. Calmed by the mineral scent of limestone in the dirt she sat on, she curled up with a hand on her stomach and rested her head against the tree trunk.

Every day she considered phoning or going down to Domaine de Valois to tell Clovis about the baby, but every day she decided she wasn't ready yet. The truth of the matter was she was scared. She knew it was wrong of her, but it was the only way she knew to protect herself and her unborn child.

Just then, a branch from the tree above fell on her head—she took it as a sign the *cerisier* didn't approve of her cowardice. Something deep in her gut agreed.

# chapter twenty-six

BY THE BEGINNING of November, Cerise was confronted with the reality that she needed help. She couldn't prune back her increasingly bare vineyards and remove the old canes alone.

For the baby's sake, she called Jorgé and asked him to come and help her. She had talked to him a few times since the end of the harvest, but even though he always asked how she was doing, she remained vague and turned the conversation to the vineyards.

"I'll bring Fiona, of course," he said.

"Are you two a package deal now?" Cerise asked. She knew Fiona hadn't returned to Ireland, and she was touched that unlike her and Clovis, their lightning-bolt romance had lasted.

"I adore her," Jorgé answered in that frank way of his she envied. "We are definitely a package deal."

The next morning, Jorgé came striding into the cellar as Cerise was barrel sampling some wine, spitting it out systematically in her trusty *crachoir*.

"Jorgé!" Her eyes lit up as she saw his familiar, reliable face in the dim light. He grinned, and they gave each other enthusiastic *bises*. "It's so good to see you." Tears pricked her eyes.

"Not just me!" he said.

Cerise glanced to the stairs at the far end of the cellar, and there was Fiona, walking briskly toward them. "I had to make sure the car was locked," she said. "Jorgé can be forgetful about such things," she said in her much-improved Irish-flavored French.

"Fiona!" Cerise gave her the *bises*.

Fiona placed a hand on her forearm, a surprisingly maternal gesture from a young woman. "Just to set things straight. I'm not here to be paid. I'm simply here as a friend, to help you in any way I can. We know what happened with Clovis, of course."

Her hands flew to her cheeks. "Everyone does, don't they?"

"You know how it works," Jorgé said. "It will be replaced by some other gossip in a few months, but we've been worried about you. I know how private you are, so we didn't want to keep checking on you, but maybe we should have…"

"Merci." She blinked back tears at their loyalty. "It hasn't been easy."

"I can only imagine." Fiona gave Cerise's arm a squeeze, which made her want to cry even more.

She shook her head. "I can't ask you to work for free, Fiona."

"You're not asking me," Fiona said. "I'm telling you."

Cerise glanced at Jorgé, who was smiling proudly at Fiona. "Fiona gets things done," he said. "I've never seen anything like it."

Cerise smiled at the love in his eyes.

He shook his head. "I still have a hard time believing it of Clovis…everything in that article. It was just so unlike him. I would never have thought he was capable of saying such stuff."

"Me neither," said Cerise. "He didn't deceive only me; he deceived all of us."

"Better to find out sooner than later," Fiona said, deciding the matter.

"And the two of you?" she asked, but just looking at the shared glow between them, she already knew.

"We are so in love," Jorgé gushed, his eyes shining as he

took in Fiona in all her fair-freckled glory. "I never thought it was possible."

She remembered feeling the same way. She thought of Clovis's childhood and her year of loss. "Lucky you—to be able to love with free hearts. Neither of you is burdened with baggage."

"Are you mad?" Fiona demanded. "No roadblocks? I grew up in a tiny Irish Catholic village. My younger brother committed suicide because my crazy-religious family could not accept the fact he was gay. How do you think my parents feel about me being with Jorgé?"

She didn't know how to answer, shocked by the reproach behind Fiona's words.

"I'll tell you how they feel," Fiona continued. "They have cut me off and told me I will be going to hell. Last I heard I'm dead to them."

"I'm so sorry…I didn't know."

"They demand I return to Ireland," she said. "And marry a nice Irish village boy and never move away and go to church every Sunday."

Jorgé wrapped Fiona in a tight embrace. "I've begged her to go back to them and forget me. I would rather lose her than cause her pain like this."

"There is no question of that." Fiona kissed him fiercely. "I know how I feel about Jorgé, and I know what kind of man he is. I'll not be a coward. Besides, what's the value in a love you don't have to fight for?"

She hadn't heard from Clovis since that day at the market. Perhaps he had given up. She could hardly blame him if he had. She wondered for the umpteenth time if maybe she should have fought harder to get to the bottom of his innocence or guilt. After a few seconds of reflection, she concluded that she simply didn't possess the blind faith in Clovis, or love, that such a fight would require. Life had taken that away from her a long time ago.

Within three days, Jorgé and Fiona became de facto members of her family. They worked tirelessly all day so Cerise could rest and do the important work in the cellar. Jorgé had established a schedule and routine in the vineyards, accomplishing twice the work of a normal person in half the time. Fiona usually helped him, and Cerise had begun to teach Fiona how to cook.

They ate lunch together every day, and often dinner. The boys begged to have them stay for meals in the evening. Jorgé and Fiona brought a sense of festivity and hilarity to the table. Cerise felt both comforted and tortured by their love and commitment to each other. She could have had that, if only… Maybe she still could, but… Her mind would spin off into all the doubts. Now, with the baby, these multiplied tenfold.

The days passed, and she still couldn't find the courage to tell Clovis he was going to be a father for the second time.

Fiona was so impressed with her simple French recipes— quiches, *coq au vin* that could be left to simmer all day while they worked the vineyards, *boeuf bourgignon*—that Cerise offered to teach her. She hadn't expected much of Fiona's aptitude. As a French woman she had a fundamental lack of faith in an Irish person's ability to cook, even one as competent as Fiona.

Fiona shocked her with her quick brain and nimble hands. She was able to repeat a recipe to perfection, even adding a few flourishes of her own.

About ten days after their fortuitous arrival, Jorgé was out pruning while Cerise was instructing Fiona on the delicate art of making chocolate mousse. Fiona had been tasked with the tricky business of separating egg yolks from the whites and then whipping the whites to the perfect stiffness. Cerise broke up pieces of a chocolate bar into a glass bowl to melt with butter.

"Do you still think of Clovis?" Fiona asked as she cracked her first egg, then carefully, as Cerise had taught her, kept the yolk in the half eggshell while letting the white drain into the bowl.

She thought of lying, but there was something about Fiona's practicality that made her tell the truth. "All the time."

"That doesn't surprise me," Fiona said, admiring the perfect yellow yolk, which she plopped, intact, into another glass bowl. "You two had something special."

"We did," she said and felt tears pricking her eyes yet again. She cried so easily these days. Damn pregnancy hormones.

"Not to mention you're carrying his child."

Her hand flew to her stomach, and her body went rigid with shock. "You can tell?" It was true; she'd had to leave the top button of her jeans open the last few days. Her heart pounded at the thought that the miraculous, private time of being able to keep it a secret had already passed.

Fiona smiled at her as she cracked a second egg. "I can. My ma's a midwife, so I know the signs. I doubt anyone else can tell yet, but they will eventually, you know."

She didn't like to think about that, but she would have to. "Wait, does Jorgé know?"

Fiona chuckled. "Are you joking? Men are clueless about this sort of thing. He thinks it's just the heartbreak that's made you so tired."

"You haven't told him?"

She clicked her tongue. "I would never do that. It's not my secret to tell."

Cerise's heart swelled up. "Thank you, Fiona. Truly. I'm still reeling myself, so the idea of starting to tell other people, even a dear friend like Jorgé…"

Fiona nodded. She paused her egg cracking and leaned on

the counter so she could get a better look at Cerise's face. "Have you told Clovis?"

Her cheeks flushed with... What? Guilt, she realized. "No."

"Why?" The question was not condemning, merely curious.

It took a good minute to find the words. "I can't even describe what I felt when I read that article. The depth of his betrayal. I felt like a fool. I felt like he had cut my beating heart from my chest. The worst thing, though, was despite all that, I still love him."

Fiona nodded, her pale eyes full of compassion.

"I wanted more than anything to believe the article was a mistake, like Clovis swore it was, but I can't trust him anymore. I hate myself for wanting to be a naive idiot so I can be with him again. If I trust him when he doesn't deserve it, I could lose everything. My vineyards, my livelihood, myself... I couldn't bear the idea of losing this child to him."

"Could the article be a mistake?" Fiona asked.

She shook her head. "I have proof he said those things to that journalist. Proof I would love more than anything not to have."

Fiona winced. "I know the situation with the inheritance is complicated, and I know you've suffered terrible losses in your life, but I don't think you realize the power you have."

"What do you mean?"

"Well, I didn't read the stupid article, so I don't know the details, but although you may not have the money he does, you legally own fifty percent of these vineyards and Maxime's house. You are pregnant with Clovis's child, and the most important thing—"

"What?"

Fiona fixed her with those translucent eyes. "He's desperately in love with you."

"Not anymore," Cerise said, her voice cracking.

"I would wager now more than ever," Fiona corrected her.

"His is the kind of love that just grows with time instead of diminishing." She sighed and turned back to her work. "I can just tell. I have no idea what happened with the journalist, but stop thinking you are the only one with everything to lose, because it's not true."

She stood motionless against the counter for a long time, her mind rearranging in a new formation with Fiona's words. "I need to be brave," Cerise burst out. "I need to tell him about the baby."

Fiona nodded, not breaking pace with her work. "Far be it from me to tell anyone what to do, but yes, you do."

# chapter twenty-seven

$\int$HE HEARD JORGÉ bang through the door again to come home for lunch. She was glad she had arranged for the boys to eat at the *cantine* at school that day. Now that she had decided, she couldn't wait another second. She had to go down and tell Clovis face to face. She met Jorgé in the front hall "I have to go out," she said. She pulled a heavy knit cardigan of Maxime's down from the coatrack. There were barely any leaves left in the vineyards, and the November cold had set in for real.

A knock on the door made both of them jump. Usually no one came by at this time of day. Geneviève? That idea now made her happy instead of annoyed. Clovis? She wondered if she had somehow summoned him with her thoughts. The skin on the nape of her neck prickled.

"Who would that be?" Jorgé frowned at Cerise.

"No idea." Cerise gestured with her chin for Jorgé to open it.

Amandine and Luc stood outside, rubbing their hands and stamping their feet with the cold. "Bonjour." Cerise gave them both the *bises*. "I was just leaving."

They stepped in the hall. "Can you just wait a second?" Luc asked. "We have an urgent question for you."

Cerise wrapped a scarf around her neck. "Okay, but quick."

Amandine studied Cerise's face closely. "Do you know where Clovis is?"

She froze. "He's not at home? That's where I was going."

"Why?" Luc demanded. "Have you heard from him? Did he ask you to meet?"

Cerise shook her head, dumbfounded.

"Even Jean doesn't know where he is," Amandine said. "He's disappeared. There has been no sign of him for two weeks."

They all stood there in silence for a few moments.

*"Café?"* Jorgé gestured the kitchen with his thumb.

"Or maybe something stronger," Amandine muttered as they filed in there.

They collapsed around the table, and Jorgé and Fiona supplied them with glasses of robust Hautes-Côtes de Beaune Pinot. Cerise also got a glass of water to sip on instead of the wine.

"So *nobody* has seen him? Cerise demanded.

"No." Luc's usually candid blue eyes were troubled. "You were our last hope, to be honest."

"He didn't even tell Jean?"

Amandine raked her blonde bangs out of her eyes. "No. Jean is worried, which makes us even more concerned. It is completely out of character for Clovis. Nobody has heard anything. How did things... How was your last conversation?"

She thought back to that morning at the market.

"We bumped into each other at the market a few weeks ago. We began to argue about the article. He was angry with me for not trusting him. Before we could get into it, my aunt Geneviève came and told Clovis off, then swept me away to a brasserie."

Neither of his friends bothered to suppress the censure in their eyes.

"You were the one who told me to stand strong against him," she reminded Amandine.

Luc turned to his friend. "What?"

Amandine's face turned red. "I was so upset with my brother and father that day, and then I stumbled on the article. I couldn't do what I really wanted to my own family, but Clovis... I was in a rage, and you know what I'm like when I'm in a rage." Her eyes shifted to Cerise. "I thought he'd betrayed you, and he was fair game."

Cerise drew in a sharp breath. "You mean you've changed your mind? Even with what I told you about Cerasus?"

Amandine raked her fingers through her bob. "I regretted it the next morning when my anger had passed. I still couldn't make sense of the article, of course, but I remembered who Clovis really is, and I knew in my gut he didn't say those things. I admit that so much of this is my fault. I'm so sorry. Right now, though, I'm terrified. Clovis was in such a state before he left...I barely recognized him."

Luc nodded. "He's been completely unlike himself ever since... I don't know what he is capable of."

Jorgé, in the meantime, must have been watching Cerise. "You look pale, Cerise. Do you need to lie down?"

Her head spun, and her stomach was threatening to send her breakfast on a return trip. "I think I may have caught a stomach thing from the boys. I'll go and rest for a bit and see if it passes. If I hear anything, I'll let you both know immediately. Can you do the same? It's important I talk to him. Extremely important."

Fiona cast her a loaded look.

They nodded and began bundling up for the cold outside. Cerise walked them out, while Jorgé and Fiona started to set the table for lunch. Usually her nausea improved when she got some fresh air, but not today.

The air in the courtyard was opaque with November fog. She wrapped her wool cardigan tightly around her torso. She couldn't remember ever feeling this cold.

"Who's that?" Amandine said.

She peered into the fog. Indeed, a man was walking toward them, dressed in a dark suit. She couldn't seem to get air into her lungs. He was carrying a large envelope. Men in dark suits were always bad news. Always. She couldn't even manage to say *bonjour* when he drew up to them.

He, too, dispensed with niceties. "I'm looking for Cerise Desloires."

"That's me." Her voice was tight.

"This is for you." The man thrust the envelope into her hand.

"What is it?"

"I'm a notary in Dijon. I was instructed by my client Clovis de Valois to draw up these papers three weeks ago."

"What papers?" she demanded.

"They essentially gift you his share of the vineyards and the house on this domaine. He has relinquished his claim to your partnership. In the case of your demise before your ratification of this agreement, his former shares in the property would pass to your sons."

"What?" A roar of panic filled her head. "Why? Where is he?"

The notary shrugged. "I'm merely a notary. He didn't inform me as to his reasons, nor would I expect him to."

"But—but why would he give me his shares?" she demanded.

He shrugged again, his face completely unexpressive. "That is not for me to answer." He spoke like a robot.

"But—"

"Take time to review the paperwork. It doesn't require your signature. The documents you need to show whole ownership are included. My professional advice is to take them to your own notary to consolidate your holdings onto one title, but that is the extent of what I can advise you."

"But the taxes," Luc said. "The inheritance taxes. Those could bankrupt Cerise."

The notary held up his hands. "It was negligent of me not to mention they have been paid in advance by Monsieur de Valois as well."

Cerise stared at the envelope, feeling bereft instead of relieved, as she would have expected. "But why...what motivated him to do this do this?"

"Madame Desloires, the logical conclusion can only be that Monsieur de Valois wished to dissolve your partnership."

With that, the notary turned, strode off, and was quickly shrouded in the mist.

Holding the envelope tightly to her chest, she spun to Luc and Amandine. "What does this mean? You must know."

Again, they exchanged grim glances.

Luc placed his hand on her shoulder. "It can mean only one thing. Clovis has finally given up."

A week went by—impossible, but it did. Time was implacable that way. Jorgé and Fiona tried to lift Cerise out of her ruminations, but they failed.

She now had the thing she'd wanted most—her independence as a winemaker—and she'd never felt more destitute. She haunted her vines, shivering in the damp fog, trying to take in that all of this was hers now. She would always finish at the cherry tree, leaning her forehead against its trunk, trying to soak up its wisdom.

There was still no sign of him, and each day that ticked by without his appearance fertilized everyone's fears. She talked with Amandine and Luc every day, and their conversations became increasingly despondent and hopeless.

Now that she owned Domaine du Cerisier outright, she

knew that—ironically—the thing she'd always wanted was no longer enough. She yearned for what she and Clovis had during the harvest. But if he did come back, which was looking less and less certain by the day, she didn't know how to tell him about the baby or what to do after that.

She wanted to at least try to make things right, but as November dragged on, Luc's conclusion that Clovis had given up on her became increasingly probable.

She found herself out by the cherry tree again, as if its solid presence could supply her with answers. It was Thursday, and the boys were in school.

She was glad Jorgé and Fiona were around so often. Alone, she didn't feel she had it in her to be the upbeat mother they needed. The next day she had to man a stand during the huge wine auction in Beaune—Les Trois Glorieuses. Her bones ached with exhaustion just thinking about it. The auction happened every year under the covered market hall, but the real event was in the streets of Beaune, which erupted into a massive party with music, drinking, and winetasting.

It was the absolute last thing Cerise felt like doing. Her stomach was becoming round—a source of delight but also consternation. Despite the heavy sweaters she could now wear in the cold weather, everyone would soon realize she was pregnant. It would take no clever deduction to determine the baby was Clovis's. Yet Clovis had, for all intents and purposes, disappeared. It was the talk of the town, from what Amandine and Luc told her.

She was certain of one thing: she did not want anyone to know about her pregnancy before Clovis, but if he didn't come back, that was going to be impossible. Her longing for him was as solid and unmovable as the cherry tree she leaned against.

He had given Cerise her independence. There were no strings attached to his gift, not even inheritance taxes. She'd taken the paperwork to Maître Gilbert, and after a painful wait in his office, which made her remember the will-reading all those months ago, she discovered that Clovis's gift had been done so thoroughly she had only three papers to sign—unheard of in French administration. She'd walked out of Maître Gilbert's study as the full and complete owner of Domaine du Cerisier.

Maître Gilbert exclaimed loudly over what he coined "Clovis's brief moment of insanity," but mainly, Cerise sensed, he was offended that Clovis had opted to use another notary.

Just before she'd left his study, the *maître* said, "You've gotten everything you wanted, Cerise. Are you happy?"

She hadn't answered then, and she couldn't answer now.

She should feel relief. She should feel satisfaction. She should feel security and vindication, but she felt none of those things. Somehow, all of that, including Cerasus, rang hollow now. It was not that she needed a man for her life to be whole—not at all; it was that she needed Clovis.

She reached her arms up and grasped the trunk of the cherry tree where it split into three main branches. She banged her forehead softly a few times against the trunk.

The tip of her index finger felt something cold and metallic. She went on tiptoe and reached farther. It was the curved edge of something… She finally freed the object from a hidden hollow in the trunk. She stared at it.

It was an oval metal container for the Flavigny licorice candies Maxime sucked on constantly. It was the same metal box he always carried in his pocket, with the pastoral scene of a rural couple reposing on a bench under a tree.

She opened the lid, and inside, wrapped in plastic, was the message she had searched for but not found.

With trembling fingers, she smoothed out the paper, a bit damp but still legible with Maxime's bold, truncated cursive.

My dear Cerise,

*If you are reading this, I must be gone, or perhaps I am still at the house, cooking up a nice* fricassée *of rabbit and you just found this box. I doubt it, though. I've been feeling chest pains and think I know what is coming for me. Don't mourn for me. If I go quickly without having to spend months living like a potted plant in some godawful retirement home or hospital ward, then I have been granted my dearest wish. I suppose that's not true. A nice, clean, quick death is my second dearest wish. My dearest wish? Ah, if you are familiar with the terms of my will, you already know.*

*I can just imagine how furious you will be when you learn I have left you and Clovis as equal partners in the vineyards. I would not have done it, believe me, if I didn't feel you two belonged together or could work brilliantly together. Also, you must realize I owed something to Clovis as my heir as much as I owed something to you for all your work and talent.*

*I know how poorly this must sit with you, but I hate to think of you alone when I am gone. You buried part of yourself in the graves of Antoine and your parents, and I want you to reclaim your full life.*

*Do not think I believe you cannot cope alone. Far from it. The issue with you is precisely the opposite: you are so self-sufficient you don't need anyone else. That is why I thought the only way was to insert the right person into your life in such a shocking fashion.*

*Why Clovis? I have known for some time that he was interested in hearing me talk about you, but I managed to always dissuade him from meeting you beyond wine events and passing in the street as he would have liked.*

*His weakness, if you could call it that, is his deep desire for a family. For all his carousing in the past, that boy is ready to commit to the right woman—as well as that woman's children. I knew this would scare you. If you two were linked through the vineyards, I reasoned, you would be obliged to work through your fear and his need.*

*I know, I know, you will say I've become a meddling old man in my dotage, but you and Clovis are the people I love most in the world. Something tells me your souls are made of the same stuff. In any case, I wanted to leave things so you both had the opportunity to see that, even if you decide not to follow through on it.*

*If I was wrong, forgive me. I am a deeply flawed person, but it all came from a place of love. I love you very much. In my heart, you were always the daughter I never had.*

*Je t'émbrasse,*

*Maxime*

By the time she'd finished the note, folded it up carefully, put it back in the container, and slipped it into the crook of the cherry tree, Cerise could feel the wet tracks of tears on her face. Of course the cherry tree. She couldn't believe she hadn't thought of looking there.

"*Merde.*" She dug her boot tip into the hard, frozen earth. She was filled with sorrow at what a mess they had made of Maxime's schemes.

Clovis could be here with her right now, surveying their vineyards from the vantage point of the cherry tree, in bed with her at night, sliding his hand surely over their growing child, warming her up with his love and caresses and secret glances and laughter.

She shivered as cold penetrated every cell in her body. Where was he?

# chapter twenty-eight

CERISE HARDLY SLEPT that night. She tossed and turned, haunted by fleeting dreams of trying to find Clovis in the fog, but he always disappeared, slipping just out of her reach. Her back ached, and her leg muscles spasmed. She kept her hand over her stomach, wracked with guilt that she had failed her baby before it was even born.

She woke heavy-eyed and exhausted, but once she got the boys off to school, she had to go through the motions of loading the car with Jorgé and Fiona as they accompanied her to Beaune to help set up her stand on the Place Carnot so the revelers could taste and purchase her wines.

Jorgé had tried on numerous occasions to talk Cerise out of running the stand that year, offering to man it himself.

The truth of the matter was it was a huge day of sales for the domaine as well as a prime opportunity to find new, local clients who often became repeat customers. Nobody wanted to see the face of someone who worked at the domaine. Everyone wanted to see the face of the actual winemaker. Now that Domaine du Cerisier was hers, she couldn't let a moment of suffering interfere with its success.

Besides, it was an honor to be invited. If she turned it down, even for one year, she knew she would not be invited again.

She thought of begging Fiona and Jorgé to stay, but Jorgé had plenty to do in the vineyards, and Fiona was going to help him and be at the house when the boys got back from school. If she showed any hesitation or weakness about manning the stand, she knew they would bundle her right back home again.

Cerise had been feeling too queasy to eat breakfast, and now her stomach protested. She hadn't met this baby yet, but one thing she knew was that when it was hungry, it was *hungry*.

Once Jorgé and Fiona left, Cerise perched on the uncomfortable stool behind her stand. The air was sharp with approaching snow. By eleven o'clock she could no longer resist the seductive scent of melted butter, garlic, and parsley emanating from the escargot tent a few meters away.

She hailed over a man wearing a band uniform with a trombone dangling off his left arm. When he answered her summons with a bemused expression, she thrust a handful of euro coins at him. "Can you go and buy me a dozen escargots? I'm starving. Keep the change."

He grinned at her. "*Bien sûr*. It's hungry work spending the whole day sitting in the cold like you are."

He returned quickly and gave all her bills back as well as a piping hot plate of escargots, tongs, and a small glass of chilled white wine.

"But I need to pay you—"

He shook his head. "I don't let beautiful women pay. Especially not ones who have a long, frigid day ahead of them."

"*Merci,*" she said, tears threatening again. She proceeded to polish off the escargots. What a kind man. She had lost much of her taste for wine since getting pregnant, so she left that untouched. White wine was reputed in Burgundy to be an energy drink in the same way as coffee, but she would have preferred a coffee.

A few bands marched by, and the festivities were becoming

louder with the hubbub of chatter and brass instruments as the hours wore on. She talked to so many people that her mouth hurt from smiling. The shivering became more violent, until it eventually stopped—but not because she'd warmed up. Rather, it felt like once her feet were numb and her torso ached with cold, her body gave up trying to shiver. She kept her gloved hands cradled over her stomach to give the baby any extra warmth.

By the afternoon her backache was worse, and as she stayed on her feet serving people wine, the ache circled around to her front as well.

Docteur Beaumont, a man who would never miss a local wine festival, especially not this one, came by around the time she began to worry about her stomach feeling tight and crampy.

He gratefully accepted a glass of Hautes Côtes de Beaune, Vieilles Vignes, and complemented her work. Over the rim of his glass he studied Cerise. His eyes sharpened, taking on that diagnostic look they had when she visited his office. She was glad for it. There was a time to be a martyr but not when her baby's well-being was in question.

"You're pale," he observed. "I don't like it. How are you feeling?"

"Not the best," she admitted. "I'm relieved to see you. My back has been bothering me, and now the pain has moved to my front."

He studied her again. "Can someone take over the stand for you?"

"No." She shook her head, feeling strangely close to tears. If only Clovis… "It's just me."

Sharp pain wrapped her midsection. She gasped. Just then her eyes met a pair of piercing blue ones and a head of thick brown hair that was taller than most of the crowd. She wondered for a split second if she was conjuring up Clovis from wishful thinking.

She clutched her stomach and made an inarticulate sound of pain. *Please let my baby be fine. Please let Clovis be real.*

He was walking toward her. *My Clovis.* He was too skinny, and the circles under his eyes were so dark they looked like bruises. Her heart beat so fast she thought it would explode, and the metal band encircling her torso tightened. A tall, pale, blonde woman stood beside Clovis, staring at her. Between Clovis and the woman, a sprite of a little girl with blonde pigtails and Clovis's eyes held each of their hands. Emily. Clovis's daughter.

"Clovis," she gasped, then the world tilted on its axis. Black rushed in from the sides of her vision. There was only Clovis's eyes. They were full of fear and incomprehension. Then, even they extinguished.

She rose up to consciousness with a sickening, swimming sensation in her head. Her eyelids felt like they were made of lead. Docteur Beaumont's voice broke through the dark.

"She's nearing the end of her first trimester, and I know for a fact she had no complications during her first two pregnancies."

"Cerise is pregnant?" That was Clovis's voice, filled with shock. *I should have told him.* "But when—"

"Sir, can you please step back." A voice she'd never heard before. "If you want what's best for Madame Desloires, you will let us do our job."

"Back away, Clovis." *Le docteur's* voice again. "I will deal with you later. Right now we must get her to the hospital."

"But—"

"Please, sir."

"Yes—yes, of course," said Clovis, and Cerise's eyelids flickered open. She wanted to see his face.

Instead it was a strange one that filled her line of vision. "*Bonjour*, Madame Desloires. You've experienced a *malaise*. Because of the baby, we're going to put you in the ambulance and get you to the hospital. I took the liberty of putting an IV in your arm while you were unconscious. If it feels a little sore there, that's why. Do you understand me?"

"*Oui*," said Cerise. Her voice came out sounding unlike her—small, scared.

They shifted her onto a stretcher, and Docteur Beaumont's face appeared in front of her. "I'll be following the ambulance," he said. "I won't leave your side."

"But your tastings…"

"Poo. We live in Burgundy, my dear, and you're a winemaker. I'm sure you can make it up to me."

"The baby?"

She caught a grim look appear briefly on his familiar features. "I don't know, but we're going to do everything we can. I promise that."

Tears began to roll down her cheeks. She reached out from underneath the blankets and grasped her doctor's hand. "Clovis?" she asked.

"I'm here, Cerise." Like magic, he appeared in front of her. "I'm going to see if I can go in the ambulance with you."

But then everyone disappeared as she was hoisted into the ambulance. The smell of antiseptic made her shake with fear. She closed her eyes and put her hand on her stomach. *Don't leave me,* she pleaded to her baby. *Please don't leave me. I love you so much, and I promise I will make things right. Please.*

The paramedic took her arm and injected something in the IV. Blackness swallowed her up again.

When she opened her eyes, it was in a room she recognized.

She was in the Beaune hospital maternity ward. She recognized the unmistakable whiff of Dettol and the squeaky sound of steps in the hall outside the door. She had spent a few days in the ward with the births of Yves and Marc. Those days were among the best in her life.

She had also spent time in the other areas of the hospital—the emergency department and the morgue. The smell was the same there, except in the morgue it was overlain with something else. Those were hours she wanted to forget but could not. Her hand slipped across her stomach. *Our baby.* The pain had gone. *Does that mean—?* She sat bolt upright in bed and cried out.

On the other side of the bed, away from the window, sat Docteur Beaumont. He bit his lip as he read a clipboard.

"The baby?" she demanded, her voice hoarse.

He looked up. "Ah! You're awake! The baby seems fine for the moment, although I have to admit I was worried."

She bunched up the pale-blue hospital sheet in her fists. "Tell me."

"I believe what you experienced is termed a threatened miscarriage. There was some blood, but it seems to have stopped, and the back and stomach pain correlate to that diagnosis as well. We tested the baby as soon as we got you here, and it seems to be all right—nice, steady heartbeat. Good movement."

"But?" Cerise knew from the caution in his voice there was a "but."

He walked over to her and took her hand in his large, wrinkled one. He took a deep breath and gave her a frank look under his bushy eyebrows. "But in my experience, it's going to be dicey for the next couple of weeks. You will need complete bedrest. You must understand this is not a suggestion; it is a requirement."

She nodded. "My boys?"

"They know you are here to rest. Fiona and Jorgé haven't told them about the baby, but Fiona told me to tell you the boys are fine and that they will of course stay at Domaine du Cerisier with them as long as needed."

She nodded. "How did you know about Jorgé and Fiona?"

"I called your house. Fiona and I had a chat. She's an efficient person, isn't she?"

"I think she's the most efficient person I've ever met." Cerise lay back, taking this all in. She held Docteur Beaumont's eyes. "Clovis?" she asked.

"It is critical you avoid getting upset or excited," Docteur Beaumont squeezed her hand for emphasis. "Which is why, as I'm sure you can understand, I have so far prevented Monsieur de Valois from coming into your room."

Her heart began to beat faster. "Oh," she said, not knowing what else to say. "Clovis is here?"

Docteur Beaumont didn't answer but sucked his pen for a moment. "Was it the right thing to ban him?" he said finally. "I still can't decide."

"I'm emotional about him," she spoke as honestly as possible for the baby's sake. "But then I'm emotional without him, too. Clovis and I have a lot to talk about."

The doctor peered over the top of his black-rimmed glasses. "That isn't much help, my dear."

She sighed. She honestly didn't know the answer to Docteur Beaumont's question. Once again, she wished her emotions were a switch she could just flip off, but they weren't, especially when it came to Clovis. "Of course I don't want to do anything that could hurt the baby, but perhaps it would be good if I could settle things between us." She yearned to see him, but why had he been with Emily and that woman, who had to be Emily's mother? Her stomach cramped at the thought that they might be together, although she could hardly blame him. Oh God. She was already emotional. It could hurt the baby...

Docteur Beaumont nodded. "Perhaps...I know they had planned to put more medication in your IV to make sure you have a good sleep tonight. Do you want my advice—my medical advice?"

Cerise nodded.

"I'll tell Clovis you need to rest and that he can come back tomorrow afternoon during visiting hours."

"But—"

"I believe that is what's best for your baby."

She felt a familiar reflex, the same she had felt when she lost her husband and parents—the need when she or anyone she cared about was in danger, this time her baby—to pull into herself and lock the door, letting no one in.

She nodded. She wanted nothing more than to tell Clovis what was in her heart and try to understand what he was thinking when he'd gifted her Domaine du Cerisier, but not if it could harm their child. She wasn't protecting this child only for her, she was doing it for him, too.

And, if she was being truthful, she was scared. She needed to do everything the doctor ordered until she knew their baby was out of danger. She didn't think she could survive another heart-wrenching loss, and she couldn't impose another one on Clovis, not if it was in her power to prevent it.

There was a soft knock on the door, and a nurse slipped in. "Hi, I'm Mathis," he said. "I'll be your nurse for the next twelve hours, and I have something for your IV to help you rest. *D'accord?*"

"*D'accord,*" she agreed, and Docteur Beaumont patted her hand, then left the room and shut the door quietly behind him.

# chapter twenty-nine

THE NEXT MORNING, even though Cerise felt far more rested than she had in a long time, she didn't feel like she could breathe until the nurses rolled in the fetal monitor, took readings, and informed her everything was looking perfect with the baby.

She didn't know how the time passed until three o'clock, the start of visiting hours, but somehow it did. Nurses and doctors came and went; a lovely Moroccan woman came to take several vials of blood, and they had a nice chat about their favorite wines; the lunch cart served a hot meal; and Cerise forced herself to eat it even though the queasiness had returned.

As the clock neared three, she could feel her heart pound with nerves. The more she tried to calm herself down, the more agitated she felt. At precisely the top of the hour, there was a soft knock at the door.

Cerise lay still in her bed. She wished she could at least sit up, but Docteur Beaumont had instructed her to lay flat on her back except to use the washroom.

She watched for the first glimpse of Clovis. Instead, however, it was Docteur Beaumont who appeared.

"Oh… *Bonjour*, Docteur." Cerise tried to hide her disappointment.

"I know it's not me you're expecting," he said, adjusting his blue plaid tie. He came to her bedside and took her hand in his. "I just had a long talk with the doctors treating you, and they are pleased with how you and the baby are doing. Every hour we can put between you and yesterday's episode is a win."

"I'm feeling better."

"Have you been lying down all the time, like I ordered?"

She nodded and adopted a mockingly obedient tone. "*Oui,* Docteur."

He chuckled. "Good. I don't think I could force you to comply with bedrest to take care of yourself, but to take care of your baby...*voilà*! It works."

Behind Cerise's smile, her mind spun with questions. Where was Clovis? Did he not want to see her? Maybe that was for the best, even though her heart told her something very different.

"You're wondering about Clovis," the doctor said—a statement rather than a question. "He's still outside your room, wearing a groove in the linoleum since yesterday."

She felt warmth flood her but also that familiar fear. She pushed it down. "I think I should see him."

The doctor studied her through narrowed eyes. "I'm not convinced. I will let him in on two conditions."

"What?"

"I sit in that chair the whole time." He pointed to the chair in the corner that he had sat on the day before. "And I will let him stay only twenty minutes. I'm going to set my timer."

She made a sound of disbelief.

"Yes, I know I'm acting like your guard. Until I know your baby is out of danger, that is exactly what I will be. This is a medical issue, Cerise. As I warned you yesterday, I do not want you getting upset. If it was up to me, knowing what I heard transpired between you two, I would prevent him from coming in here altogether."

"I understand, but what we have to say to each other—it's private," she tried to explain.

"Precisely. My presence should curb any distressing exchanges. Do you agree to my conditions?"

She grimaced at the truth in what he said. "*Oui*. For my baby."

He nodded and left, only to return with Clovis following close behind.

Finally. She didn't know if he would angry, dismissive, or hurt, but she stretched out her hand toward him by instinct.

She couldn't see him properly until he neared the bed, but when he did, she was struck by how different he looked from her Clovis of the harvest. His mouth was stern and his eyes distraught.

Still it was him—this man who had broken down almost all her defenses and made her love him. She wanted to encircle him with her arms but had to lay still. He was also the man who was quoted in that article. He might also be the man who had given up on her and reunited with the mother of his child.

He stood beside her bed while Docteur Beaumont settled in the armchair and pulled some folders from his leather bag. Clovis eyes flicked over to him.

"He's staying," she explained. "I can't get upset because of... because of the baby, so this is his way of ensuring I stay calm."

Clovis nodded, his eyes fixed on her. He hadn't taken her hand. She saw his chest expand beneath his sweater as he gulped in a mouthful of air. "The baby?"

There were so many questions contained in those two simple words.

"The baby is fine for the moment," the doctor answered for her. "However, we need to get Cerise over the next two weeks with no excitement or upset, as I explained. Is that understood?"

Clovis glanced at the doctor, then looked back at Cerise and widened his eyes. She had never thought they would be sharing a joke at this moment, yet even now, that spark of humor arced, binding them together somehow.

"Understood," he said.

She suppressed a laugh. She had missed laughing with him.

Incongruously, they smiled at each other. How she'd longed to see Clovis's smile, but then it faded and became something far more complex. "The baby…is it our baby?"

She nodded, that familiar guilt rising in her yet again. "Yes."

His face was the sun breaking out from behind a cloud. "We're going to have a baby?" Now he took her hand. The rough feel his calluses jumpstarted her heart.

She nodded and realized her expression probably reflected his. It was going to be all right. Except…

His blue eyes darkened. "When did you find out? Did you know you were pregnant when I left?"

It would be so easy to lie. Only Fiona and Docteur Beaumont knew the truth, and even though Docteur Beaumont couldn't help but overhear, Cerise knew he would never contradict her. Patient confidentiality, not to mention his innate loyalty. Still, she knew Clovis, whatever he had done, deserved to know the whole truth.

"I knew several weeks before you disappeared," she whispered.

His body went completely still.

"I'm sorry. I should have told you right away. It was so wrong of me." She squeezed his hand, feeling desperate. There was no response, but at least he let her hold on. "Please say something."

He wouldn't—or perhaps couldn't—meet her gaze.

"I thought I knew how much you despised me." His nostrils flared. "But this…I could never have anticipated that you would exclude me from this."

She squeezed his hand even harder. "Clovis," she said, louder this time, to get him to look at her. "You have to believe me—"

The doctor must have noticed her raised voice and sensed the tension in the room. "Enough of this," he said briskly, putting his folder down and striding toward Clovis. He firmly, inexorably, took Clovis's arm and escorted him out of the hospital room, shutting the door behind him. He came back a few minutes later.

"Clovis has left the hospital," he said. Cerise felt the sting of tears on her cheeks.

"But—"

"Cerise, I will not have him—or anyone else, actually, but especially him—upsetting you."

"There's more I need to say to him. I did something unforgiveable."

"You'll find most things can be excused in this life if enough love is applied to the situation. Is it worth risking the health of your child?"

"No."

"Can it wait?"

She lifted her shoulders helplessly. "I don't know. I think maybe it's already too late."

He took her hand. "You're an adult. You've proved that many times over, more than any person should have to. I'm not doing this to patronize you. I have seen many cases like yours before, and not becoming emotionally excited or stimulated is frequently a deciding factor."

She didn't say anything, but her body knew the truth of the doctor's argument. Even now her heartbeat felt slightly off, and her head had begun to ache.

"Can I recommend to Clovis to hold off seeing you until you are out of the hospital and, more important, out of danger?"

She nodded. "Can you explain to him that I want...that I need to talk to him, but that... Well, can you explain the medical thing?"

"I already have," the doctor said with kind eyes. "I will do everything I can to impress upon him that this situation is only temporary."

She had no choice but to nod her agreement.

A day slowly passed without word from Clovis, then another. She talked to the boys on the phone, and they came to visit with Jorgé and Fiona every day.

Docteur Beaumont checked on her regularly and declared himself pleased with how she and the baby were doing. He never failed to add that she mustn't change a thing for the moment.

On the fourth morning, Geneviève swept into the hospital room with a glossy shopping bag from Galeries Lafayette under her arm.

She kissed Cerise roundly before plopping down on the chair with a sigh.

Cerise had called her aunt, who had been vacationing in Biarritz now that those American tourists (her words) had left, the day after Cerise had been taken to the hospital. She'd told her everything about the baby and Clovis. Geneviève had been deeply troubled by Cerise's health but overjoyed about the baby. As for Clovis, she'd already consigned him to the devil.

"Well!" she exclaimed now. "You certainly keep me on my toes, *ma puce*! A baby! I cannot tell you how thrilled your uncle and I are about the baby. Are you resting?"

"Yes. Docteur Beaumont is making certain of that."

Geneviève sniffed. "You're still seeing that country doctor?"

Cerise lifted an eyebrow.

"Ah well. He always had common sense as far as I can remember, which is more than I can say for many of his colleagues."

"He's banned Clovis from my room."

"*Ça alors*, I'm starting to think he's a very good practitioner after all. What could Clovis do at this point but upset you, and hasn't he done that enough?"

She knew after seeing Clovis that she'd hurt him just as deeply as he'd hurt her. The destroyed look in his eyes pierced her heart every time it flashed through her memory. She sighed. "I don't feel as if I know anything anymore, Tata, to tell you the truth. I miss him, though. I miss him so much. I should have told him about our baby right away."

Geneviève narrowed her eyes. "I thought he betrayed you."

"I don't know," she said. "The way he was when we were together—my heart tells me that is the real Clovis, and that man never would have betrayed me."

"The evidence points to the contrary."

"Yes, but I never gave him the chance to prove his innocence. I thought I had an excellent reason for that, but now... You must think me an idiot."

"No..." Geneviève said slowly. "Nobody could ever think of you as an idiot. Do you know the one thing enduring love requires?"

"Obviously not, or I wouldn't be alone. What?"

"Bravery."

She turned this over for a moment. "Explain that, Tante. Please."

Geneviève glanced down at her fingers, adorned with several large diamond and sapphire rings. "I'm not saying you should do this with Clovis, because that article was horrific, but to create something that endures you have to be brave enough to love in the face of logic and fear. Do you think it was easy for me to stay with your uncle when I found out, only a few months before our marriage, that I could never carry a child?"

"Tante... I had no idea."

Geneviève nodded. "My doctor discovered my issue during testing for something else entirely. He was aware of my engagement and told me right away that…well, that I would never be able to give your uncle a child." She took a deep breath and met Cerise's eyes. "That was a different time, you realize. A large part of a wife's role—especially a wife to someone like your uncle—was providing heirs."

"Did you tell him right away?"

Geneviève nodded. "It was the hardest thing I've ever done. I was sure he would want to call off the wedding. I mean, he was the heir to a winemaking dynasty, as you know. The idea of marrying a barren woman when he could have any number of eligible fertile brides, well…it was unthinkable."

"But you told him anyway?" She had already revised her old opinion of Geneviève and had begun to see there was so much beneath the aggravating veneer of her aunt. But this…she never realized just how brave he aunt had been.

"Yes. I couldn't build love on a lie. Because I loved him, I had to tell him."

"What happened?"

Geneviève blushed rosy under her foundation. "He was still single and informed me he would remain so until I consented to marry him."

"Wow."

She shrugged. "Cowards can't truly love, *ma chérie*."

Cerise sat back. She thought back to her reflex of retreating into herself and bolting the door when she felt threatened. How she hadn't wanted to even listen to any of Clovis's apologies and protestations of innocence. She wondered if that had been sensible or just chicken-hearted.

"Now!" Geneviève removed something from her glossy bag. "I bought you a silk *peignoir* and a hair dryer. Even with the baby glow, you look a fright, *ma chère*."

# chapter thirty

GENEVIÈVE'S VISIT LEFT Cerise needing time to think. It took several hours for the doctors and nurses to come and go, and then the lab techs to take more blood, and then dinner. It wasn't until the lights were turned off for the night and she lay back in the dark that she was alone with her thoughts.

She hadn't been brave. That knowledge kept circling since her aunt's visit.

Her reaction after reading the article—even after the initial shock had passed—had been cowardice as much as it had been shock and self-preservation. There was, of course, ample reason to be wary and angry, but she'd been absolutely unwilling to consider that Clovis might be telling the truth when her own instinct, not to mention that of his friends, felt he was incapable of such a betrayal.

She had built the battlements around her heart to be too impenetrable. She was scared of being taken for a fool, scared of being controlled, scared of letting someone in her life who could disappear.

It wasn't as if she would have let Clovis get his way for everything he wanted, but she could have been open to at least listening to his side. She had let fear take the lead, refusing to listen to his apologies, keeping her pregnancy a secret from him, withdrawing into herself.

This realization was a cold, hard thing to accept in the sterile dark of the hospital room.

It was probably too late, but she had to be brave and honest with herself from now on. The look in Clovis's eyes when he learned she'd hidden her pregnancy from him… She'd almost certainly blown her chances. Then again, Geneviève had been certain she no longer had a chance either. It didn't matter. The whole point of being brave was loving even when there was no hope of it being reciprocated.

She sat up, flicked on her light, and pressed the nurse call button.

Within seconds the door flew open and a lovely, warm nurse named Solange burst in.

"Everything all right?" she asked.

"Yes…well, no, but everything is fine with me and the baby. I was wondering if you could get me a pen, paper, and envelope?"

"What?" Solange asked, confused. "Why?"

"It's to tell a man—the father of my baby—I love him."

Solange's deep brown eyes popped wide open. "*Ça alors!* In that case I'll be right back. Once you're done, give it to me, and I will make sure it's sent off. Do you need to mail it?"

She considered. She couldn't give it to Docteur Beaumont, and she didn't know when Fiona and Jorgé were coming to visit. "Yes," she said. "I suppose I do."

Within seconds Solange had returned with all the writing materials and a conspiring wink. "You ring me as soon as you're ready."

Cerise smiled and nodded. She was still terrified of declaring herself, but Clovis deserved to know she loved him with every fiber of her being. Besides, Maxime always said being brave wasn't a lack of fear; it was being scared and acting anyway.

She couldn't know if he would come back to her—that was his choice. She could hardly blame him if he didn't. It didn't matter; she had to tell him the truth anyway.

A whoosh of life rocketed through her body as she wrote, smashing the walls she had constructed to protect herself.

*Mon amour,*

*I probably have no right to call you that anymore after pushing you away and not telling you about our child.*

*Just as things were becoming serious between us, that article gave me the perfect opportunity to retreat into solitude and take no risks with my heart. It was awful and I still don't understand how it came to be, but that doesn't change I was a coward.*

*It has taken me this long to realize what I've done, but I want you to know that even at my angriest, I never for a second stopped loving you. That love drove me insane and made me angrier, but I couldn't stop.*

*I know I'm probably too late. From what I saw there is a good chance Emily's mother and you are back together, and you will finally get the family of your dreams. I will always wish your perfect family had been built with me, but when you gifted me your shares in Domaine du Cerisier, I could understand why you had given up on us.*

*Besides, I love you enough to want your happiness above all, even above my own.*

*Remember that grape crown you set on my head at your* paulée? *I wish I had kept it instead of throwing it back at you when*

*Amandine showed me the article. I would have kept it to remember that brief moment in time when I was your harvest queen and we belonged to each other.*

*I love you, Clovis. I wish you happiness. Can you do me one last favor? Can you go to the domaine, taste Cerasus, and tell me what you think? It should be bottled, and I need to know if it's time. There is no one I trust to do this except you.*

*There has been talk of letting me go home in a few days, but in the meantime, rest assured I will do whatever it takes to ensure this child of ours is cared for in the best way I know how.*

Je t'aime,

*Cerise*

She folded the letter and wrote the address for Domaine de Valois on the front, then buzzed for Solange, who took it away with a wink.

She fell asleep with tears on her cheeks but, for the first time in a long time, an open heart.

The days dragged on. They were enlivened only by visits from the boys when Fiona and Jorgé brought them in.

There was no word from Clovis, but Cerise reminded herself that sometimes in Burgundy it took longer for a letter to arrive in the next village than to arrive in Africa.

She couldn't expect a response anyway, even though her

heart longed for something different. She had sent him the letter because she wanted him to know how she felt. He didn't owe her an answer.

Jorgé had stayed to work at the domaine the day Cerise told Marc and Yves during one of their visits to the hospital they were going to have a baby brother or sister.

"Who is the baby's father, Maman?" Marc asked, watching her closely.

"It's Clovis," she answered, unsure what Marc's reaction would be.

"Clovis!" Yves cried. "*Fantastique!* Why isn't he here?"

Marc didn't react one way or another. He just watched her.

"I've seen him." She kept her answer purposely vague.

"I would think he would want to be here all the time!" Yves said.

Fiona and Jorgé knew why Clovis had been banned from the hospital room by Docteur Beaumont, but they didn't know about the letter. Fiona produced a ten-euro bill from her pocket and handed it to Marc. "How about you take Yves down to the cafeteria, and you can both buy a drink?"

"Orangina?" Yves asked, easily diverted.

"Just this once, as a treat," Cerise said.

Marc nodded, understanding the subtext, and ushered Yves out of the room.

Fiona pulled the chair beside the bed after they left. "Any news from him?"

She shook her head, frustration and longing warring under her breastbone. "Nothing. Have you heard anything?"

Fiona grimaced.

"What?" she demanded.

"Not much, just that his daughter and his—his daughter's mother are staying at his house."

"Are they back together?" She tried to keep her voice calm

but wasn't sure if she succeeded. Part of Cerise expected them to be, as she had written in her letter, even though her heart hurt at the thought.

Fiona shrugged. "Nobody knows, although there has been a lot of speculation."

She felt like she couldn't breathe. "I'm sure he's furious with me. When I told Clovis I knew about the baby but didn't say anything—his stillness, Fiona. It was terrible. And then Docteur Beaumont banished him from visiting me for good. I don't think he'll ever forgive me, and I don't blame him."

"I don't think that's the right question to ask," Fiona said, her words thoughtful. "I think the right question is have you forgiven him?"

That, at least, she knew the answer to.

"*Oui*. It felt safer to push him away instead of listening to him. I should have been brave enough to trust my own instinct that the Clovis I knew wouldn't have told the journalist about Cerasus. I'll probably never know what happened—how the journalist found out about my secret wine—but I know in my heart it couldn't have been Clovis. I guess deep down part of me always knew. I've decided to believe in him, but I'm too late."

"Cerasus?" Fiona echoed, her voice hollow.

"Hadn't I told you about that part?" She sighed. "I had started working on a wine that I was taking out of the appellation system—a risky wine that was unfiltered and without sulfates. It was my secret project to not stay limited by my appellations and to pave a more secure future for Domaine du Cerisier. I told only Clovis about it. Nobody else knew. I believed that because the journalist had written about Cerasus, Clovis had to have betrayed me."

"Cerasus," Fiona repeated. "I know about it."

"From the article?"

"No, I never read that."

"Then how?"

"From you," Fiona said, still in a distant tone of voice.

"That's impossible."

"No. It's not. Clovis didn't tell the journalist," Fiona said, still in that distant tone of voice. "I told the journalist about Cerasus. It wasn't Clovis; it was me."

She gripped the raised arm of her bed. "What?"

"It was me who told the journalist about Cerasus." Fiona went deathly pale. "This was all my fault."

"How did you possibly find out about Cerasus? Nobody knew. I didn't tell you. I never told anyone except Clovis."

She shook her head. "You did; you just didn't know it. I was going to the cellar to meet Jorgé one night, and when I crept in, I overheard a bit of your conversation with Clovis—the part when you were explaining the wine. I didn't hear anything about it being a secret, though, and then I heard... Well, I knew I should wait for Jorgé *outside* the cellar and that we should go somewhere else."

It hadn't been Clovis at all. "I put him through hell," she murmured to herself.

"I'm so sorry," Fiona said, a pleading note in her tone. "I had no idea, I swear. I was just so impressed by you and a little riled up at how slavish the journalist was when he talked about Clovis, so I just wanted to show that chauvinist the innovation and brilliance in the vineyards were yours."

Cerise opened her mouth, but no words came out. The past three months were breaking apart and rearranging themselves in an entirely new design.

"I ran off at the mouth," she continued. "Just like my ma is forever telling me not to do."

"He was telling the truth," Cerise marveled. "All that time he was telling the truth."

"Yes. I am sorry. If I had known the mention of Cerasus was

so important, I would have said something right away. I was so angry about the story Jorgé told me that I refused to read that stupid article. I didn't realize—"

"I need to see him." She sat up again but then remembered she had sent him the note and he hadn't responded. He had terminated their partnership by giving her everything she wanted. Clovis had showed her he was done.

Besides, if he was trying to make a go with Emily's mother, she couldn't jeopardize that. Not when there was a child involved. But there was a child involved with her now, too.

She dropped her head into her hands. She could be at home with him right now. She could have said yes to him and, in doing so, said yes to life together.

# chapter thirty-one

AFTER WHAT SEEMED like an eternity, Docteur Beaumont finally decreed that all danger had passed and Cerise could go home on the condition she rest and not work in the vineyards.

She phoned Jorgé immediately and arranged for him to pick her up at noon once the doctors had signed her release.

There had still been no word from Clovis.

She had a new future in front of her, and she was determined to face it with courage, but it felt hollow. Maybe one day they could be friends again. It would never feel like enough, but it would be better than nothing.

Solange was on the nurse rota the morning of Cerise's discharge and jollied things along, never asking whether she had heard from the baby's father. Instead, she chatted on about how wonderful Jorgé and Fiona and her boys were as Cerise pulled on some clothes Fiona had brought. She had to leave her jeans undone at the waist. All of that was true, and Cerise felt her heart surge at the idea of being with them again in time for Christmas.

"Who's picking you up?" Solange asked once she had helped her slip on her coat.

"Jorgé," she said.

"I'll check and see if he is charming the nurses at the station."

Cerise chuckled. "Probably."

"If he's there, I'll get him to come in here for you. How about you sit on the bed while you wait. It's still not good to be on your feet too much."

She nodded and sat on the bed after Solange left. She placed her palm flat over her belly. "I'm so lucky to have you," she whispered to the baby. Even though she couldn't have Clovis, she had his child, and she loved it fiercely. *"Je t'aime."*

Solange popped back into the room. "I've found your chauffeur!" Her face was flushed pink. "How are you feeling?"

"Fine." She smiled back. She would work on finding happiness again, or at least contentment.

"All right, I'll send him in!" she chirped and vanished.

Jorgé didn't appear in the doorway. There, in his place, was Clovis.

She gasped.

"I don't want to upset you." He held up a hand. "I would never want to do anything to hurt our baby. That's why I didn't immediately run here when I got your letter. Nothing but concern for you and our child, and…well, the specter of Docteur Beaumont could have prevented me from doing that."

"You got it?" she asked.

He nodded, his blue eyes shining.

She didn't see indifference in that gaze; she thought she saw its opposite, but perhaps that was just wishful thinking. Cerise felt suddenly flustered. "The baby's fine. The only thing I'm feeling seeing you is…" She laid her hand on her heart, feeling its strong rhythm. "Oh, my heart. My heart is so happy, but I don't know if it has any reason to be."

His lips quirked up, tremulous. "So is mine," he whispered, not moving but looking at her as though drinking her in.

"I know I have no right to ask, but I need to. Are you and Emily's mother together?"

He shook his head. "How could we be, when I'm in love with you?"

"Are you?" She gasped. "Even after—"

He stopped her short by rushing over and sweeping her into his arms. "I was so angry, so frustrated with you not believing me, but never did I stop loving you." His voice was muffled in her hair.

"But I thought... Fiona said—"

Cerise felt rather than saw him shake his head. "Emily's mother has started seeing a new therapist who has been extremely helpful, and when she said she wanted to bring Emily to stay with me, of course I said yes. I was staying near them in England for a few days at the end of my fruitless trip to find the journalist. He seems to have dropped off the face of the earth for all I can tell. They left yesterday, but on their next visit I want more than anything to introduce Emily to you. She's going to be our baby's big sister, after all."

She was enveloped in his arms. She took a deep breath and closed her eyes, feeling that final puzzle piece snap into place. "*Je t'aime*, Clovis." Cerise tightened her arms around his torso. "I'm not always going to let you have your way, but I'm determined not to shut you out anymore. That was gutless of me."

"I pressured you," he said. "I realized after I left on my wild goose chase that you had every right to dictate how you want your life to be. I was working through things from my childhood that were not your burden to take on. I apologize for that."

"Why did you gift me the vineyards?"

He smiled. "I didn't want the partnership to stand between us anymore. I used to think it was the thing, sometimes the only thing, that bound us together, but then I realized it was driving us apart."

"Luc and Amandine told me it was because you'd given up on me."

"They couldn't be more wrong. It was an essential step in getting my harvest queen back."

Their lips found each other, and he exhaled softly. She could explore the feel of his lips on hers forever. Home.

"I'm ready for a new vintage," she said when they finally came up for breath. "By the way, I just found out it was Fiona who told the journalist about Cerasus. She overheard that part of our conversation in the cellar. I'm so sorry—"

"Ah!" he said, stepping back to fish around in his jacket pocket. "I almost forgot!" He extracted a half bottle of wine called a *chopette*. From the other pocket he pulled two wineglasses. He put them on the hospital table, uncorked the bottle, and poured a bit for each of them. "Just a small taste."

She nodded. Clovis passed her glass, then took his. *Santé* was the usual cheer, but somehow today it didn't feel quite right.

She clinked her glass against his. "I love you, Clovis de Valois. Hopelessly."

He blinked. "I love you, too, Cerise Desloires. Completely."

They took a sip. It was early, but the promise was there of a fullness that would develop into something sublime.

She grabbed a paper cup from the table beside her hospital bed and spat the wine into it.

"What?" Clovis asked. "It's incredible."

"Baby," she reminded him.

"Right." The smile that wreathed his face made all the lonely nights and confusion and heartbreak worth it.

"We made a wonderful vintage together," she said, stepping into his arms again.

"I take no credit. I didn't have anything to do with Cerasus." Clovis shook his head.

"We made love that first time against the barrels."

His dimple indented deeply as he laughed. "We made much more than that." His hand was strong and sure as he slid it over the slight curve of her stomach and splayed his fingers. "I'm definitely sharing credit for this production."

"And you thought it was the vineyards that bound us together." Cerise kissed his neck.

He chuckled. "I was wrong."

She grabbed his hands. "Let's get out of here. I'm worried if we hang around, they'll make us stay the night and…well, we have to be careful, but I would love to sleep in the same bed as you."

He nodded. "Oh! I forgot the last thing."

"What?"

He opened the backpack he had dropped on the chair when he came into the room. He drew out the vineyard crown from his *paulée* and placed it in her head.

Cerise reached her hands up. It was dry now, of course, but still miraculously intact. "You kept it?"

"I picked it up off the ground that night. You're going to learn that I can be a bit sentimental. My friends tease me mercilessly about it."

It still fit her head perfectly. "I will never throw this at you again. Promise."

"I can guarantee you'll be tempted."

"Yes, but then I will remember this moment, and I won't," she said. "I'm sure I'll give you plenty of reasons to throw it away."

"But then I'll remember this moment, too." He leaned down and kissed her again. It felt like a promise.

"Let's make a life full of these moments."

With their fingers intertwined, and the crown still on Cerise's head, they strolled out of the hospital—and into the rest of their lives.

*La Fin*

311

# the grapevine

Interested in receiving Laura's French recipes, sneak peeks at her new work, as well as exclusive contests and giveaways, insider news, plus countless other goodies? Sign up for Laura's Grapevine newsletter and join our fantastique community.

Click here: http://bit.ly/LauraBradburyNewsletter

# merci

*A Vineyard for Two* is the first fiction I have published (though I have definitely written a few others), so the learning curve was steep. Thank you to Liza Palmer, author extraordinaire, for telling me just when I was about to throw in the towel that it was normal for new things to feel terrible and gross at times.

Thank you as always to my amazing Surrey International Writers' Conference tribe, especially Kathy and Karen, who surprised me at my last signing and are always there cheering me on.

To my Paris Authors Group. I love our "rising tide" mentality, and I could not do this without our mutual mentorship and support (and love of France!).

Pamela Patchet is not only my beloved friend but also my ideal reader and an incisive, thoughtful beta reader. She also wields a trident, so, you know, RESPECT.

Sally is the best collaborator and takes care of so many things so I can carve out time to write. She is also a fantastic editor and is hilariously honest when she needs to be (i.e., "there is a lot of hair patting going on in this scene, REMOVE").

Thank you to Samantha, Maggie, and Pam for beta-reading *A Vineyard for Two*. Your comments were thoughtful and so helpful. You have made this book better.

Thank you to Franck, who is so relieved I am finally writing a book that does not feature him. Same with my girls, Charlotte, Camille, and Clémentine, who have never read any of my memoirs but provide me with daily inspiration, laughs, and pride.

My readers are absolutely the best. I love our "Grapevine" community. The input they provide is invaluable as I develop every one of my books. Lynette, you will see you're included in these pages! My Grapeviners had input on everything during the "building" of this book—the cover, excerpts, the title (cf. Lynette), so I see *A Vineyard for Two* as a group effort. In any case, I could not write a word without this group of quirky, intelligent, and passionate readers.

Would you, too, like to become a Grapeviner and be repaid in sneak peeks, special contests, delicious recipes, and so many other goodies? To join, just go to www.bit.ly/LauraBradburyNewsletter.

To my crazy-talented and fascinating girlfriends, who inspire and support me every day. To my *ami de coeur* Charlotte Buffet, who has endured me peppering her with random questions about the nitty-gritty of the harvest and winemaking calendar. Any mistakes are mine, not hers.

To my PSC and transplant families around the world: you are the bravest, best people. I am thankful every day that our paths have crossed. Sign up to be an organ donor!

And, of course, to Nyssa, who saved my life by donating 63 percent of her liver in 2017, as well as to all the transplant team at the U of A hospital in Edmonton, the incredible nurses on 3G2, and my wonderful transplant team in Calgary. Neither this book, nor me, would be here if it wasn't for you.

# author's note

Just a few logistical notes from *moi*.

I know the inheritance dilemma imposed on Clovis and Cerise does not adhere strictly to the reality of French law. I purposely diverged from this as I have sat through FAR too many meetings in notaries' offices in France hearing about every aspect of the arcane concept of *usufruis* as it applies to French wills. I have a law degree from Oxford, and I still couldn't make heads or tails of it. I couldn't possibly inflict this on my readers, so I simplified things for the sake of a readable story.

I have tried to be as accurate as possible with the winemaking calendar, although Yannis's accident would most likely have happened later on in the vinification process. However, I quizzed my winemaker friends in Burgundy before adding it in, and they said it could possibly happen when it did in *A Vineyard for Two* in an unusually hot year.

Keep in mind that my French is purposely regional (i.e., "Tata" for aunt instead of "Tatie," which seems to be more common in southern France) and at times colloquial (i.e., *Je te paie le café?* is something we say all the time in Burgundy).

As for the scene when Clovis cleans up after Yves's barforama, this may seem a tad out of place for some readers, but it came from a conversation I had with my sisters and then my book club about what we found truly romantic. The inspiration stemmed from a night when I had an anti-rejection medication–induced migraine and woke up in the middle of the night to decorate our bathroom in an *Exorcist*-style vomit fest.

Franck got up, put me into the shower, got me into clean pajamas, then put me back to bed while he proceeded to scrub the bathroom with bleach. Franck and I have been lucky enough to experience plenty of romance (as you can read about in my bestselling Grape Series memoirs), but his actions that night were amongst the most romantic things anyone has ever done for me.

Love, just like everything in life, is in the eye of the beholder.

To learn more and sign up for my dynamic newsletters full of exclusive content and recipes, visit www.bit.ly/ LauraBradburyNewsletter.

If you enjoyed *A Vineyard for Two*, then you will love my bestselling, romantic, and escapist memoirs, the Grape Series.

Turn the page for an excerpt of *My Grape Year*, voted number one in Buzzfeed's "18 Feel-Good Books That Will Make You Believe in Love."

## Sneak peek of
## Chapter One
# My Grape Year

*A*T THE AGE of seventeen in a last-minute twist of fate, Laura Bradbury is sent to Burgundy, France, for a year's exchange. She arrives knowing only a smattering of French and with no idea what to expect in her first foray out of North America. With a head full of dreams and a powerful desire to please, Laura quickly adapts to Burgundian life, learning crucial skills such as the fine art of winetasting and how to savor snails.

However, the charming young men of the region mean Laura soon runs afoul of the rules, particularly the no-dating edict. Romantic afternoons in Dijon, early morning *pain au chocolat* runs, and long walks in the vineyards are wondrous but also present Laura with a conundrum: How can she keep her hosts happy while still managing to follow her heart? Follow along on Laura's journey to *l'amour* in *My Grape Year*.

# chapter one

## RULES FOR 1990–91
## OUTBOUND EXCHANGE STUDENTS—
## THE FOUR "D"s

1. No Drinking

2. No Drugs

3. No Driving

4. No Dating

*By signing this contract, I hereby accept my role as Ursus Youth Ambassador for the 1990–91 exchange year abroad and agree to abide by all four of the "Rules for Exchange Students."*

The other outbound exchange students around me were scribbling their signatures on the forms.

*No Drinking.* I knew I was heading to Europe, Switzerland, if everything went according to plan, and even though I was drawn by the history and beauty and exoticism, I was also hoping to be able to enjoy a nice glass of beer or wine from time to time. I was seventeen and would be graduating from high school in three short months, so I hoped they wouldn't take this rule too seriously in what my grandmother always referred to as "the old country."

*No Drugs.* I seriously doubted that marijuana was as ubiquitous in Europe as it was on Vancouver Island, Canada, where it self-seeded in many people's back gardens. And since I had no intention of ever trying any other type of drug, this rule wasn't an issue.

*No Driving.* It would be weird to no longer be able to drive nor enjoy the independence that came with that. Still, like many Canadians, I knew how to drive only an automatic and didn't like traffic very much, so I could live with this rule.

*No Dating.* This rule bothered me the most. It had just been explained to us that as Ursus Youth Ambassadors we would have to be available and open to all people we encountered during our year abroad. Having an exclusive romantic relationship would interfere with that goal. Also, the Ursus Club hosting us would be responsible for our welfare during our year in its country, and that would be far simpler to ensure when we students remained single. I could see the logic of it all, but my romantic life during my high school years had been seriously disappointing, if not to say practically nonexistent. My heart longed for romance and love.

Still, I felt as if the whole world was out there waiting for me, and I needed to take the step to meet it. If that meant signing this contract, then I would do whatever it took.

I picked up my pen and signed my name.

The men's polyester pants were off-gassing in the stuffy hotel room. The scorched smell of synthetic fabric tickled my nostrils. March was generally a cool month in Victoria, so the hotel staff hosting the annual Ursus District Convention hadn't anticipated the heat wave. The Rotary and Lions clubs, similar community service organizations, had recently begun to welcome female members, which I was sure had lessened the polyester quotient. Ursus, though, stubbornly remained a men-only group, aside from their female International Youth Exchange Ambassadors like me.

A makeshift fan had been unearthed and stuck in the corner of the room, but sweat trickled inside my navy wool blazer, which had already been festooned with at least forty pins. Pins were the currency of the incoming and outgoing exchange students and were traded with the fervor of stocks on Wall Street.

The interview was almost over, thank God. If they liked me, I would get the final confirmation that I would be spending the 1990–1991 academic year as an exchange student in what I hoped would be my first choice of host country, Switzerland. There was only one available spot in Switzerland, and it was contested hotly every year. Belgium, my second choice, was better than nothing. Germany was my third choice, but I knew I definitely didn't want to end up in Germany. I'd never found blond men attractive, and I vastly preferred wine to beer. It was a crime that Italy, France, and Spain weren't options. I could completely envision myself at some Spanish or Italian bar, dancing on the tables after a night fueled by sangria or Prosecco—though I'd apparently signed away my rights to drink either of these.

"I see Switzerland was your first choice, Laura," the head of the committee observed.

*Was? Not is?*

Every one of the ten or so men around the table had a copy of my application in front of him. "Can you explain your reasons for that?"

I had answered this question so many times in previous interviews that I could do it in my sleep. "One of my main motivations for going on a year abroad is to learn a foreign language," I said.

"Switzerland has not one but *three* official languages—French, German, and Italian. I would love to be exposed to more than one language during my year as an Ursus Youth Ambassador." Actually, I was hell-bent on a year abroad because I sensed this huge, marvelous world waiting for me beyond the mossy shores of my island home, and I vibrated with the need to meet it.

The Ursunian who was chairing the interview cleared his throat. "That is an excellent answer, Miss Bradbury. However, we just received the news that the Switzerland spot was nabbed by another district." The men exchanged shocked looks at this breach of fair play.

*What?* What about my fantasies of racing up and down the Swiss hills like Maria from *The Sound of Music* and warming myself up with some lovely cheese fondue and wine in a wooden chalet afterward, preferably with an entourage of handsome Swiss men? I knew I would have to deal with my disappointment later; right then wasn't the time. I dug my nails into my palms and smiled brightly. "I'll go to Belgium, then."

"We do have several spots there. I just feel we should let you know, though, that more than half of them are in the Flemish-speaking part of Belgium."

*Flemish?* I had been so sure I was going to Switzerland that I hadn't even considered the possibility of being sent to Flemish-speaking purgatory.

I flashed another smile. "Of course, I would make the most out of any placement," I said. "However, French is Canada's second official language, and growing up here on the West Coast, I have always regretted the fact that I have never learned to speak it fluently. I hope to go to McGill University in Montreal, so obviously French would be a huge advantage for me."

There was no need to mention that French had actually been my worst subject all through high school, and that I'd had to drop it after Grade 11 because it was torpedoing my GPA. Or that I ran out to the quad after my Grade 11 provincial exam for French and yelled, "Thank God! I will *never* have to speak French again in my life!"

A slighter, bald man piped up. "You may not be aware of this, Miss Bradbury, but there is no way for us to guarantee where you will be placed. We send over the files for the incoming students, and it's up to our Belgian brothers to allocate them as they see fit."

I struggled to maintain my bright-eyed demeanor.

"There's always France, I suppose," mused the head man, as though thinking aloud.

My head snapped in his direction. "I understood there were no exchange spots available in France."

He cleared his throat. "That *was* the case, but there has been a...ah...development."

My heart began to somersault. *France?*

A tall man at the opposite end of the table, who had been picking something fascinating out from under his thumbnail, jerked his head up. "With good reason!" he said, paying attention now. "Every exchange we arranged in France has ended in disaster. The families didn't even bother to come and pick up our students from the airport, or they suddenly decided that they were sick of hosting and locked the child out of the house or left on vacation without them. We couldn't possibly jettison another student into—"

The chair cleared his throat meaningfully. "I have a letter here from the Ursus Club in Beaune, France." He waved the letter, which from what I could see was written in elaborate cursive with a fountain pen. I longed to get a closer look—it possessed a tantalizing whiff of the exotic. "They say that one of their students is being hosted this year by our district, so they would welcome one of our students. Just one student, you see. It would be on a trial basis. They sound sincere."

"Don't believe them," snarled the tall man. "I was president of our club the year our poor student was abandoned at the airport in Paris. He had to take a plane back to Seattle the next day. Try explaining *that* to his parents!"

"We must believe them," the chair insisted. "Ursus spirit demands we have good faith in our French brothers. Besides, Miss Bradbury here strikes me as a competent sort of person who can deal with extreme situations. I wouldn't even mention the possibility of France to most of our outgoing students."

"I—I…" I stuttered, wondering how I was going to disabuse him of this notion. I couldn't imagine any horror worse than leaving for a year abroad only to have to return to Canada the next day with my tail between my legs. Yet…France! I had always wanted to see Paris and the Eiffel Tower and learn how to drape scarves properly.

"George"—the tall man's voice was stiff with displeasure—"throwing this nice young lady here to the French would be like throwing a lamb to the wolves, and I for one—"

"Neil," the head man said in a quelling tone, "there is an open space for France, and it needs to be filled. Miss Bradbury has explained how urgently she wants to learn French. She is mature and full of positive energy. I have complete confidence in her."

*What is the word for "shit" in French? Merde?* My mind whirred as I tried to find a way to extract myself from this fix.

But then I thought about red wine. Little cafés. Baguettes. French men were supposed to be very charming, weren't they? In any case, they had to be an improvement on Canadian boys. It could be a disaster, or it could be even better than Switzerland. In any case, I decided, it was definitely better than spending a year learning Flemish.

"I'd be delighted to take that spot in France." I straightened my shoulders.

All the men except Neil nodded approvingly at me as though I had just performed a selfless and heroic act. Darn. Had I?

The chair erased Switzerland and Belgium from my application and wrote "FRANCE" on it in large capital letters. He scrawled something in his notes.

"That settles it, then! You'll be heading to France in August, Miss Bradbury. I hope you have an excellent year, or shall I say a *bon voyage?*" He chuckled at his own joke.

"Thank you," I said, "or shall I say *merci?*" This got a laugh out of all the men, and they stood up and stretched their polyester-clad legs to indicate that I was dismissed.

I must have missed the sound over the whir of the fan and the muffled scrape of chairs against the carpet, but when I think back to it now, I am convinced there must have been a mighty creak. There had to have been, because at that precise moment my entire life shifted on its axis.

*To purchase*
*My Grape Year*
http://bit.ly/2IxCJ7i

# about laura

Laura Bradbury is the author of five bestselling memoirs—the Grape Series. *A Vineyard for Two* is the first book in her fictional Winemakers Trilogy.

Laura published her first book—a heartfelt memoir about her leap away from a prestigious legal career in London to live in a tiny French village with her Burgundian husband in *My Grape Escape*—after being diagnosed with PSC, a rare autoimmune bile duct/liver disease. Since then she has published four more books in the Grape Series about her enchanting adventures in France. *A Vineyard for Two* is her debut in fiction.

Now living and writing on the West Coast of Canada with a new liver and three Franco-Canuck daughters (collectively known as "the Bevy"), Laura runs three charming vacation rentals in Burgundy with her husband, does all she can to support PSC and organ donation awareness, and speaks on creativity, fear, and moving toward life no matter what. She writes about all these things in her blog. She is working on the two sequels to *A Vineyard for Two* in her Winemakers Trilogy, more Grape Series books, and a cookbook based on the Grape Series, due in fall 2020 from Touchwood Editions.

# find laura online

### The Grapevine Newsletter
http://bit.ly/LauraBradburyNewsletter

### Website
www.laurabradbury.com

### Facebook
www.facebook.com/AuthorLauraBradbury

### Twitter
twitter.com/Author_LB

### Instagram
www.instagram.com/laurabradburywriter

### Pinterest
www.pinterest.ca/bradburywriter

### BookBub
www.bookbub.com/authors/laura-bradbury

### Goodreads
https://www.goodreads.com/LauraBradbury

# Books by
# Laura Bradbury

### The Winemakers Trilogy
*A Vineyard for Two:* http://bit.ly/AVineyardforTwo

### The Grape Series
*My Grape Year:* http://bit.ly/2GNTSt9
*My Grape Paris:* http://bit.ly/2v2vjTP
*My Grape Wedding:* http://bit.ly/2v3gy2X
*My Grape Escape:* http://bit.ly/2v000sF
*My Grape Village:* http://bit.ly/2GRw1EC

### Other Writings:
*Philosophy of Preschoolers:* http://bit.ly/2RKXaxJ

CPSIA information can be obtained
at www.ICGtesting.com
Printed in the USA
LVHW041217020520
654897LV00003B/502